We asked readers what they love about

Danielle Steel

'Danielle's books always make me feel **strong, inspired and happy** – truly a page-turning experience' *Liz*

'She has a remarkable ability to write different stories at an **amazing pace**. Every time I pick up a book I know that I'm going to be taken through **highs and lows**' *Gillian*

'I feel like I've **travelled the world** through her descriptions of the places in her books' *Ann*

'Every book **gets you hooked** from page one' *Julie*

'Danielle Steel takes me to another place with her masterful story-telling ... **Absolute reading pleasure** from the first page to the very last' *Holly*

'I have **drawn immense strength** from the characters in many of her books' *Sarika*

'I love how she puts **her whole heart** into her writing' *Corina*

'I just love getting lost in her books. I can **stay up all night reading one**, just to know how it ends' *Kimmy*

'Danielle is such **an inspirational writer**, whose experiences are carried into the books. When I read each book, I feel as though **I am there with the characters** . . . They have gotten me through some very tough times and I would be lost if I didn't have one of her books in my hand' *Katie*

'Danielle Steel's books are **the perfect escape** from reality. Every time I read her books I'm transported to another place, ready for a new adventure' *Kelly Ann*

'I have been reading Danielle Steel books for fifty years or more and have kept every one – she is **my favourite author**' *Christine*

'**Gripping** reads that you **can't put down**' *Joanne*

'Her stories are **beautiful** and **gut-wrenching** and **totally unforgettable**. She has to be one of the best in the world' *Linda*

In His Father's Footsteps

Danielle Steel has been hailed as one of the world's most popular authors, with nearly a billion copies of her novels sold. Her recent international bestsellers include *Turning Point*, *Silent Night* and *Blessing in Disguise*. She is also the author of *His Bright Light*, the story of her son Nick Traina's life and death; *A Gift of Hope*, a memoir of her work with the homeless; and the children's books *Pretty Minnie in Paris* and *Pretty Minnie in Hollywood*. Danielle divides her time between Paris and her home in northern California.

BY DANIELLE STEEL

Blessing In Disguise • Silent Night • Turning Point • Beauchamp Hall
In His Father's Footsteps • The Good Fight • The Cast • Accidental Heroes
Fall From Grace • Past Perfect • Fairytale • The Right Time • The Duchess
Against All Odds • Dangerous Games • The Mistress • The Award
Rushing Waters • Magic • The Apartment • Property Of A Noblewoman
Blue • Precious Gifts • Undercover • Country • Prodigal Son • Pegasus
A Perfect Life • Power Play • Winners • First Sight • Until The End Of Time
The Sins Of The Mother • Friends Forever • Betrayal • Hotel Vendôme
Happy Birthday • 44 Charles Street • Legacy • Family Ties • Big Girl
Southern Lights • Matters Of The Heart • One Day At A Time
A Good Woman • Rogue • Honor Thyself • Amazing Grace • Bungalow 2
Sisters • H.R.H. • Coming Out • The House • Toxic Bachelors • Miracle
Impossible • Echoes • Second Chance • Ransom • Safe Harbour • Johnny Angel
Dating Game • Answered Prayers • Sunset In St. Tropez • The Cottage
The Kiss • Leap Of Faith • Lone Eagle • Journey • The House On Hope Street
The Wedding • Irresistible Forces • Granny Dan • Bittersweet • Mirror Image
The Klone And I • The Long Road Home • The Ghost • Special Delivery
The Ranch • Silent Honor • Malice • Five Days In Paris • Lightning • Wings
The Gift • Accident • Vanished • Mixed Blessings • Jewels • No Greater Love
Heartbeat • Message From Nam • Daddy • Star • Zoya • Kaleidoscope
Fine Things • Wanderlust • Secrets • Family Album • Full Circle • Changes
Thurston House • Crossings • Once In A Lifetime • A Perfect Stranger
Remembrance • Palomino • Love: *Poems* • The Ring • Loving • To Love Again
Summer's End • Season Of Passion • The Promise • Now And Forever
Passion's Promise • Going Home

NON-FICTION

Pure Joy: *The Dogs We Love*
A Gift Of Hope: *Helping The Homeless*
His Bright Light: *The Story Of Nick Traina*

FOR CHILDREN

Pretty Minnie In Paris • Pretty Minnie In Hollywood

Danielle Steel

IN HIS FATHER'S FOOTSTEPS

PAN BOOKS

First published 2018 by Delacorte Press,
an imprint of Random House,
a division of Penguin Random House LLC, New York

First published in the UK 2018 by Macmillan

This paperback edition published 2019 by Pan Books
an imprint of Pan Macmillan
20 New Wharf Road, London N1 9RR
Associated companies throughout the world
www.panmacmillan.com

ISBN 978-1-5098-7759-1

1 3 5 7 9 8 6 4 2

A CIP catalogue record for this book is available from the British Library.

Typeset in Charter ITC by Palimpsest Book Production Ltd, Falkirk, Stirlingshire
Printed and bound by CPI Group (UK) Ltd, Croydon, CR0 4YY

Visit **www.panmacmillan.com** to read more about all our books
and to buy them. You will also find features, author interviews and
news of any author events, and you can sign up for e-newsletters
so that you're always first to hear about our new releases.

To my wonderful children,
Beatie, Trevor, Todd, Nick,
Sam, Victoria, Vanessa,
Maxx, and Zara,

My wish for you is
to honor the past and your history
and those who came before you,

Cherish the present and embrace it,
and be brave,

And have faith in the future,
respect yourselves,
and always be true to yourself,
and may you find your soulmates.

I love you,
Mom/DS

IN HIS FATHER'S FOOTSTEPS

Chapter 1

On April 6, 1945, the Nazis began evacuating Buchenwald concentration camp, on the Ettersberg Mountain, near Weimar, Germany. The camp had been in operation for eight years, since 1937, and two hundred and thirty-eight thousand prisoners, men, women, and children, had passed through the camp by then. Fifty-six thousand prisoners had died there: Czechs, Poles, French, Germans.

On the sixth of April, U.S. troops had been in the area for two days, and the Nazis wanted all the prisoners out of the camp before the Allied forces arrived. It was a labor camp, with a crematorium, a medical facility where horrific medical experiments were conducted, and horse barracks to house the prisoners. Stables which had once held up to eighty horses were lived in by twelve hundred men, five to a bunk. There were additional buildings for the men. And a single barracks for the women, which could accommodate up to a thousand female inmates.

Most of the women prisoners were sent to Theresienstadt, once considered a model camp, used as a showplace for visitors and the Red Cross. The women who were mobile enough to go were moved by train or on foot. Those who weren't remained in the barracks, ignored at the end. As many male prisoners as could be handled were evacuated too. They were to be moved deeper into Germany, or sent to other camps farther away. The evacuation continued for two days, as the prisoners wondered what would happen next.

On April 8, Gwidon Damazyn, a Polish engineer who had been at the camp for four years, used the hidden shortwave transmitter he had built, and sent a message in Morse code in German and English. "To the Allies. To the army of General Patton. This is the Buchenwald concentration camp. SOS. We request help. They want to evacuate us. The SS wants to destroy us." Working with Damazyn, Konstantin Leonov sent the same Morse code message in Russian.

Three minutes later, they received a response. "Kz Bu. Hold out. Rushing to your aid. Staff of Third Army."

As soon as the message was received, Russian inmates stormed the watchtowers with weapons they had hidden and killed the guards. The others in charge rapidly retreated and fled rather than face the advancing U.S. Army. There were twenty-one thousand prisoners left in the camp after the evacuation, only a few hundred of them women.

Three days later, on April 11, 1945, troops from the

U.S. Ninth Armored Infantry Battalion, from the Sixth Armored Division, part of the U.S. Third Army, entered Buchenwald. It was the first concentration camp to be liberated by American forces. Other camps had already been liberated by Russian forces advancing through Poland.

Later in the day, the U.S. Eighty-Third Infantry Division arrived at the camp. None of the U.S. soldiers were prepared for what they found there, walking skeletons staring at them, some too weak to move or stand, others cheering and shouting as tears ran down their cheeks. Their liberators cried too. The prisoners attempted to lift them to their shoulders but were too weak. Several died as the Allies rolled into the camp, or minutes later. Starvation and the illnesses resulting from it, as well as the Nazis, had been their enemy for years.

The American soldiers entered the barracks and were horrified by what they found, the stench and the filth, the decaying bodies too weak to leave their beds, the people the retreating Germans had intended to kill, but hadn't had time to.

As the soldiers entered the main barracks, a tall, ghoulishly skeletal man staggered toward them waving his arms. His head had been shaved, the filthy camp uniform he wore was torn, which showed his ribs. He looked like a corpse and it was impossible to determine his age. He was desperate as he approached them.

"The women . . . where are the women . . . are they all gone?" he asked.

"We don't know yet. We haven't found them. We just got here. Where are they?"

The man pointed in the direction of another barracks and started to stumble toward it.

"Hang on." A young sergeant put out a hand to stop him, and then caught the man as he began to fall. "How long since you've had food or water?"

"Five days."

The sergeant gave an order to two of his men standing near him and they hurried off to comply. The mayor of nearby Langenstein was to be commanded to supply food and water to the camp immediately. Another officer had already radioed for medical personnel. Every single member of the camp looked like the walking dead. "I'll take you to the women's barracks," the newly liberated prisoner volunteered although he could barely stand up. Two soldiers helped him into a jeep. He was almost weightless as they lifted him. They tried not to react to the stench. His boots had the toes cut out and the soles were worn through. They were from the body of a dead man, killed by the Nazis. He directed them toward the women's barracks, and when they got there, the women looked even worse than the men. Some women were being carried by others, and as many of them as could were coming out of the building to watch the American troops explore the camp. They had no idea what to expect now, but they knew it could be no worse than what they had lived through so far. Some had been transferred from other camps, all had been assigned to hard labor, and several had undergone unimaginable medical experiments. Many of them had died.

The prisoner directing the soldiers in the jeep introduced himself before they stopped at the women's barracks.

"I'm Jakob Stein," he said in fluent English, with a heavy German accent. "I'm Austrian. I've been here for five years." They stopped at the women's barracks then and one of the soldiers lifted him out of the jeep so he wouldn't fall. He hobbled toward two of the women and spoke to them in German. "Emmanuelle?" he asked with a look of panic as the soldiers stared at the women in horror. They were ravaged and barely alive. "Is she gone?" Jakob asked with a grimace of terror on his gaunt face. The soldiers wondered if she was his wife but didn't ask. They tried to smile at the women walking toward them so as not to frighten them.

"She's inside," one woman with blue-gray lips said hoarsely, pulling the shreds of an old blanket around her. They were more filthy strings than anything that could keep her warm, and her eyes blazed with fever. She was shaking and stumbled into the arms of a soldier who lifted her into the jeep.

"We have medics coming," the private told her, "doctors." She looked terrified as he said it and shrank away from him. They had no way of knowing what she'd been through, but a festering open wound that ran down the length of her leg was part of it. By then, Jakob had hobbled into the women's barracks, as the officer driving the jeep radioed for medical assistance for several hundred females and described where they were.

It was a long time before Jakob emerged carrying a woman who looked close to death. He stumbled several times but didn't drop her. She was barely larger than a child and couldn't have weighed more than fifty or sixty pounds. One of the soldiers took her from Jakob and set her down in the jeep. She tried to smile, but was too weak.

"I thought they sent you away," Jakob said with tears in his eyes. He spoke to her in French.

"They didn't see me in my bed. There are less than half of us left." It was easy to see that she would have died on the march to Moravia or been crushed on the train.

"The Americans are here now," he said in a comforting voice, and she nodded and closed her eyes. "Everything is going to be all right." She opened her huge green eyes and looked at him, and then at the soldiers, and smiled. They could see the tattoo with her camp number on the inside of her naked forearm. Jakob had one on his arm too. They all did. They were numbers here, not people. No one in the camp had been considered human. They were to be eradicated. Jakob and Emmanuelle were both Jews. She was French and had been deported from Paris with her mother and younger sister. Her little sister had been killed when they arrived at the camp and her mother had died of illness a few months later. Other women had watched their families and children murdered. They were only kept alive if they were strong enough to work. Emmanuelle's hands were filthy, her nails broken stubs with dirt under them. She had worked in the gardens, and had given Jakob pieces of potatoes and turnips from time to time when she met him. She could have been killed for it.

"I want to take these two women to get medical help," the soldier next to Jakob said, "you too. We've got trucks coming for the others, they'll be here in a few minutes. Our medics will take care of them. Will you tell them that? The Nazis are gone. No one is going to hurt them now." Jakob translated what he'd said in French to Emmanuelle, then German, and Russian, which he appeared to speak fluently as well. The women nodded, and the jeep took off toward the main part of the complex with Jakob, Emmanuelle, and the other woman, who had slipped into unconsciousness by then. Jakob was holding Emmanuelle's hand, and the soldiers noticed that they all had a dead look in their eyes. They had been through an unspeakable hell for as long as they'd been there. None of the Americans could fully understand what they were seeing, and the residents of the camp didn't have the strength to explain, but they were walking proof of what the Nazis had done to them.

A medical tent had already been set up by then, and a soldier escorted Jakob and Emmanuelle inside. Another soldier carried the unconscious woman. As soon as Emmanuelle was being tended to by an army medic, Jakob hobbled back outside to help the soldiers with explanations about the locations of the camp offices and other barracks. There was a mountain of naked corpses the Nazis had wanted to have buried before they left, but hadn't had time to see to it. The soldiers were devastated as they entered the dormitories, and medics followed them, carrying litters to bring out the sick and the dead. Jakob stayed with them for a long time, to be as helpful as he could, translating for them. And after that, he went back to the tent to find Emmanuelle. She was his friend, and the food she had stolen for him had sustained him. More than that was unthinkable here. Having a friend was rare enough, particularly a woman. She had been very brave to give him what she did. She had almost been caught once, when a guard suspected her of putting a potato in her pocket, but she had let it drop to the ground, and it was so small and rotten, the guard hadn't bothered with it. He had hit her with a whip on the back of the neck and moved on. She had picked it up again before she left, when she'd finished work.

The medic tending to her asked her name, and Jakob supplied it. "Emmanuelle Berger. She's twenty-three years old, from Paris. She's been here for almost two years."

"Is she your sister?"

"No, I'm Austrian. We're friends." The young soldier nodded and made note. Eventually, they would have more than twenty-one thousand histories to take, but the Red Cross would help them do that. Families and survivors would have to be reunited. This was only the beginning, and just in the short time they'd been there, prisoners had continued to die. For some, the Americans had come too late. For others, like Emmanuelle, just in time. The other woman from her barracks had died while they were examining her.

The following day, April 12, the Eightieth Infantry Division came to take control of the camp. Medical units had been arriving since the day before, responding to emergency calls from the Eighty-Third Infantry. They'd never seen anything like it. It was a camp filled with living corpses who were barely clinging to life. How they had survived was beyond imagining. They were using all their translators to communicate with the freed prisoners, who spoke many languages, and after a cursory examination by the medics, Jakob had continued to help them where he could, since he spoke English, German, Russian, and French.

The next day, the press corps arrived and were photographing everything. One team was making newsreels of the freed prisoners. This was hard evidence of just how inhuman the Nazis were. These weren't prisoners of war, although it would have been inexcusable treatment of them too. These were civilians who had been brought from all over Europe and incarcerated in the camp. The army already knew there were other camps like it but Buchenwald was the first they'd seen.

The mayor of Langenstein had done as he'd been ordered to do, and food and water were brought to the camp to feed the survivors. Both were dispensed with meticulous caution by the Red Cross and medical personnel, as too much of either could kill the starving prisoners if taken too quickly. The army had buried the corpses—there was no way to identify them, other than by their numbers, although books had been found in the camp office, with careful records the Nazis hadn't had time to destroy before they left. And there were extensive records of experiments in the medical facility too. But all of that would be gone through later. In the early days, they were treating the survivors medically and trying to save everyone they could. Many died in the first few days, but with food and medicine, some of the sturdier young ones started to look less like the living dead. General

Patton had come to visit the camp himself. And both the Red Cross and film crews had arrived in great numbers. Field hospitals had been set up immediately.

Emmanuelle told them that she was twenty-three years old, and the only survivor of her family. Jakob was twenty-five. His entire family had been exterminated. His grandparents and two younger sisters had been shot and killed when they arrived at the camp and his parents had died months later, unable to withstand the rigors of hard labor. Jakob was the only one left.

Within days after they were liberated, the sickest survivors had been taken from the field hospitals to army hospitals, a small number to local hospitals. The rest eventually moved to other facilities, where the Red Cross was also set up to help them get back to their countries wherever possible, or to try to locate members of their families in other camps, as the Allies liberated them. And in each camp, the conditions were as horrifying as those they'd seen at Buchenwald.

The camp survivors who had no home to return to were identified as "displaced persons." Some wanted to go to Palestine, which was not an easy process. Quotas into other countries, including the United States, made leaving Germany difficult.

Jakob had requested to be transferred with Emmanuelle to a facility the army had set up for survivors, a few miles from the camp. Once there, Emmanuelle looked like a young woman again in the clothes they had given her, although she was not healthy yet. But she no longer looked like a dying child. Neither of them stood in line at the Red Cross tent for reunification. They had no one to look for and no one to go home to. They had been at the displaced persons camp for a month when they were told that Jewish American relief organizations were offering to help survivors relocate, and American sponsors were willing to pay for their transportation and help them find jobs in the United States. Immigration into the United States was complicated by quotas, but the War Refugee Board, established a year before, was working with refugee organizations that provided sponsors to give the victims of the camps new homes, whenever possible.

Jakob and Emmanuelle were talking about it one afternoon, as they sat in the May sunshine. Neither of them had any idea where to go, or what to do next. The war in Europe had ended a week before, but Jakob had nothing left in Vienna. Everything had been taken from them when they'd been deported, their money, his family's bank, their home, a schloss near Salzburg his family had owned for two hundred years. He had nothing now. He had been forced to leave university after the Anschluss, when Jews could no longer attend classes, and his father had been made to turn over their bank to the Third Reich. Jakob was alone in the world, and he didn't want to go back to Vienna to stand in the ashes of everything he had lost.

Emmanuelle had lost much less materially. Her father had died when she was a small child. Her mother had been a seamstress in an important fashion house in Paris and took in sewing on the side, which Emmanuelle often helped her with. Her mother had lost her job shortly before they were deported, and one by one, her private clients had stopped coming to her. They were too afraid to give her any business because she was Jewish. Their neighbors, who had been lifelong friends, had turned them in. Emmanuelle never wanted to see any of them again. The neighbors had taken over the Bergers' apartment, with the permission of the prefecture of police. Emmanuelle had nowhere to go, and no home to return to, and she didn't want to see Paris ever again. But they couldn't stay in the army facility forever. They'd have to go somewhere eventually.

"You don't want to go back to Paris?" Jakob asked her as they sat in the sunshine, while he smoked a cigarette the soldiers had given him. The Americans had been very generous with them, with food and chocolates. She was wrapped in a wool shawl from the Red Cross. She was so thin she was always freezing. She shook her head.

"For what? Our neighbors took our apartment because it was bigger than theirs. I think that's why they reported us." He nodded. Many Austrians had done the same thing, turned on Jews whom they had known all their lives, Jews who were often pillars of the community, like his family had been. Suddenly greed and jealousy had created a mob mentality that no one had thought possible in civilized communities and sophisticated cities. Being Jewish had become a death sentence overnight. His family had never been religious, nor had Emmanuelle's mother, but they were Jews nonetheless.

"Maybe going to America would be a good thing," Jakob said cautiously in French, and she shook her head again with a terrified expression.

"What would I do there? I don't know anyone, and I don't speak English. I couldn't get a job."

"The Red Cross workers are saying that the sponsors will help people find housing and work and be responsible for them until they can take care of themselves."

"I want to stay in France, just not Paris. Are you going to America?" She was sad as she asked him, since he was her only friend and had taken good care of her in the past month. They were always together and the American soldiers respected him. He had been helpful whenever he could, and he could speak to them in English, which she couldn't.

"I don't know," he said. "I don't have anyone there either. But I have even less here. I don't know what kind of job I could get. I was going to work at our bank after university. I'm not sure what I could do now. I didn't finish my studies."

"I stopped going to classes after the lycée. I wasn't

very good in school," she said shyly. "All I know how to do is sew."

"You can get a job doing that," he reassured her. "And you don't need to speak English to be a seamstress." She nodded agreement, but America seemed frightening and too far away. She had never dreamed of going there, and it sounded like a nightmare to her now, although the soldiers had all been very nice and very respectful of her. And Jakob liked them too.

In the past month, they had both gotten stronger and healthier. She had gained a few pounds with wholesome regular meals, although her stomach had revolted at first. She was no longer used to eating normally, and she frequently had stomach pains and so did he. But his body craved the food they were given and he devoured it. He was tall and thin normally, so you couldn't see much weight gain yet, but his face looked less skeletal, and his eyes less sunken. His hair had grown out a little and was very dark.

She now had soft blond baby curls instead of her shaved head, but they both looked like people who had been to hell and back, even if they were on the road to recovery now. Jakob had trouble with his feet from the chilblains he had gotten every winter, with boots that had been falling off his feet, and had open toes and holes in the soles. Both the Red Cross and the army had provided clothes for the prisoners too. Some of it was a little odd, and none of it fit well, but they now had warm, clean clothes. All their prison garb had had to be burned. It was filled with lice and the stench was overwhelming. Jakob knew he would never forget the smell of the barracks, their bodies and their clothes, and the corpses left in mountainous piles outside, until they were buried.

Emmanuelle said she still had nightmares every night. He was the only one who understood what she'd been through. Despite what they'd seen when they arrived, the soldiers had no idea what it had been like when the Nazis were there and the camp was fully functioning. It had been hell on earth and there had been many times when she had hoped she'd die rather than have to live another day. And yet they had gotten through it, she for two years, and Jakob for five. There had been no predicting who would survive and who wouldn't. They had found dead prisoners in their bunks every morning, sometimes lying side by side with them, with dead, unseeing eyes.

Jakob went with her to talk to one of the Red Cross workers again about the possibilities open to them. They could choose to repatriate to their own countries, but both of them had nothing but bad memories of their last days there. Emmanuelle and her mother and sister had spent three months in a stadium after they were taken from their home, before leaving for Buchenwald. And the Steins had lingered for months in a holding facility outside Vienna.

"We have sponsors for both of you, if you want them, through the American relief organization I mentioned to you before. And the War Refugee Board is doing all they can for displaced persons. We have one sponsor in Chicago, and another one in New York," the Red Cross worker said kindly. She didn't add that they had to be well-connected people to get through the red tape and quotas.

"Could we go to the same place, or have the same sponsor?" Jakob asked cautiously, feeling suddenly shy with Emmanuelle. He didn't want to seem presumptuous, but he knew she'd be too afraid to go to America alone. For a brave girl who had been through the worst experience imaginable, she was fearful now about crossing the Atlantic to a new home.

"Are you married?" the Red Cross worker asked Jakob, and he shook his head.

"No, we're friends."

"The sponsors won't do that. Couples have to be married, or else sign up singly and be placed with whoever is able and willing to take them. We have to submit their profiles to the people offering to be responsible for them, and they choose who they want. The rules are strict about all of it. Most of these people have volunteered to help through their temples," she explained. "We have sponsors in other cities too. We have a number of participating organizations in Chicago, Los Angeles, and

Boston. Do you have relatives in any of those places?" They both shook their heads.

"We have no one except each other." They didn't even have passports, and their citizenship in their respective countries had been canceled because they were Jews, but the United States had offered to give them passports as displaced persons, if American citizens were taking responsibility for them. She gave them each a sheet of information and they went back outside to talk about it some more. "We can't stay here forever," Jakob reminded her. Sooner or later they had to make a decision about where to go. He didn't know why but he felt a strong pull to a new life in New York. He talked about it to one of the soldiers later, when he offered Jakob a cigarette.

"What's it like there?" Jakob asked the private he was smoking with. He had chatted with him before.

"America is a land of opportunity. I'm from Brooklyn. My uncle is a butcher, I was working for him before the war. But I think I want to move out West when I go back. There are good jobs there."

"Where's Brooklyn?" Jakob had never heard of it.

"It's part of New York City. You'd like it, it's nice. Brooklyn, Queens, Manhattan, Staten Island, the Bronx, it's all part of New York City. Man, what I wouldn't give right now for a hot dog and a beer in Times Square, and a night on the town." He smiled knowingly at Jakob, who laughed. They were the same age.

"I'm thinking about signing up for one of the sponsors who are offering to find us jobs and lodgings through Jewish relief groups."

"Can your girlfriend go with you?" he asked sympathetically.

"I don't think so, unless we're married. She can sign up too, but she might go to another city. Boston, Chicago, or Los Angeles. I don't think she wants to go. She's afraid to be so far away from where she grew up, but it can't be worse than here." He glanced around them as he said it, and the soldier felt sorry for him. Jakob still looked ravaged and old before his time. He had trouble walking and had been beaten with sticks so often that he was bent over despite his youth. But at least he was alive. So many more had died in the last month, from typhoid, typhus, tuberculosis, yellow fever, dysentery, and starvation. And many were suffering from depression and delusional disorders too, from what they'd been through.

"Maybe you two should get married," his American friend suggested and Jakob nodded. He had thought of it himself, but had no idea what Emmanuelle would think of the idea. He hadn't dared suggest it to her. He liked it, but it seemed too soon to offer that as a solution. It seemed extreme to him too, but leaving her in Germany would be hard. There were also some complicated opportunities to go to Palestine, but he had no desire to go there. New York sounded better to him, if they could get housing and a job from benefactors.

He ate with Emmanuelle in the mess hall that night, as they did each evening. He saw that she looked tired and worried. Most of the other women didn't know where they were going either, and many of them were trying to get news of their relatives in other camps. All they had to go on were rumors they had heard about where they were, or clues from someone who had seen them several years before. There was still chaos in every camp once they were liberated, and most of the freed prisoners had nowhere to go.

He waited a few more days to talk to her, and finally dared to broach the subject. "I was thinking, if we get married, the same sponsor will have to take us both, as a couple. And I could take care of you once we get to New York. That way you wouldn't be alone." She looked at him in surprise.

"What if we hate it there? How would we get back to Europe?"

"We'd have to save our money," he said, "but what do we have to come back to? I have nothing left in Vienna, and how do we know our own countries would take us back? Our fellow countrymen were happy to turn us in and get rid of us. The French as much as the Austrians. Our countries were occupied, but many of our friends seemed to be willing to cooperate with the Germans. It might not be easy for us here," he said, and she nodded. She had thought of that as well.

"Do you want to get married?" she asked him so softly he almost didn't hear her. He nodded and took her hand in his.

"You saved my life, you stole food for me, Emma. You could have died for it. Your doing that gave me hope when I had none left." She smiled at what he said.

"Is that enough reason to get married?" But they both knew that if they didn't, they might never see each other again. He was the only familiar face now in a sea of strangers, except for the women she knew from her barracks, and they would be gone soon too.

"People have married for less," he said sensibly. "And I promise I will protect you." He could say that now, whereas a month before he couldn't have. He could be gallant now, which for an instant reminded him of his old life, where men took care of women, and shielded them. All they had been able to do in the camp was survive, if that.

"What if you don't want to be married to me once we get to New York? You might meet an American girl and fall in love." She looked worried and he smiled and held her hand tighter.

"I don't need an American girl, I'm already in love," he said, and she blushed and looked very young, despite her still too thin face and the dark circles under her eyes.

"I love you too," she said quietly. "I just thought you only considered us friends."

"We will grow to love each other more when we know each other better. We can have a new life in a new place where they want to help us. It's a good beginning." She nodded agreement. They walked in silence for a while, and then she stopped and looked up at him.

"Yes," she said simply, but he hadn't spoken. He was thinking about her, and the opportunities they could share.

"Yes, what?" His mind had been a thousand miles away.

"To what you said . . . what you asked me a little while ago." She didn't want to say the words herself, and he smiled as he understood.

"Emmanuelle Berger, will you do me the honor of becoming my wife?" he asked her formally, dropping to one knee on the dusty path as he said it. She smiled down at him and nodded.

"Yes," she said in a whisper, "I will." He stood up and kissed her gently then. She was so frail he was afraid to break her if he took her in his arms. He was no sturdier than she was, but he was young and strong, and her injuries had been more severe than his from the beatings she'd been given when she didn't work fast enough. She'd been on a burial detail before she worked in the garden.

He put an arm around her shoulders and walked her

slowly back to her barracks, which was not far from his own in the army camp. "We'll go back to the Red Cross tomorrow and see what they have to offer us. Then we'll go to the chaplain, and ask him to find us a rabbi." There had been several rabbis wandering around the camp, to talk to Jewish prisoners. "Good night, Emmanuelle," he said and kissed her lightly again. "Thank you." She smiled shyly at him, and then slipped into the barracks to join the other women, as Jakob smiled, put his hands in his pockets, and walked back to his own.

Chapter 2

Three weeks later, when the Red Cross and the American relief organization in New York had processed their papers, Emmanuelle and Jakob were put on a train to Calais. From there they would take a ferry to England and then another train to Southampton to board the RMS *Queen Mary* to make the crossing to New York. There were to be fourteen thousand troops on board returning to New York, in cabins fitted for three soldiers in each. And fifty-eight civilian passengers had been allowed to book passage, Emmanuelle and Jakob among them, thanks to the Jewish relief organization and their sponsors' connections.

They had been free for seven weeks by then. Emmanuelle still had short blond curly hair, and Jakob had what looked like a military crew cut, and was surprised to see that there was gray in his hair now. He looked more than two years older than she, and they both thanked the people at the Red Cross for their help when they left. All their documents were in order, they had identity papers to travel with through France and

England, provided by the army. The paperwork they had was in lieu of passports and identified them as displaced victims of war, seeking asylum in the United States. They had affidavits from their sponsors, Rachel and Harry Rosen in New York. A small studio apartment had been rented for them, and they both had jobs working in Mr. Rosen's factory. He was in the garment business and made women's dresses. Jakob had no idea what he was going to do there, maybe something in finance, since he had written his CV, which mentioned his studies of both business and finance in Vienna, and he had listed his family's bank for work experience. But he couldn't worry about that now.

From Southampton, they would be setting sail to New York on the *Queen Mary,* a ship that had been used to carry troops during the war. She had been recently repainted from military gray during her wartime service, although there was still a six-inch gun attached on deck.

Despite the removal of the silver, china, and art from her peacetime decor as a passenger vessel, she was an elegant ship, one of the fastest on the seas during the war. There was still an aura of grandeur about her, which reminded Jakob of his trips with his parents as a child. They had traveled on the *Normandie* once. It was an exquisite ship and had been a lot of fun. And he imagined this time the voyage would be simple and rugged, and the cabin they were assigned very small. The relief organization had booked their passage, which the Rosens were paying, in steerage. It was the first of June, and they had been married by a rabbi the week before. He was an army chaplain and had wished them luck, and reminded them that they deserved a good life after all they'd suffered.

"The crossing will be our honeymoon," Jakob said grandly.

With fourteen thousand troops and only fifty-eight civilian passengers, they felt lucky to be on board. When they reached the ship and boarded it, holding their small cardboard suitcases with their few belongings, they found that they were sharing the cabin with another couple. It was barely big enough to move around in, so they left their valises on their bunks, and went up on deck to watch the ship set sail. They had been warned that there were still mines in the water, and the crew would have to be vigilant. There was still a sunken U-boat in the mouth of the harbor and they would have to maneuver around it. Jakob sighed as they headed out to sea and he took his wife's hand.

"I think we're going to like New York," he said confidently, and she smiled up at him. She worried more than he did, and liked how positive he was. They still barely knew each other, and had had no opportunity to consummate their marriage. It wouldn't be possible to do so sharing the cabin with another couple. Jakob was disappointed by that. But they had survived the war and were sailing to freedom. That was enough. They had time to discover each other more intimately when they got to New York.

The crossing was smooth at that time of year, and the weather warm. They sat in old battered chairs in a small area on deck, looking at the ocean together. They saw dolphins on the second day, and on the third day, the captain made an announcement that they had passed the danger zone, and there would be no more risk of mines in the water from then on. The war was over for them. They were safe at last, on their way to their new home.

The crossing took eleven days, considerably longer than usual. It was a fully loaded ship. And on the last night, they sat together, looking up at the stars. Jakob kissed her and held her close. He put his suit jacket on her as she shivered in the chilly night air. They were due to arrive in New York by morning, and tugboats would guide them in. Among the fifty-eight passengers, only ten were immigrants, due to the stringent quotas. The others were Americans who had gotten trapped in Europe during the war and were desperate to return to the States. Jakob and Emmanuelle had been told that before the war they would have gone to Ellis Island, but it was being used as a detainment center for Germans, Italians, and Japanese. Instead they were being sent to an old army camp, near Oswego, New York, which was designated to process immigrants. They would be there to make sure their papers were in order, and for additional medical exams and vaccinations. The Rosens were planning to meet them in New York City after Oswego. They were as curious about the young couple as Jakob and Emmanuelle were about them. Whatever they were like, the Steins were infinitely grateful to them. Without sponsors in America, their life in Europe would have been a dead end, for a long, long time, with jobs scarce and the economy shattered. A new life in America was just what they needed.

Jakob could hardly sleep that night, as he waited to reach New York Harbor. He wanted to see the Statue of Liberty from the ship to prove that they were in fact there. He could never have dreamed seven weeks earlier that they would have a new world waiting for them in New York.

They knew they would have to undergo a superficial physical examination by officers of the U.S. Public Health Service on arrival, would be checked for trachoma, an eye disease, as well as other contagious diseases and mental disorders, and an hour or so later, they would board a small bus with the other displaced persons to go to the camp at Oswego. And after a day or two, they would be free to go.

Eventually they went to their cabin, deep in the bowels of the ship, and they got into their respective bunks. Emmanuelle slept fitfully, and heard them drop anchor at five in the morning. Jakob waited as long as he could stand it, and then put his shoes and coat on over his pajamas and went upstairs to stand on deck to see if he could spot the Statue of Liberty and the lights of New York. And when he got to a higher deck there she was, the statue that had been a gift from France, and had become the symbol of peace and freedom, and a welcome to the United States before they even set foot on land.

Emmanuelle woke up a little while later, and guessing where he was, she went up to look for him. He wasn't hard to find. He was standing at the railing, contemplating his new city, and he smiled when he saw her approach.

"What are you doing up here?" she asked him gently.

"Nothing," he answered at first, and then corrected himself. "Saying hello to our new friend." He gestured toward the statue, as Emmanuelle took his hand and held it. They were in this together and it was the only option they had, and the best one, by far.

It was still dark when they went back downstairs to bed, to get another hour or two of sleep. They had a long day ahead. He slipped into the narrow bunk beside her and held her. The other couple were fast asleep. Emmanuelle and Jakob drifted off, and woke up as they felt the ship move again as the tugboats slowly brought them in. They dressed quickly and went upstairs to watch, and there were tears in Jakob's eyes as they glided slowly into New York Harbor and tied up at the dock. Their bags were already packed, and they waited as they had been told to do, and finally an officer came to get them for the medical inspection. He had another couple with him, who were older than the Steins. The other passengers had left the ship by then, and after the exam, Emmanuelle and Jakob followed them downstairs, across the passerelle, and off the ship to the dock, where the bus was waiting for them. They had their small suitcases in their hands. The military troops had been leaving the ship en masse since they docked. And the few civilian passengers had left in cars that picked them up. Jakob followed Emmanuelle onto the bus. The other man did the same with his wife, and there were three other couples they hadn't seen before. They thanked the officer who had helped them, and he handed them their papers, which had been stamped, making their entry into the United States official, and he wished them luck. He didn't know where they had come from, but it was easy to see that they had been through a lot.

None of the couples spoke as they headed to Oswego, wondering what they would find there. When they arrived, it was an ordinary army camp, with barracks for immigrants and displaced persons, who were moving around freely and talking animatedly to each other. There were signs in several languages telling them where to go, and they walked into an office where their travel papers were examined again and handed back to them.

Emmanuelle's eyes looked huge and she whispered to Jakob in French, "What if they refuse us?" He squeezed her hand and told her that wouldn't happen now, and he was right. Emmanuelle had expected something to go wrong all along the way, but nothing had. The entire trip had gone smoothly. They walked into a large reception area, with their papers in hand. People were milling around, and every imaginable language was being spoken. They could hear Russian, French, German, there were many Italians, and several clusters of men with Irish accents. There were a handful of Poles and some Czechs, and they were handed information packets containing everything they needed to know. They were examined again that afternoon, tested for TB, syphilis, and leprosy, and given the smallpox vaccinations that were required in the United States.

During the exam, Emmanuelle had seen the doctor notice the number on her arm. He seemed puzzled, and asked her about it in halting French. She said it had been her identification number at Buchenwald concentration camp. He hadn't seen any yet. And afterward, Jakob said that the doctor who examined him had said the same.

"Maybe we're the first camp survivors to arrive," he said. He wasn't self-conscious about it, but Emmanuelle was. She hated the constant reminder of the camp, and had been wearing long sleeves ever since they'd been given clothes when they left. She wore a shirt whenever she went to shower, so the other women couldn't see her arms. "You should be proud of it," Jakob told her. "It means you survived the worst that the Nazis could dish out. It's a sign of courage and strength and victory of good over evil." To Emmanuelle, it was a physical reminder of two years of sorrow, pain, and loss. And she had physical scars that were evidence of it too. Jakob had those as well, the marks of many beatings, where he had been clubbed and whipped and bludgeoned, a broken shoulder that hadn't healed properly and was noticeably higher than the other, and a broken arm that the camp medical staff had refused to set and said that Jews had no right to medical care and had called him vermin. His wounds meant nothing to them. He still felt the effects of them.

By the next day, they had completed all their entry procedures with the Bureau of Immigration, and all they had to do was wait for the member of the relief organization to arrive, to drive them to New York the following morning.

There were hundreds of people in the large reception area, some of whom had been there for longer, either due to their health or something missing from their papers. There were women and children, and there was an area for them to play outside, and they could see many children through the window. It was a relief to see healthy, happy children again, a sight they hadn't seen in so long. They were told where the dormitories were and assigned two bunks side by side since they were married, and there was a large dining hall where meals were served.

They went to find their beds after a while, and saw the long row of cots and double bunks. Their beds were in a distant corner, and there was a window nearby where they could look out at the campgrounds and the country-side beyond.

There were people their own age bunked around them, but Jakob and Emmanuelle kept to themselves. And a little while later, Emmanuelle went to take a nap while Jakob looked around. All immigrants to the United States had to come through here now, since Ellis Island was occupied. And by the time they went to bed that night after a plentiful dinner in the dining hall, they were both exhausted from the emotions of their arrival and concerns about what lay ahead.

The next day, a member of the relief organization arrived as promised, and brought a letter of welcome from the Rosens. Emmanuelle and Jakob were ready to leave as soon as the relief worker showed up. She was to drive them to the studio apartment the Rosens had rented for them on Hester Street on the Lower East Side.

Once there, they could see that it was a Jewish neigh-borhood, since the signs in all the storefronts were in Hebrew. There were kosher butchers and bakeries and grocery stores all around them, which meant nothing to Jakob. His family wasn't practicing and didn't get kosher food. His parents had had a French chef for many years before the war and had looked down at Orthodox Jews. Emmanuelle said they weren't Orthodox either, and her mother didn't care what they ate, although she lit the candles and sang the prayers on Shabbat, because she liked the tradition, and Emmanuelle and her sister, Françoise, helped her with the candles and chanted the prayers with her.

The address the woman stopped at was a narrow battered-looking building, with a long flight of steps to enter it, and more once they were inside. Their apartment was on the sixth floor and there was no elevator. The building was noisy, and there were the sounds of children playing and babies crying. It was a sound Emmanuelle and Jakob hadn't heard for years. The sounds of normal family life. Emmanuelle looked shocked. She had forgotten what that was like. The children at the camp were mostly silent, afraid to attract notice to themselves. Most of the children at Buchenwald were killed when they arrived, since they weren't big enough or strong enough to work. They only kept them alive if they were over twelve or thirteen, and a good size, big enough to be useful workers on the labor details. Both of them were quiet as they listened to the voices in the building, and at last, they reached the apartment.

It was a single tiny furnished room. Everything in it was basic and old. There was a bed that folded into the wall, as the woman showed them. There was a set of sheets, a few frayed towels, two thin pillows, two cooking pots in the kitchen, a dented kettle, and the furniture looked ancient and well-used. But it had everything they needed. They set their bags down and looked around. The apartment faced into a courtyard and was dark, with no direct sunlight. Jakob realized that the rent must have been dirt cheap, but it was a roof over their heads, and at least it wouldn't be expensive once they had to pay for it themselves, after a year. They would have saved enough money from their jobs by then, which was the arrangement they had made with the Rosens. They expected Jakob and Emmanuelle to become self-supporting by the end of a year. Their gift to them had been their passage, entry papers, a studio apartment for a year, and a job for each of them. They had to pay all other expenses themselves, food, medical, clothes, transportation. In his letter to them, Harry Rosen had said it was the best he could do. Jakob was grateful to the Rosens. They had saved them from living on charity in their own countries, and perhaps not being able to find jobs at all, or a place to live at a price they could afford.

After they had looked around and seen the minuscule bathroom, which was infinitely better than sharing a latrine with more than a thousand people, they went back downstairs with the relief worker to her car. She drove them to the garment district where Harry Rosen's factory was located. It was on West Thirty-Seventh Street, in an old brick building. They took a freight elevator upstairs, while the relief worker explained that the other couple the Rosens were sponsoring had arrived the day before, and had an apartment in a building less nice than theirs. She said that it was kind of the Rosens to sponsor two couples, and Mr. Rosen had given them jobs as well.

They waited for him in a reception area for twenty minutes, and finally he appeared. He was a round, short, bald man with smiling eyes. He was wearing a shirt and tie and a shiny gray suit, and stuck out a hand to each of them. Jakob was able to speak to him in fluent English to thank him, and Emmanuelle was tongue-tied the moment she saw him. She was terrified that he would change his mind and send them back. Harry looked startled by how well Jakob spoke the language, with a faint British accent, instilled in him by the elite schools where he'd been educated. And Jakob assured him that Emmanuelle would learn quickly and make every effort to do so. He was giving her English lessons himself.

Harry told them that they would be starting their jobs the next day at eight A.M. He was taking Emmanuelle to his sewing staff, so she could show them what she could do with embroidery, beading, her delicate hand sewing, and how well she could work with a sewing machine. She would be one of several sewers. And Jakob asked his new boss then to what job he had been assigned, and added that his strength was anything to do with math and finance, after periods of time when he had trained at his father's bank.

"We have an accountant for all that," Harry said, looking busy. "I didn't know that you spoke English so well," Harry said, looking faintly apologetic.

"I put it on my CV," Jakob said matter-of-factly. Even if he was taking charity, he was still a man, and worthy of respect.

"I guess I didn't read it carefully. Anyway, you're on our maintenance team. It's the best I could do. But it's a job and you'll get paid." He brushed him off.

"We're very grateful to you," Jakob reiterated for both of them, and Emmanuelle nodded. She had understood. Her English had improved a little while on the ship, with Jakob's help and diligent lessons, although she was too shy to speak. Jakob spoke English to her now whenever he could, so she would get accustomed to hearing it.

They left a little while later, walked around their neighborhood after the relief worker dropped them off, bought a few groceries with a small amount of cash they'd been given by the relief organization. And then they went back to their apartment, which smelled musty the moment they walked in. But however small, it was home.

Emmanuelle couldn't help wondering how long they'd have to be there. Even the apartment she had shared with her mother and sister had been better, and bigger, but all of that was behind them now. They just had to make the best of this, and if they worked hard, maybe one day they would be able to afford a nicer apartment. At least they were safe now. Emmanuelle never felt secure anywhere anymore. The worst had happened to them both before, and she was terrified it could again, even in New York.

Emmanuelle cooked dinner that night, and discovered that three of the burners on the stove didn't work, and one of the saucepans had a tiny leak. The equipment was the most rudimentary but she didn't let herself focus on that, as she put the meager leftovers from dinner in the tiny icebox. Jakob watched her do it, trying not to remember how different his life had been. It was a thought which haunted him from time to time, his parents' beautiful home, the elegant, generous grandparents they'd visited, the chateau that the Nazis had occupied, the people who had tended to them in all their houses, many servants, important art, his parents' lavish lifestyle, and now he was reduced to this. But they were alive, and no one else he knew or was related to was. He was the last survivor of a lost world. He would have liked to share it with Emmanuelle, who'd had a much simpler life in Paris.

Their first night in the apartment was the first one they'd spent alone since their marriage six weeks before. Emmanuelle looked shy when he helped her make the bed with the frayed sheets with mended tears in them, and moments later, they slipped into it, after taking baths, and discovered each other's bodies as man and wife. He was gentle and loving with her, and they were tender with each other's scars. Afterward, she lay peacefully in his arms and felt safe for the first time in years. Her nightmares were not as bad that night. Jakob had become her haven and the hub of her entire world.

After their loving night together, they rose early. He made coffee and she made toast. They arrived at work on time, and Jakob was shocked when the man he was assigned to help handed him a set of overalls. He discovered within minutes that he was the assistant to the janitor, which used none of his talents, experience, or education. He was given a mop and a pail, and the lowliest jobs were assigned to him, including cleaning toilets and all the really dirty work. He spent the whole day mopping and scrubbing, and emptying garbage cans. He said nothing about it in complaint to Emmanuelle, when he saw her briefly at lunchtime. He asked her how her job was, and said nothing about his own. She told him honestly that the clothes were cheaply made, and she was sewing pearls, beads, and appliqués of roses onto ugly blouses, but the work was easy for her. She saw the crushed look in his eyes and guessed at the humiliation he was enduring but he'd been through worse, and there was no other choice for either of them.

They met the other couple the Rosens were sponsoring. Both of them were German. They had been in Auschwitz, had lost families too, had been married before they were deported, and had no children. But unlike Emmanuelle and Jakob, they were bitter and angry about their misfortunes, their time in the camps, and their jobs with the Rosens. They commented that their sponsor was using them as slaves. Their names were Hilda and Fritz. They had assigned her to wash dishes in the cafeteria, and he was on the crew that kept the factory machines running. His overalls and hands were streaked with grease and oil, and there was a smudge of it on his cheek. He had been an engineer before the war.

Jakob wanted a better job than janitor, but none had been offered. It only served to make him more determined to do well in the future, and make more money, so they wouldn't be at Harry Rosen's mercy forever. And he agreed with Fritz. Harry was using them as slave labor, but rather than bemoan their fate, it made Jakob eager to work toward a better job.

He was silent when they took the subway to their apartment that night, and he helped Emmanuelle to get dinner ready. She was unskilled in the kitchen and he wasn't much better. Her mother had done all their cooking, and a fleet of servants and a master chef had done his in Vienna.

They ate some spaghetti and a tomato salad, and didn't want much else. They had barely enough money to buy food. Emmanuelle was resigned to her assignment at the Rosen factory, but she could tell that Jakob was unhappy. He said he liked his supervisor, but hated the menial work he was doing. He had expected better opportunities in America, and greater challenges, which was why he had talked Emmanuelle into coming. He felt responsible now that it wasn't what they'd hoped.

"You'll find something else, when we fulfill our obligation to them," Emmanuelle encouraged him. They had signed a contract to work for Harry for a year, and he intended to hold them to it. He'd said as much when they met him. And it was obvious to Jakob that Harry had managed to kill two birds with one stone. He seemed like a generous man for sponsoring them, but was paying them and the other couple substandard wages, and using them to the fullest. They were willing to work hard, but Jakob wanted to look for better employment that used his skills as soon as possible. But for now, he would be cleaning toilets and whatever else was required of him for the next year.

It was July and crushingly hot in the factory and offices, with no air-conditioning. And in August, they finally met Rachel Rosen, Harry's wife. She treated

Jakob and Emmanuelle with disdain. She was pretentious and overdressed, and looked at them as though they were lesser beings. It terrified Emmanuelle, who was afraid she'd have them fired, and then they would have no jobs and no apartment. She never felt secure, despite Jakob's reassurance that the relief organization would help them if that happened. Emmanuelle trusted no one except Jakob, and she no longer believed in a kind destiny, or even a merciful God, after two years in the camp.

But whatever happened, they had to stick it out for a year, and they were careful not to jeopardize their sponsorship. They were trapped, and kind and respectful to everyone at the factory. They did their jobs without complaint and were well liked by all.

*

By the time they were approaching the one-year mark of their arrival and sponsorship by the Rosens, they were struggling financially, and could barely afford their food and minor expenses for the two of them. And they had a shock when they discovered that Emmanuelle was pregnant, which hadn't been in their plans—far from it. They couldn't afford a baby on the salaries they were making from Harry Rosen. And Emmanuelle was afraid to have children. What if it all happened again?

She had continued to have stomach problems, and

went to see a doctor at Jakob's urging, and was told she was pregnant. An examination and a blood test had confirmed it. She was panicked when she told Jakob that night. He wanted children, although she didn't, not for many years, until they could afford them. Jakob was worried about how they would support a baby, and thought of getting a second job at night. He tried to calm her fears to no avail. And two weeks later, she told him about an opportunity one of her coworkers had mentioned. Some of the other sewers were French and she chatted easily with them. The woman she spoke to told her that the wholesale jewelers and diamond merchants in the West Forties were always looking for runners, whom they used to deliver diamonds to other dealers or pick them up. It was a responsible job, not just as an errand boy. The runners had hundreds of thousands of dollars' worth of precious stones in their hands daily. The job required that a runner be trustworthy, and he might learn the jewelry business in the process, which would be lucrative if he were paid commissions.

The wholesalers used mostly young boys as runners, but Emmanuelle wondered if it was something Jakob could do instead of scrubbing floors and toilets at the factory. Their contract with Harry was almost over, and they were barely making enough money to take over the rent for their apartment, and now they had a baby coming.

Jakob was intrigued by the idea of the jewelry business, although he knew nothing about it, other than what he'd seen his mother and grandmothers wear before the war. At Emmanuelle's urging, he began handing out his résumé to all the jewelers in the diamond district during his lunchtime. The jewelry district was a few blocks north of the garment district where they worked. He skipped lunch to do it, and two weeks after he'd started, he got a call at home that night, and one of the jewelers where he'd left his résumé asked him to come in the next day to talk to him during lunch.

Jakob took his only suit with him to work the following day, and changed quickly at the time he normally had lunch, and walked the ten blocks to the jeweler's address on Forty-Seventh Street. It was a small store with an unimpressive front, and when he went in, an older woman asked how she could help him, and went to get Israel Horowitz in the back, when Jakob said he had an appointment with him. His heart was pounding as he waited, and a moment later, a gray-haired man emerged from a locked doorway, and looked Jakob over appraisingly. The owner was in his sixties, and asked Jakob to come with him into the back room, after shaking hands with him. He had a heavy accent, which Jakob recognized as either Czech or Polish, but they spoke English to each other, and Jakob followed him, looking subdued. They walked into an office, and Israel Horowitz sat down at his desk. He had a serious face and kind eyes, and he looked at Jakob intently. Neither of them spoke for a moment.

"Why do you want a job as a runner?" The jeweler finally broke the silence as Jakob gazed at him respectfully. "You're old for that. We usually use fifteen- or sixteen-year-old boys, eighteen maybe. Our rabbi finds them for us. They draw less attention than a grown man walking around with diamonds in his pocket."

"I need a better paying job than the one I have," Jakob said honestly.

"What are you doing now?" Israel asked him. "You didn't say on your résumé."

"I'm an assistant janitor at a garment factory," Jakob said without pretense or artifice. "I came here from Germany a year ago with my wife. The factory owner sponsored us through a relief organization." The elderly man nodded and his blue eyes were intense as he stared at the younger man.

"You were deported?" he asked gently.

Jakob nodded. "Yes, from Vienna."

"And your family?" he asked in a respectful tone.

"We all went together. They sent us to Bergen-Belsen first, and then we all went to Buchenwald." Bergen-Belsen was a transit camp, where deportees were held and then sent to other camps. Jakob explained, "Buchenwald was one of the worst. It was a concentration camp, everyone was assigned to hard labor, as my wife

45

and I were. They killed people constantly if they thought you didn't work hard enough. Or they sent you to an extermination camp to be gassed. And many people died of starvation and disease," Jakob said quietly.

"And your family?" Israel asked.

There was a heavy silence in the room as Jakob tried to quell his emotions when he answered.

"I'm the only survivor. My grandparents, parents, and two younger sisters all died there. I have nothing to go back to in Vienna now, except bad memories." There were tears in the older man's eyes when he nodded. It was a story he had heard too often in the past year, since the war ended, about relatives and friends in Europe. Too many had waited too long to try and get out, and couldn't, with tragic results.

"My wife and I are from Warsaw. We came here twelve years ago, in 1934, when we saw what was coming. No one wanted to come with us. They didn't believe that the Germans would succeed at what they wanted to do. We lived in civilized countries, no one could imagine it. But those were barbaric times. My family owned the largest jewelry store in Warsaw, and we came here with very little and got a small start. None of my family survived the war. Everything there is gone now for us. Our relatives were sent to Auschwitz, some to Dachau. What did your father do before the war?" Israel asked with interest. He liked this plain-speaking, obviously well-educated, well-brought-up young man. Looking at him, it was difficult to believe he was only twenty-six. He was mature far beyond his years, and the salt-and-pepper hair was misleading. He looked at least thirty-five. But they had a common bond with the losses they had suffered. The main difference between them was that Jakob had been in the camps himself, while Israel had left in time and had lived out the war in New York.

"My family owned a bank," Jakob answered him, "which my great-grandfather started. It's gone now of course. The Nazis took it right after the Anschluss, when, as you know, Germany annexed Austria, and occupied it, which they had said would be a peaceful move for the benefit of Austria. But soon after, all Jews were removed from their jobs and homes, and deported. And now our homes are gone too. Everything. I have nothing now."

"Your wife too?"

"She's French, she also lost her family. We met in Buchenwald. She came here with me. Our employer sponsored both of us and another couple. It was difficult for them to do, but they knew someone on the War Refugee Board."

"And paid you next to nothing for a year, and treated you like slaves." He had heard stories like it before. In some cases, sponsorship was not the charitable act it appeared.

"We're grateful to them anyway," Jakob said politely.

"Our contract is over in a month. We will have to pay rent for our apartment." He hesitated for a moment, and didn't want to sound pitiful, but Israel Horowitz had been honest and open with him, and he seemed like a sympathetic person. "And we have a baby on the way. I need a better job." The jeweler nodded again and didn't comment.

"What do you know about diamonds?" he asked Jakob.

"Nothing, except what I saw my mother and grand-mothers wear, and I never paid much attention to their jewelry," he said with a smile. "Everything I know is about finance and economics. I was preparing to work at the bank when I graduated from university."

"And they forced you to leave the university after the Anschluss?"

Jakob nodded in response. "But I worked at our bank during holidays from school. I only had one term to go to finish my studies when I left."

Israel Horowitz nodded again, and looked pensive for a moment, before looking back at Jakob, sitting across his desk.

"I had a son your age. He died in the war. We became American citizens after we came here. David volunteered right after Pearl Harbor. My wife begged him not to. He was killed at Iwo Jima. We have no other children. She hasn't been well since he died. She used to work in the store with me, but now she can't. We have no other family now after what happened in Europe. I could use a young man like you to help me, if you care about this business. Do stones interest you at all? It's a fascinating trade. I could teach you a great deal, if you want to learn. This could be a 'mitzvah,' a blessing, for both of us. What does your wife do?" He assumed that her background and education were similar to Jakob's, which was not the case, although it didn't matter to either of them, and Jakob had never loved and respected anyone as much in his life. She was a genteel, gracious person despite her simpler background.

"She sews at the Rosen factory. She's a seamstress. And I'm very sorry about your son."

Israel nodded in acknowledgment. "I hear Rosen runs a sweatshop. Maybe eventually, we could find her a job here. Most of my business is with other diamond wholesalers. We only sell to the trade. I have two diamond cutters who work for me, they came from Belgium and have been here for a long time. They're very good at what they do. We're well respected in the industry. How soon are you available?"

"In four weeks," he said, his heart pounding again with excitement. He didn't know what Horowitz would pay him, but the opportunity sounded like a good one. He wanted to fulfill his contract with the Rosens to the letter. It seemed only fair and honorable. They had brought them to America after all, even if working and living conditions had not been ideal. Without them, he and Emmanuelle wouldn't be in New York.

Israel Horowitz stood up then and held out his hand. "You have a job then. I'll start you as a runner, and you'll have to learn the rest. There's a lot to learn about this business, and I'll teach you everything I can."

Jakob was overwhelmed with gratitude as they shook hands. He quoted a salary to Jakob then, which was double what the Rosens were paying him, and he would be able to pay rent for their small apartment now with ease, and buy better groceries. They needed to with Emmanuelle pregnant, she was still much too thin. He had filled out a little in the last year, but she had barely gained a few pounds. Her stomach gave her too much trouble to gain weight and she was sick now with the pregnancy, which worried him. He couldn't wait to tell her about the job he had just gotten, with even a possibility for her one day. She was going to have to work after the baby was born, they couldn't afford to give up her salary, although he wished she could stay home, but there was no way they could do that yet. Maybe one day. And in the meantime, they were going to try and find a babysitter in their neighborhood, who wouldn't charge too much to watch the baby while Emmanuelle worked.

Israel walked Jakob to the front of the store, and they shook hands again. Both men looked pleased, and Jakob was so excited about the job, he wanted to leap as he ran back to the factory. He was fifteen minutes late from lunch, the interview had taken a long time, but if they fired him at the factory now, he didn't care. He had a wonderful new job! He couldn't wait to tell Emmanuelle that night.

His supervisor growled about his tardiness when he got back, and Jakob apologized and went straight to work, and finished on time. He didn't see Emmanuelle until the end of the day when they left work together, and he told her all about the interview on the subway ride back to the apartment.

"And he said he might have a job for you one day." Jakob was beaming at her. This was a dream come true for them, with double the salary for him, just when they needed it most. But Emmanuelle looked worried as soon as he mentioned the job for her.

"I don't know anything about diamonds or jewelry. I only know about sewing. And it wouldn't be smart for me to work for him. What if he gets angry at you and fires both of us? We'd be in a desperate situation." She was anxious about everything now, and always imagined the worst case. She trusted nothing and no one, except him. The war had left her frightened that bad things would happen to them.

"Why don't you try to get a better sewing job then? You don't have to stay at Rosen's." And he didn't want her to. Her skills were too refined for the factory, and Jakob was convinced she'd be paid better somewhere else. They couldn't pay her less, and Horowitz wasn't wrong when he said Harry Rosen ran a sweatshop. He had saved them from Germany, but he hadn't proven to be a kind man, and the deal had worked best for him.

"No one's going to hire me now that I'm pregnant. I have to stay until the baby." It was due in December, and she hadn't told the Rosens yet. She was three months pregnant, but it didn't show, and as thin as she was, it probably wouldn't for a long time. And sewing and sitting all day, she could work until the end of her pregnancy, although Jakob didn't like the idea of it for her. The first few months had been rough and had added to her stomach problems from the camp.

"Maybe after the baby is born, Mr. Horowitz can find you a job," Jakob said hopefully. He could hardly wait to start. In only four weeks. He had to scrub and clean and haul garbage for another month, but after that he would work looking like a gentleman and be treated like a human being. It was a gift from God.

They celebrated that night, with a simple dinner Jakob cooked for her, although she could hardly eat it. They were both happy, and he thanked her, since applying for a job with the wholesale diamond dealers had been her idea, and a good one. By nine o'clock, she was fast asleep in his arms. She had been exhausted ever since she'd gotten pregnant. It had put a big drain on her already delicate system.

Her doctor had said that it would take years for her

to recover from what she'd been through at the camp, if she ever did fully. Two years of starvation and brutality had taken a heavy toll on her, and Jakob's experience there had marked him too, but he was stronger. His psyche had bounced back more readily in the past year. He had a positive attitude about life, which nothing had shaken, although he worried more than he used to. But Emmanuelle was tormented by her anxiety that something like what happened before could happen again.

Jakob reassured her, but fear was her constant companion now. She even worried about the baby, that something would be wrong with it, or it would die before it was born, or it would be taken from them after. She had lost everyone she had loved, except Jakob, and her fears were focused on him too. There was nothing she could do to stop it.

*

Two weeks after his meeting with Israel Horowitz, Jakob gave Harry Rosen notice. He took it badly, in the vein of "how dare you, after everything I've done for you!" He threatened not to let them keep the apartment, which was rent controlled and all they could afford at the moment, but finally he relented and said they could stay there for another year, as long as they paid their rent promptly, which Jakob fully intended to do. And Rosen was slightly mollified that Emmanuelle was staying, at the absurdly low rate he was paying her as one of his seamstresses. He was well aware of her talents, and preyed on their gratitude and sense of obligation to him for sponsoring them initially. Jakob warned him that Emmanuelle was pregnant and having the baby in December, and Harry said he expected her to work until the end of her pregnancy, and return to work two weeks after the birth.

Jakob didn't answer him and wanted his wife out of Harry's clutches. But for now, at least he had escaped, and who knew where the job in the diamond business would lead him. Hopefully, far away from Harry Rosen and men like him. But Harry had been the gateway to his future, and for that Jakob was grateful. And on his last day at the factory, he politely shook hands with his supervisor, thanked him, and left. Emmanuelle was waiting for him outside, and Jakob looked jubilant as he joined her. His new life had just begun. He wanted it to be a better life for both of them, and their baby.

Chapter 3

Jakob started his job with Israel Horowitz on the Monday after his employment ended at Harry Rosen's factory. He appeared at Israel's office in the only suit he owned, with a clean shirt Emmanuelle had washed and ironed, and an expensive-looking navy blue silk tie she had made for him. She had sewn it easily with her nimble fingers from a fabric remnant she had bought at a shop on the Lower East Side. Jakob looked like the banker he might have been when he arrived for work, and Israel smiled when he saw him. He was a handsome young man, and he had the grace and bearing of his upbringing.

Israel, or Izzie, as he asked Jakob to call him now, spent the morning showing him around his office, and then introduced him to his two diamond cutters, who worked in a room in the back. They spoke Flemish with each other but they spoke French and German too, and conversed easily with Jakob, and were happy to meet him. Izzie showed Jakob what they were working on. Both had diamonds on their work table. One was cutting a six-carat stone, which Izzie explained was an F color, and qualified at VSI, which meant very slightly included. He told Jakob that the interior flaws were so slight they could only be seen through a jeweler's loupe, and the color was nearly perfect. The other diamond cutter was working on a four-carat stone, of lesser color with more inclusions, which he was setting into a ring with small pavé stones. It was for a well-known retail jeweler on Fifth Avenue.

"The finest color is D," Izzie explained to Jakob, "and flawless is what they call a stone with no internal inclusions. Come, I'll show you." They returned to his office where he opened the safe, and took out a small white paper packet folded many times, to protect its contents. And as soon as he unwrapped it, a round cut stone of blinding clarity lay on the paper on his desk. "That is as close to a perfect stone as you will ever see. It is eight carats exactly, with no inclusions. It's been certified as D flawless. It's very rare. Six diamond wholesalers own it together. I'm brokering the deal, and we just came to an agreement with the man who's selling it. I need you to take it back to one of the other investors. We're selling it to Cartier, for a very nice profit," he explained to Jakob. "The office you need to take it to is four blocks from here. Put it in your inside pocket, and go straight there. Call me when you get there, and then come back."

"That's it? That's all I have to do?" Jakob was fascinated by the business and the beauty of the stones he had just seen. They reminded him of a ring his mother had worn that had belonged to her own grandmother. It was a diamond, larger even than the one Izzie had shown him. Jakob had never paid much attention to it, although he recalled now that it was very pretty, and gone forever, along with everything else the Nazis had stolen from them.

"If I told you what this stone is worth, what we just paid for it, and what we're selling it for, you'd be shaking in your shoes all the way to that office. Go fast, look straight ahead, and deliver it. I'm trusting you with an important stone as your first assignment from me. Now, go." He handed him a piece of paper with the address and the man's name, and Jakob's stomach tightened as he realized the responsibility he'd been given. He tucked the stone into an inside pocket, as Izzie had told him to do, and left the store a moment later, went directly to the delivery address, called Izzie from their office when he got there, and was back ten minutes later, mission accomplished.

"Good," Izzie said, smiling at him. "You didn't sell it on a street corner and run away to Brazil. Very good. I'm proud of you," he teased him, and Jakob laughed. He liked him and liked working for him, and he realized now that it was going to be interesting. It wasn't banking, but there were large sums of money involved, despite the un-impressive look of Izzie's office. It was a small operation, but they brokered some important stones and turned over more money than Jakob would ever have guessed.

He had another smaller, less important stone to pick up later that afternoon. Two dealers wanted to sell it to Izzie, who wasn't impressed, and sent the package back to them via Jakob twenty minutes later after he had looked at the stone from all angles with his loupe, and shone a special light on it. "Junk," he said to Jakob and showed him why. "There's more 'stuff' in that stone internally than my cutters' ashtrays. I don't sell stones like that. If I did, Cartier wouldn't buy from me." He had several important retail customers, and a number of private ones, and a reputation to protect. The merchants he did business with trusted him and respected his "eye," honesty, and judgment.

By the end of his first day, Jakob felt as though he were part of an exciting business, and he had learned a lot from Izzie. He told Emmanuelle all about it over dinner that night.

"What if somebody steals a diamond from you while you're delivering it?" She looked worried again. She hadn't realized how valuable the stones were that Jakob would be picking up and delivering.

"Then Izzie will kill me when I get back to the office, and you'll be a widow and get to find a rich, handsome husband like you deserve," he teased her. Tears filled her eyes as soon as he said it, and he put his arm around her.

"I was just joking with you, sweetheart. Nothing will happen to me. I'm not wearing a sign that says what I'm carrying, and all the other jewelers are very close. I don't have far to go." He told her about the D flawless diamond and how beautiful it was, and then he mentioned his mother's and looked sad himself for a moment.

Emmanuelle had never lived around that kind of wealth so it was hard for her to imagine, and at first it had worried her about him. She was afraid that she wasn't fancy enough for Jakob, given the family he came from, but he didn't seem to care. It bothered her more than it did him. He loved her just the way she was, although he did wish she would worry less. Sometimes her angst was so convincing it was contagious and he got swept up in it too. But he was loving his new job, and all he had to learn, and his new boss was generous about teaching him. It made Jakob sorry for him again that he had lost his son, and he was clearly enjoying having Jakob around and sharing his knowledge of the diamond business with him, which Jakob found fascinating. And he suddenly realized how important his mother's jewels must have been, and how valuable. He'd never thought about it before. His father had been very generous with her, and she had inherited some important jewelry from her grandmother.

Izzie had mentioned that his wife rarely left their home anymore, since they'd lost their son. She was ill and depressed, but Izzie appeared to be a cheerful, positive person, who was trying to keep moving forward despite his son's death.

For the next two months, Jakob soaked up everything he could about the diamond business, and Izzie sent him on errands constantly, delivering stones to other dealers, or picking them up. And he told Emmanuelle about it at night.

She was six months pregnant by then, and she couldn't conceal it anymore. The baby was a good size, and she hoped it would be a boy, since there were no members of Jakob's family to carry on his name. He said he didn't care. He just wanted it to be healthy, and the birth easy for her. She was eating better now and felt better than she had in months. She still had nightmares but less often.

Jakob had her come to the store one day after work so he could introduce her to Izzie. He was very proud of her. The next day Izzie commented on how gentle and beautiful she was. She looked so delicate that he couldn't imagine her surviving what she'd been through, or that anyone would want to do such brutal things to her. He was pleased for them about the baby, and he was generous with Jakob.

In September, Izzie had handed him an envelope of cash and told him to buy himself another suit and some new shirts. He needed more than one suit to wear to work, and there was enough money for Jakob to buy gray slacks and a blazer too, and a new dress for Emmanuelle. They'd had fun shopping uptown all Saturday afternoon, rode back downtown, dropped off their purchases at the apartment, and went to the movies afterward.

It was hard for Jakob to envision their life with a baby. They had grown so close in the year and a half since they'd been married that he could no longer imagine his life without her, and maybe it would be that way with the baby too. The apartment would be cramped for the three of them, but they didn't want to move. They were saving every penny they could.

After fourteen months of working for him, and now with a baby coming, Harry Rosen had refused to give Emmanuelle a raise. She knew by then that all of his employees hated him. He was stingy with everyone. Hilda and Fritz, his other sponsees, had left as soon as their contracts ended. They were working in a German restaurant uptown, and doing well. She was cooking, and he was waiting on tables, and said he was making a lot of money on tips.

In October, Emmanuelle fainted one afternoon at work. One of her coworkers called Jakob at the office, and he came to pick her up and took her to the doctor. They told her that she should slow down and possibly stop working until the baby came, but she didn't want to lose two months of salary, and insisted she was fine. Many of the women at the factory were pregnant—they were calling it the Baby Boom, with lots of women having babies right after the war, and Harry Rosen had no policy in place to protect the women or their jobs. He worked them just as hard as everyone else, and expected them to return to work two weeks after they gave birth. If they didn't like it, they were easy to replace, so Emmanuelle was hanging on to her sewing job for dear life.

Her English had improved, but she still had a heavy French accent, which most people found charming. Jakob continued to correct her and gave her lessons whenever he had time. She always spoke to him in French, and he indulged her in that. It was all she had left now of her history and heritage, the language she had spoken as a child and before the war. After that, she'd learned German in the camp, and had to speak English in New York. She was relieved to speak to Jakob in French at home, and she was going to speak to their baby in French.

"You don't miss speaking German?" she asked him late one night as they lay in bed, and he rubbed a hand over her belly, which was a good size now. She was still very thin, but the baby was growing, and Jakob could feel it kick a lot when she cuddled up next to him at night.

"No, I'd be happy if I never had to speak German again," he said. "It has too many bad associations for me now. It makes me think of the camp." She nodded—she felt the same way whenever she heard people speaking German. There had been an influx of German immigrants since the war, and in their neighborhood, she heard German and Yiddish spoken constantly, particularly among the old people who had been there for a long time, but it always gave her a chill. Her nightmares were finally subsiding, and she felt peaceful waiting for the baby.

Izzie invited them to Thanksgiving dinner at his apartment on the Upper West Side. It was the Steins' second Thanksgiving in the States and they hadn't celebrated the first one. They were shocked when they met his wife, Naomi. She was a wraithlike creature with a distant, vague expression. She was sitting in a dimly lit sitting room when they arrived, and barely looked up when Izzie introduced them. She nodded and forced a wintry smile. She was dressed all in black, and there were photographs everywhere of their late son, who had been a handsome boy and looked like his father. It was hard to discern what Izzie's wife had looked like before grief had decimated her. She was so pale she looked like a ghost herself and her eyes were two pools of sorrow. She walked like an old woman, and it was hard to imagine her married to a man as energetic and vital as Izzie.

He carried the conversation with Jakob all through dinner, and Emmanuelle attempted to chat with Mrs. Horowitz, who answered in monosyllables and retired to her bedroom without touching the Thanksgiving meal that Izzie had prepared and served. He did everything at home now, and talked to his wife as though she was part of the conversation, but she refused to engage. She had buried herself alive with her son. Even Jakob and Emmanuelle's impending baby didn't warm her, and she kept her eyes averted from Emmanuelle's maternal shape as though just seeing it caused her pain. It had the opposite effect on Izzie, who was excited for them.

"I think I'll have to become the baby's adopted grandfather, if you'll let me." Jakob and Emmanuelle loved his taking an interest in their child. It was nice being able to share their joy. "You should rest for a few weeks before the baby comes," he said sternly. "You'll be busy and exhausted after that."

"I have to go back to work two weeks after, or I'll lose my job, and they expect me to work until the day I give birth," Emmanuelle said, sounding worried.

"Your boss is a monster," Izzie said with strong disapproval, and Jakob agreed with him.

"Half the factory workers are pregnant, and he's angry about it."

"He can't fire all of you. At least stay home for a month after the baby is born. Who are you going to leave it with when you go back to work?"

"Our neighbor downstairs said she'd take care of the baby for us. She has a six-month-old, and she doesn't mind taking care of both of them. She wants very little money for it, so we can afford her." Their budget was still very tight, but they were managing with Jakob's new salary as Izzie's runner. They'd been able to buy what they needed for the baby and borrow the rest from neighbors and women that Emmanuelle worked with who had had babies too and had things their infants had already outgrown.

Emmanuelle was planning to nurse until she went back to work. Her doctor said it was better for the baby, and it would save the money for formula until they had no choice. They had to think of everything and calculate every penny, which wasn't unfamiliar to her from her life before the war, but it was an entirely new experience for Jakob. He had adapted to it, although it had been a huge adjustment for him at first. He had never had to worry about money before or even think about it. He had had everything he could possibly want when he was growing up. And he wanted some of the same advantages he'd had for their child, such as an excellent education, a secure home, and parents who weren't frantic about having enough money to put food on the table. He wanted their children to feel safe. And he wanted more than one child, which Emmanuelle was fiercely opposed to. She was still convinced that the Holocaust could happen again, even in America. She firmly believed it, despite everything Jakob said otherwise. It seemed inconceivable to him. And she kept insisting that given the dangers for Jews in the world, one child was enough. He hoped she would change her mind over time, but at the moment she was very firm about it.

Their Thanksgiving with the Horowitzes was warm and touching, even after Naomi disappeared to her room to rest. They stayed and talked to Izzie for a long time, and then went home and talked about how nice it had been, and how much they liked him.

And then, before they knew it, it was December. The baby was due on the eighteenth, a Wednesday, and Emmanuelle worked the entire day on her due date, and nothing exceptional seemed to be happening when she left work. Jakob met her outside the factory at the end of the day, fiercely annoyed that her boss and supervisor hadn't agreed to give her some time off before the due date. She told everyone she'd see them tomorrow, since there was no sign of impending labor, and her doctor had seen nothing promising the day before when she went for her appointment. The factory was going to be closed on Christmas Day to acknowledge the Christian workers, but they didn't have the day off on Christmas Eve, and her coworkers had teased her that even if she had the baby on Christmas, their boss would expect her back the next day. Their standard policy was two weeks after delivery, although some women had taken three after a Caesarean section, without their employer's consent.

She was moving more slowly than usual when Jakob met her, but said she was just tired after a long day. She had been up and down the stairs between the workrooms and the factory several times, which angered him even more.

"You should all go on strike," he said, as they walked to the subway, and he held her arm. It was snowing and he didn't want her to fall. He wished he could afford a cab, to make things easier for her. They had celebrated the first night of Chanukah the night before, and she had lit the candles and sung the prayers as her mother would have. It had brought tears to her eyes as she sang, and Jakob joined her and they held hands alone in their tiny apartment. Izzie had wished them a happy Chanukah and given them the first dreidel for their baby, which Emmanuelle said she would keep forever.

Jakob had celebrated Chanukah with his family too, in Vienna. For them, it had been a gala affair with friends and relatives around the table all dressed in black tie, and exchanging gifts. But his family had always been very open and non-religious and they had a Christmas tree every year as well. Emmanuelle had never had one, and didn't think it would be right now when Jakob suggested it, not even a small tabletop one. She felt that they had to honor all of those who had died for their faith, and not muddy the waters with Christian traditions that weren't theirs, even if they were in America now.

She was out of breath and could hardly make the six flights of stairs to reach their apartment when they got home. She had been doing it every day, but it was getting harder and harder, and Jakob was surprised that the stairs and her job hadn't brought on early labor. He rubbed her feet and ankles when she lay down on their bed, before lighting the candles again for the second night of Chanukah. She needed to rest for a minute first. They chanted the prayers together again. And after that, he told her to sit while he made dinner. He wanted her to take it easy.

The baby was still high, which the doctor said was normal for a first baby, and it wouldn't come down until she was actually in labor, so the fact that it wasn't lower down didn't mean it would be a long time before she delivered. It could happen any day. They had said that a two-week span before or after her due date was considered normal, so it could still be two weeks away. Jakob hoped not for her sake. She looked exhausted and was grateful to sit while he made dinner. Afterward she helped him do the dishes, and then he insisted she relax, take a bath, and go to bed. It was bitter cold out, and he thought they should stay home as much as possible and had stayed home over the weekend. He didn't want her slipping and sliding on the ice and snow, or going up and down six flights of stairs more than she had to, to go to work.

"If you haven't had the baby by then, we're going to have a nice cozy weekend," he told her, "and you are going to stay in bed, while I wait on you hand and foot. Your wish is my command." She smiled as he said it, and fluffed up the pillow behind her. "Do you want me to run your bath?" They knew they were lucky, since many apartments like theirs had no bathrooms of their own, and shared a common one with other apartments on the same floor. She was grateful they had one for themselves.

She got up eventually, and soaked in a warm tub for a while, which felt heavenly, while Jakob read one of the books Izzie had given him about diamonds. He had learned a lot about the business in the last five months and was eager to know more. When she came to bed in a pink flannel nightgown she had made with lace at the collar, he smiled. She looked like an enormous pink balloon with graceful arms and legs and her pretty face above it all. It was hard to believe she was having a baby, she looked so young. He took a shower after her bath, with a hand-held shower he'd installed himself, and he was wearing pajamas she had made for him out of the best Egyptian cotton, like the ones he used to wear.

He had just gotten into bed and turned to her to say something when he saw a strange expression on her face, like a grimace of pain, and then it was gone.

"What was that?" he asked her, concerned.

"I don't know. I think the baby just made a knot or

something, or put a foot in the wrong place. Maybe it's just trying to make room, but there's none left." He nodded and kissed her and picked up his book again, and as he did, he saw her wince again, harder this time, and instinctively she grabbed his arm. Her eyes were worried when she met his. "That really hurt. Maybe something's wrong."

"I think you're having a baby one of these days. Maybe the baby is fed up and wants to come out." They had told her what to expect in labor, and it didn't seem like that. According to what the nurse had told her it was all very predictable and regular, contractions which started slow at first, and got stronger much later, that one could time and were regular intervals apart. What she'd just had was a massive pain that took her breath away, and a feeling of pressure that made it even worse, as though everything inside her was being squeezed in a vise.

"Should we call a doctor?" he asked her.

"It's probably something I ate."

"A watermelon perhaps," he said, looking at her, and they both laughed. But it was her due date, so he didn't want to ignore it entirely, and he kept an eye on her between chapters as he read. After a few minutes she fell asleep, and he tucked the covers around her with a tender look, and kissed the top of her head with the silky long blond hair that had grown back. It was fanned out across the pillow. He finished reading, and was about to turn off the light, when she gave an awful moan, which he recognized as one of her nightmares, but when he glanced at her she was awake. "Are you okay?"

She shook her head and fought to catch her breath. It was almost a full minute before she could speak. "I'm having some kind of awful pain. It's really bad, Jakob. It feels like the baby is trying to come out sideways and breaking everything on the way." She was panicked, tried to sit up and couldn't. It hurt too much, and when she pushed back the covers she saw blood on the sheets. She had nothing to compare it to, no mother or aunts or grandmother or sister to talk to, and this was nothing like the predictable, genteel process she'd been told to expect. This was violent and so agonizing she couldn't even stand up. She looked at Jakob in terror as the vise squeezed everything inside her again.

"Let's call the doctor," he said, trying to appear calm, but terrified by the agony etched on her face. She thought it had happened too quickly to be normal labor, and like her, he had no idea what to expect. He fumbled for the number she had written down for him weeks before, and called. He got the answering service, and the operator told him to hold. It was eleven o'clock at night by then, and the doctor came on the line quickly. Jakob identified himself and described what Emmanuelle was experiencing, and said she was in too much pain to talk or even stand up.

"You need to get your wife to the hospital. I'm already there with another patient. I'll be waiting for you. You need to leave home right now." He wanted to ask if the doctor thought something was wrong, but he didn't want to frighten Emmanuelle even more.

"He said we need to come to the hospital now," Jakob said gently, and she frantically shook her head.

"I can't get up. It hurts too much," she said through clenched teeth.

"You have to," he said firmly, wondering if he should call an ambulance, but it would cost a fortune. He didn't think her life was at risk, she was just in terrible pain. "I'll carry you. Don't move." He leapt out of bed and put his clothes on as fast as he could, with his coat on over them, laced his shoes and wrapped her in a blanket and picked her up as she screamed at him not to move her or touch her. He felt like a monster as he ignored her pleas, turned off the light with her in his arms, and walked out of the apartment. Even nine months pregnant, Emmanuelle was light as a feather, and she was crying as he hurried down the stairs with her in his arms, trying to reassure her.

"You'll be fine," he kept saying over and over. He just wanted to get her to the hospital, so they could do something about the pain. He could tell that she was having the agonizing pains every couple of minutes, and when he reached the street, carrying her, he held her tightly and hailed a cab that was passing by. He settled her on the seat, and got in on the other side, told the driver to take them to Beth Israel hospital, and turned to look at Emmanuelle. Her eyes were closed and she was grimacing through another pain.

"Is she all right?" the driver asked, glancing at her in the rearview mirror.

"She's having a baby," Jakob said, holding tightly to her hand as she looked at him with tears running down her cheeks, convinced that everything was going wrong. The baby had to be dying to be giving her so much pain, but she couldn't even speak to tell Jakob how it felt.

"I've delivered two in my cab," the driver said, racing through the snow, and going through two red lights. "They named one of them after me." He smiled and Jakob nodded as he kept an eye on Emmanuelle, who was getting worse by the minute. It took fifteen minutes to get to the hospital at full speed, and her condition had degenerated dramatically by then. He paid the driver quickly, scooped Emmanuelle up in the blanket and walked into the emergency room with an air of desperation, and a nurse spotted him immediately. He looked like a madman, with his hair askew and Emmanuelle sobbing in his arms. The nurse grabbed a gurney, signaled for two attendants to help them, and they got Emmanuelle onto it and wheeled her into an examining room, as Jakob gave them the name of her doctor, and they said they'd find him right away. He followed them into the examining room, not sure if he should be there, but he wanted to know what had gone wrong. None of this was what they had been told to expect. Birth was a normal, natural process, and not the violent agony that he was witnessing Emmanuelle going through.

They ignored him standing in a corner of the room, still in his coat, unwrapped the blanket, took off her blood-stained nightgown, and slipped on a hospital gown, as she started to scream and wave frantically for Jakob to approach. He did hesitantly, not wanting to interfere, as the nurse encouraged her and kept telling her that everything was fine. Another nurse had gone to have the doctor called, and the first nurse did an internal exam as blood gushed from Emmanuelle and tears rolled down Jakob's cheeks as he watched, terrified to lose her. What if she was dying? How would he live without her? She was all he had left, and the nurse smiled as she finished the exam.

"You're doing beautifully, Mrs. Stein," she told her. "You can start pushing in a few minutes, and we're going to have a baby in your arms before you know it." Emmanuelle was waving frantically, and screamed with another pain as the doctor walked in and the nurse reported her findings to him. "She's almost at ten, she may be there by now. They just got here," she told him calmly, and the doctor turned to smile at Jakob.

"You're lucky you didn't have the baby at home. You cut it very close."

"She just started having pains less than an hour ago." And then Jakob lowered his voice, so Emmanuelle wouldn't hear him. "Is something wrong?"

"Not at all." The doctor smiled pleasantly as he washed his hands in the sink. "Why don't you wait in the fathers' waiting room. We're going to get to work. We'll take her up to the delivery room now. She can start pushing soon. We'll come and find you as soon as the baby is born. Everything is going fine." Emmanuelle let out a horrific scream as he said it, and Jakob looked as though he didn't know whether to go to her and refuse to leave, or do what they told him. She sounded as though she was being torn in half, and the doctor pointed to the door, as the nurses got Emmanuelle onto the gurney under protest, and the doctor gave her a shot for the pain. They all looked busy and Jakob knew he had to leave, and he felt as though he had betrayed and abandoned her when he did.

The fathers' waiting room was down the hall, and he could hear Emmanuelle screaming as they rolled her away. He felt sick as he listened to her, it reminded him of the camp, and women who'd undergone ghoulish experiments. What was happening to her couldn't be normal, it wasn't supposed to be like this. But he had never known a woman who'd had a baby before, and no one had ever discussed it with him. He was sure that Emmanuelle hadn't expected this either. She would have warned him if she'd known there would be this much pain. And he wondered if the doctor had been lying to him and something was wrong, but they had all looked very calm in the room, except his wife, writhing in agony and screaming his name. He had never felt so helpless in his life, and he felt like a murderer for having done it to her, and for causing her so much grief.

There were three other men waiting in the room when he walked in. One was reading a newspaper, the other had a book with him, and the third was asleep slumped in his chair. The one with the book looked up and smiled at him, and saw instantly Jakob's panic and despair.

"First baby?" he asked Jakob, and he nodded.

"This is our third. First babies take a long time. You've got plenty of time to go to the cafeteria and get something to eat." There was a pot of coffee in the room, and the thought of food after what he'd just seen made him feel sick. And even worse that it might take a long time. How would she stand that if it did? She would never forgive him for it, he was sure.

The man with the newspaper lowered it and smiled at them both. "This is our fifth. We already have four girls. We came in early this time, my wife had the last one at home. I delivered it." Jakob felt weak at the realization that he was in a room full of pros, and tried to relax as he perched uneasily on a chair, hoping they'd come to give him good news in a few minutes, that it was all over, and both mother and baby were fine. But half an hour later, no one had come. A nurse had come in to refresh the coffeepot, and the sleeping father had gone out to get something to eat. They told him he had plenty of time. And when Jakob asked, the nurse said there was no news of his wife, but they would tell him right away when his baby was born, and he could see it through the nursery window and visit his wife. He felt completely out of control and wondered how she was and if the shot for the pain had helped.

The man with four daughters was the first to get news an hour later. The head nurse said he had twin girls, which was unexpected, and he groaned and then laughed.

"Six girls," he said with a shocked expression, and left the room shaking his head and wished Jakob and the other father good luck.

"I don't care what we have as long as my wife and the baby are all right," Jakob said anxiously to the other man, who looked at him sympathetically.

"They'll be fine." Jakob didn't want to tell him how awful it had looked when they took her away, and how unprepared she had been for what she had to face. It had never occurred to him that it would be as bad as that.

He had been there for two hours, and was ready to crawl out of his skin when the man expecting his third child was told he had a son, and mother and child were doing fine. He left the room beaming, and wished Jakob luck. And then he was alone in the room, and dropped his head into his hands, praying for her. After everything she'd been through, she didn't deserve an agony like this. His eyes were closed, and he was thinking about her when he heard someone walk into the room and looked up. A nurse was smiling at him.

"You have a beautiful eight-pound, fourteen-ounce son, Mr. Stein, and your wife and baby are doing fine. They're in the recovery room now, and we'll bring her down to a room in about an hour. She's a little groggy right now. They'll bring the baby down in a few minutes and you can see him at the nursery window. Congratulations," she said and left the room, as Jakob sank deeper into his chair with shaking legs. He was overwhelmed with relief. All he could think about was Emmanuelle. He wished he could go to her, even if she was asleep, and then they came to tell him that his son was ready to meet his dad, and he walked down the hall to the nursery on legs that felt like rubber.

When he got to the window, they were holding up a beautiful baby boy, all pink and perfect, in a blue nightgown, tightly swaddled in a blue blanket, wearing a little blue knit cap. He was sound asleep and looked just like Emmanuelle. Jakob had never seen such a beautiful sight in his life, and he stood staring at him until the nurse put him in a bassinet with blue bows on it and rolled him away, and Jakob walked back to the waiting room, thinking about his son, wishing he could tell his parents, who would have been so proud. They had no one to share this with except each other.

It was another hour before they told him that Emmanuelle was in a room and he could see her for a few minutes. She was dozing when he tiptoed in, but her eyes opened when he bent to kiss her, and she smiled. Everything he felt for her, and all the worry of the past few hours, was in his eyes.

"He's beautiful. Are you all right? Was it terrible?" She hesitated and then shook her head. Instinctively, she knew it was one of those secrets one was supposed to keep from men.

"It was fine . . . he was very big, and he was sideways for a while . . . that's what I felt when we were at home, but then he came down normally when they helped him." They had used forceps, which she didn't tell Jakob either, he didn't need to know.

"He looks just like you," he said and kissed her again. He had never loved her more, and he could sense that it had been much harder than she was telling him. He had wanted it to be easy for her, and it had been anything but that. "What are we going to call him?"

"Max," she said, after Jakob's father, and Julien for hers. It was Jewish tradition to name children after family members who had been lost, and Jakob's more recently than hers.

"He looks like a Max, and you're the most beautiful woman I've ever seen. Thank you for our son, and everything you went through tonight." No one had warned her, and he thought she had been very brave.

"It was worth it," she said, her eyes fluttering closed. Maybe that was why no one told the truth about it, because in the end, the pain didn't matter. The baby was worth it all. "I love you," she said and drifted off to sleep as Jakob watched her. Then he left her, and went back to the nursery window to see his son. He was sound asleep too. They had told him that he could see them both at nine o'clock the next morning. He left the hospital and walked all the way home in the snow. It was four o'clock in the morning, and he was thinking of the people they had lost, his parents and grandparents, her mother, their sisters, and now they were a family of their own. He had a son, and he knew how proud they would have been of him and happy for them. He and Emmanuelle and Max were a family. He was smiling as he walked home. It was the best night of his life.

Chapter 4

Emmanuelle and the baby stayed at the hospital for five days, which was a standard maternity stay. Jakob had hoped that having Max would make her more confident about the good things in life and bring her peace. She was ecstatically happy with their son, but at the same time motherhood heightened her anxieties about the bad things that could happen. What if he got sick or was kidnapped, or became handicapped or injured when he got older? What if he died or a war came, and another Holocaust? What if Jews were singled out again for persecution and deported?

She still firmly believed it could all happen again, no matter what Jakob said to reassure her. He worried about it himself at times, but not to the degree she did. He was more concerned about their financial situation, about providing for them, and making life secure for his wife and son. She worried less about money than about her son winding up in a concentration camp, as they had, for the same reasons of discrimination. And nothing convinced her otherwise. She was deeply marked by her years at the camp and all she had lost there. So was Jakob, but it manifested itself differently. He was always worried about money and providing for them. He had never had to worry about money as a young man, and now he did, constantly.

Her nightmares started again the night after Max was born, now she had a tiny being she loved to focus her terrors on. She wanted to do everything she could to protect him. But if the worst happened again, how could she? Her mother hadn't been able to protect Emmanuelle's little sister, Françoise, from being shot, nor could Emmanuelle protect her son if the world went mad again, and they took her, Jakob, and Max. What could she do now to protect her son from a dangerous world and an uncertain future? It tormented her as she held him and nursed him. He looked so innocent and at peace at her breast, and she already loved him more than anything in the world.

Jakob said something to Izzie about it when he went back to work. He explained that though Emmanuelle was a sensible woman, she was certain the Holocaust would happen again, even in the States.

"You have to get her to stop thinking that way," Izzie said. "She's young, she can't ruin her life like that, or yours, or your son's. This is America. It could never happen here. This is the land of freedom and equality. The Nazis could never have gotten control here, and they never will. It was a phenomenon that happened in Germany. They had a gang mentality, and followed Hitler blindly. This country is all about justice. No one wants to kill the Jews here. That's why we came. I know what you both went through was horrible but you're safe now, and so is your baby. It's only been a year and a half since you were liberated. She'll drive the poor kid crazy if she is terrified about another Holocaust all the time. Let's hope she'll calm down in a few years. Try to do everything you can to help her."

"I will," Jakob said. He had his own terrors to contend with, and their son would probably be affected by his fears about their security too. "I have a favor to ask you, Izzie. We need to have the baby circumcised. Normally, we'd have a bris, but we don't really have close friends here. You're my closest friend, and Emmanuelle and I don't go to temple. My family never did. We weren't religious, we were culturally Jewish, but not practicing. Do you know a mohel through your temple who would do it? You could be there too if you like."

"Of course." Izzie was touched to be asked. "I'll call our rabbi right away."

"Thank you. They'll be in the hospital for three more days, and then they'll come home, and we'll find out what parenthood is really like," Jakob said, grinning. Normally, a circumcision would be performed on the eighth day after birth, but since Jakob wasn't religious, he was happy to have the mohel do it whenever he could.

"Don't expect to get a good night's sleep for the next five years, maybe ten," Izzie kidded him. "First you have night feedings, then you have nightmares, after that you have a drink of water they need at two in the morning. After that they want to sleep in your bed for about two years, then there's a gorilla under the bed, or an elephant in the closet. Eventually they sleep through the night, but by then you can't because you haven't in so long. I hope you got some sleep before the baby was born, because you won't for a long time." He was laughing as he said it, and Jakob grinned, and suspected it was all true.

Izzie called his rabbi for him after that, and got the name of the mohel who would perform the circumcision at home. Emmanuelle was afraid the baby would bleed too much, and Jakob reassured her that the mohel did it all the time. She was ready to protect him with her life and he was only two days old.

Jakob called the mohel and he promised to come to their apartment on the eighth day, and Jakob told Emmanuelle when he visited her that night after work. She looked content with the baby in her arms, and as though she had been a mother forever. He made a comment about having another one and she said again that Max was all they needed, and he realized it was probably too soon after the delivery to talk about more babies. But he would love to have a little girl too, or another son. Seeing Max made him realize that a family of several children would be wonderful, and they would be less focused than they would be on an only child, which might prove to be hard on Max. Izzie had said that too, and when his son, David, had died, their whole world had caved in around them, and Naomi hadn't recovered from it and probably never would. Jakob didn't want that to happen to them, God forbid.

When Jakob left the store on his first day back at work after Max's birth, Izzie handed him an envelope, and Jakob looked at him in surprise.

"Put that in the bank for Max," Izzie said in a gruff voice. "He can use it when he's older," he said and patted Jakob on the shoulder as his eyes filled with tears. Izzie had been so good to him ever since he'd come to work for him. He was even more moved when he opened the envelope after he left work. There was a check for five thousand dollars in it, made out to Jakob. He was stunned—it was an enormous amount of money. He told Emmanuelle about it as soon as he got to the hospital, and she was equally amazed and touched. It was more money than Jakob had seen since before the war. Izzie was coming to Max's bris with the mohel from his temple when they got home. He was becoming like a father to them, and Jakob was like an adopted son for him. It was a blessing for them all, and would be a blessing for Max one day to have a surrogate grand-father, since he had no real ones. They sat and talked about it quietly for a long time, about how blessed they had been to find him.

"I wish he would hire you to work in the store, instead of your working for that cheapskate Harry Rosen," Jakob said. She had to be back at work in ten days, and hadn't even left the hospital yet, but in Rosen's mind since she wasn't digging ditches, she could come to work and sew. Izzie hadn't offered her a job. Jakob hoped he would sometime, but he was afraid to ask after all he'd already done.

"I'm all right at the factory," she said, the baby in her arms. He wanted to nurse all the time, and her milk was starting to come in. She had a lot of it, but was going to stop nursing when she went back to work, and she was already sad about it. She loved feeding him, and holding him, and watching him sleep. She had held him all day, and hated it when the nurses took him to the nursery to check his vital signs. He was healthy and she glowed every time she looked at him. Jakob was proud of both of them and hated to leave at the end of visiting hours but they would be home soon, and he could be with them all the time.

On Tuesday they went home. Jakob picked them up at lunchtime, and they took a taxi back to the apartment.

It was a long walk up the stairs for Emmanuelle, who still had stitches from the birth. Jakob held the baby while they walked up slowly, and Emmanuelle sat down on the steps several times. They finally reached the apartment, where Jakob had set up the bassinet next to their bed, which he had left open, so Emmanuelle could lie down as soon as they got home. He had bought enough food for several days and filled the small icebox. And then he went back to work by subway, and the downstairs neighbor, who was going to babysit for Max while his mother was at work, came to see the baby and help Emmanuelle. Her name was Hannah Friedman, and Emmanuelle had agreed to pay her three dollars a day to take care of Max. It was a big chunk out of her salary, but she couldn't afford to stay home with no salary either.

Emmanuelle wanted to help Jakob, and they saved every penny they could. There would be no movies anymore, and no dinners out, even on special occasions. They had to be serious now, for their son, although they had never been frivolous about money. And Jakob had already started to set aside money for his education before he was born. He wanted him to go to the best schools, and get the very best education. He didn't want him ever to be a janitor, or even to work in the diamond market. He wanted him to work in a bank one day, or be a lawyer or a doctor. He never wanted him to be poor and worried about money, as they were. Jakob had read about restitution for some people who had lost valuable properties and art in the war, but they had to have documentation and he had none. Everything was lost, and he didn't qualify for restitution. They would just have to save everything they could for their son. That was Jakob's primary goal now.

The mohel came to do the circumcision three days after Emmanuelle and the baby came home. Izzie and Jakob watched as the mohel did his job. Emmanuelle couldn't and cried the entire time, while she held Max, and the mohel gave him a drop of wine to soothe him. He cried for a few minutes and then settled down. The nurse had warned them that he'd be fussy for a few days afterward, especially when he had a wet diaper and it burned him on the incision the mohel had made. But he had done a good job of it. And Jakob was satisfied that they had done what they needed to.

It broke Emmanuelle's heart to leave the baby every day when she went to work, and she loved the weekends when she could care for the baby all day herself. Jakob helped her, and had become an expert at changing diapers. They had to buy formula when Emmanuelle weaned him, which was an added expense too. They figured it all out down to the last penny. Jakob was grateful when Izzie gave him a raise in January. It all helped.

In April, Izzie called Jakob into his office, opened the safe, and carefully unwrapped a stone that he said was extremely rare. It was a flawless twenty-carat fancy intense yellow diamond. He was considering going in on it with four other dealers, with the intent to sell it immediately to an important jeweler. He was planning to invest a considerable amount in it, and Jakob was dazzled when he saw it. Jakob took it around to the other dealers at Izzie's request, and then brought it back to Izzie.

It took three weeks to make the deal and in May, the five diamond dealers bought it, and two weeks later sold it to a retailer they knew was interested and had a customer for it. Izzie made a hefty profit on it, and gave Jakob a commission, since he had dealt with the other dealers, and Izzie said he had been very helpful. Jakob was shocked when he saw how much Izzie had given him. It was half his annual salary, but they had sold the stone for a big price, at a huge profit, and Izzie had the largest ownership of anyone in the group.

"This can be a very lucrative business," he said to Jakob as he handed him the check. "You still have a lot to learn, but I think you have a feeling for it." Jakob took it seriously and enjoyed it, and he was impressed by the stones and the amount of money that changed hands. Izzie's storefront was unimpressive, and he wanted to keep it that way. The real business all happened in his office, with the important stones he bought in collaboration with other wholesalers, and how fast they moved them. "You should stay in the business," he told Jakob, "you'll make money at it." Jakob could see that, and was grateful for the opportunity Izzie was giving him. And from then on, Jakob was part of all Izzie's deals, and made a commission on all their transactions. It altered his income considerably. In July, he told Emmanuelle that he wanted her to stay home with the baby. The increase in his salary was more than what she was making sewing for Harry Rosen.

"Are you serious?" She looked worried. "What if Izzie gets tired of you, or you have an argument and he fires you?" Jakob smiled at her reaction—he was used to her negative responses, always imagining worst-case scenarios.

"We couldn't live on your salary anyway. If that happens, we both have to go out and find good jobs that pay us well. So I think it's safe for you to quit Rosen's now. You've been there for two years, and you'd make more money scrubbing floors than decorating his ugly blouses and sweaters." She didn't disagree, but she was nervous about giving up a job, and being totally dependent on his commissions from Izzie. In the end, Jakob convinced her, and she gave Harry Rosen two weeks' notice that she was leaving. Even after two years of hard work and dedication, he told her how ungrateful she was for his sponsoring her, but she had given him his pound of flesh by then, and he knew it.

She thanked him the day she left, and he grudgingly wished her luck. She was sad to leave her fellow sewers but thrilled not to have to work anymore, and to be able to stay home with her baby. Max was now seven months old and a strapping baby. She could hardly make it up all six flights of stairs carrying him and his stroller when she took him out. He was a happy child, always smiling and laughing, and he squealed with delight when he saw her or his father. He loved Izzie too, who met them in the park sometimes on weekends, and adored playing with him. Max was a joy to all who knew him.

"He'll be an important man one day," Jakob would say firmly, as though trying to instill him with his own dreams for the boy. "He'll work hard, and get a good education, and have a big job."

"What if he wants to be an artist or a musician?" Emmanuelle would tease him.

"He'll have to talk to me about it," Jakob would say sternly. "He has generations of bankers in his bloodline. He'll be a rich man one day," Jakob said, wishing that for him, which Emmanuelle knew was no guarantee that he'd be happy. She wanted her son to do what he wanted and believed in, and follow his passions. But Jakob was so serious about business, making money, and loved what he did for Izzie, that he was setting a good example for his son. Jakob was only twenty-seven years old, and had been in America for two years, but he was steadily building a nest egg for his family from the commissions he made. He put everything in the bank, except what they needed to pay rent and buy groceries. Emmanuelle made her own clothes and the baby's. She spent nothing they didn't have to.

They celebrated Max's first birthday during Chanukah, and invited Izzie to dinner. Emmanuelle lit the candles and chanted the prayers and covered her head while she did, and Jakob and Izzie wore yarmulkes. Max watched them in fascination, and at the end of dinner, Emmanuelle served the birthday cake she had made, with two candles on it, which included "one to grow on." They had a wonderful warm evening together.

Emmanuelle and Jakob spent a quiet New Year's Eve at home, and, after Max fell asleep in his crib, toasted each other with a small bottle of champagne Jakob had bought. He had outgrown the bassinet months before, and she had returned it to her neighbor.

"We should go out to dinner more often," Jakob said, as they sat on their small couch with the sagging springs with his arm around her, and sipped the champagne he had gotten them. It brought back memories for him, of New Year's in Vienna with the best champagne lavishly poured and beautiful women in evening gowns dancing at his parents' home, or when he was out with friends in the best nightclubs. It was a life he'd never know again.

"It's too expensive," Emmanuelle said about going out to dinner.

"It would be good for us," he said reasonably. They were both young. She was only twenty-five, and they never went anywhere, and were always saving money. Izzie had chided him for it recently and reminded him that they were too young to stay at home all the time. They needed to have some fun. Jakob had made enough money now to take her out occasionally, at least to a neighborhood restaurant, but they were happy at home and Emmanuelle preferred to cook rather than to spend money.

They finished the champagne—they'd had two glasses each—went to bed and made love, and were asleep in each other's arms by two A.M. An hour later, Max woke up for his night feeding, and Emmanuelle put him in their bed with his bottle, and he went back to sleep with them. The phone woke all three of them at seven A.M. on New Year's Day. It was Izzie, and Jakob was shocked when he realized he was crying.

"What happened? What's wrong?"

"It's Naomi. She had a heart attack last night and died before the ambulance could come. They tried to revive her, but they couldn't. She's had heart problems since David died. She just couldn't face living without him, no matter what I did. He was her whole life. We're burying her tomorrow." It was a day later than it would have been normally, but they couldn't bury her on New Year's Day. "We'll sit shiva for her tonight if you want to come. You can bring the baby." He knew they never left him, and it would cheer him up to see the chubby smiling baby he loved as much as a grandson.

"We'll be there," Jakob said. "I'm so sorry." He told Emmanuelle what had happened when he hung up. She had gotten out of bed to get Max's bottle, and got back in to hold him. They had both seen so much death in the camp, sometimes she felt numb to it, but she was sorry for Izzie, who loved his wife and had no one left now.

They went to the Horowitzes' apartment on the Upper West Side by subway that night. Emmanuelle was wearing an elegant black silk dress she had made without a pattern, remembering one of her mother's simple designs, her head was covered, and Jakob was wearing a black suit, and one of the ties she had made for him. The baby was wearing a little black velvet suit she had made for his birthday with a white satin collar and a little black satin bow tie, and black patent leather shoes she had bought in a secondhand shop, where she bought her own.

The apartment was crowded with mourners when they got there, old friends of theirs, men whom Izzie did business with, and members of their temple. The rabbi was there, talking to Izzie about the service the next day. Izzie's business was going to be closed all that week while they sat shiva for Naomi. He looked devastated. She was his only living relative. He had now lost both his son and his wife. He embraced Emmanuelle and Jakob with tears rolling down his cheeks and looked as though he had aged ten years overnight. Naomi was only fifty-nine years old, but her spirit had died when her son did. She had no relatives either, and Izzie was alone in the world now, except for his friends, and the young couple he had grown so fond of. Jakob was almost like a son to him. They stayed until the last guests left, and Emmanuelle helped him wash the dishes and glasses. Many of his friends had left food for him, there were baskets all over the kitchen, and the refrigerator was full of casseroles he was never going to eat. He looked bereft as Jakob consoled him.

They stayed until nearly midnight while the two men talked quietly, and Emmanuelle held the baby while he slept, and then they went home. The service was to be at noon the next day at the temple, so people could come from work at lunchtime, and they were going to bury her at a Jewish cemetery on Long Island, where their son, David, was also buried. Mother and son would be together again, and it seemed unbearably sad as they went home that night and put the baby to bed in his crib. They lay in their bed holding each other, and Emmanuelle looked at her husband.

"If you die, it would kill me," she said in a strangled voice and he held her tighter to reassure her.

"Nothing's going to happen to me, not for a very long time," Jakob said quietly, and they fell asleep in each other's arms, and woke to a bright winter sun the next day, the day of the funeral.

The service for Naomi was beautiful, the cantor sang and the whole congregation was there. The Horowitzes had both been active in their temple, particularly before their son's death. And many people came to the cemetery for the burial ceremony. They each threw a small shovelful of earth into the grave. They rode back to the city with Izzie, who was devastated. Their friends returned to the Horowitz apartment after the burial. And it was many hours before Jakob and Emmanuelle left. Izzie had the limousine he had hired take them home. It was a relief to get out of their black clothes and play with their baby before they put him to bed. Emmanuelle always spoke and sang to him in French, and Jakob in English. They wanted him to be bilingual. The one language they weren't planning to teach him was his father's native German. Neither of them could bear hearing it anymore. And Jakob refused to speak it except when he had to in business.

Jakob spent the rest of the week at home with them since the office was closed. They went on long walks together, and had quiet nights. Jakob wanted to go to a movie with her, but she didn't want to leave Max with their neighbor since her baby was sick with a bad cough and she didn't want Max to catch it. She always had some excuse not to leave him. Jakob played with him while she cooked dinner.

It snowed again over the weekend and they made a snowman for Max in Washington Square, which he loved. He was a happy child with two adoring parents who loved him, and each other. It was a perfect life. And on Sunday, Izzie came for lunch, and it cheered him up to be with them. It had been a hard week, and now he had to get used to life without his wife. She had withdrawn from the world three years before, but now he was truly alone. He was grateful to have Jakob and Emmanuelle in his life, and their baby. Jakob said it would do Izzie good to get back to work the next day. Jakob was looking forward to it too. He was a diamond dealer now, and he liked it. He was glad they had come to the States two and a half years before. It had been the best decision he'd ever made, that and marrying Emmanuelle. He looked over at her and smiled after she put the baby down for his nap.

"I love you, Mrs. Stein."

"I love you too," she said and melted into his arms, and they wound up in bed making love a few minutes later, before the baby woke up. It was a confirmation of life, which they both needed. They were young and alive, and they loved each other. They had much to be grateful for. The past that had brought them together was slowly fading as they built new memories together. And Emmanuelle hadn't had a nightmare in months. She smiled most of the time now, and Jakob loved her more than ever.

Chapter 5

It took Izzie time to get used to living alone, without Naomi. He made it a weekly ritual to come to lunch with Jakob and Emmanuelle on Sundays, and he had asked Max to call him Grampa as soon as he could talk. The young family and he filled a need for each other. They had created a family without a connection by blood, but their attachment to each other was deep and heartfelt.

Jakob was doing well in the diamond business under Izzie's tutelage. He had learned his lessons well and his knowledge of banking and finance helped too. He made sensible decisions and gave Izzie good advice, which he valued. And with the commissions he earned, his savings were growing.

When Max was four, they moved into a two-bedroom apartment in the same building and felt as though they had moved into a palace compared to their tiny studio. They bought secondhand furniture and Emmanuelle upholstered it herself. The apartment they moved into became available when one of the older tenants died. Jakob and Emmanuelle painted it themselves.

"Why don't you move into a nicer building?" Izzie had suggested, but Emmanuelle didn't want to.

"She wants to stay where we are," Jakob explained. The neighborhood had improved slightly in the five and a half years they'd been there. The building was no better, but they knew everyone in it, and it felt like home to them. The rents were incredibly cheap and what they could easily afford. Emmanuelle never liked spending too much money.

Izzie was about to turn seventy by then, and had had some health issues, but nothing serious. He worked longer hours now that he had no one to go home to, and Jakob often stayed late with him. They discussed stones that Izzie was considering buying, and Jakob advised him to buy a particularly large stone on his own, without being part of a group of dealers for once. The profit he made on it was enormous when they sold it at auction, and it became part of a bidding war between Harry Winston and Van Cleef & Arpels. The stone went for four times what they had expected. It was a windfall for Izzie, and Jakob's commission on the deal was huge. Izzie was always generous with him. He had been thinking of making Jakob a partner, since he had no son or other relatives to leave the business to. But even without a partnership, Jakob had a sizable amount in the bank now, and Izzie advised him to buy real estate. He had been doing that for years himself, and had made a great deal of money on it. "You can't go wrong with apartment buildings," Izzie had told him, and when Max turned five, Jakob started looking at buildings in their neighborhood, and found one he wanted. After he checked it out thoroughly, he told Emmanuelle about it.

"Buy a building? Are you crazy?" She looked shocked.

"We have money just sitting in the bank, earning interest, and Izzie says real estate is always a great investment," Jakob said calmly.

"He can afford to, he's a rich man. We aren't. What if you lose everything, or he fires you?" Jakob smiled at the familiar refrain. She had stopped predicting a war in New York a few years before, but she still imagined disaster at every turn whenever he tried to get her out of her comfort zone. Spending money terrified her. She liked knowing they had money in the bank and was afraid of investments she considered risky. If they lost what they had, what if they couldn't buy food or pay for Max's school? He was in kindergarten in the neighborhood but Jakob wanted to send him to college one day and had been saving for it since he was born.

"Think of the money we'd make on rents, if we buy a building," Jakob reminded her.

"Or what we'd lose if everyone moves out, or they hate us and we have to put up with furious tenants all the time. Everyone hates their landlords," she said, painting the usual bleak picture he was used to. He told Izzie about the building the next day and he heartily approved, except for the location.

"Why don't you buy a building uptown? It will be worth a lot more one day. No one wants to live on the Lower East Side, except the old Jewish people who live there now. You need younger tenants who can afford to pay higher rents, like you."

"One day, the neighborhood will improve. Look at Greenwich Village, it gets more popular every year."

"To the Bohemians. Go where the real money is. What about the Upper East Side?"

"I'd have to pay too much for the building. The buildings in our neighborhood go for nothing," Jakob said practically.

"Do what your gut tells you to do," his friend and mentor encouraged him. He had great faith in Jakob's nose for business. He had an instinct for good deals.

Jakob closed the deal for the building he wanted a few months later, and saved the sunny three-bedroom apartment on the top floor for himself and his family. The building had an elevator which made it both more convenient and more valuable. And as he expected, Emmanuelle had a fit when he told her the news. It was always her initial reaction. Eventually she calmed down and saw the merits of the purchase, because she had faith in him too. But it always took time for her to get there.

It took him six months to talk her into moving into

the new apartment. She insisted it was much too big for them, they didn't have enough furniture, they didn't need a third bedroom since they weren't going to have more children, and he didn't need a home office, nor did she. It was wasteful and frivolous.

"You can use it as a sewing room," he said about the extra bedroom. She still made all her own clothes, and Max's, even the corduroy pants he wore, and the little suits he wore to school that made him look more like a French child than an American. The only ties Jakob wore were the beautiful ones she made for him, from expensive silks she found in fabric remnant stores. She had made several for Izzie too as gifts, and he loved them. Jakob had tried to convince her to start a business selling them but she didn't want to. She was a homemaker, a mother and wife, and didn't want to be a businesswoman. She left that to him. But she finally, grudgingly, moved into the apartment, after she and Jakob painted it. She refused to hire a painter to do it. He bought her a beautiful new sewing machine and put it in the third bedroom as a gift the day they moved in. She loved it, and took over the room almost immediately, and all her objections to their new home were forgotten.

It was a beautiful apartment, and the building was clean and in good condition, with tenants who were willing to pay higher rents than those in the building where they'd lived before, and it was four blocks closer

to Max's school. He went to a public school in the neighborhood and was a bright boy.

"How did it go?" Izzie asked Jakob the Monday after
they moved in.

"She loves it. But it'll probably take her ten years to
admit it, and Max loves his new room. He'll like it even
better as he gets older and wants to have friends over.
And at least Emmanuelle isn't predicting a Holocaust in
New York this time, or a war. She's just worried that we'll
get rats in the building and all the tenants will move out,
and we'll go broke because of all the unrented apartments. That's easier to deal with than world politics."
They both laughed at her predictable reaction. And six
months later, she admitted to Jakob that she loved the
apartment. It had southern exposure and was sunny all
the time. It was a far cry from the dismal studio they'd
moved into when they first arrived. Their new apartment
was still a lifetime away from what Jakob had grown up
with, but Emmanuelle said that it was twice the size of
her mother's apartment in Paris, the one that their
neighbor had coveted enough to report them to the local
police as Jews who had passed unnoticed until then.

The building was a good investment, and Jakob was
happy to own it, and continue building the security he
was trying to amass for them, so he could stop worrying
about money one day. He wondered if that day would
ever come. The war had left him with his own fears about

being poor, not being able to support his family, and not being able to do enough for Max or pay for a good college for him one day. He was still working on all of it. At thirty-two, he was providing for his family, earning substantial commissions, had bought government bonds, and owned a piece of income-producing real estate that he thought was a good investment. But he didn't feel totally secure yet. He wanted to buy more buildings. He didn't have the money to do it yet, but he was sure he would one day. He and Emmanuelle were both frugal, and careful how they spent their money. And with their joint decisions, Izzie's business was growing too, and they had made some very important purchases and sales in the past two years.

When Max turned seven, Izzie took him to the top of the Empire State Building, and showed him the view as far as the eye could see. They looked at Central Park, lower Manhattan where Max lived, New Jersey, Staten Island, Long Island.

"Do you see all that? One day, when you're grown up, you can own as much of all that as you'd like. There's no limit to what you can do. First you have to go to college, and then you can do business like your daddy. You can own anything you want. If you're a smart businessman, and you save your money, you can have whatever you choose to. It's up to you."

"Can I buy the Yankees?" Max looked at him in wonder.

"You could, if you wanted to. You'd have to buy some other things first, and sell them for a lot of money, and then you could buy the Yankees," Izzie said seriously.

"Good. Then that's what I'm going to do." He looked determined as he said it. Other boys wanted to play baseball, but he wanted to own the team. Izzie smiled at him and ruffled his hair, and hoped Max would remember what he'd told him one day. The secret to life was not believing in limitations. If you believed in yourself, you could do whatever you wanted, and accomplish whatever you dreamed. He had said the same things to his own son when he was Max's age. And David would have been a smart businessman too.

As soon as they got home, Max exploded into the apartment and announced to his parents that he was going to buy the Yankees. "Grampa Izzie said I could," he said, jutting out his chin with an intense look. "He said I can do whatever I want to do."

"If you go to college first," Izzie reminded him, and Jakob grinned. He recognized the philosophy and didn't disapprove. He believed in having big dreams too. When he'd arrived in New York he wouldn't have believed that he'd own an apartment building one day, and now he was about to buy his second one, although he hadn't said anything to Emmanuelle about it yet. And Izzie had teased him and called him a slumlord when he'd discussed it with him, but he approved too. Real estate investments were always a good thing, as long as the building was sound, and the neighborhood was decent and had the potential to improve, and Jakob was convinced that the Lower East Side did. He insisted that it would be gentrified one day, like Greenwich Village, where the rents had begun to climb steadily. The area around Washington Square had become a great investment, and so had lower Fifth Avenue. Izzie had even thought about buying an apartment there himself. He liked the idea of being closer to the Steins, and always spent time with them on weekends.

But Emmanuelle looked annoyed when Izzie left. "He shouldn't fill Max's head with crazy dreams, like buying the Yankees one day. That's not realistic, it would cost millions."

"How do you know he won't make millions one day? He could," Jakob said about their son.

"Doing what?" She scowled at her husband. "Buying real estate on the Lower East Side, like you?" She still thought his wanting to buy buildings was risky and foolish, even if she loved the one they lived in.

"Maybe he'll buy and sell bigger real estate. It never hurts to dream big. Look how far we've come in the eight years we've been here. This is America. Anything is possible."

"And what if something happens to Izzie? You'll be out of a job, and who knows what kind of job you'll find afterward."

"Maybe I'd get a bigger job than I have now." She gave him a dark look and disappeared into her sewing room. She always took refuge there when she disagreed with him, which she only did when they talked about his investments.

He left work early the next day, to meet with the owner of the building and negotiate with him. They were still too far apart on the price, but Jakob was sure he could get him to lower it, and he told Izzie where he was going when he left. They were expecting a stone to be delivered that afternoon. They had hired a new runner several years before, but lately, they got most of their deliveries by armored car, and Izzie didn't need Jakob to be there when it came in, and he wanted to check on their diamond cutters that afternoon. They had moved them off-site to a separate workshop the year before, and hired three more cutters, because they had so much business.

Jakob took the subway downtown to his neighborhood, and spent two hours with the owner of the building, discussing its weak points and its strengths. Jakob walked through it with him, and pointed out several issues that concerned him. He had done his due diligence thoroughly, and at the end of their inspection tour, the man came down in price to where Jakob wanted him, and with a handshake they concluded the deal. Both men were pleased. Jakob had an intelligent, gracious way of doing business, like his father and grandfather before him.

He was feeling happy about the deal as he walked home, and was going to tell Emmanuelle that night, and he was startled to see her looking pale and flustered as soon as he walked in.

"Where were you?" she asked him in a strained tone.

"In a meeting, with a building owner down here. Why? What's wrong?"

"Something happened to Izzie. Florence called about a dozen times." She was the receptionist at the office who had replaced the older woman they'd had before, when Jakob started. The first one had retired and moved to Florida.

"What do you mean something happened to Izzie?" Jakob was frowning and looked instantly concerned.

"I don't know. I thought it was his heart, but it isn't. He's at Lenox Hill Hospital. He's been there for two hours. It sounds serious. Florence was crying when she called."

"That doesn't mean anything. She cries when she gets a cold." Jakob picked up the phone and dialed the hospital, worried about him. And all the emergency room nurse would tell him was that Izzie was there, and they hadn't determined his condition. The doctors were with him. As soon as he hung up, Jakob grabbed his coat and headed to the door.

"Call me and tell me what's happening," she shouted

as the door closed behind him, and she heard him clatter down the stairs. He didn't wait for the elevator, which was always slow. He hailed a cab as soon as he reached the street, and the ride uptown seemed endless. He paid the fare when he got there, tipped the driver, jumped out of the cab, rushed into the emergency room, and asked for Izzie at the desk. They asked him his relationship to Mr. Horowitz, and after hesitating for only a fraction of an instant, he said he was his son. And with that, a nurse led the way to the cubicle where he was being examined. As soon as Jakob saw him, he could see what had happened. His face was drooping severely on one side, his arm and leg hung limp on the same side, and he couldn't speak. He'd had a massive stroke. Jakob strode to his bedside and took Izzie's good hand in his own, and Izzie squeezed it tight.

"You're going to be all right," Jakob reassured him in a gentle tone. "Just take it easy." There were machines hooked up to him, and after a few minutes, the doctors asked to speak to Jakob in the hall. He bent and smiled at Izzie before he left and promised to be back in a minute, but the news they shared with him wasn't good. Izzie had had a brain hemorrhage, and they were worried about swelling on his brain. They had administered medications and were considering surgery to alleviate the pressure. If they didn't, they were afraid of a second stroke. And another one might kill him.

"We're going to wait another hour or two and see how he's doing. I really don't want to take him into surgery just now. He's not strong enough yet."

"What are his chances if you operate?" Jakob asked the doctor bluntly.

"Fifty/fifty, at best. He's not so stable, and he has a weak heart. If he has a heart attack on top of this, we'll lose the battle before we start. It's smarter to wait, but he could have another stroke while we do." It was a bad situation either way, and he called Emmanuelle to tell her before he went back into the room, and told her not to tell Max anything yet.

"Of course not," she said, sounding deeply upset, and Jakob was too. But nothing showed on his face when he went back into the cubicle to stand beside Izzie and hold his hand. His eyes were closed, and he looked like he was sleeping, but he opened them as soon as he heard Jakob and felt his hand on his own. His eyes were full of questions that he couldn't express.

"They said you're a feisty old bird, you're going to be fine, and you just want to be here to flirt with the nurses and get sympathy. And they told me to get you out of here as soon as I can." Half of Izzie's face smiled, and he squeezed Jakob's fingers tightly. He pulled up a chair and sat down next to the bed, and spoke to Izzie in soothing tones. He didn't want to make anything worse by exciting him too much, and after a few minutes, Izzie closed his eyes again and dozed off. A nurse was in the room, checking the monitors, and the doctors came back several times in the next hour, but nothing changed. He seemed to be sinking into a deeper and deeper sleep. A buzzer went off shrilly a few minutes later, and half a dozen doctors and nurses rushed into the room.

"He's coding!" the first nurse shouted at the others as a doctor pumped his chest, and Jakob watched the monitor, saw his heart start beating again, but as soon as they stopped, it slowed down. He didn't dare ask what was happening, he didn't want to distract them. It was obvious that Izzie was in extremis and fighting for his life. They gave him a shot of something straight into his chest, and Izzie opened his eyes briefly, looked at Jakob, nodded slightly, and then closed them again, as though to tell Jakob that everything was fine, but clearly it wasn't. The alarm went off again twice, and then his whole body seemed to go rigid, and more doctors came into the room and told Jakob to leave. He slipped outside and paced up and down the hall for the next half hour, and finally two doctors came out to see him. Their first words were "We did everything we could," which said it all. Jakob looked stricken as they told him Izzie had had another massive stroke and a heart attack. He was seventy-two, which wasn't old, but all his vital organs had given out at once. Jakob felt like he was in shock as he listened to them. Izzie had been fine that afternoon when he'd left the office, and now only hours later, he was gone. He didn't know what to do for a few minutes, and they told him how sorry they were. They called Jakob Mr. Horowitz, which confused him, and then he remembered he had said he was Izzie's son so he could get in to see him.

Jakob went back into the room to see him before he left. Izzie was lying peacefully on the bed, and Jakob touched him gently, but his hand already felt cold to him. He had loved Izzie like a father, and he knew that Izzie had loved him like a son. He had turned everything around for him after they'd met and Izzie had hired him. He couldn't imagine his life without him now. Jakob had spent almost every day with Izzie for the past seven years, and he was woven into the tapestry of their lives. He knew Max would be heartbroken to lose him. They all would be, and an important member of his community was gone.

Jakob told the hospital that he would call them as soon as he made arrangements, and he bent to kiss Izzie's forehead, and then he left, as tears streamed down his cheeks, and he went outside to hail a cab. He didn't have the heart to call Emmanuelle from the hospital and tell her over the phone. But as soon as he walked into the apartment, he didn't have to say a word. She knew from the expression on his face. His best friend and mentor had died. He had been the only father figure Jakob had since the war, and he'd been wonderful to them. He couldn't imagine his life without him now. Emmanuelle quickly took him in her arms and held him as he cried like a child. Fortunately, she had already put Max to bed, and he was sound asleep.

They sat and talked that night for a long time. He had to plan the funeral, but he didn't know where to start. There was no one else to do it. Izzie had no other family. Jakob called Izzie's rabbi that night, to let the congregation know, and he agreed to do the service once Jakob organized it. There was suddenly so much to think about. The service, the cemetery, the obituary, so people would know when the funeral was. Everyone in the wholesale diamond district would want to come. He was the most respected man in the business. Eventually Jakob would have to close the office. And they had a safe full of stones Izzie had bought in the last few months, and Jakob had no idea what to do with them now. If he sold them, who would the money go to? Izzie had no relatives and no beneficiary to his estate. He had said it many times in recent years. He had no one to leave it to, with both Naomi and David gone, and he had a sizable estate, with real estate investments, his apartment, and the business. It was all racing through Jakob's mind as he clung to Emmanuelle.

"Calm down," she said gently. She could see he was in shock. "We'll deal with all of it tomorrow. Max will be in school all day. I'll help you. We'll get everything organized." Despite her fearful nature, she was always there for him and solid as a rock in hard times. Then she would instantly put her own anxieties aside and support him.

"And then what? What am I going to do without him?" Jakob asked, feeling lost. He felt like a child without the man who had championed him, taken him under his wing, and taught him so much. Izzie had only been dead for an hour. He couldn't imagine the world without him, and for once Emmanuelle was right. Jakob had just bought a building that afternoon, and he was out of a job. But that was the least of his problems. His biggest problem was losing his closest friend.

He lay awake for most of the night, thinking about him, and all he had to do the next day. He wanted to do everything right for him, the way Izzie would have liked. But he wasn't even sure what that was. He would have to figure it all out in the morning. After a sleepless night, he finally got up at six o'clock, but he was still too distraught to see his son, or be calm about it, and he hid out in their bedroom until Max had left for school. Then he and Emmanuelle sprang into action, and made all the calls they had to, to organize the service for the next day. He wrote the obituary with all the information he had and dictated it to Florence over the phone, and she had the runner take it to *The New York Times*. They closed the office for the day, and he arranged to have the funeral home pick up Izzie's body at the hospital morgue. By three o'clock when Emmanuelle had to pick Max up at school, everything major had been done. The rest were details. And he'd had Florence call Izzie's lawyer and notify him. He called Jakob after that, but Jakob didn't take the call. There was time to talk to him later, they needed to get through the funeral first.

The rabbi had it all arranged and had called the cemetery for them. Jakob felt like he was in a daze, and as he sat in their living room looking stunned, he realized that this was also the funeral they had never had for his father. He was suddenly mourning both men at once, and everyone he'd lost. He could do for Izzie what he had never been able to do for them. When they'd died at Buchenwald there was no way to honor them, but at least for Izzie he could do it right.

He was still sitting there when Max got home. He and Emmanuelle told him together, and he sobbed in their arms. "He was my grampa," he said, hiccupping on a sob as his parents cried too.

"I know. We all loved him. Sometimes people just die sooner than we expect. He wasn't very old, but I think he was very sad after he lost his son and his wife," Jakob said while hugging Max.

"Who'll take me to baseball games now?" Max asked through his tears, considering the practical aspect, and Jakob smiled.

"I will," he promised, although he wasn't a big fan.

"You don't know anything about baseball," Max said in despair.

"You can explain it to me."

"Can I still buy the Yankees when I grow up?" He looked worried about it, as though the magic had gone out of his life, and for all of them.

"You can do anything Grampa Izzie said you could," Jakob said and meant it. He didn't want Max to lose or ever forget the courage and confidence that Izzie had tried to instill in him.

"But it won't be any fun if he's not there when I own them," Max said softly.

"Yes, it will," his father said, sounding stronger, for Max's sake. He had to be strong for him now, just as Izzie would have been, if Jakob had died. "He'll always be with you, and you'll always remember him. He would want you to buy the Yankees. You can do it for him." Max nodded and believed his father. They sat together for a long time that night, and Jakob put him to bed. Max had stopped crying but he looked very sad, and Jakob stayed with him until he fell asleep, and then returned to the living room to find his wife. It had been a rough day, and they were both deeply affected by the death of their friend.

Jakob barely managed to sleep that night, and he went to the temple early to meet with the rabbi, who had the service organized. They had printed a program with a photograph Jakob had supplied and Florence had brought them. It was a great picture Jakob had taken a few months before, of Izzie laughing, looking handsome and like the master of his world, the way he would want to be remembered.

Emmanuelle arrived with Max shortly after. The temple was full to bursting by the time the service started. They had all seen the obituary in *The New York Times,* and diamond cutters, jewelers, diamond dealers, and wholesalers were there, a crowd of his old friends that Jakob didn't recognize, and everyone he'd met in the business with Izzie in the past seven years. Their two original diamond cutters sat in the pew just behind him, the more recent ones were farther back. Emmanuelle and Max were in the front row with Jakob. The service was very moving, for a man everyone had loved and respected. And they all went to the cemetery afterward. Jakob felt drained by the time he got home. He had shaken hands with everyone at the temple and the cemetery, and his wife and son had stood beside him, as the family Izzie had adopted once he lost his own.

"It was beautiful, and just what he would have wanted," Emmanuelle said gently, as she handed him a cup of coffee. He took a sip and set it down, and remembered that he hadn't eaten since breakfast, but he couldn't have touched food now. His mind and his stomach were both upset. And he had told Florence he would go into the office the next day, to try and organize things. It would take time to shut the business down, and he had to go through Izzie's papers. She said Izzie's lawyer, Marvin Rosenbaum, had called several times. He had promised to call him in the morning and he did as soon as Jakob got in. Jakob knew he had been Izzie's lawyer and advisor for thirty years. He had come to the funeral, but Jakob had only shaken his hand and hadn't spoken to him. There were too many people around.

"Hi, Marvin, I'm sorry I didn't call you yesterday, I just couldn't, there was too much going on."

"I understand. I want to come by and talk to you about what you do next. There's a lot to think about and plan."

"I know. We'll have to close without him, but it will take some time. He's got a safe full of goods I'll dispose of, but I have no idea what to do with the proceeds now."

"Why don't we talk about it when I get there. Does eleven o'clock work for you?"

"It's fine," Jakob said, feeling overwhelmed again. He looked at the inventory of what was in the safe, and there was even more than he had remembered, and some very important stones Jakob had encouraged him to buy as short-term investments, that he owned outright, without the participation of other dealers, so he wouldn't have to split the profits. Jakob looked harried and upset when Marvin arrived. He followed Jakob back into Izzie's office, and they both sat down, with Jakob at Izzie's desk, where he'd been since he arrived that morning, although he felt like an imposter, sitting in Izzie's place.

"One thing you'll be pleased to know is that Izzie left everything in good order," Marvin said immediately. "He knew what he wanted, and how he thought it should be handled and distributed. He was a very practical, decisive person, which will make things easier for you now."

"It'll still take me a few months to shut it all down, or at least two," Jakob said sadly.

"Is that what you've decided?" The lawyer looked surprised.

"What other choice do we have? We can't run it without him."

"I think you could," the lawyer said fairly. "He thought so too. I think he'd be disappointed that you want to close. That isn't what he had in mind."

"What did he have in mind? With no heirs, what else can we do?"

"He has heirs," the lawyer said quietly, and Jakob looked startled.

"I thought he had no living relatives after Naomi died."

"That's true, he didn't." The two men looked at each other for a moment, and Jakob didn't understand.

"So who did he leave it all to?" He had no girlfriend, he had never gone out with another woman after his wife died.

"He left everything to you," the lawyer said calmly as

Jakob stared at him in disbelief, "with an educational trust for your son." Jakob didn't say a word for a long time as tears filled his eyes. He was overcome with emotion.

"That's not possible. How could he do that? I thought he'd leave everything to charity, or the temple," he said when he could speak again.

"He didn't want to do that. He knew you could run the business without him, and he wanted you to. He left it all to you. His apartment, the real estate, his stock portfolio and investments, and the business. It's all yours now. I tried to reach you yesterday before the funeral to tell you."

"Oh my God." Jakob was stunned.

"There's more than enough to pay the estate taxes. It's all yours, Jakob. It's what he wanted, and he was enormously relieved once he made the decision. I thought he was going to tell you, but apparently he never did." Jakob looked like he was going to faint for a minute, he was too shocked to even be pleased. He wasn't sure he knew enough about the business to run it properly, but apparently Izzie thought he did. It was the greatest compliment anyone had ever paid him, and by far the biggest gift. It would change their lives forever, and Max's future. Suddenly he thought of the verse in the Bible that talked about returning beauty for ashes. He had lost so much in the war, and now Izzie had repaid him by leaving him everything he had, and the business he had so carefully built for forty years.

"He said you helped him a lot with some difficult decisions and gave him sound advice. He had great respect for your abilities in business. He said he knew it would be in good hands," Marvin said respectfully.

"I hope he was right," Jakob said, thinking about everything he had just inherited. He would have to think about what to do with it. He didn't have to close the business. He could run it the way Izzie would have wanted to. They were partners forever now.

The lawyer left a few minutes later after handing Jakob a copy of the will. He said they could talk again in a few days after Jakob had time to read and digest it, and he could answer any questions that Jakob had. After he left, Jakob went back to Izzie's office and stood staring at the empty chair. He could almost see him there, smiling, the way he looked after he made a great deal, so pleased with himself, and suddenly Jakob smiled, thinking about him and all that Izzie had left him.

"Thank you, my friend," he said out loud to the empty chair, and then left Izzie's office and went back to his own. He picked up his coat and told Florence he was leaving for a few hours. He hailed a cab and gave his address. He had to tell Emmanuelle what Izzie had done for them. They would never have to worry about having enough money again. Izzie had seen to that, and even

Max's future and education were assured. And whatever she said as a reaction when he told her, a war was not going to break out in New York, and they would never live through a Holocaust again. Of that he was sure.

Chapter 6

For the first few weeks after the discovery of what Izzie had left them, both Jakob and Emmanuelle were in shock. Decisions had to be made, some of them quickly. The purchase of the building Jakob had negotiated on the day Izzie died went through. There was no valid reason not to buy it—it was a decent investment, the structure was in sound condition, the apartments were all rented to good tenants, the neighborhood was mediocre but familiar to them since they lived there, and Jakob felt certain it would improve. They could afford something much more substantial now, but he had no reason to renege on the deal, so he didn't, and he could always sell it. Emmanuelle would no longer be angry about it, or even frightened. There was so much more to consider now in both their immediate and distant future.

They thought about moving into Izzie's apartment, but Emmanuelle strongly preferred staying downtown on the Lower East Side, in the area where they had lived since coming to the States, in a neighborhood that was almost entirely Jewish. A month after he died, they put Izzie's apartment on the Upper West Side on the market at a fair price and it sold quickly. There was nothing in it they wanted except for a few mementoes they kept out of respect for him. They kept all the photographs of him and his family, and sold the rest at auction. There was nothing of value in it, and the apartment needed remodeling. They had no regrets about selling it. And although they had options now, they liked the apartment they'd moved into two years before, and decided not to move. Jakob said sometimes he felt he would like to move to Greenwich Village, or someplace a little more upscale, but he continued to own their building as an investment, and Emmanuelle flatly refused to move. She needed time to adjust to their new circumstances. She'd never known financial security before, and the reality that they could do almost anything they wanted was new and unfamiliar to her. In her eyes, in her anxious moments, now they just had more to lose. Jakob understood that about her so he didn't push her to make any sudden changes, but what Izzie had bequeathed them made a big difference to him. He decided not to sell any of Izzie's real estate investments. They were all good properties, and lucrative to own, and would only continue to appreciate in value. He didn't want to make any major changes in the business, and he knew that with wise and cautious ongoing investments, his family would be secure now, and Max would have everything they had dreamed of for him. Izzie had spared them all a lifetime of worry. It was an unspeakably generous gift.

"We're not going to start going crazy now, are we?" Emmanuelle had asked him with rising panic. She was thirty-two years old, Jakob thirty-four, and they had solid ground under their feet now, nine years after they had arrived in New York with forty dollars in their pocket, having lost everything they held dear. They had hoped to do well and find a safe home in America, but they'd never even dreamed of something like this. "I don't want to move to a fancy apartment, or wear diamonds and furs, or show off," she insisted. "I want Max to grow up with the same values we have. And he should know that he could lose the money, and have to start over like we did, if he's not sensible and careful with it."

"I don't want him to live in fear," Jakob said thoughtfully, "that's what Izzie gave us, the gift of not having to be constantly afraid anymore." They had both been living in terror ever since they'd been deported, in his case for the last fourteen years, and in hers for twelve. It had marked them forever, but the reign of horror and fear was long over. They had the luxury now of making choices, and deciding how they wanted to live, while the money and the business continued to grow.

Emmanuelle vowed to make no changes, and continued making her own clothes, which were prettier than what she found in stores anyway, and she made Max's until he objected that what she made for him was too nice or too fancy, and he wanted what everyone else had. It pained her to put him in store-bought clothes, although she purchased them from stores on the Lower East Side in their neighborhood, in secondhand shops whenever possible. She objected strenuously when Jakob bought a few good suits, but they reminded him of his father and made him feel important and successful when he went to work. He told her it was good for business, so she relented. She still cleaned the apartment herself and balked at going out to dinner, saying it was a waste of money. And although he loved knowing that they were secure now, there was an element of fear for Jakob too, that someday they could make a bad investment and have serious reverses. He stuck to real estate for the most part, as Izzie had advised him, and bought several more buildings. He owned six on the Lower East Side. And looking at them, and the way they lived, no one would have suspected that he was a man of considerable means. He was discreet above all.

The business continued to flourish without Izzie, and Jakob bought bigger and bigger stones of his own, and sold them at astounding profits that surprised even him. It seemed as though whatever he touched made money. It was a gift, and Izzie had been right about him. Jakob was a smart businessman and knew just when to take a risk and when not. And a year after Izzie died, Jakob asked Emmanuelle to come into the business with him.

"What would I do there?" She was startled by the suggestion, but she didn't dislike the idea. Max was eight and in school all day, and she had less to do at home. "I don't know anything about diamonds."

"I didn't either when I started," he reminded her. "You're the one who pushed me to apply for a job with the diamond dealers, and Izzie taught me everything. Florence is getting married, you could be the receptionist, greet the diamond merchants who come to see me, make the appointments. I'd love having you near me. We'd see more of each other, and you can leave in time to pick Max up at school." Jakob had considered putting Max in private school, but Emmanuelle didn't want him going uptown, and Max didn't want to leave his friends in public school.

"I'll think about the job," she said, cautious about every decision, but in the end she agreed, and once she started, she loved it. They left for work together every morning after they dropped Max off at school, took the subway uptown, and at night they had more to talk about, and he always explained to her what he was doing. When someone left an exceptional stone with him, he showed it to her, and had her look at it through the loupe, explaining to her about the inclusions, the clarity, the cut, and the color. She had a better eye than she knew, and within a few months she could usually guess the size of a stone and the color from across the room. She was a natural, and he loved working with her every day. It brought them even closer.

They had never had many friends. They worked hard, spent as little as possible, and their experiences during the war set them apart from most people. They didn't want to talk about past history, it was too traumatic, and their everyday life was based on hard work. Their every waking moment outside of work revolved around their son.

Max started to complain about it when he was twelve. It hadn't bothered him until then, and suddenly it did. His friends didn't have doting parents like him, and didn't worry about everything their children did. And they didn't fret about every penny they spent. His friends' parents all seemed like a lot more fun than his own. They had owned Izzie's business for five years by then, and he was still a cherished memory for Max, who couldn't wait to start high school in two years, and was beginning to like girls.

"What's wrong with him? I never complained about my mother the way he does about us," Emmanuelle said to Jakob on the subway on their way to work, after they'd had an argument with Max at breakfast. He wanted to join a baseball team, and Emmanuelle thought the equipment was too expensive. Max had no idea what they had inherited from Izzie, and his parents always seemed frightened about something.

"He's growing up," Jakob said, although he didn't enjoy the arguments either, and they were becoming a daily occurrence. Max was always ready to do battle with them. He was a good boy and got good grades, but he was eager to spread his wings.

"He's only twelve," Emmanuelle said, frowning. "If I'd spoken to my mother the way he does to me, she'd have sent me to bed without dinner." Jakob's parents had been more lenient and they had never talked about money, they hadn't needed to. Neither did he now, thanks to Izzie, but it had become a habit with Emmanuelle after years of poverty and fear. He and Emmanuelle still had a wartime mentality, which wasn't surprising given their experiences, after losing everything. It was impossible to feel totally secure, no matter what they had in the bank, the solidity of the business, or the property they owned. They had lived through an entire world crashing down around them, which no one had thought possible.

Jakob bought everything jointly in both their names, which terrified Emmanuelle, who was sure he'd lose it all, and she'd be responsible for their debts. He had finally convinced her that owning things jointly was a good thing, and something he was doing for her.

They had spoken to Max about the war in Europe, because they thought it was important and part of his history too, and he knew they'd met in a concentration camp, but they had never gone into detail about their experiences, and thought it was too terrifying for a boy growing up in a warm, comfortable home in New York. What had happened to them would have been unimaginable to Max.

He had studied the Holocaust in school, but the worst of it had been glossed over, and Jakob had assured him that nothing like it could ever happen again, which Emmanuelle still disagreed with, but she kept her fears to herself. Jakob knew that for her, nothing had changed. And she had staunchly refused to have more children, in case they ever had to flee again, or were deported. It would be hard enough with one child, she wouldn't risk it with two. There was no talking her out of her position. Jakob understood by now that she would spend the rest of her life in fear of being deported again, and losing everything, because they were Jewish. They had brought their son up with no religious training whatsoever, since neither of them practiced their religion. She still lit the candles for Shabbat, in memory of her own childhood, and they exchanged gifts for Chanukah, but it went no further. Jakob went to temple once a year on Yom Kippur, in honor of the family he'd lost. Most of Max's friends in the neighborhood were going to make their bar mitzvah in a year, but he had no training for it, and was glad he didn't have to spend hours studying Hebrew. He preferred to spend the time playing baseball, and his friends thought he was lucky.

*

When Max was almost fourteen, in 1960, and his father was forty, Jakob took him on a tour of the neighborhood one day, and showed him all the buildings he owned, all seven of them within a four-block radius of their home. He tried to explain to him the value of real estate and solid investments.

"When your mother and I came to this country after the war, we had nothing. We were sponsored by people we didn't know. I had a job as a janitor and your mother as a seamstress in a factory. We had an apartment smaller than your room, and a bed that came out of a closet. A year later, I got a job with Izzie, and he taught me all about the diamond business. But we worked hard for what we have now, and Izzie left us the business, which was incredibly generous of him. When you grow up, after you go to college, you need to find a good job, work hard, save your money, and put it in things that are solid. There is no fast way to make money, no crazy deals with a lot of risk. The way to security is to be smart, work hard, and save your money." It didn't sound like a lot of fun to Max, and he never saw his parents do anything frivolous, or enjoy themselves. They never took a vacation, and he thought they were very dull people, worried too much, and paid far too much attention to him. They were constantly on him to study harder, get good grades, and watched closely who his friends were and were quick to disapprove of anything they thought dangerous or high risk.

"Why don't you buy buildings in other neighborhoods?" Max asked his father on their walking tour. He was surprised by how many buildings they owned. He'd never known before and thought they were poor, as his mother always said. Jakob didn't tell him about all of Izzie's real estate, which he still owned. "Instead of seven buildings down here, why don't you buy two or three buildings uptown in a fancier neighborhood?" Max asked him, and his father smiled. His son had bigger dreams than he did. Jakob had learned to play it safe. And Izzie's real estate represented far more money than he wanted Max to know about at his age.

"It's better to invest in what you know," Jakob said firmly. "We know the neighborhood down here."

"Everyone here is Jewish," Max said practically. "Why do we have to live in a neighborhood which has all one kind of people?"

"It's familiar," Jakob said for lack of a better answer, "and your mother likes it here."

"Isn't that kind of like a ghetto? The way they used to do in Europe hundreds of years ago? In America, everyone is mixed in." But New York had its little enclaves. There were entirely Italian neighborhoods near them, and Chinese on Mott Street. The Irish had their own neighborhoods. And there was an area uptown where all the Germans seemed to live. And Russians were in another part of town.

"Maybe it seems like a ghetto, but it isn't. We're all free to be here, or to live somewhere else. We're not restricted to any one area. But it's comfortable being with your own people." Max looked as though it sounded stupid to him, but he was impressed by the buildings his father owned, and real estate made sense to him too, he just didn't think all their buildings should be in the same neighborhood and that everyone around them had to be the same religion or from the same ethnic background. It seemed so limited. He had been taught in school that the country was a giant melting pot of people who had come from everywhere. John F. Kennedy was running for president, and the American Dream was everyone's ideal. Max's parents still seemed so European to him, so steeped in their own fears and traditions. The war in Europe had ended fifteen years earlier, but he could tell that it still affected both of them, and the choices they made every day. He spoke fluent French because his mother had taught him, but he was an all-American kid. He felt no ties to their histories in Europe. They had no relatives left there, and he'd never been there himself.

He didn't see why he had to be affected by their experiences before they came to this country, or even by the fact that they had been so poor at first. At nearly fourteen, he couldn't conceive of what they'd lost there. Appropriately for his age, Max was looking to the future, while his parents were still looking over their shoulders and running from the ghosts of the past.

*

In Max's senior year of high school, Jakob helped him apply to the colleges he had chosen. It was a long list of illustrious academic institutions, mostly Ivy League schools: Princeton, Harvard, Dartmouth, Yale, Duke, Columbia. He had good grades and was well thought of by his teachers. But Max wasn't sure he'd be accepted by his top choices. He'd gone to public school all his life in his own neighborhood, and didn't have the advantage of private schooling. When Izzie died, Jakob had wanted to switch him to a private school uptown, and Emmanuelle had objected. She didn't want him going to school so far from home, out of their neighborhood, and she said that private schools were snobbish, and he would be ridiculed for being Jewish. Jakob was afraid she might be right and had finally given in, but with some regret for his son and the opportunities he might be missing. He had tried to convince her again when Max started high school, and got nowhere, and Max didn't want to leave his friends by then, and added his own objections to his mother's. So he had remained in public school, and even if his grades were outstanding, and his recommendations from his teachers excellent, getting into one of the Ivy Leagues wasn't a sure thing. With the trust Izzie had left for him, and what Jakob had now, they could afford to send him to a top college, if he could get in.

Emmanuelle was worried about his leaving home. She had suggested Brandeis University, and other predominantly Jewish colleges, but Max was ready to break out of the mold he had grown up in, and wanted to explore a broader world. He had his heart set on the schools he was applying to, and even if he got into Columbia in New York he wanted to be in the dorms. He didn't want to live at home anymore. As far as he was concerned, he was all grown up.

They sent all of his applications out before the December deadline, and he turned eighteen before Christmas. They had to wait until March to see where he was accepted, and he was on edge for three months. In his heart of hearts, Max was already gone. He made plans with three friends from high school to go out West for a month in the summer. They were going to roam around on their own and go to San Francisco and LA, Yosemite, Yellowstone, and the Grand Canyon. They were going to go where the spirit moved them. He had thought about

Europe, where he'd never been before, but both his parents objected. The thought of him going there upset them. The memory of what had happened there, even though twenty years before, was still too vivid for them, but they agreed to let him go West instead. One of the boys had been given a car for graduation, and they were going to drive, sleep in tents in national parks, and stay at youth hostels in the cities they went to. It was definitely not a luxury trip, and it was going to be Max's first taste of independence away from his parents. He had never left them for more than a few days for his entire life, and he couldn't wait. The thought of it kept him going for all the months waiting to hear from the colleges he'd applied to. Jakob and Emmanuelle were as eager as he was to see where he got in.

When the letters came, he was accepted at his top four choices, and waitlisted at three others. He was on top of the world, and the decision was easy for him. He accepted the offer from Harvard the day it came in, and his parents were relieved that he'd be in Boston, which wasn't far away. They said they could visit him for an occasional weekend, although it was the last thing he wanted. He didn't want his parents hovering. As far as he was concerned, they had done enough of that for the past eighteen years. He wanted to be free now, and they just had to get used to it. It hurt his mother's feelings every time he said it.

"Well, are you ready to have a college boy?" Jakob asked Emmanuelle the night Max accepted the offer from Harvard. Max had gone down to the street immediately with his acceptance letter and mailed it himself. It was an emotional moment for them, but they were very proud of him, and Izzie would have been too.

"How did he grow up so fast?" Emmanuelle said sadly. It seemed like only yesterday when he was a little boy. It had happened in the blink of an eye, and suddenly he looked like a man, and thought he was, although to them, for many years to come, he would still be a boy.

"He can hardly wait to get out of here," Jakob said with a bittersweet smile. They had been in the States for almost twenty years by then, and married for the same amount of time. And Jakob was doubly sorry now that they hadn't had a second child. It would have taken the edge off Max's leaving, but a second child would have left soon too. Eventually, they all did. And Jakob thought but didn't say that he had only been two years older than Max was now when he and his family were deported and sent to the camp. At Max's age, he had enjoyed the same freedom, and had been thrilled to go to university and get away from his parents.

"He's ready to fly," Jakob said with a sigh. "That should be a lesson to us. Maybe we should take a vacation this summer while he's traveling out West." Emmanuelle nodded but didn't seem convinced. She liked staying close to home. Her family had been that way too. She had gone to Normandy in the summer with her mother and sister, but never for very long. They didn't have the means to travel, and her mother had to work all the time. Jakob's family had been all over the world. He had often gone with them, and had been to vacation spots all over Europe. Those places were only names to him now.

"We could go to New Hampshire or Vermont if you like," he suggested. The few vacations they'd taken so far, to Florida or New England, had always included Max, but no more. He would want to be at home in New York over school holidays to see his friends.

His graduation from high school was emotional for both of them. He looked so tall and handsome in his cap and gown, and so much like his paternal grandfather. He was very distinguished-looking for a young man, and he was thrilled to be out of high school at last. They took him to dinner at Peter Luger Steak House in Brooklyn with half a dozen of his friends. And two weeks later, the four boys set off for California with their sleeping bags and camping equipment, backpacks, and a cooler, with the radio blaring as they waved to their parents standing on the sidewalk. Jakob had given Max travelers' checks and cash, and a credit card, which Emmanuelle disapproved of, but Jakob wanted him to have enough to fly home if he needed to, in case something went wrong.

Then they went upstairs and the apartment was deadly

quiet and they both looked mournful and felt like marbles in a shoe box, as they rattled around in the silent apartment. Their life was empty without him, and as Jakob had feared from the beginning, all their hopes rested on him. Their joy in life was their only child, and now they had to figure out how to live without him. They had been lucky to have him for so long, but all of that was going to change now. It already had.

Jakob came home with a surprise for Emmanuelle the next day. He told her that he had made reservations at a small inn in New Hampshire owned by an Austrian couple. They had only half a dozen rooms. He had heard about it from one of the jewelers he dealt with who said it was a charming place and they went every year. The proprietors had left Salzburg in time, before the war; they served traditional Austrian food, the waitresses wore dirndls, and the countryside around it was spectacular. He had reserved a room there for a week, and had managed to keep it a secret from her. After he told her, he took a small box out of his pocket. He had selected the stone carefully, and had it mounted in a ring for her in a rectangular emerald cut. It was a D flawless stone in a simple platinum setting, and she gasped when she saw it. He put it on her finger and it looked huge on her delicate hand.

"Are you crazy? How can I wear something like this? Why did you do it?" There were tears in her eyes as she looked at him. She was a woman who never asked anything of him, cared nothing about material things, and never wanted to show off. She loved her husband and son and wanted nothing more.

"That's for putting up with me for twenty years. The stone is twenty carats and you deserve it. You should have an even bigger one. I'll get you a thirty carat for our thirtieth anniversary. And I expect to see this on your hand every day," he said, smiling at her.

"In the subway?" She looked horrified and he laughed.

"You can turn it around, or wear gloves. You've earned it, my love. Happy anniversary!" It took the sting out of Max's leaving, which had been his intention. Emmanuelle stared at the beautiful ring on her hand all that evening. She couldn't imagine wearing such a large stone every day, and its quality made it sparkle even more. To please him she wore it to work the next day, and smiled every time she saw it. It made him happy to see her wear it. It was hard to believe they'd been married for twenty years.

They left on their vacation that weekend, and put their runner in charge of the office. He was competent enough to answer the phone and inform clients that they were on vacation for a week. The inn in New Hampshire was everything Jakob had hoped for. The Austrian owners were charming, and their daughter helped them run it, the food was excellent and plentiful, and the other guests kept to themselves. They spent the days climbing over rocks and discovering waterfalls, they went on long walks and mountain hikes. There was skiing in the area in the winter, and in summer the countryside was lush and the mountains beautiful. It felt like a honeymoon to both of them, and made them feel young again. Jakob was forty-five years old and Emmanuelle was forty-three, and it made them feel even closer to spend time together, to make love in the morning and before they fell asleep. They found a peaceful lake with no one around, and swam naked, feeling like two kids. At the end of the following weekend, they hated to leave.

Max called them the night they got home. He was in Yellowstone National Park with his friends and said he was having fun. He could hear that his parents sounded happy and his father told him they had just had a wonderful vacation in New Hampshire and Max was happy for them. All three of them had to try their wings now. It was a brave new world. Spending a week alone together had recaptured the romance in their relationship. As soon as they got home, Emmanuelle put her spectacular new ring back on. She had left it in the safe in the office during their trip. She wasn't embarrassed now when she wore it, and appreciated the love that had inspired Jakob to give it to her.

"Nice ring, Mrs. Stein," he commented when he saw it on her hand while she made dinner the day after they got back. She smiled and flashed it at him. She looked sexy and happy and relaxed after the week they'd just spent together, and they both laughed and he kissed her and pulled her into his arms with a mischievous look. "Maybe Max going away to school won't be so bad. We can make love whenever we want." Emmanuelle looked up at him and smiled and Jakob saw the girl he had fallen in love with all those years before. In his eyes she hadn't changed. She was as beautiful as ever, and he loved her even more.

Chapter 7

When Max got to Harvard at the end of August, it was infinitely better than he had even dreamed. The campus was beautiful, the classes he had signed up for were interesting, and he liked his roommate. He was planning to be an economics major eventually, and selected his classes accordingly. His parents had come with him to settle him in and see the campus after everything they'd heard about it. It was a big moment for them too. But they had barely set down his bags when he was ready for them to leave. He wanted to explore the campus on his own and meet the other young men in his dorm, without his parents tagging along. Emmanuelle and Jakob both looked emotional when they left. As they got back in the car they'd rented for the drive from New York with all Max's bags and boxes, Emmanuelle glanced at Jakob with concern.

"Did you see his roommate's name?" she asked him. Their names had both been posted on the door to their room, along with everyone else in the dorms.

"Steve MacMillan, I think. Why? Does it sound familiar?"

"That's not a Jewish name. He's a Christian. Do you think he'll be nasty to Max because he's Jewish?" Jakob smiled and shook his head as he started the car and pulled away. They had a long drive home to New York.

"I hope not. I don't see why he would be. College is a melting pot for all kinds of races and religions. These kids don't care about that. They're just excited to be at Harvard." Max was no exception. He was thrilled.

"I hope you're right." She wasn't sure, but trusted what Jakob said, and they talked about what they'd seen and how happy Max was to be at Harvard. He and his room-mate had seemed to hit it off immediately, and Steve had a friend from school down the hall. They had both gone to Exeter, which was a first-rate boarding school, and his friend had come in to visit too, with his roommate. The four boys had been planning to walk around the campus together when their parents left, which couldn't be soon enough for them.

Jakob and Emmanuelle were planning to come up to Cambridge for parents' weekend in October, and knew it would be a long two months without Max until then.

"They looked like nice boys," Emmanuelle said softly, already missing her son.

"I'm sure they are," Jakob said, thinking how proud Izzie would be of him. Max's Harvard education was going to be entirely thanks to their old friend, although thanks to Izzie, Jakob could afford it now too. And by then, the four boys were already bicycling around the campus, looking for people they knew, and eager to meet new ones. Their adult lives had just begun.

*

Steve MacMillan was from San Francisco, and his parents were divorced. His mother was remarried and had two more children, and his father was single, a real estate developer who now lived in New York. Steve told the others that they could all go down to the city for a weekend and stay at his father's place anytime they wanted. He said his father had a cool bachelor pad and traveled a lot, which sounded enticing to his friends.

Steve's classmate from Exeter, Jared Barclay, was from Boston, but his parents lived in London and Switzerland for part of the year. His father was an investment banker for private clients, and his mother was an anti-trust attorney. She had taken a two-year sabbatical to write a book, and he was an only child like Max.

And Andy Peterson was from Texas. His family was Peterson Oil and he was the oldest of four kids.

They were a bright, affluent group, all of whom had had top grades in school or they wouldn't be there.

"I'm from New York, no brothers or sisters. My father is a diamond wholesaler, which is not what I want to do when I graduate," Max said, and the other three laughed. "My father is Austrian, from Vienna, and my mother is from Paris. They came to the States after the war." There was silence for a moment as the implication sank in. With a name like Stein, he was obviously Jewish, and if his parents had come to America after the war, some seriously bad things could have happened to them, but no one dared ask. Max decided to fill in the blanks for them. "They met in Buchenwald concentration camp."

"Wow, that had to be rough," Steve said, looking impressed. "Do they talk about what it was like?" He was curious now.

"Never. I learned more about it in school than from them. They both lost their whole families and are the only survivors. They met and fell in love in the camp. And then they came to the States after the war." He made it sound a lot simpler than it was. He had seen the tattoos on his parents' arms many times and was used to them. "My father's family were bankers in Austria. He got into the diamond business here."

"Interesting," Steve said. "My father buys crap land all over the country and sells it for shopping malls. It's the new big thing. The land is all over the place, Oklahoma, Arkansas, in the South, Texas, wherever there's a lot of land he can buy cheap and sell for malls. He says it's the wave of the future. It's not what I want to do when I graduate either. Wall Street sounds a lot better to me."

"I can't decide between business school or law school after this, but I guess we've got time to figure it out,"

Jared added. "And before graduate school, where are the females around here?" He grinned and the others laughed.

"Radcliffe!" they all said in unison and they all cheered.

"Yeah, screw graduate school," Andy said. "Where do we go to meet girls?"

The four boys felt at ease with each other, and none of them cared that Max was Jewish. It was irrelevant, and they thought what he'd said about his parents was interesting. He didn't look Jewish, not that they cared. They were all handsome boys, and couldn't wait to experience college life, and all the social activities that went with it.

Steve and Max were in two of the same classes, they discovered when they compared schedules. Andy said he was going to be a science major when it came time to decide. He was thinking about medical school but wasn't sure. He wasn't interested in the family oil business. None of them wanted to follow in their fathers' footsteps. They wanted victories and paths of their own.

Their first few weeks at Harvard were demanding and intense. None of them were used to working so hard, having so many assignments, and juggling so many classes. The two boys who'd been in boarding school were better prepared, but even they had to struggle to keep up. They had dinner together at night, and went to the library to work on their assignments. There were women in their classes but they didn't have time to date in the early weeks of school.

Andy was the first one to ask a girl out. He met her at the library, and the other three teased him mercilessly when he went to pick her up for their first date. But he declared her a dud when he got home. At least he'd tried. And Steve met a girl he liked in one of his classes, but she said she had a boyfriend at home and wanted to be faithful to him. College life was not proving to be as fruitful romantically as they had hoped. It was serious business, particularly at a school like Harvard.

By the time his parents came up in October for the parents' weekend, Max had had C's on three papers and a quiz, and realized he had to work even harder. Their professors were tough and set a high standard. But this was what Max had wanted, and Jakob and Emmanuelle agreed that he looked happy, and they liked his friends.

The week after the parents' weekend, which only Max's parents and Andy's father had come to, they all went to Steve's father's apartment in New York. He was out of town, and Max didn't tell his parents he would be in the city or they'd be upset if he didn't come to visit, and stay with them.

They had a fun weekend. Steve looked up a friend from Exeter who was at Columbia, and they visited him on campus, and went to a party with him. Steve's father showed up late Saturday night, and was there when they got home. He handed them each a beer, and talked about the land he'd just bought in Arkansas for a shopping mall. Max was intrigued by everything he said. He wanted to tell his father about it.

On Sunday afternoon, they took the train back to Boston, and finished their weekend assignments late Sunday night. They all looked tired the next morning when they left for class.

By Thanksgiving, they were fast friends, and went everywhere together. Max had pulled up his grades and was getting B's. For the moment, A's appeared to be out of reach, although Steve had managed to get one. Jared had the best grades, but he studied on most weekends, instead of cruising for girls, which seemed a high price to pay for grades. Max wanted to have more fun than spending the whole weekend in the library.

He was happy to see his parents when he got home for Thanksgiving, and they were thrilled to have him back, even for four days. He headed straight out to see his friends who were home for the weekend too. Some were going to City College, others to state schools. A few were going to good colleges out of state, and two were at Jewish universities. He was the only one at an Ivy League school and they teased him about it, but it was great to see them. The next day, he had traditional Thanksgiving dinner with his parents. His mother had cooked. She had become an expert at Thanksgiving dinner over the years, and afterward Max told his father about meeting Steve's father, and the land he was buying to turn into shopping malls in the Midwest and Southwest.

"Apparently, he buys the land dirt cheap and builds a shopping mall on it, then sells it. He says it's not complicated and the profit margin is fantastic. Maybe that could be something for you," Max said, looking excited, and Jakob smiled at him. Max was running with a high-flying crowd with a lot of money at their disposal and fancy ideas. Jakob knew nothing about land prices in Oklahoma and Arkansas, and didn't want to lose his money on a bad deal. "You should look into it, Dad. It might be a lot more lucrative than buying buildings here, and you're not selling them anyway. This is higher volume, faster turnover, and big money from the sound of it." Max was enthusiastic and Jakob was amused. He had been in college for three months and was already coming up with investment ideas for him. He was clearly on the right track, and had a passion for business. He wanted to do big things when he grew up.

"I'll check it out," Jakob promised, and Emmanuelle scolded him when they went to bed.

"Don't start taking investment advice from our eighteen-year-old son," she chided him, "or we'll be broke in a year." It was exactly the kind of project she hated, far from her home turf, in a field they knew nothing about, and highly speculative. Buying apartment buildings in their own neighborhood on the Lower East Side was much safer, even if the profit margin wasn't great. The greater the risk, the higher the profit, and all the downsides that went with it. He'd expected her to disapprove and wasn't surprised.

But Jakob called Lenny, a successful developer he knew in New Jersey, after the weekend, and asked him what he thought about it, and credited his son with the idea. The developer had bought several very expensive stones from him and Izzie, and Jakob trusted his advice. He had done extremely well on some speculative projects, and shopping malls in the Midwest sounded right up his alley.

"He's a smart boy," his friend told him. "That's where the money is these days. It's considered high risk, but it isn't really. How far wrong can you go with bad cropland at rock-bottom prices and turning it into a shopping mall for a big profit? I bought one myself last year. It's a little gold mine. I sold it in six months and doubled my money, and the construction is simple and straightforward. You pour some concrete, and presto magic, you have a shopping mall six weeks later. It's not quite that simple, but damn close. It sounds like your boy has a bright future in land development."

"His roommate's father is doing it, and Max is excited about what he's heard. Do you think I should invest in something like that?" Jakob had faith in what he'd tell him.

"In your shoes? Hell, yes. I'm sure you have enough cushion to take a chance, and there's not that much risk involved. Tell you what, the next time I hear about one I like, I'll give you a call. You can decide then. Your son is on the right track. He's a bright kid." Jakob was impressed that Max had picked up on something so potentially profitable, although he still wasn't sure he'd want to do it. His little apartment buildings were a safer investment, although they didn't represent a profit until he sold them, and he hadn't yet. He was waiting for the neighborhood to improve even more. Shopping malls were a lot faster, from everything his friend Lenny had said.

He assumed he'd hear from him in a few months and was surprised when Lenny called him two weeks later.

"I just heard about one of those shopping mall deals we talked about. It's in Kansas, near a popular suburb of Wichita. It sounds good to me, and I know the developer personally. He's looking for investors. I'm going to put some cash in myself. The real money is if you do it without partners, but then the risk is higher." Just like buying diamonds. He told Jakob how much money was involved, and he could afford to put in that amount without selling any of his buildings. It was a good test of the market. And Izzie's investment portfolio had been conservative and solid, and had done well. He could afford to speculate a little, or even a lot, although Jakob wasn't a gambler by nature.

"All right, I'm in," Jakob said, and Lenny said he'd have the developer send him the prospectus and the paperwork on it.

A week later Jakob had given the principal developer the money, and he was told not to expect any return on his investment for six months, maybe a year. They were hoping for four times their investment, which sounded good to Jakob, and he told Max about it when he came home for winter break. He was excited to hear it and thrilled his father had followed his advice.

"But don't say anything to your mother. She gets nervous about things like that. I don't like keeping secrets from her and I'll tell her eventually, just not yet."

"Sure, Dad," Max said easily, but it made him feel very adult to have given his father investment suggestions. He had just turned nineteen. He was loving Harvard, and had recently met a girl he liked. It was nothing serious, but she was smart and pretty, and he'd taken her to dinner and a movie. She was from Atlanta, and had gone home for Christmas. He was meeting people from all over the country and the world, and he wanted to go to Europe in the summer with Steve MacMillan. His father was renting a villa in the South of France, and the boys wanted to get Eurail passes and move around. He mentioned it to his father, who frowned.

"Why don't you and Mom ever go to Europe?" He'd asked before but never got a clear answer from him. Everyone he knew at Harvard had been to Europe many times, but he never had, which was odd since he had European parents.

"It's not a vacation spot to us. It's our past, and a very painful one, for both of us. I understand why you'd want to go there, and there are so many beautiful cities, and so much history. But I think it would break your mother's heart to go back. And I'm not ready for it either." He had never been as honest with Max, but he was an adult now, or close to it.

"Even all these years later?" Max asked gently, and Jakob nodded.

"Those kinds of memories don't fade, not entirely. And I think being in the cities where it started would bring it all back. Your mother had nightmares for years afterward." Max had seen their scars and was familiar with them, but only the physical ones. The others couldn't be seen or measured, especially by someone so young.

Max didn't press the point, and they managed to have a few family meals with him, while he was in New York for the holidays. The rest of the time, he was out with his friends. Jakob didn't mention the land development deal in Kansas to Emmanuelle until after Max had left. He forgot about it, with the joy of having his son at home. Once the apartment was quiet again, he told her about the land development investment over dinner one night, and she was horrified.

"Why would you do something like that? You don't even know what the land looks like or where it is. What do you know about Kansas? That's just throwing money away, blindfolded." Jakob smiled as she said it. "What are you smiling at?"

"At least you didn't tell me the Russians are going to drop a bomb on New York, or we're going to wind up in prison camp in New Jersey and lose the business."

"That too," she said in a huff and left the table. She gave him the cold shoulder for two days. He had told her they might make four times their investment on it, and he hadn't put too much money into it. It was more of an experiment to test the waters. She always forgave him eventually, and he suspected she would again. She hated it when he rocked the boat, and he knew that about her. It didn't upset him or slow him down anymore. He was a smart businessman and had done well for them, which she knew too.

They spoke to Max several times a week—he called frequently from college. He went to Florida with his friends for spring break, so they didn't see him, and they had finally agreed to let him go to Europe with Steve in the summer. They couldn't keep him from it, and Max had insisted. His mother didn't like the idea, but Jakob had talked her into it. He said they couldn't expect Max to avoid Europe for the rest of his life because of their war experience. It just wasn't fair to him, and she finally relented. It made her think of Paris herself, and she was nostalgic for several days. She played old French records she had bought in thrift shops and hardly ever listened to. There were some things about Paris that she still missed, just as Jakob missed Vienna and everything he had loved about it. It was such a beautiful, gracious city, until the Nazis occupied it and the whole world had caved in and collapsed.

Max was coming home for three weeks before leaving for Europe, and they were looking forward to it. His grades for the semester had been good, and he'd managed to date several girls though no one he cared about particularly. He was hoping for a few "scores" in Europe, with beautiful young European girls, maybe in the South of France. The boys were excited about the trip, and Max was grateful that his parents had agreed to it, knowing what it represented to them. But he thought he might understand them better if he saw the cities where they had grown up. And they were planning to go to Spain and Italy too, and London if they had time. Steve had seen all of it before, but never on his own, traveling with a friend. He had always gone with one of his parents. So the trip was a symbol of independence for both of them.

*

Two days before Max came home for the summer, at the end of freshman year, Lenny called Jakob at the office to report on their investment in the site for the shopping mall in Kansas.

"I thought you'd like to know how we did," Lenny said in a cryptic tone Jakob couldn't decipher. "I'd say our little project performed pretty well. Apparently the site was a perfect choice in that suburb. We made ten times our investment, Jakob. How does that sound to you?" Jakob was stunned for a minute and couldn't respond as he digested it. "They sold it lock, stock, and barrel to a Japanese firm, looking for holdings in the States."

"Good God," Jakob said, grinning. "Beginner's luck!" He couldn't wait to tell Max and Emmanuelle. And he hadn't sold anything to do it. If he'd made a larger investment his profit would have been even greater.

"The developer we invested with is a good guy. He's going to do one in New Jersey in a few months, and another one in Louisiana. I'm going to go in on both. Let me know if you're interested. The price of entry is a little higher but the ratio is going to be even better, fewer investors, and the locations are excellent."

"I think I'd like to do it again." Jakob was almost reeling with pleasure when he hung up. He told Emmanuelle that night, and she had the grace to admit she'd been wrong.

"That's why you're the businessperson in the family

and I'm not. I don't have the stomach for it or the under-standing."

"Thank you for trusting me," he said kindly.

"I didn't," she reminded him and he laughed.

"I think Max is going to be the businessman in this family very shortly. This was his idea, not mine, the theory at least. I called a client about it, a land developer, and he told me this is the wave of the future and where the money is right now, so I took a shot at it, with very good results." She smiled at him, and he kissed her. When Max came home, he told him, and thanked him for the good advice.

"That's what Steve's dad does for a living, and he's made a fortune on it. Just don't go crazy with it, Dad, or you'll be building shopping malls all over the country. But I'll bet that eventually, if you sell your buildings in our neighborhood, you could make some very interesting investments with the money, with higher returns." Jakob smiled at how businesslike his son seemed, and how grown up suddenly. And Max didn't tell him that they had added another location to their trip that was mean-ingful to him. It was a pilgrimage he had decided he had to make, and Steve had agreed to go with him. Max was going to tell his parents when he got back.

*

The money from his investment was back in Jakob's hands two weeks later, and he signed on for the project in New

Jersey, but not the one in Louisiana. There were fewer investors this time, as Lenny had said, and he was one of them again too. They expected results by the end of the year. They were short-term investments with big profits and a certain risk, but Jakob could afford it, and he was fascinated by it, and pleased with what he'd made so far.

After Max left, the house was too quiet again. They were used to it now. When he was there, it infused life into the apartment, and their life, and then it all went dead again once he was gone. Jakob saw a number of people, all men, through his work and his days were full. But Emmanuelle had remained shy and her entire life revolved around her husband and son. She'd made a few friends among the mothers at Max's school, but didn't see them anymore, after he graduated. For all of her years since they'd come to America, Jakob had been her best friend, and he and Max her whole existence.

Max had promised to spend a few weeks at home when he got back from Europe, before he went back to Harvard for sophomore year, and he promised to stay in touch while he was away in Europe so they wouldn't worry. The boys were starting in Paris, and Emmanuelle was excited about it, although knowing that her son would be in the city where she grew up and not being there with him was bittersweet for her, but she just couldn't do it. She had given him a list of landmarks that had been meaningful to her, and he promised to visit them all, and Jakob had done the same with Vienna, including the house where he and his family had lived when he was exactly the age Max was now, and for all his growing up years. Emmanuelle and Jakob didn't talk to each other about it, but it meant a lot to both of them. In a way, Max was retracing their footsteps in the sands of time, and making his own. It was a rite of passage for him, and touched his parents' hearts, whether they admitted it or not. Interwoven with so many painful memories, it was too hard to put into words.

Chapter 8

Their trip to Paris was more than anything Max could have ever dreamed of or hoped for. They stayed at a small student hostel on the Left Bank, and he had his mother's list of important locations in his pocket, but first he and Steve did the standard tourist sights. They walked down the Boulevard Saint-Germain, had coffee at Les Deux Magots. They went to Notre-Dame and Sacré-Coeur, where they looked out over the city. They walked through the Louvre, saw the Grand Palais, and walked around the Palais-Royal. They stood outside the Ritz hotel and the Plaza Athénée but didn't feel dressed up enough to go inside. They visited churches, and smaller museums, walked in the Tuileries and Bagatelle and the Bois de Boulogne, and stood at the Trocadéro with the Eiffel Tower squarely before them, and rode up the Eiffel Tower for an even better view. They spent three days visiting everything, and took a Bâteau Mouche down the Seine to admire the bridges and monuments. They saw the ceremony in honor of the Unknown Soldier, from the First World War, complete with military band, which happened every day under the Arc de Triomphe, and they ate macarons at Ladurée.

And then they started on his mother's list. Max stood outside the lycée where she had gone to school and saw schoolchildren in bright blue smocks leaving their classes, and he could envision his mother there as a child. He went to Berthillon for ice cream, the park where she used to play, the carousel she loved, the bistro where his grand-mother took his mother and aunt for dinner as a special treat. He went to her favorite museum, the Jeu de Paume, and last on the list, he stood outside the house where they had lived, and wondered if the same people who had taken her apartment still lived there. She had told him the story with tears in her eyes. It was more than she had ever shared with him before, and gave him new insights into her and why she was so frightened of disaster all the time. Her whole world had come tumbling down when she was eighteen. That would be hard to recover from, and he was old enough to begin to understand that now.

He was in awe of the sheer beauty of Paris and the history it represented. And he felt some kind of visceral tie to it through his mother, since he was half French. It was the first time he had felt any personal association with France, but now he did, as though a part of him belonged there, especially since he spoke fluent French, and had translated for Steve during the entire trip. Max was thoroughly American, yet part of him felt French now too.

He walked through the Place de la Concorde and dozens of smaller squares, admired sculptures in the parks, and stood at the Champs-Élysées, looking at the Arc de Triomphe at the other end, with the French flag flying under the arch, and then walked down the Avenue Foch with the beautiful Napoleonic buildings and saw people who lived there out walking their dogs. He couldn't even imagine living in a city so beautiful, after growing up on the Lower East Side of Manhattan, which was battered, ugly, crowded, noisy, and dirty, and had no charm at all. He suddenly realized how his mother must miss the sheer beauty of where she'd grown up, along with her language, customs, and traditions. And he had never seen a sky as beautiful. It looked like a painting above the elegant architecture and monuments of Paris. It was almost too perfect to be real. Their visit was meaningful and just long enough to have fun, go out at night, and speak French to the girls they met. Max was Steve's interpreter with every girl, but most of all he had loved seeing the places from his mother's childhood. Steve had come with him to most of them, and was respectful when Max fell silent, too moved to speak, as he was in front of the apartment building where his mother and her mother and sister had lived. The trip to Paris had been perfect from all points of view and much more than he'd expected.

They took the train from there to Barcelona and Madrid, went to all the museums and churches, ate dinner at midnight, watched gypsies dance the flamenco, spoke bumbling Spanish to local girls, and enjoyed making fools of themselves unashamedly with all the abandon of youth, occasionally with success.

The next location on their itinerary was harder to get to, but an important one for Max. They visited West Berlin and Munich, went to beer gardens and more museums, and parts of Berlin reminded him of Paris. Their last German destination was up in the mountains. Max was quiet in the train on the way there and wondered if coming here had been a terrible mistake and was an intrusion into a part of his parents' lives they didn't want him to know since they never spoke of it, or very little. Instinctively, he hadn't told them he was coming here and he could feel his chest tighten as they approached their destination, and Steve saw the look on his face.

"You okay?"

"Yeah," he said. He hadn't said why they were going there, but Steve had understood it from what Max had said when they met, and he had agreed to come along, out of curiosity and for moral support for his friend.

They took a cab from the train station, and asked the driver to wait for them, and Max walked through the arch at the entrance, with Steve walking silently behind him. A sign in English and several other languages,

French, Russian, and German, said "Buchenwald," and explained that most of the camp had been demolished in 1950, but the crematorium, the medical facility, and the watchtowers had been preserved. There were photographs of barracks with captions that said the barns were designed as stables for eighty horses, and inhabited by twelve hundred inmates, five to a bunk, with one toilet for a thousand people. The sign said simply that two hundred and thirty-eight thousand people had been prisoners in the camp over time while it had functioned, and fifty-six thousand had died there at the hands of the Nazis. Men, women, and children, most of them Jewish of multiple nationalities, were deported from their countries. And there was a monument where the trenches were, where the bodies had been buried, fifty-six thousand of them. The thought of it, and the sheer numbers, were staggering, and the boys said not a word as they read the sign.

Max and Steve walked silently to the monument and stood there for a long time as the full impact hit him that three of his grandparents, four of his great-grandparents, and three aunts who had been children at the time had died there, and he was standing at their grave. This was not just the place where his parents had met. It was where their lives had changed forever, their families had been destroyed, and civilization and humanity had vanished into darkness.

After they stood there speechless for a while, they walked to the crematorium where women, children, and old people and some men had been cremated. Max was crying openly, and Steve put an arm around his shoulders. Somehow, just being there, they both knew that their lives would never be quite the same again. It was a phenomenon that explained to Max everything about his parents that they had never said. It wasn't a place or even a simple tragedy, it was a horror of such massive proportions that the normal mind couldn't even absorb it—one race choosing to wipe out another with cruelty and genocide on a mass scale. But even that didn't explain it when you thought of little children being killed and innocent people whose lives had been taken from them and wantonly destroyed.

They finally turned back, and returned down the path they had come, as Max wondered how often his parents had walked this same road, under threat of death with every move they made, and beatings that had caused the scars he had seen on their bodies and never fully paid attention to. It was all too clear what had happened to them.

Now it was a place of memory and respect. Its shame had been transformed into a memorial for those who had died there. It seemed like a miracle to him that his parents had survived at all, and found each other. It was a mystery as to who survived, and a tribute to the human spirit for those who did. There were photographs of the liberation of the camp by the Third Army too, and Max looked at them intently on their way out, wondering if he'd see his parents. The corpse-like figures standing behind the barbed wire were unrecognizable as normal people, and he knew he wouldn't be able to distinguish them if they were there. He gave a last look over his shoulder, and got into the cab with Steve. The driver didn't speak to them on the way back, he knew how it affected people to go there. It was always the same. And many people who visited had lost family members there. They paid him and he left them at the station, they caught the next train, and it was a long time before Max spoke again as he looked at his friend.

"Thank you for coming with me. I never understood anything about my parents until I came here," he said, wiping tears from his cheeks. "I don't know how anyone could do things like that, or how they made it through. I always thought my mom was a little weird and over-protective, and worries way too much. Now I realize she's a saint, and so is my dad. How could they not hate everyone after something like that? And they're both such loving people." Neither of them was bitter and Max admired them even more now. Steve couldn't understand what they'd just seen either. All they wanted to do now was get out of Germany as fast as they could. Max could see why his parents didn't want to come back. The good memories weren't strong enough to drive away the bad ones. The terrible memories were too powerful, even for him twenty-one years later.

They caught a train to Vienna that night, and arrived in the majestic beauty of the city that was a little jewel. The architecture and monuments were grandiose and exquisite. It was the last of the pilgrimage for Max. He went to all the places his father had told him about, the bank, their home, the opera, favorite restaurants, gardens, the places he had loved as a young boy and later as a young man. And standing outside their enormous, elegant family home, he understood what his father had come from and how dramatically his life had changed, how much he had lost. Jakob never complained, or talked about it, was never bitter, always kind. His life on the Lower East Side was a universe away from how he had grown up and lived before the war. Only fate and a kind man like Izzie had changed things for him again, but he would never again live as he had. A whole world of elegance, opulence, graciousness, and beauty had been destroyed.

Max's heart ached for his father as they left Vienna and took the train to Italy the next day. The atmosphere was too heavy for Max in Vienna, the realizations too strong. It was a relief to get to Italy where there was no history for him. They went to Venice with all its charm and beautiful churches, Florence with the incredible art,

Rome with its utter insanity and joy. The boys had a wonderful time, but they both knew they would never forget what they'd seen in Germany and the camp at Buchenwald. Max had grown up on that day and learned who his parents were. He saw them differently now and knew he always would.

They arrived at Steve's father's rented villa in Saint-Paul de Vence, exhausted but elated. For Max particularly it had been an extraordinary trip, but Steve had enjoyed it too. It had solidified their friendship, and Max was glad he hadn't been alone.

They spent two weeks with Steve's father and had a fantastic time. They went to nightclubs in Monaco and Cannes, dinner in Saint-Paul de Vence and Antibes, swam in the Mediterranean and in the pool at the Hotel du Cap-Eden-Roc, and spent a day on a friend's yacht. It was the most amazing trip of Max's life.

Steve stayed in France with his father for a few more weeks before school started and Max flew back to New York. The two boys hugged when they left, shared everything they felt about what they'd experienced without words. Max thanked Steve's father for a terrific time. He thought about all of it on the flight to New York. It was a Saturday, and his parents were home when he walked into the apartment at six o'clock that evening. They knew he was due back that day, but didn't know what time, and Max went to his mother and hugged her so tight she could hardly breathe as tears rolled down his cheeks with all the love he felt for her and everything he had never understood before.

"It's nice to see you so happy to be back." She beamed at him. "Was it wonderful?" He nodded and sat down, holding her hand.

"We went there, Mom," he said as his father stood watching them, not sure what was going on or why Max was so upset if he'd had such a good trip with his friend.

"To Paris?" she asked him, looking confused.

"We went to Paris and Vienna, and a lot of other places," he said, glancing from his mother to his father. "I went to everywhere on both your lists. We went to Germany too." Her brow furrowed as he said it. "We went to Buchenwald," he said softly, and it felt as though all the air had been sucked from the room, as both his parents stared at him in horror.

"It's still there . . . intact?" She could hardly speak. He had catapulted her into the past with a single word.

"No, just the crematorium, the medical facility, the guard towers, and a monument to the dead. The rest was taken down fifteen years ago. But there are photographs of it and of the liberation. I don't think I could ever have understood without going there," he said with tears still rolling down his cheeks, and his mother pulled him tightly into her arms and held him. She was crying too. She had never wanted him to see the evidence of what they'd been through. He didn't need to know, but in fact, he did. For himself, and for them. It was an important part of who they were.

"You didn't need to see that, or even know about it," she said in a raw voice, as Jakob sat down on Max's other side and put an arm around him.

"Yes, I did. How were you both able to live through that? How can something like that happen? Now I know why you're always afraid there's going to be another war, or people are going to deport Jews again." Now it all made sense. It was all too real to them and would be forever. How could it not be?

"They're not going to," his father said firmly in a strong voice.

"I hope not. But I can see how you'd think that. When you see Paris and Vienna, and how beautiful they are, how civilized, and where you both lived, and then you see that place, how they could take normal people and put them there like animals and kill them, how could you ever trust anything again?"

"Sometimes we don't." Jakob spoke for both of them. "But that was an aberration, a mob of very sick people who took control. The world won't let that happen again. I believe that, and I think your mother does too."

"I do now," she said softly, "but it took a long time. You never forget something like that. And we shouldn't. The world needs to remember what happened there, and in all the camps like it. I just didn't want you to see it. I love you so much," she said, holding him again and smiling through her tears.

"I'm glad I did, and that we went." For the first time in his life he had wanted to be Jewish and stand up for those people who had been tortured and died there. But they would have killed him too if he had been alive at the time.

They had dinner together that night and talked about it, and he told them about the rest of his trip. He had loved Venice and Barcelona and the Uffizi in Florence, Rome, and everything about Paris, and especially the girls he'd met in the South of France, he said, laughing. He kissed them both and went to bed early, and Jakob looked at his wife with all the power of their memories, after Max went to bed. Their son had grown up. He was a man now, and had learned a hard lesson about the world, and his parents. He wasn't a child anymore.

Chapter 9

Jakob's second land development deal, in New Jersey, was far more profitable than the first one in Kansas. He and Lenny made a small fortune from it, and continued to invest in shopping mall construction all over the country. The best ones turned out to be in Texas, and by that time, Max had graduated with honors from Harvard. Jakob had doubled the fortune Izzie had left him, and he felt ready to sell his apartment buildings in his neighborhood. He could make much more money with other investments, the buildings were a headache to run, and developers were hoping to gentrify lower Manhattan, just as he had predicted they would one day. He sold all his buildings there within a year, except the one they lived in, and made a killing on them. He had included Max in some of his investments the year after he graduated. It was 1970, Jakob had just turned fifty, and they were both very rich men, more than Emmanuelle could grasp or even wanted to think about. She liked their small life, and her job in his office, and going to work with him on the subway every day. Anything more than that made her anxious and she didn't want to know about it.

Max was only twenty-four years old, but he had gotten an apartment in a trendy building on the Upper East Side, full of young people his age and older, and had set up an office with an assistant, where he was making investments with the profits he had made on some of the deals Jakob had included him in. His father was in awe of his son's instinct for business, and his determination to make money, invest it, and multiply it again. Jakob was never sure what motivated him, but Max knew. He never wanted to be as poor as his parents had been when they arrived in New York or were when he was a young boy. If it hadn't been for the money they'd inherited from Izzie, they'd still only be modestly comfortable, or maybe even poor. And having visited their history in Europe, he shared some of their fear now. What if they lost everything again? He wanted to get to a place financially where that wasn't possible. He liked women and had friends, but he was driven to work hard and do business and amass a fortune that nothing and no one could take from him. He remembered how his parents had scrimped and saved through his whole youth, how they always worried about money and were afraid, his mother making his clothes instead of buying them, secondhand shoes as a child, the things they couldn't do, the vacations they didn't go on, the baseball uniforms and equipment they couldn't afford. He never wanted to be deprived again. Just as his mother hated risk, he had hated being poor and never wanted to be again.

And yet his father had gone from being extremely wealthy while he grew up to having nothing after the war, and he was content now to have a great deal of money in the bank, but he and his wife continued to live simply. His new wealth was barely visible except in a few things he occasionally bought for himself, like good suits. Max's mother still made her own clothes with her sewing machine and preferred it that way. She didn't want to spend money on things she could do herself, like clean her house. They were a strange dichotomy, a conglomeration of contradictions, and to make Jakob happy because he'd given it to her, Emmanuelle wore her twenty-carat D flawless diamond ring every day. They had pieced their life together like a patchwork quilt in a way that worked for them. But that wasn't what Max wanted. He wanted the best of everything. He liked earning it himself, and was proud of it. Each successful investment felt like a victory to him. And making money was almost like a drug. He couldn't get enough of it.

His friends from college didn't have the same fire in their bellies he did. Steve worked for his father, but screwed around a lot. His father had bought him a Ferrari for graduation, and he chased women all the time, which distracted him from what Max considered the main event.

He was missing opportunities to make as much as his father, but Steve didn't mind. He had set the bar low for himself. Andy had decided on medical school, and his family had so much oil money it didn't matter if he never made a dime. And Jared was in law school but wasn't crazy about it, and had no real passion for the law. He was considering some kind of work involved with the environment. Max was the only one out in the world, making real money on his own. His single-minded focus worried his parents at times, but no one could stop him and it was what he wanted to do, and he was good at it. Jakob thought there were more important things in life and didn't care about being the richest man in the world. He had enough, although he continued making investments that turned out well, but not on a monumental scale. He felt that he was just very lucky, and the time he spent with Emmanuelle was precious to him. She had never been a greedy woman, and was almost more comfortable being poor, or pretending to be. The only sign of wealth she allowed herself was the diamond ring on her hand. Being wealthy embarrassed her, so she never admitted to it, and still pretended to be poor.

Max had suggested to his father several times that he sell the diamond business. He didn't need it anymore. He had more than enough income-producing investments without it, and why not retire early and concentrate on his portfolio rather than going to work every day?

"Because I enjoy my business," Jakob said simply. "It gives your mother and me something to do every day and a place to go. And I think it would be disrespectful to Izzie to close it. He left me everything so I could continue what he started, as his son would have." This made no sense to Max at all. He was twenty-seven by then.

"He's been dead for twenty years, for God's sake, Dad. He can't have expected you to run his business forever."

"Why not? It still makes money every year. We've got a good reputation. We've expanded, and we sell to some of the best jewelers in the world on a piece by piece basis. It doesn't make as much as real estate development. But everything I do doesn't have to make a fortune. Your mother and I have more than enough and the rest will go to you. And you're making more money than I ever dreamed of. Where's the limit here? How much is enough?"

"I haven't figured that out yet," Max said seriously. "I'll let you know when I do."

"Your mother is hoping you settle down one of these days. You're still young so you don't need to worry about it. But at some point, you'll meet a girl you're crazy about and want a wife and a family. You'll have to spend time with them too."

"That's why I don't want to get married yet. I don't have time except for what I'm doing. This is the right time for me to be doing it. Later, I can think about a wife and kids, not now." Jakob didn't disagree, but he wondered if his son would ever be able to slow down at the rate he was going, or want to. He acted like he wanted to be the richest man in the world one day. He wondered if they had done that to him, by being so worried about being poor when he was young. Max was driven, and the more he made, the more he wanted. He wasn't extravagant, or stingy. He was just a money machine and an extremely good one. He was in the business press frequently now with his successful deals. Jakob thought that his own father, a banker, would have been impressed by him, but a little startled by him too. Max was taking success to extremes.

*

Three years later, shortly after Max turned thirty, Emmanuelle started having stomach problems again, similar to those she had had for years after the war, and even after her pregnancy. She began losing weight at a rapid rate and couldn't eat, and her doctor put her in the hospital for extensive tests. She was fifty-four years old, which wasn't old, and Jakob could tell from what they weren't saying that stomach cancer was a possibility, while Emmanuelle kept insisting it was a recurrence of the stomach problems she'd developed in the camp. But there was no reason for it now, and no explanation other than a truly frightening one.

Jakob was at her side for every exam they'd let him attend, and she was in the hospital for three weeks, undergoing grueling tests. Everything had come back negative so far, but she was continuing to get worse. Every possible bacterial infection had been ruled out. They hadn't been to Africa or any tropical place, and Jakob went home in tears one night, begging God to save her. They hadn't been through all they had in order for her to die now, at such a young age. It made him think of Izzie's wife dying at fifty-nine, and how ravaged Izzie had been by it. Nothing in Jakob's life would make sense without her, and Max was frightened too, and had flown back from meetings in Taiwan to see her. She looked terrible. Her complexion was gray, and her already slight frame had become skeletal in a matter of weeks. It reminded Jakob of how she'd looked in Buchenwald.

At her insistence, they finally let her go home, because they didn't know what else to do. No medication had worked, no test had been conclusive, and she confided to Jakob that she thought they were letting her go home to die, but she informed him with an iron look in her eyes that she had no intention of dying, and she was going to get better. He wanted to believe her, but he didn't. This time it was Jakob who thought the end had come, and they were going to lose the war.

She stayed in bed for the first few days after she got home, drinking milkshakes until they made her sick. She ate mashed potatoes with every meal. And with grim determination, she got up and cleaned her house four days after she got home, and then went to sit at her sewing machine. She had decided to make new curtains with some fabric she'd been saving.

"What in God's name are you doing?" Jakob asked her when he got home. "You should be in bed resting." She was too weak to go to the office with him and seemed very frail.

"I'm tired of resting, and I don't like our curtains. I never did. I'm making new ones." She was using an elegant beige damask, and she said she was planning to make pink satin curtains for their bedroom when she finished. After that, she got up and dressed every day, put on makeup, combed her hair, cleaned the apartment, worked on the curtains, went out for a walk in the afternoon every day, and cooked dinner at night. At first, Jakob thought it was some terrible sign that she was nearing the end, and clinging to life by a thread, but she had decided to choose life, not death.

She slowly got stronger, and started to put on weight again. After a few weeks, she went for longer walks, and was visibly healthier. And six weeks after she'd come home, she announced that she was going back to work with him. When he refused to let her, she showed up at the office anyway. She had come by cab, a luxury she normally never allowed herself. He tried to send her home but she wouldn't go, and she stood in his office with a look of rage, at him, at the mysterious illness that had nearly killed her, and she refused to be beaten by it.

"I survived Buchenwald, dammit. I'm not going to let my stomach kill me, or some disease they don't even have a name for. I'm through being sick. I won't have it," she said with purpose and marched back to her desk, where she started answering the phones and making his appointments again. At the end of the day, she looked exhausted, but no worse than she had for months. In fact, she looked better. And little by little she improved, and three months after she'd been released from the hospital, she looked almost normal again, had her strength back, and had gained ten pounds. They still had no idea what she'd been suffering from, but whatever it was, she had refused to be beaten by it, and she was winning. Jakob smiled at her one night as he looked at her.

"You're the strongest woman I've ever met." He could see now why she had survived the camp, she had simply refused to let them kill her. She didn't want to die. And he had come to a decision while she was sick and he told her about it now. "I want to sell the business."

"Don't be ridiculous, you're too young to retire." She dismissed the idea immediately.

"No, I'm not. I'm fifty-six years old. I've worked hard for thirty years, after five years of hard labor in the camp.

That's long enough. I made myself a promise that if you survived, I was going to retire. We're going to travel and have some fun, and do all the things we've never done, while we're young enough to enjoy it." She thought about it for a moment, and this time she nodded. What he said made sense to her.

"What if we get bored after a few months? Then what? Or if we lose our money?" She said it out of habit, not real belief, and he knew that about her.

"We won't and if we do, we can start another business, or I'll get a job. But that won't happen. And there won't be a war, we won't get deported. Let's have some fun for a change. Maybe Max is right and we should go to Europe. We don't have to go to Germany, why would we? But I'd like to see Vienna again, and go to Paris with you, if you want to. We could travel in Italy. We've never taken time out to have fun. We were always working, and you never wanted to spend any money." He looked at her, and she smiled ruefully. "We have more than enough. Let's enjoy it. And when we get back, let's move to a new apartment. We've been here for twenty-five years, and I want to sell the building." It was the only one on the Lower East Side he hadn't sold yet. "We can stay downtown if you want to, maybe on Fifth Avenue, or move uptown near Max. But I think we should enjoy life and do some new things." He had thought about all of it while she was sick, and she wasn't ready to admit it to him, but she liked what he was suggesting. Two days later, she agreed. She had been thinking the same things during her illness, that if she died now, there would be so much she hadn't done. And she wanted to enjoy Jakob while they were both young enough and strong enough to do it.

He put Izzie's business on the market, with only a faint pang of guilt, and she spent weeks planning their trip to Europe. One Saturday afternoon, they went to an open house for an apartment on lower Fifth Avenue near Washington Square. They fell in love with it, and made an offer immediately. She had spent her whole life being frightened, and she didn't want to be afraid anymore, of illness, or death, or wars, or persecution, or another Holocaust. She wanted the rest of her life to be about living, not about fear, which was a kind of death in itself. She had been afraid to spend money, and of being poor, or losing everything they had, or something terrible happening to Max or Jakob. Terrible things had happened, and they had survived them. Now it was time to look forward and get past them, and enjoy what they had. She had figured it all out when she was sick, and so had he.

They told Max that they were going to Europe in June, and Jakob told him he was selling the business. Max was happy for them. It was what he had been telling his father to do for years. Jakob said they would be moving into a new apartment in September, after Emmanuelle decorated it to her satisfaction, and then they were going to sell the building they were living in. It was the last building he still owned on the Lower East Side. Their days of poverty were over, had been for a long time, and they were finally willing to acknowledge it.

"Good for you, Dad," Max said and hugged him. "I'm proud of you."

"What about you? When are you going to start living instead of just making money? Any sign of romance in your life? I keep reading about you at Studio 54 and El Morocco with beautiful girls. Have you met anyone you care about yet?" Studio 54 had just opened and was the secret hangout of young, racy New Yorkers.

"I'm trying hard not to care about anyone," Max said with a smile. "I'm not ready yet. Maybe when I'm thirty-five. I have a lot I want to do first."

"My life would have meant absolutely nothing without your mother," Jakob said with feeling. "I realized that again when she was sick and I thought I might lose her. You and she are all that ever really mattered to me. Don't miss out on that, Max. Maybe not now, but eventually you'll need someone to give your life meaning and make it all worthwhile. Until that happens, it's all meaningless."

"I know, Dad," Max said but Jakob knew he didn't, not until it happened to him. "But I just haven't met anyone I care about, not enough to settle down and marry, and have kids with."

"It'll happen. You can't predict when. One day you'll meet the right woman. A woman who makes your heart beat faster every time you look at her." That's how he had felt about Emmanuelle since the day they'd met, and still did. Max nodded and didn't comment. His mother nagged him about it all the time, and he accused her of being a Jewish mother when she did. But in the meantime, he was glad that his parents were taking time to enjoy their life. They had earned it and worked hard all their lives, and had been through so much together. He had never forgotten his pilgrimage to Buchenwald.

*

Jakob sold the business to his two original Flemish stonecutters, and agreed to let them pay him slowly over time so they could afford it. He thought Izzie would have liked that, and it made him feel less guilty for selling. They closed on the apartment on Fifth Avenue near Washington Square in a beautiful pre-war building. He received an offer on his last Lower East Side building a week before they left for Europe, and he accepted it. He sold the building for six times what he had paid for it, and probably could have gotten more if he'd pushed, but he didn't want to. The man who bought it was thrilled.

They had dinner with Max the night before they left for Europe. It was going to be a trip back in time for both of them, but they felt ready for it now, to face the ghosts of their past, as Max had twelve years before, the first time he'd gone to Europe, while he was in college. They were starting in Paris, and staying at the Ritz. Jakob had insisted they were going first-class everywhere, and Emmanuelle would just have to put up with it. He was not going to stay in small miserable hotels just so she could brag about how much money they'd saved when they got back. It still pained her to spend money, but she'd agreed. When they arrived at the Ritz, she was bowled over by how luxurious the hotel was, how elegant their suite, all done in beautiful brocades, with rooms filled with antiques, and fresh flowers in every room, chocolates, and macarons from Ladurée.

"This is what we've worked for, for thirty years," he reminded her as he put his arms around her and kissed her. "Consider it a belated honeymoon."

They walked all over Paris together, to all the places that were meaningful to her, and others he wanted to see. They stood outside where she had lived, and she cried thinking about her mother and sister, but it was a peaceful feeling coming back here, as though she were putting old ghosts to rest, and was no longer tormented by them. She was glad they had come back to Paris. She had needed to see it again and hadn't realized it. There had been so much violence in the way she'd left, and she'd never been back since, to say goodbye to the people and places she loved. She walked into the butcher shop across from her home, and saw Flore, the daughter of the owner. She was heavier but looked the same. They had played together as children. She recognized Emmanuelle immediately and they both burst into tears and hugged each other. She owned the butcher shop now, had inherited it from her parents, and said she had four children, and three grandchildren. Emmanuelle asked her in a pained voice if the same people were still in their old apartment, the ones who had denounced them to the police as Jews and got them deported. Flore said they had moved away years ago, right after the war. The entire family had been denounced as collaborators and paraded through the streets with shorn heads, and after that they left, and Flore had no idea where they went.

"There's a nice family there now with two little girls," Flore reassured her. "I always think of you and Françoise when I see them." She had heard years before that Emmanuelle's sister and mother had died in the camp. People said Emmanuelle had survived, but she never came back to Paris, and no one knew where she went. "I always wondered where you were, but I didn't know how to find you."

"I had no one to come back to, and nowhere to stay," Emmanuelle said quietly. "I met my husband at the camp, and we got married after it was liberated. We went to America together. I have a son, but no grandchildren yet." She smiled, and introduced her to Jakob, who was warm and gracious when he shook her hand. She was happy to see that Emmanuelle was alive, in good health, comfortable, and not alone in the world. It had been such a terrible time for all of them, and even worse for their Jewish friends.

They talked for a little while longer, and then Jakob and Emmanuelle left, walked around the neighborhood for a while, and then back to the hotel. It struck her that many shops and bistros near her home were still the same. In many ways, Paris hadn't changed. She loved that about the city, that there were establishments that had been in the same place, in many cases run by the same family, for a hundred years.

She loved seeing all the familiar landmarks and monuments, the Place de la Concorde, the Champs-Élysées, the Arc de Triomphe, the Invalides, Napoleon's war monument in the Place Vendôme. They were the sights of her childhood and adolescence, the places she had gone with her parents, and later with her mother and sister. Even the smells of Paris were familiar to her. And she had always gone to Ladurée with her grandmother for hot chocolate and macarons for a special treat. It was one of the few memories she had of her since she had died when Emmanuelle was very young. And she remembered things she had done with her mother and sister that she hadn't thought about for years.

She took Jakob to all the places that Max had visited

when he had gone to Paris for the first time when he was in college, and now she could see them for herself. It wasn't the agony being there that she had feared it would be. On the contrary, it comforted and soothed her, and felt like coming home after thirty-six years. How she had left no longer seemed as important as the fact that she had grown up there. When they left, she felt calm and at peace.

Jakob felt the same way in Vienna when they got there. He showed her all the favorite places of his boyhood, the parks, and the monuments, the places where he had played, and their enormous elegant home. It was a club now, and he stood outside for a long time, and showed her the windows where his room had been. She had always known that he had grown up in wealth and luxury, but she had never fully understood to what extent, and all that he had lost, until she saw the family bank and his home. The bank was still a financial institution of some kind, but he didn't want to go in when she suggested it. He wanted to leave the past in the past, and he looked sad as they walked away from his home. She tucked her hand into his arm, and he looked down at her with deep emotion, tears brimming in his eyes.

"I don't mind losing the house so much as all the people I loved in it." It was incredible to realize that an entire family had disappeared, had been wiped out, except for him. It was what the Nazis had wanted, and nearly succeeded in doing, and in many instances they did. In their case, he and Max were the only ones left to carry on his name. And since she was a woman, Emmanuelle's family name had ended with her.

They only stayed in Vienna for two days. They had accomplished what they'd gone there to do. In essence, they had come to say their farewells to their cities, their childhood homes, and the people they had lost. They had never had a chance to do that. And now finally, they were ready to bury their dead and move on.

From Vienna, they flew to Rome, which Emmanuelle only remembered vaguely from a trip there once with her mother and sister, and Jakob still remembered fairly well. The atmosphere was electric. Everything was chaotic, with a holiday feeling to it. From there they drove north to Florence and Venice, which she didn't know but Jakob did. He had traveled a great deal in Europe with his family, and their last stop was Lake Como, which she thought was one of the most romantic places she'd ever seen. They spent four days there, relaxing and walking, looking at the mountains and the lake, and talking about where they'd been. But both of them had been more peaceful since they'd been to their respective homes and cities. It had done them both good to see them again. And they were both sad when it was time to leave.

After Lake Como, they flew from Milan to New York. They had much to do when they got home. Jakob had to conclude the sale of the building they had lived in, and Emmanuelle had to get their new apartment ready. Jakob had work to do getting ready to hand over his business. He wasn't sure what he was going to do after that, although he was still interested in more land development deals. They had dinner with Max their second night back. He seemed busier than ever, and very stressed, and told his father about a new land offering in Illinois for another shopping mall. Jakob was interested in the deal. He'd been worried he wouldn't have enough to do once he left his business, but he was busy all week and they were thinking about taking a cruise that winter. Suddenly, they were turning into world travelers, but it was what they had wanted to do. They had gently left the past behind them in Europe, and now they were ready for the future, and whatever it would bring.

Chapter 10

Jakob and Emmanuelle moved into their new apartment in September, and it took until the end of the year to hand over the business. They took a Caribbean cruise in January, and planned a trip to Hawaii and Mexico in the spring.

The cruises they took introduced them to new people and places. They were waited on hand and foot, and they came back every time having made new friends and discovered foreign destinations they would never have gone to otherwise. Jakob still felt guilty about not going to work every day, but once they were away, he enjoyed it immensely. They'd been traveling constantly for almost a year after he left the business, and came back for Max's thirty-second birthday. His mother noticed that he had a gleam in his eye when they had dinner with him. There was something he wasn't telling them, she was sure, but she couldn't figure out what it was. She said something to Jakob about it, on the way home to their new apartment, and he said it was her imagination. And then he saw it in the paper, on the society page two days later.

It was a picture of Max with a beautiful young woman in an elegant white evening dress on his arm and the caption under it said that they were going to the Christmas dance given by the young woman's parents. Her name was Julie Morgan and she was a spectacular-looking girl. The column said she was one of the three Morgan girls who were currently taking New York by storm.

Emmanuelle saw her son in the social columns frequently, so there was nothing unusual about it, but he was smiling broadly and looked absurdly happy in the photograph, and she had a strange feeling that this young woman wasn't just the girl of the hour. She was clinging to him, and he was leaning toward her in a very familiar way. Her hair was swept up in a shower of blond curls, she was almost as tall as he was, and she was wearing a diamond necklace. She didn't look like just any girl. He called Emmanuelle that afternoon to thank her for his birthday dinner, and she tried to sound nonchalant when she asked him about the column.

"I saw you in the papers today."

"I went to a Christmas party with a girl I met recently," he said casually.

"She's very pretty. Someone special?" He laughed when she asked him. He knew her better.

"Stop playing Jewish mother, it doesn't suit you. And the answer to your question is I don't know yet. I just met her. She seems very nice. She and her sisters are very popular at the moment. Her parents give fabulous parties." She thought it was interesting that he had responded "I don't know yet" to her question, instead of the usual emphatic no she'd been getting from him for years. She told Jakob about it that night and showed him the picture. He glanced at it for an instant and nodded.

"Are they engaged yet? Should I be calling her father?" he teased her. They both knew their son better than that. His romances never lasted more than a few weeks or months, and then he'd be off to another project and another girl.

"I'd be happier if it said they were giving a Chanukah party," she commented drily and Jakob laughed at her.

"Not likely with a name like Morgan. But we have ourselves to blame for that. We should have sent him for Hebrew lessons and had his bar mitzvah if that's what you wanted. We don't go to temple, so why should he?"

"He may not care, but maybe she does." He glanced at the newspaper photo again and shook his head.

"Doesn't look like it. If she were hanging on to him any tighter, she'd have cut off the circulation in his arm." She was wearing long elegant white gloves, and she was smiling radiantly. "His friends are always Catholic or Episcopalian. He has a knack for finding them anywhere. We never made a point of his being Jewish, so neither does he. Do you really care?" Jakob asked her, serious for a moment, and she answered honestly.

"Maybe. It's his heritage, even if we're not religious. And I wouldn't want him to convert for some Christian girl, if that's who he falls in love with."

"Maybe she'd convert for him," Jakob said sensibly. "Why don't we wait to see if he's serious about this girl, before we worry about who's converting for whom."

"If he marries a Christian, their kids won't be Jewish," Emmanuelle said, looking worried, since the mother had to be Jewish, in order for the children to be Jewish too.

"Be sure to remind him the next time he calls you," Jakob said, making fun of her.

"I asked him today if he's serious about her and he said he doesn't know yet. Usually he just says a flat no," she said, pursuing the subject.

"I think you're getting ahead of yourself here." But her instincts were better than he gave her credit for and she had a feeling about this girl. She was very good-looking, and there had been something about Max at dinner that had never been there before. He was excited about something and she could sense this girl was it.

There was a photograph of them again a few days later. He had taken her to El Morocco on New Year's Eve, and she was wearing a sexy, low-cut black dress in the picture, and the photograph showed them toasting each other at midnight and kissing. She showed Jakob again over breakfast and he nodded.

"I don't think she's the first girl he's kissed."

"New Year's Eve is different," she insisted, and he went back to reading his newspaper. He wasn't going to get wound up over some girl Max was dating. They never lasted long with him, no matter how many times he was in the papers with them.

But the next time they asked him to dinner, he asked if he could bring Julie and Emmanuelle reported it to Jakob immediately.

"He wants to introduce her to us. That's a sure sign that she's important to him. Normally, he won't let his dates near us."

"Then we'd better behave and make a good impression," Jakob teased her, but now he was intrigued too.

Jakob made a reservation at La Côte Basque, which they went to for special occasions, and when they got there, Max and his date hadn't arrived yet. Jakob and Emmanuelle sat at the table waiting, and they were fifteen minutes late. When they came, she was wearing an expensive red silk dress that Emmanuelle thought was much too short to look respectable, but she was an extremely pretty young woman, with exquisite features, milky white skin, big blue eyes, and masses of blond hair piled high on her head. She looked like a model, and Max seemed besotted with her. He held her hand for most of the evening, except when they were eating, and she was very polite, responded to questions they asked her, but she seemed to have no particular interests. She spent the entire dinner staring adoringly at Max, and giggled when he spoke to her, which Emmanuelle found irritating and somewhat immature. But she was undeniably beautiful and Max seemed crazy about her.

She said her family lived in Connecticut, and she hadn't gone to college, but she was on a number of charitable committees with her mother and older sister. She said her younger sister had gone to college, but had dropped out in sophomore year. Max didn't seem to care. She liked to ride horses, went to Europe with her parents every year, and had made her debut in New York five years before. Emmanuelle did the calculation, and since girls were debutantes at eighteen, according to tradition, that meant she was twenty-three, nine years younger than Max. His mother had no concrete objections to her except that she was very young and seemed a little silly, and she wasn't Jewish. She would have liked to see him with someone slightly older, a little more serious, and who had gone to college. And she would have preferred it if Julie were Jewish. But a debutante from Connecticut was not likely to be a Jewish girl. And Max seemed to hang on her every word. Her family had invited him for a weekend at their ski house in Vermont in two weeks. After thanking them for dinner, the young couple left right after dessert. They were meeting friends at Studio 54.

"It's serious," Emmanuelle said as soon as they were out of earshot. And Jakob didn't disagree with her. He just didn't think it would last. Max's romances never did. "I wish she were Jewish," she said wistfully. "I wish she'd gone to college. What would they talk about for the next fifty years? Men don't think of that when a girl is as pretty as she is." And it was obvious that Max was very taken with her, for the moment at least. The fact that he'd brought her to dinner with his parents spoke for itself, or maybe he felt obliged to, since he had met her parents at their Christmas dance for four hundred people, and they'd invited him to go skiing with them in Vermont.

"Let's not get worked up about it yet," Jakob said calmly as he paid the check, and a few minutes later they left the restaurant.

The following day, there were photographs in the paper of all three Morgan girls and the men they were dating. Pamela, the oldest, was dating the scion of an important Boston banking family, and Belinda, the youngest, was dating a famous movie actor. Julie had been photographed with Max again, and the caption read "Youngest tycoon in town Max Stein," and they referred to him in the article as the most desirable bachelor in New York. None of it was his parents' style. They thought he should be more discreet, about both his success and his love life, but he was young and handsome and went out a lot. Max was the image of his Viennese father and grandfather. He had their dark-haired, blue-eyed good looks. Emmanuelle was green-eyed and fair.

For the next several months the newspaper coverage continued. Max and Julie were in the papers almost every day, and had become the darlings of the press. Emmanuelle didn't like to see it, and thought he should conduct his romances in private, but they had been seen together in public too often to be able to avoid the photographers now.

It was hardly a surprise in May when he told his parents he was deeply in love with her. They had been dating for five months and he told them over Sunday lunch in their new apartment that it was serious and he wanted to propose.

"Already? Don't you think it's a little soon after five months?" his mother said, looking anxious. "She's awfully young, Max."

"She'll be twenty-four in June. That's old enough. We don't want to wait."

"What do her parents think?" Jakob asked him calmly.

"I think they like me," he said innocently. He would certainly be able to provide for her, but his parents weren't sure what she'd be bringing to the table, other than her family name and a pretty face.

"How do they feel about your being Jewish?" his father asked him.

"They haven't said anything. I'm not sure they care."

"Have they asked you to convert?" his mother wanted to know.

"No, they haven't. And I haven't asked her to. We're not religious, so it would be hypocritical of me to make her do that. She's Episcopalian, and they go to church, but I don't think she's very religious. She never goes to church when she's with me."

"I've only met her once," Emmanuelle said, "but she doesn't seem like a serious person to me. Life can be hard at times, and you need someone who can weather that with you. When we met her, she only talked about her horses, going to Studio 54, and organizing fashion shows for the Junior League. Is that what you want, Max? You need someone who can help you in your career, take care of your children, and support you in hard times." What she was saying was reasonable, but her son looked amused.

"You mean like if there's a war, Mom? Or another Holocaust?" He had heard her say it too often on every subject while he was growing up. She always predicted disaster, although he understood why and had compassion for them.

"Your mother's not wrong, Max. Things happen that you don't expect. Difficult things sometimes. It doesn't take a war to have something bad happen. You need someone solid who can go through that with you. Young people don't always see that. I'm not sure she's mature enough to give you the kind of support you might need."

"It's my job to take care of her," Max said nobly, which

was what they had taught him, but they wanted him to get something in exchange, and neither of them could envision Julie being anything but frivolous, beautiful, and very spoiled. It didn't seem like a solid foundation for a marriage to either of them. Max didn't want to hear it. "I'm going to ask her to marry me in the next couple of weeks. I just wanted you to know. I've made up my mind. Do I have your blessing?" He gave them no choice.

They both hesitated for a moment and then nodded. He had made it clear they had no right to object. And why would they? But he was marrying a Christian, and what seemed like to them a very indulged young girl. It wasn't what they had wished for him. But saying so would have alienated him from them, possibly forever.

"Would you consider waiting a few more months to be sure?" his father asked him, and Max shook his head.

"I am sure. That's why I'm here today. I know you want the best for me. But I know what I'm doing. We love each other, and she's a great girl. We have a lot of fun together, and we both want to have kids, like three or four." He could afford them, they knew, but he would have no time for them if he continued his career at the same pace, and neither of them could see Julie bringing up four kids with no help from him.

"You're going to have to slow your work down a little if you want a wife and children," his mother said seriously. "They'll need you around, or sooner or later she'll get upset, and you won't even know your own children."

"Stop seeing disaster at every turn, Mom. We'll have nannies, I can afford them, and I want her to spend time with me when I'm not busy, and that's what she wants too. I don't want her being a slave to our kids and changing diapers all the time." The one thing Emmanuelle was sure of was that there was no risk that Julie would be spending much of her time changing diapers. "We're going to have a lot of fun, you'll see." It was the second time he'd said it, and Emmanuelle glanced at her husband and then at her son.

"Marriage isn't always fun, Max. I love your father, but things happen. It's not fun every day."

"You two have had an unusual experience. Your whole world fell apart. That's not going to happen to us, or anyone in this country today." Buchenwald had moved him deeply, but it had nothing to do with the life that he and Julie were going to lead once they were married. But that wasn't what his parents were worried about. Julie just didn't seem like a serious, solid young woman to either of them. She only wanted to play.

"We love you, we just want you to be happy," his mother said as he stood up after lunch.

"We will be. I promise." He smiled at both of them. His announcement hadn't gone quite as smoothly as he'd hoped, but they weren't going to object. He was thirty-two years old and they weren't the kind of people to forbid him to marry the girl of his dreams, which Julie was. He had never been as in love as he was with her, and she was too.

There was a long silence after he kissed them goodbye and left the apartment, and Emmanuelle glanced at her husband.

"So, what do you think?"

"I think the same thing you do," he said unhappily. "I think he's making a mistake, but there's nothing we can do about it. And I don't even care that she's not Jewish. She's a lightweight. I wouldn't leave a dog with that girl, let alone three or four kids, no matter how many nannies he gets for her. And what does she need nannies for if she doesn't have a job? Why can't she take care of the kids herself?"

"She's not the type," Emmanuelle said. "She seems very spoiled. I'm sure her parents indulged her, and she was brought up by nannies herself." And then she thought of something else. "And why are they so obsessed with 'having fun'? We never thought about that. Marriage isn't about fun, it's about supporting each other."

"We never thought about it because we were too busy trying to put food on the table to feed our son. They don't need to worry about that." He looked at his wife long and hard then. "I don't think it's going to work."

"Neither do I," Emmanuelle admitted, "but if we tell him that, he'll never speak to us again." She didn't want to lose her only son to a superficial, possibly not very bright girl who might turn him against them.

"Do you think we should be telling him that?" Jakob asked her.

"No, I don't. Unless you don't want to see him again for the next ten years, or until she divorces him and proves us right."

"I hope that never happens," Jakob said quietly.

"So do I. I just don't have a good feeling about her. She's a party girl. That's great when you want to go dancing at Studio 54, it's not who you marry. I guess we never taught him that." Max had always dated nice girls, but the girl he married had to be more than that, and this one wasn't. Jakob nodded agreement, and they were both upset for the rest of the afternoon. They went for a long walk together. He was their only child and they didn't want to let him down, but they were worried for him, and he couldn't see why.

*

Julie had had a similar conversation with her father over brunch with her parents. She had told them that she and Max wanted to get engaged. They weren't surprised and Mike Morgan had already checked Max out with a full financial investigation.

"I never expected any of my daughters to marry a man with the last name of Stein," he said honestly, "but he checks out perfectly. The guy is worth millions, and he's done it all himself, with a little bit of help from his father. He's very bright and ambitious, with a great reputation. He's going to go far. And he's a Harvard graduate. You're going to have a very comfortable life," he said, looking pleased, and then as an afterthought, "Do you love him?"

"Yes, I do," she said demurely. He was handsome as well as smart. And they'd been fooling around a lot lately; she was on the pill, which her parents didn't know. She had pretended she was already married to get it.

"Do you think he'd be willing to convert?" her father asked her.

"No, I don't, and I don't want to ask him. He's not religious, and he's never gone to temple, but he's proud of being Jewish. It's a cultural thing with him. And his parents were in a concentration camp. He wouldn't want to offend them." Mike nodded, and then thought of something else.

"He hasn't asked you to convert, has he?"

"Of course not."

"Good. Just make sure you don't, and if you have kids, he has to agree to their being raised Episcopalian like us."

"I'm sure he would."

"We'll put it in the prenup," Mike said confidently. "Has he proposed yet?"

"No, but I think he will soon." She wouldn't have slept with him if she didn't think he would. He'd been hinting at it. And she'd made him wait four months until she gave in. It had driven him crazy.

"He'd better treat you right, or he'll have me to deal with," he said menacingly and she nodded.

"He will, Daddy. He already does." Her mother hadn't spoken during the exchange between father and daughter, but she nodded approval the entire time. She liked Max, he was very bright and charming, and had good manners, and Julie would have a good life with him, and everything she wanted. That was important to them. It was what she wanted for all her daughters, and Julie was going to be the first to marry. She had done well, except for the fact that he was Jewish, but he was a handsome man with a ton of money, and that was good enough for them.

"We'll give you the wedding of your dreams, baby, just say the word." And Julie knew they would. Her father gave them everything they wanted. He had made a fortune in commodities years before and had been making money hand over fist ever since, and he lavished it on his wife and daughters. He was a very generous man. And he respected Max's ability to turn water into wine too.

*

She reported to Max that afternoon that her parents were thrilled. "How were yours?" she asked him.

"The way they always are. Serious, and a little scared. It's understandable in their case, but they love you," he lied to her. "They're very happy for me." It was all she needed to know. He wasn't going to share their concerns with her, and they were going to prove them wrong anyway. As he saw it, his parents were always worried about something that never happened, and never would. He had lived with it all his life. "Tonight at my place?" he asked and she giggled.

"Why, Mr. Stein, I don't know what you mean. I'm a good girl."

"Tell that to someone else," he teased her, "I happen to know you're the best. And very soon you are going to be Mrs. Max Stein." He had every intention of making an honest woman of her, and a very happy one. He had already chosen the ring and was picking it up that week, at Harry Winston. He didn't want to get it through his father. The Morgans would think it was tacky to get a diamond wholesale. It had to be from a jeweler like Cartier, Tiffany, or Harry Winston. He had picked out a six-carat round stone for her, and was paying a fortune for it. But he knew that was what she expected, and he wanted her to have what she wanted for the rest of her life. He wanted to make all her dreams come true.

The doorman announced her from downstairs that

night, and Max asked him to send her up. He was naked when she rang the bell of his bachelor pad on Fifth Avenue, with the penthouse view of Central Park. His parents thought he was crazy to buy such an expensive apartment, but he could afford it and women loved it. She was naked and in bed with him two minutes later, and the best part of it to both of them was that she was almost his wife, but didn't act like one in the meantime. She was the sexiest girl he'd ever been with and knew just how to drive him insane. How could he go wrong with a wife like her?

Chapter 11

Max proposed to Julie the day he picked up the ring at Harry Winston, five days after he spoke to his parents about her. He took her to dinner at La Grenouille, and then back to his apartment, where he had champagne and strawberries waiting for her. He kissed her and then slipped the ring on her finger as they were admiring the view on his terrace, and she managed to look astonished, although she had suspected it would happen that night, when he took her to dinner at La Grenouille. She'd hardly been able to eat, she was so excited about seeing what the ring would look like. It was just what she had hoped for, and it looked beautiful on her finger and was exactly the right size. He didn't tell his parents that he'd bought it or where, because he knew his father would have insisted he could get it for him wholesale at twice the size and half the cost with fewer inclusions and a better color, all of which was probably true, but he knew Julie would expect the fancy jeweler's name to go with it, and he didn't want to disappoint her, or have her father think that he was cheap.

She spent the night with him at his apartment, as she

did every night now. She had her own one-bedroom apartment in the city on Seventy-Ninth Street that her father had given her, and her younger sister was staying there to cover for her, in case their parents called. And in the morning, Julie and Max both called their parents and told them the news. The Morgans were delighted and the Steins said all the right things, but they were sad as they listened on both phones in their apartment.

"Mazel tov!" his mother said, and then he put Julie on the phone and she burbled about how beautiful the ring was, and told them how much she loved their son and how happy she was. She sounded like a sixteen-year-old on the phone, and Emmanuelle looked at Jakob when they met in the kitchen.

"Well, he did it," she said grimly, looking disappointed. "All we can do is hope for the best. How is she going to bring up children? She sounds like one herself."

"She'll grow up," Jakob said hopefully. "You were a year younger than she is when you married me," he reminded her and Emmanuelle was stunned to realize it. She had nothing in common with this spoiled girl.

"But look what we'd been through. And I was her age when I had Max." They both fell silent remembering it. It seemed like only yesterday.

Their engagement was announced in *The New York Times* the following week in the Sunday edition, and they set the date that week. They were going to get married the day after his birthday in December, right before Christmas. She wanted the wedding to be at her parents' estate in Greenwich, and they were estimating about six hundred guests. She planned to have sixteen brides-maids, and both her sisters as maids of honor. Max would have to come up with as many groomsmen. He asked Steve MacMillan, his Harvard roommate, to be his best man, and Andy and Jared would be in the wedding too. The groom and both fathers were going to wear white tie, and everyone else black tie. It was going to be a formal affair, and then they were going to Tahiti for their honeymoon. Julie had told him she had always wanted to go there, so he promised they would.

Julie kept saying that they hardly had enough time to plan it all. She went straight to Bergdorf with her mother and sisters to pick a dress days after he'd proposed. They were expecting there would be ten or twenty engagement parties in the coming months. Planning the wedding was going to be Julie's full-time job until December, and Max was already stressed trying to figure out how to plan his business trips around their engagement parties. But he'd make it work somehow. Julie expected all her women friends to give her bridal showers.

The only thing the Steins had to do was host the rehearsal dinner, which they were told would be about a hundred people, mostly family and those coming from distant places, and Emmanuelle had no idea where to have it. Jakob promised to help her, and they eventually settled on a room at The Plaza. The hotel would provide the food and flowers as well, and music if they wanted, although there wouldn't be dancing the night before the wedding.

"Can we afford it?" Emmanuelle asked Jakob when they got the estimate. She was horrified by what it was going to cost them, but she didn't want to embarrass Max either by having it at a less luxurious place.

"Yes, we can." Jakob smiled at her. "And you're not allowed to make the hors d'oeuvres yourself or arrange the flowers, to save money," he teased her. "This has to be first-class all the way. He's our only son, and hopefully it will be his only wedding." But neither of them believed that as Jakob signed the contract with The Plaza.

Emmanuelle refused to go shopping for a dress, and insisted on making one herself. She found some navy blue lace at a shop near their apartment and made a dress with long sleeves and a matching jacket. She always wore long sleeves so no one could see her number. And Jakob ordered a set of tails from his tailor and tried them on for her when they arrived in September. He looked incredibly elegant and she could easily imagine him dancing in a ballroom in Vienna. He was going to have the first dance with Julie's mother, and Mike Morgan would dance with Emmanuelle.

The two couples had met in August to discuss the details of the wedding. It was going to be a grand affair with heated tents and chandeliers, and paths lined with snow and candles. They had hired a well-known wedding planner, and it sounded like a coronation ball at Buckingham Palace to Jakob and Emmanuelle, but their son and the bride were happy, which was all that mattered. They were going to celebrate Max's birthday at the rehearsal dinner. The Morgans were flying in a famous band from Las Vegas to play dance music for the young people in a separate tent after midnight at the wedding and they booked a twelve-piece orchestra to play during the reception. The Morgans had thought of everything and spared no expense, including luxurious buses to ferry all the guests to Connecticut from the city. They didn't want anyone driving if they'd been drinking, before or after the wedding, particularly since the bride's friends were young and wild, and all in their early twenties. Max's friends in their thirties were more sedate.

Mike Morgan had lived up to his promise. He was giving his daughter the wedding of her dreams. And Max went along with all of it. The only thing he wanted was for Julie to be happy.

*

The Big Day came after four months of engagement parties. Max commented to Steve that he felt as though he'd been out in black tie almost every night for months, and he could hardly keep up with his work. He was constantly on and off planes to get to meetings between parties, and arriving late, half dressed, ill-prepared, and hungover. He could hardly wait for the parties to end and the wedding to be over, so he could get back to his normal work routine without interruptions. But he didn't say that to Julie. Emmanuelle thought he looked exhausted whenever she saw him. They'd been invited to many of the parties, and she was invited to all of the showers but only went to two, a kitchen shower and a lingerie shower. She'd never been to anything like it before, and was astonished by the elaborate, expensive gifts the bride was given, and how all her friends were competing to give her the best bridal shower.

She and Jakob had decided to give the couple their everyday china as a wedding gift. Max and Julie had chosen it at Tiffany with the rest of the items on their registry, and the Steins were stunned by the expense of the china too. Emmanuelle didn't even want to think of what the Morgans were spending, and was sure it was close to a million dollars for the wedding.

Much to Emmanuelle's relief, the rehearsal dinner went off smoothly. She wrote all the place cards herself in her careful European handwriting, since she didn't want to pay someone to do it. She made a long-sleeved black taffeta gown which molded her slim figure for the rehearsal dinner. She wore her long blond hair in a loose bun and looked elegant, with a pair of diamond earrings

Jakob had given her for their twenty-fifth anniversary, and the big diamond ring he'd given her for their twentieth. They had no family jewelry to give Julie as a wedding present, since the Nazis had taken all of it in Vienna, but Jakob bought his daughter-in-law a very pretty, simple diamond bracelet from their former diamond cutters. The Morgans had given Max a diamond dress set from Tiffany as a wedding gift, and a platinum watch from Cartier for his birthday.

Emmanuelle was relieved when the rehearsal dinner was over. And the next day, the Morgans sent a limousine to bring them out to Greenwich early so they could dress for the wedding, and put them in a beautiful guest suite. There were a fleet of hairdressers, makeup artists, and manicurists there for the bridesmaids and the wedding party, and they sent a hairdresser to the Steins' room, but Emmanuelle said she preferred to do her own. She swept it up in a smooth French twist and did her own makeup. The wedding looked more like a circus to her, with the three enormous tents on the Morgans' back lawn, for the ceremony and the reception. Later, when Emmanuelle saw the bride, Julie looked exquisite. She was wearing a white satin gown with a white mink collar and cuffs, and a long lace veil that trailed fifteen feet behind her. She knew that her son would be bowled over when he saw her.

She and Jakob took their places on the groom's side in

the front row of chairs that had been set up, and when the music started, Mike walked his daughter down the aisle, and Max stood waiting for her at an altar entirely made of lily of the valley, which she also carried in her bouquet. The bridesmaids wore deep purple velvet gowns, trimmed in dark mink, and carried violets. All the flowers had been flown in from South America. The mother of the bride was wearing an emerald green gown by Oscar de la Renta, and Emmanuelle's navy lace gown looked lovely and appropriate. Jakob was very proud of her. He looked like a prince in a fairytale in his tails, and Max like a young knight in shining armor waiting for his fairy princess.

There was an unreal quality to all of it, and *Vogue* magazine was there to photograph the entire event. Many of the guests were well-known socialites and prominent people. Emmanuelle recognized none of them except the governor of New York and his wife, and two senators who had arrived from Washington on the front lawn by helicopter.

Emmanuelle and Jakob watched their son say his vows to Julie with tears in his eyes, then Julie said hers, the minister declared them man and wife, and they walked jubilantly down the aisle after they kissed and everyone applauded. The band struck up, and the celebration began. It was expected to last through breakfast the next morning.

There were speeches and toasts at the wedding dinner, and both fathers made touching tributes to the couple, and Emmanuelle cried as she listened to Jakob's. He was so dignified and elegant, and Max remembered as he listened how embarrassed he had been as a child that both of his parents had foreign accents. He had wanted them to be like everyone else, but they were always different. He knew they loved him, but he felt suffocated by them at times and by how much they cared about him. He felt guilty just remembering it. His father's speech was eloquent in his remaining Austrian accent tinged with slightly British English, and he wished the bridal couple a lifetime of happiness, and many children. Then the best man gave a very funny toast, and both of Julie's sisters followed. The evening seemed to go on and on and on, and the bride's mother was bowled over when Jakob did an elegant Viennese waltz with her. It reminded him of the ballrooms of his youth. Then he danced with Emmanuelle, and they became the most elegant couple on the floor. Max acquitted himself well too, having been taught to dance as a boy by his father, as something he might like to know one day, and it came in handy at his wedding. He and Julie were on the dance floor all night.

It was a beautiful wedding and a perfect evening. After thanking the Morgans profusely, the Steins went back to New York in the limo that had brought them. Only the young people were staying to dance until breakfast. They had kissed and hugged Max and Julie goodbye before they left. They weren't flying to Tahiti until the following afternoon.

"Oh my God," Emmanuelle said as she took off her shoes and leaned back in the limo, "that had to be the wedding of the century. Thank God we never had daughters." But they would never have dreamed of putting on a wedding like that, nor spending that kind of money. Jakob agreed it must have cost well over a million dollars once they saw the food and the flowers. There were several caviar stations set up on ice sculptures, and a profusion of white orchids on every table. They hadn't missed a single detail. And there were party favors at each place for every guest, a Tiffany silver frame with the date engraved and a photo-graph of Max and Julie. "I just hope they'll be happy after all that." Jakob nodded and yawned and smiled at her.

"I loved dancing with you. We should do that more often," he said happily.

"We could become professional wedding guests," she suggested and he laughed. "Can you imagine, the Morgans are going to have to do that two more times for their other daughters?" The thought of it and the effort and money it took was horrifying. They were very indulged young women, with no sense of the value of money. The party favors alone had cost a fortune, not to mention everything else.

They reached their apartment at three-thirty in the morning, and Emmanuelle was thrilled to take off her dress, take down her hair, and put on her nightgown. Jakob appeared a moment later in his pajamas, as his wife was brushing her hair and she stopped to look at him with a serious expression. "I hope they'll be as happy as we are." But it didn't seem likely. There was no substance to Julie and no depth, and after knowing her for nearly a year, they had never had a serious conversation with her, and Emmanuelle suspected that Max hadn't either. She wondered how he could be so oblivious to it. All he seemed to care about was her youth and beauty, which was all she had to offer.

"Come over here and prove to me how happy we are," Jakob said to her as she put down her brush and went to sit on the bed beside him, and he leaned over and kissed her. And then she slid into bed beside him, and he turned off the light and put his arm around her. This was where she felt safe, with the man she loved, and nothing else mattered. "I'm the luckiest man alive," he whispered to her and she smiled in the dark.

"I love you, Jakob," she said peacefully.

"I wish our son had married someone like you," he said sadly.

"Maybe he will one day," she said, thinking about watching him exchange vows with Julie, "but not this time," she said with a sigh, and she snuggled closer to her husband and drifted off to sleep in his arms.

Chapter 12

Max called his mother as soon as they got back from their honeymoon in Tahiti three weeks later. He wanted her and Jakob to come and see the house he had bought near Julie's parents in Greenwich, Connecticut. They'd looked at other communities as well, but Greenwich was the one she liked best, and he wanted her to be happy. And he could live with the commute. They were estimating that the house would be ready to move into in June. They had work to do, and Julie had hired a well-known decorator to pick the furniture and fabrics. She was going to be busy with the decorator for at least the next six months, working on the house. In the meantime, they were living in what they considered cramped quarters in his bachelor apartment in the city. He was planning to keep it after they moved, so they'd have a place to stay after late nights in town. Julie's younger sister had taken over her apartment.

Max's parents hadn't seen the new house yet. He had wanted it to be a surprise initially, and to show it to them when the decorating was complete, but it was obvious now that it was going to take months to do. Julie was fully prepared to make a massive project of it. Max said they'd had a fabulous time in Tahiti, and Emmanuelle was touched to be asked to see the new home, even if it wasn't finished yet. Max and Julie were spending Friday afternoon there with the contractor and decorator, and he suggested that his parents come out then, at the end of the day. She thought it was exceptionally nice of him to have bought a house exactly where Julie wanted to live, close to her family. It was typical of Max, who always went the extra mile to make the people he loved happy. Even though he was busy and traveled constantly, he did it with her too, and he was attentive to his father. He called them as often as he could, even if it was sometimes only for a few minutes between meetings. She thought Julie was a lucky girl to be married to him, but nothing had prepared them for the house they drove up to on Friday afternoon.

They passed a small lake on the property on the way to the house. The gates at the entrance were impressive, and the driveway seemed endless. There were trucks and workmen in front of the house when they arrived. They'd started work on it the previous week, and Max had said there was a fair amount to do in the house, and they were also redoing all the landscaping, which Julie had hated, and putting in a pool. They would be lucky if it only took six months, but he hoped they would at least be able to move in by the summer, and they could finish the outside work by the end of the year.

After they parked behind three vans that belonged to the electrician and the contractor's Mercedes, Emmanuelle stood looking at the house in wonder when they got out of the car. The estate had belonged to a famous architect who had designed the house for himself, but Julie thought it was too old-fashioned and dark and depressing. They were putting floor-to-ceiling windows in almost every room and changing everything. But it was the size of the house itself that stunned Emmanuelle. It was huge. She had no idea Max had bought a home like that, he had only closed on it weeks before the wedding so they hadn't had time to talk about it in depth. The architect who had owned it had died recently at the age of ninety-seven, and the family had been eager to sell.

"It must have cost a fortune," she whispered to Jakob as they made their way to the front steps, and he smiled at her.

"He can afford it," he reminded her.

"But it's so much to maintain." Emmanuelle was well aware that it would take an army just to clean it.

"They're young, they'll manage, and they want kids." Jakob was always willing to look at the bright side, and make excuses for those he loved, but it seemed awfully big to him too.

Max and Julie were standing on the top step with the

contractor and an architect who had blueprints in his hands, and Julie was looking upset about something. Max shook hands with both men and the meeting ended, just as he saw his parents coming up the stairs. He came halfway down the steps to greet them.

"Welcome to The Orchards," he said, which was the name of the estate. He smiled broadly, and Julie disappeared for a minute, and then returned looking petulant.

"This is quite a place," his father complimented him. It was after all an accomplishment to be able to buy a home that size. At his age, they had still been struggling, although Izzie had died a few months later, and everything had changed. But Max had made it all himself, which was a huge achievement.

"The house is so big," Emmanuelle said as they walked inside, and she saw the twenty-foot ceilings. Max put an arm around his wife's shoulders.

"Julie is upset because they don't want to put a skylight where she wants it. We've been arguing with the contractor about it all day. We told him he has to find a solution." Julie launched into an explanation then about what they were going to put where, what furniture, what rugs, what light fixtures. They were putting in an elevator, and they were going to do the living room in pastel colors like a summer garden. They were going to plant rose gardens all around the house, for an indoor/outdoor effect. Emmanuelle glanced at her son then as they walked around, wondering what he thought of it, but he looked happy, and he had given Julie carte blanche to do whatever she wanted. She sounded like a little girl decorating a dollhouse, not a woman whose husband had just bought her what had to be a ten-million-dollar home on a vast estate. Emmanuelle was speechless. Then they walked upstairs and Julie showed them bedroom after bedroom. Emmanuelle counted eight of them.

"What are you going to do with all these bedrooms?" Emmanuelle asked in amazement as Max put an arm around his wife again and smiled at his parents.

"We're going to fill them with our children. We want lots of babies," he said confidently, as Julie pointed to the master bedroom and showed her mother-in-law where she was going to put her closets, which were going to be almost the size of her parents-in-laws' whole apartment in New York. Emmanuelle noticed that Julie had made no comment about all the children Max said they were going to have. She was more excited about her walk-in shoe closets.

"That's a lot of children," she said to her son. One had been enough for her, but Max had all the faith in the goodness of life that came from growing up in a safe country and a peaceful world with loving parents. "We want five or six kids," he informed his parents, and Jakob nodded. If they could afford it, so much the better. He had wanted more himself, even with their restricted means, and would have made it work but had never been able to convince Emmanuelle. He wasn't sure she would have agreed to have children at all, if Max hadn't been a fortuitous accident.

"Do you want that many too?" Emmanuelle asked Julie directly, and she nodded, and then showed them the pink marble bathroom they were keeping in its original state. It looked like it belonged in a palace, and was worthy of a queen. But Julie was a princess to Max, and he treated her like one. She was wearing jeans and sneakers, as she ran around the second floor, showing them bedrooms and bathrooms, dressing rooms, a study for Max, the view into the garden, and the extensive apple orchards beyond that the house was named for. There were five gardeners to maintain them and the manicured gardens around the house, Max said proudly. Upstairs on the third floor, there were additional smaller bedrooms for the staff, and two huge guest suites.

"You can stay here with us whenever you want," Max told them generously, and they knew he meant it.

"And we're just six miles from my parents," Julie said happily. She reminded Emmanuelle again of a little girl who was playing house, not a grown woman planning to make a home for her husband and bear many children. But Max seemed to love the childish quality about her. He knew that she could be a femme fatale in the bedroom. She was the sexiest woman he'd ever been with, and also a young ingénue whom he could direct as he wanted. She was willing to take all guidance from him, and if he wanted six children, that seemed fine to her too. Emmanuelle couldn't help thinking that they had no idea what they were getting into, but they'd have to figure it out along the way.

Max had stepped into a far bigger world than his parents, and was comfortable with it. He was a very successful man, and their home was a symbol of it. So was his wife. She looked at the ring on her mother-in-law's hand, and said she hoped that Max would give her one like that someday, and not for their twentieth anniversary. Julie wasn't afraid to show off her husband's wealth, nor her father's. The size and number of closets she wanted were ample proof of that. There was going to be an entire wall of cedar closets for her furs, and a huge built-in safe for her jewels.

They spent an hour walking around the house and the grounds, and Emmanuelle and Jakob hugged him and congratulated him before they left and drove back to the city. Max and Julie were meeting friends at a restaurant in Greenwich, and staying at her parents' home that night, and meeting with another landscaper at The Orchards the next morning. It was an enormous project.

Emmanuelle was silent for the first few minutes after they got in the car, and they were already through the main gates when she turned to Jakob.

"Our son is crazy. What is he going to do with that house and all those bedrooms? I don't even want to know what it cost him, and what it's going to cost him now while they pull the place apart and redesign it. What's wrong with it the way it is? It's a gorgeous house. And he's letting her have whatever she wants." His mother clearly didn't approve of that and thought her daughter-in-law needed to be reined in. She was like a child out of control who could eat all the candy in sight and was determined to do so.

"He loves her," Jakob said simply. "He wants her to be happy."

"That's not happiness, it's greed. It's not even good for her to be so indulged. She'll turn into a monster."

"No, but a very spoiled woman," he agreed. "Her father got her off to a good start on that," he said, remembering the wedding.

"Is that what you did with me? Let me do whatever I wanted so I'd be happy?" she asked, looking at Jakob curiously, as they reached the highway.

"You were only happy if we *didn't* spend money," he said, teasing her, but there was truth in it, and they both laughed.

"I can't understand anyone their age or at any age, having a house like that, or wanting the responsibility of it. It's going to be such a burden for them. And they'll need an army of people to staff it," Emmanuelle commented reasonably.

"It's not a problem for her," Jakob said realistically. "Max has all the responsibility, she has all the fun." He wasn't crazy about that either, but he didn't think the situation was as disastrous as his wife did. He thought Julie would mature in time, hopefully before too long, if they were serious about having many children. But for now, she wanted to play and have fun all the time, and made no attempt to hide it.

"Maybe he bought that house so she doesn't complain when he's away so much of the time," Emmanuelle said pensively. "The house and the kids will keep her busy."

"If she spends time with them," Jakob said wisely. He was just as uneasy as his wife about what Julie intended to do, and what kind of partner she would prove to be for their son. But there was nothing they could do about it. The deed was done. No one wanted their advice, and Max hadn't asked for it. It wasn't in his nature. He wanted their unconditional approval, not their suggestions about his life, which seemed normal even to them. He was a grown man, and had done brilliantly so far. They had no right to complain about anything he had done. He had always been a good son to them. And all they could do now was hope Julie would grow up quickly.

*

Three weeks later, his parents were planning their next trip, a cruise to South America, when Max called them with the news. Julie was six weeks pregnant. She had gotten pregnant on their honeymoon, maybe even the first night. The baby was due in late September. He said he wanted them to be the first to know. His mother congratulated him, and tried to make it sound as though she meant it. She was happy for him, but worried too. Julie didn't seem ready for motherhood, but maybe one never was until the baby got there. She was thinking about it seriously and trying to absorb the news when Jakob walked into the room and saw her.

"Something wrong?" He looked instantly concerned when he saw how pensive she was as she looked at him.

"She's pregnant."

"So, real life begins," he said. "How does Max feel about it?"

"He's delighted, thrilled, over the moon."

Jakob smiled then, remembering. "So was I, when you were pregnant. I was terrified, but I was thrilled too. I was so afraid something would happen to you or the baby. We were such innocents," he said and came to kiss her.

"I was so shocked by how hard the delivery was. No one ever told me," she said, remembering it still vividly. "I hope the baby will be all right, and Julie will turn out to be a better mother than I fear," she said simply.

"We didn't know anything about it either," Jakob reminded her. "No one does with a first child."

"No, but they have relatives to tell them. We were totally on our own." He nodded and then smiled at her.

"You don't look like a grandmother to me. You're much too young and sexy to be anyone's grandmother," he said and kissed her again, and let his hands rove over her body, and she laughed like a young girl.

"You're very badly behaved for a grandfather. Aren't you supposed to be dignified now?"

"I hope not. Maybe it will be nice to have a grandchild," he said as he led her slowly toward their bedroom. She was smiling as she followed him onto their bed, and they forgot about Max and his family, and for a time thought only of each other and the love they shared.

*

Julie was fortunate and felt well through her entire pregnancy. She met with the decorator daily, making plans and choosing furniture and fabrics. Max had set up an account so she could buy whatever she wanted for the house, and she stayed in Greenwich with her parents when he was out of town, working all over the country, looking at land to buy. He bought two oil wells in Houston with the profits from one of his biggest sales in Oklahoma. He never talked to Julie about business, just about the house. She wasn't interested in his work, and had never pretended to be, just in him.

During the summer, all her friends gave her baby showers with adorable little outfits and toys. They had decided not to find out the sex of the baby. Max wanted a boy, but he said it didn't matter since they wanted five more children anyway, and if they missed the first time, the second one would be a boy. Julie said she wanted whatever made him happy. He was ecstatic whenever he came home to her after a trip, and he loved watching their baby grow inside her. He thought she was even more beautiful than before. She looked remarkable, and was full of energy, and still playing tennis in July.

They moved into their new home after the July Fourth weekend. There was more work to be done, mostly outdoors. The house itself was nearly complete, and the master suite and nursery were ready. Her incredible dressing room, with motorized racks so she could view anything she wanted, was ready too. She loved showing the house off to her friends. They were planning a huge housewarming party as soon as the baby was born in September. Julie wanted to wear something fabulous, and not be pregnant at their party, so they'd waited.

The baby nurse they'd hired arrived on September first, three weeks early, to get everything set up the way she wanted it. The relief nanny who would take care of the baby on weekends came a week later, and the two women sat in the nursery, talking for hours in their starched white uniforms. They were both English, and another nanny was arriving in December when the baby nurse left. Julie said she wanted one of them on hand at all times, so she would be completely free and at her husband's disposal whenever he was home. She didn't want him returning from a trip and having to wait while she took care of a crying baby. She was first a wife and then a mother. Max liked the idea. He didn't want to play second fiddle to a baby.

"Did you ever feel like that?" Emmanuelle asked Jakob after Julie explained it to them, and they pretended to agree with her.

"Of course not, we took care of him together. I changed diapers better than you did," he teased her. They'd had no problem managing one child between the two of them, and Max had been an easy baby. "But they have a much bigger life than we did," he said fairly. "I didn't travel for business the way Max does. We were two adults and one baby in a tiny apartment. We had nothing to do except our jobs, and nowhere to go. We couldn't even afford to go to dinner and a movie. Maybe Max really does want her free and entirely to himself when he comes home."

"I think it's an excuse so she doesn't have to deal with the baby. She wants to go to the city and see her sisters and friends."

"She'll probably fall in love with the baby when she

sees it," Jakob said optimistically, "that's what happened to us." He smiled, remembering the sweetest time in their lives.

"I want to come out and spend time with my grand-child too, and I don't want those women interfering." She thought the nannies Julie had hired looked stiff and cold, when she visited Julie in Greenwich one day, to see how she was. They were from a fancy agency and looked professional. The baby nurse even wore white stockings with her white uniform and a starched nurse's cap.

"It's just a different world from ours," Jakob said quietly, although there had been nannies in his old life too and he had been brought up by a very strict German one.

Julie had also told them that she had decided not to nurse. That would interfere with her being free for her husband too. She didn't want anything to come between them. And by Labor Day, she couldn't wait for the baby to be born. There was a heat wave and she said she was tired of lugging it around, and there was nothing she could do anymore except sit in the pool at her parents' house. Max was still traveling, but he had promised to slow down a few days before her due date. He wanted to get all the meetings in that he could now, in case the baby came late. But Julie had been so active up to that point that the doctor didn't think she'd be overdue. She was young and healthy, and he expected the delivery to be easy, and Max had promised to be there. He had said he'd take Lamaze classes with her so he could help her at the delivery, but he was never in town on the right days, so one of her sisters went with her. Julie said she was sure it wouldn't work anyway, and she wanted drugs instead. And she had an exercise coach scheduled to start two weeks after the delivery. She wasn't going to sacrifice her figure for the baby, and she'd been careful to gain very little weight.

Two weeks before her due date, they moved to Max's apartment in the city, so they could get to the hospital quickly. She didn't want to have the baby in Greenwich, and had continued to see her obstetrician in town after they moved. She met her friends for lunch, and went shopping with her sisters. She had dinner with her parents at 21, and went to a party at Studio 54 a week before her due date and danced for an hour with assorted friends before she finally sat down. She had a few contractions afterward but nothing happened, and she told Max about it the next day, since he was out of town the night of the party and came home the day after.

"Maybe we should go dancing to get things started," he teased her. "I have meetings in Houston in two weeks, and I have to be there, so our son better not show up late. I need him to be on time," he said, and patted her belly. Every part of her still looked thin and lithe except her huge bump, which looked like a beach ball under the short dresses she wore to show off her legs. Her face was beautiful. She was the picture of youth and health. Even Emmanuelle had to admit she looked spectacular. She had movie star good looks and it was easy to see why Max was dazzled by her.

In the last few days before her due date, she kept buying clothes and toys for the baby. She had nothing else to do, while both nannies waited in Greenwich. Once the baby was born, Max was going to drive her and the baby straight from the hospital to The Orchards. The doctor said that if everything went well, and he was sure it would, she'd only have to spend a day or two in the hospital.

And true to his word, two days before the baby was due, Max came home from meetings in Detroit, and said he wasn't moving until the baby came. They had fun going for walks in Central Park on the weekend and out to dinner every night. He tried to make love to her but it was too uncomfortable for both of them, and he was afraid of hurting the baby, so they used more creative options to give each other pleasure. Much to her annoyance, her due date passed. She was two days late, while Max took conference calls at home in the morning and then went to his office. He had a staff of six now to help him keep all the balls in the air on the deals he made. He was so busy that she worried that he'd have to leave town again before the baby was born. He called her almost every hour from his office to see how she was and if there was any sign, but there was nothing. She was utterly fed up, and drove herself to Greenwich to swim in her parents' pool on a particularly hot September day, and didn't tell Max where she'd gone. Her mother was surprised to see her when she showed up, and scolded her for driving, but she'd wanted to pick some things up at the house, and she promised to go back to town after a quick swim and lunch with her mother. She was just leaving to go to her own house when her water broke in a gush as she was standing near the pool. Julie looked panicked.

"Ohmygod, what do I do now, Mom? Max is going to kill me, he doesn't know I drove out here." The doctor had told her not to leave the city two weeks before.

"You call your doctor," her mother said firmly. "I'll drive you to the city as fast as we can get there. Labor probably won't start for several hours. It doesn't happen that fast, especially the first time." Her mother handed her a stack of towels to wrap herself in, and went to put on clothes and get her purse and car keys. And Julie called the doctor, told him what had happened and where she was. She didn't want to call Max until she was back in the city, so he wouldn't panic or have a fit that she'd driven to Greenwich. The doctor told her to go straight to the hospital to be examined as soon as she got back to town, and assured her that everything would be fine, but not to waste time getting there.

She was already having mild contractions when she got in her mother's Jaguar, with a thick pile of towels under her so she didn't ruin the upholstery. She was quiet and nervous on the drive back, but nothing frightening happened, and the contractions were no worse than they'd been for the last two hours.

"I'm scared, Mom," she said softly as they crossed the Triborough Bridge into the city, and she was grateful she hadn't given birth in the car. She wanted Max to be there and everything to go smoothly.

"Don't be." Her mother smiled at her. "You'll be fine, dear. At your age, it's a piece of cake. I always had easy deliveries and I'm sure you will too."

"The baby looks huge, Mom. And what am I going to do after that? I have no idea how to be a mother, or what to do for it."

"You'll learn as you go. We all do. I didn't know what I was doing either when your sister was born. And somewhere along the way, maternal instinct kicks in. And you have those two nice nannies to help you too."

"I don't want Max to think I'm an idiot and don't know how to take care of his child. You're supposed to know these things." She was more afraid of being a mother than of giving birth, which seemed bad enough after the movies they'd shown in Lamaze class. Her sister had almost thrown up after one of them, and said she never wanted children, and Julie was beginning to feel the same way. It had all sounded so romantic when Max said he wanted babies with her, but ever since she'd gotten pregnant she'd been terrified that she had no idea what she was doing. She loved being his wife, but motherhood sounded so much harder.

"Trust me, it all comes naturally. I was younger than you are when I had my first one, and your age when I had you. I promise, you'll be fine. And Max will be a great father." Julie nodded. The contractions were starting to get worse, but they were only a few minutes from the hospital. She wanted to call Max to tell him. She didn't want him to know she'd gone to Greenwich, and she'd had to leave her car there. But the nannies could pick it up for her later, and she'd be back there now in a few days, after the baby came.

They got to the hospital five minutes later, and her mother walked into the emergency room with her. Julie called Max while they waited for the doctor.

"My water broke," she told him nervously, "and I'm at the hospital so they can check me, but nothing much is happening. I'm having some contractions, but nothing major. I'll call you after the exam," she said and he sounded excited and happy.

"I've got a conference call in ten minutes. I'll get off if something big is going on. Call me after you see the doctor." He didn't offer to come then, he was busy.

"Something big is going on!" she snapped at him. "I'm

having a baby!" She was on the verge of tears as she said it, suddenly terrified, wondering what she'd gotten herself into.

"Let's just be sure it's now, so I don't come up there for nothing," he said, and got off a minute later. The doctor's exam was discouraging.

"You're two centimeters dilated, you've still got a long way to go. You can go home now, and come back when the contractions get stronger, probably not till tonight. My guess is things won't really pick up till after midnight." It was only three o'clock then. "There's no point in your being in the hospital for all that time. Go home and relax, take a nap, don't overeat, and call me when something changes." She called Max and told him, and her mother drove her home to his apartment. Max said he had a busy afternoon, but she could call him anytime, and if nothing was moving he'd be home around six or seven so he could get his work done. Her mother had to get back to Greenwich. They were having dinner guests that night. She dropped Julie off with a big smile.

"Just take it easy. Rest, dear, you'll need it for later. And I'll come in to meet my grandchild tomorrow." She kissed her and drove away, and Julie went upstairs to the apartment, and burst into tears as soon as she walked in and closed the door behind her. She was scared stiff of what lay ahead of her, both the delivery and the child she was about to have forever after. She couldn't remember why she'd thought this was a good idea, but she had done it to make Max happy, and now he wasn't even there to comfort her. He was at the office, as he always was.

She lay on their bed and dozed for a while after she stopped crying, and then she got up and washed her hair. She'd had a manicure the day before, and she put on makeup before Max came home. He walked in at seven-thirty with Chinese food for both of them, but even the smell of it made her feel sick now and she couldn't eat it. The contractions had completely stopped, but with her water broken, she knew they would start again sooner or later, this time for real.

They lay on the bed together and watched TV, and she fell asleep again, and woke up at eleven, while he was watching the news. She had such a big contraction that her whole belly turned into a rock and she felt like she was being strangled. She was lying on the bed in her underwear and he could see her whole stomach tighten, and Max put his hand on it.

"Wow, that was a big one," he said, looking excited. She tried to sit up and couldn't. Gravity was against her with the weight of the baby, and then another one hit her. It had gone from nothing to severe in a matter of seconds, but they weren't far from the hospital, and her bag was already packed. He helped her off the bed, and she went to the bathroom and threw up while she had the next one. Max called the doctor, and reached him through his answering service immediately.

"He said to come in now," he repeated to Julie with an elated smile.

"I feel awful," she said and looked it. Her mother had said it would be a piece of cake, and it wasn't. It was the worst pain she'd ever had. Max handed her the dress that was lying on the bed and helped her put it on, while the pains kept coming. She was doubled over when they left the apartment, and as he had the doorman get them a cab, Julie started to cry. He was holding her up, and the doorman wished them luck as she got into the taxi and they drove away. She could feel the baby pushing down now with a force she couldn't stop. Max ran to get a wheelchair when they got to the hospital, and he pushed her into the emergency room. She looked at him and the nurses with wide eyes.

"I need DRUGS!" she screamed at them. "Somebody help me!" Max looked paralyzed as two nurses took charge of the wheelchair and one of them told her to calm down.

"Your doctor's waiting for you, and we'll get you an epidural as soon as he tells us to," the nurse said in a soothing tone.

"I feel awful . . . where is he?" She looked desperate, and Max ran along beside her, holding her hand as they took her up to labor and delivery. She threw up as soon as they moved her onto the bed, and started crying hysterically while they cleaned her up. "I'm dying," she said to her husband, who had tears in his eyes—he had no idea how to help her. "I can't do this . . . please . . ." She had his hand in a viselike grip. The doctor walked in seconds later and explained to Max quietly that she was probably in transition, and close to delivering. Everything had started at once and happened so fast. It was all out of control, Max thought, and so was his wife.

The doctor examined her and she screamed at him between sobs and contractions, and he shook his head at the nurse, then spoke to Julie calmly. This was all routine to him, but not to Max, who felt sick watching her writhe in agony with every pain, and no one could get her to calm down.

"Julie," the doctor said clearly. "You're at nine, you can start pushing in a few minutes. We can stay right here in the labor room if you like. Everything is going beautifully. I can feel your baby coming down, you're doing a great job."

"I want DRUGS!" she shrieked at him. "Give me something for the pain . . . I can't do this!" She looked from the doctor to Max, who felt utterly helpless.

"You're doing great. It's too late for an epidural. It started too fast before you got here. That happens sometimes. You can push the baby out in a few minutes." She had another monster contraction, and he examined her while she did, and she let out a bloodcurdling scream. Max stood beside her to comfort her, but she couldn't stand having him touch her. She was in too much pain. "You're at ten now," the doctor reported, and told her how to start pushing. Max watched her with tears rolling down his cheeks and he didn't even know it. She gave a mighty push and then screamed again and fell back against the pillows. Her legs were wide apart, and one nurse was next to the doctor watching the baby crowning, while the other nurse stood at Julie's side encouraging her, and Max held her shoulders. Her entire focus was on pushing now as all four of them in the room cheered her on. She gave two more mighty pushes, and the baby slid out of her with ease and started crying. She was a beautiful baby girl and Max was sobbing as he looked at his daughter and kissed his wife. She lay looking at him with a glazed expression, as the doctor cut the cord and handed the baby to the nurse, and told Julie what a beautiful baby girl she had.

They wrapped her in a pink blanket and asked Julie if she'd like to hold her. She shook her head no, and they handed the baby to Max. He looked awestruck as he held her. She had stopped crying as soon as she heard his voice. Julie looked at them as though they were strangers.

"You told me I could have an epidural," she said to the doctor accusingly.

"It was too late by the time you got here," he said honestly. "Sometimes it just goes too fast, especially if your water broke hours before. You went straight to ten within minutes." From the first severe pain to their baby's birth, the whole thing had taken fifty-five minutes. The doctor said she'd have had the baby at home if she'd waited any longer, and they had come in very soon after the first pains. He said it was rare for a first baby to come that fast.

"That was the worst thing I've ever been through," she said, looking straight at Max, and he was terrified she'd never forgive him. He wanted lots more children, and a son after this. But he already loved his daughter, and after he handed the baby to the nurse, he sat down next to Julie and spoke to her soothingly and told her how much he loved her while she cried. She was traumatized by the birth, and didn't even want to hold the baby.

He went to the nursery to hold his daughter while they cleaned Julie up, and the labor nurse told him that it happened that way sometimes. "Women don't expect it to be so hard, and resist the baby for a day or two, and then they get over it, and adjust to motherhood. It's tough when it happens that fast and everything feels out of control." He nodded, relieved by what she told him, and he stayed with Julie for another hour until she dozed off after a shot they'd given her to calm her down. Then he went home to get some sleep himself. He stopped to look at the baby again before he left. He had never seen anything so beautiful. They had agreed on names weeks before. They were naming her Hélène Françoise after Emmanuelle's mother and sister, according to Jewish tradition, and Julie had no objection to it. She had said she liked the name.

When he got home, he lay in bed thinking about everything that had happened, how hard it had been on Julie, how violent it had seemed for a few minutes, how exquisite their baby was, and how much he already loved her. As he drifted off to sleep, he said a prayer, hoping she would have a long and happy life, and that Julie would forgive them both quickly.

Chapter 13

Max called his parents as soon as he woke up in the morning to tell them that their granddaughter had arrived, and weighed eight pounds five ounces, a good size. And despite her reservations, Emmanuelle cried as soon as he told her and so did Jakob. They asked if they could see the baby that afternoon. Emmanuelle was deeply moved to hear that they were giving her her great-grandmother's and great-aunt's names.

"How is Julie?" his mother asked with womanly concern.

"It was fast, but very hard. She's a big baby, but it was all over in an hour, from first pain to first cry. Poor Julie took a beating, though. It was worse than she expected, and it went so fast they couldn't give her any drugs." It sounded familiar to his mother, but the moment Emmanuelle had seen Max, she knew it had all been worth it. "She was really upset last night, and they gave her something to sleep after the baby was born." That didn't sound entirely right to his mother, but she didn't want to pry. "I'm going over there now. Why don't you

247

come this afternoon? She should be feeling a lot better by then, and we're going back to Greenwich tomorrow." Julie was at Lenox Hill Hospital, not far from Max's apartment. Emmanuelle promised to be there, and they had a present waiting for the baby. It was a silver comb and brush set, like the one she'd had as a little girl. They couldn't wait to see her.

When Max got to the hospital, he opened the door to Julie's room gingerly, not sure what he'd find, and what kind of shape she'd be in, and if she'd be holding their baby in her arms like a Madonna. He found her on the phone, talking to her mother, telling her how horrendous the birth had been. She smiled and waved and blew him a kiss. Her hair was combed and she looked impeccably groomed and had on makeup. There was no sign of the baby in the room.

"Where's Hélène?" he asked, as she hung up. The infant was already a person to him, with a name.

"She's in the nursery," Julie said easily. "I had a bunch of calls to make to tell everyone and I didn't want to wake her. Since I'm not nursing she doesn't have to be here every minute."

"I want to hold her," he said, looking disappointed. He'd been looking forward to it since he woke up. "My parents are coming later. They can't wait to see her, and my mom was thrilled about the name."

Julie smiled at him. "I'm sorry I was so awful last

night. It was the worst thing I've ever been through," she said, still horrified by the memory of it. "I can't believe they wouldn't give me an epidural. It was barbaric." But women had been going through it for centuries and survived it. "My mother had natural childbirth all three times. She's a saint. But I'll never do it that way again. If we have another baby, I want to be out cold and have a C-section." She sounded definite about it. He was afraid to ask her if she'd held the baby yet.

"What do you mean 'if' we have another baby? I hope Hélène is the first in a long line of Stein children. I know it was rough last night, but please don't give up just yet." He bent down and kissed her, and she looked like herself again, young, fresh, and almost recovered from what she'd been through. It was as though the agony of the night before had never happened.

"I know, we'll have others," she said, "but let's not rush into it right away. You'll get your son." She smiled at him.

"I'm thrilled with my daughter. I'll bring her in from the nursery," he said, but before he did, he took a small package out of his pocket and handed it to his wife. "I hope this makes up a little for last night," he said, feeling humble. She unwrapped a dazzling diamond bracelet from Van Cleef & Arpels. He put it on her, and it exploded with brilliant lights in the morning sun.

"Wow!" She looked pleased and left the bracelet on for everyone to admire. "That makes it all worthwhile!"

He was disappointed by her reaction, but he didn't say it. The baby should have made it all worthwhile, and the pain of giving birth should have faded the moment she saw their child. That was what women always said, but maybe it wasn't true. In Julie's case, diamonds always helped. He kissed her again and left for the nursery, and came back a few minutes later with the baby sound asleep in a see-through plastic bassinet, with her name on a pink card: Hélène Françoise Stein. The baby was wrapped in a pink blanket over a pink and white night-gown, with a little pink cap to keep her head warm. She looked like a little rosebud, and Max wanted her to wake up so he could hold her.

"She is soooo beautiful," he said, staring at her ador-ingly. "She looks like you," he said, glancing at her mother, and Julie looked pleased. She was staring at the diamond bracelet and obviously loved it. He would have bought a bigger one if he'd known how hard it would be, and he was grateful she hadn't decided to stop at one, after last night. She'd had him worried for a minute.

The baby finally stirred and cried, and he picked her up. She was a tiny cozy bundle. He made an attempt to change her diaper, and a nurse came in to show him how, while Julie watched and left them to it. She had had a stream of phone calls all morning, and her mother and sisters arrived at noon to visit on their way to lunch. They all said the baby was exquisite, and listened to

Julie's horror story, while Max went out for a cup of coffee
and ran into their two nannies in the hall. They had come
to see their new charge, and declared her gorgeous after
they'd seen her. They said Julie had asked them to come
in case she needed help with the baby that afternoon,
and he was startled. They had the hospital nurses for
that, but it made him realize that she didn't feel confident
yet. She had admitted to him she knew nothing about
babies and was afraid of doing something wrong.

When her sisters and mother left, Max went back into
Julie's room, and the two nannies followed. They took
turns holding the baby, and Max wanted to get his hands
on her again. He felt like he had to stand in line. The
room was suddenly crowded and he wanted to be alone
with his wife and child. Finally he asked them to wait
outside.

"I thought we might need some help," Julie said,
looking embarrassed after they left.

"I think we can figure it out. She's pretty easy. For
now, all she does is sleep, pee, and poop," he said, smiling.

"I'm afraid to hurt her or drop her, she's so tiny," Julie
said.

"She seems pretty sturdy," Max said, and sat down
next to Julie on the bed. "I'm really sorry about last night.
I'm sorry it was so awful."

"It's okay," she said, looking at the bracelet that was
her reward—not Hélène, who was the real prize. "I never

thought it would be that bad. They say you forget in time."

"I hope so," he said and kissed her. He was dying to do it again. He wanted a whole family of babies like Hélène. This was only the beginning.

"Let's enjoy her for a while first. It all happened so fast before." She'd stopped taking the pill right before their wedding and two weeks later she was pregnant. The thought terrified her now. She didn't want to get pregnant again too soon, and was thinking about taking the pill again for a while, but she didn't say anything to him, in case he'd get upset.

The nursery nurse took Hélène from the room to check her vital signs and their two nannies went with them. Max lay next to Julie, thinking how blessed they were. They both dozed off for a while, and as soon as they woke up, his parents arrived with pink flowers and balloons and their gift for Hélène, and a little pink dress Emmanuelle had made in case it was a girl, with a matching coat and hat. It was lovely, and looked very French, and Julie was delighted. Max was beginning to think she liked the clothes and gifts and fuss more than the baby. They spotted the diamond bracelet on her arm, and were stunned by Max's generosity to his wife.

Max went to get Hélène from the nursery while they chatted with Julie, and she told them how awful the delivery had been, and he was back a minute later with the baby. They were in awe of how beautiful she was. They each held her and Emmanuelle nuzzled her neck, and admired her soft blond curls.

"She looks a little like my sister," she said in a hushed tone. The phone rang constantly while they were there. The two nannies came in to check on them several times, as did the nurse from the nursery, and the paternal grand-parents left them in peace after half an hour. There was a lot going on. Julie was walking around the room by then, and was bouncing back quickly from her ordeal. She stopped to look at the baby in the bassinet several times and touched her cheek with one finger, and looked at her fingers and toes, but Max hadn't seen her holding her yet. She was warming to her slowly, as the nurse had predicted the night before.

Emmanuelle didn't say anything until they got to the street outside the hospital, and then she looked at her husband.

"He spends too much money on her. Did you see that bracelet? He'll ruin her, and she'll expect it. All right, the delivery was difficult, but they didn't amputate her legs without anesthesia." Jakob laughed at what she said as they headed toward the subway. "Birth *is* difficult, but the baby is the reward. She's making him feel guilty." Emmanuelle didn't look happy about it, and Jakob didn't disagree with her. "And why are those two nannies hanging around like vultures? They need to be alone and get to know each other with their baby. That's why I thought we should leave."

"She's young and spoiled. We knew all that before. Motherhood isn't going to change her overnight. It will eventually, but it takes time. She's hardly more than a child herself."

"A child with a very fancy diamond bracelet!" she said, and he laughed again, and they talked about how beautiful the baby was all the way downtown.

*

Max drove Julie and the baby home to Greenwich the next day. The nannies were waiting for them, and took the baby to the nursery immediately, while Julie walked around the house, thrilled to have the delivery behind her, and to be back in their palatial home. Her sisters came over, and her parents, since her father hadn't seen the baby yet, along with one of Julie's friends. There was a constant flow of people in and out, and Max felt as though he couldn't get a moment alone with Julie or the baby once they were home. He sat in the nursery, holding Hélène, and gave her a bottle and changed her. But there were so many people in the house interfering that it was a relief to leave for Houston three days later and get back to work. He was gone for a week, and had been to Los Angeles and Des Moines after Houston. He swore that Hélène had grown in the week he'd been away, and he was delighted to find that Julie was back to herself again. She looked as if nothing had happened. Her body had sprung back into shape almost immediately. She was working out with her trainer every day, and often drove over to swim in her parents' pool. The minute he walked into the house, she leapt into his arms. The nanny on duty had Hélène, and Julie was free to cater to his every whim, and she did.

"I like this," he said. He had thought she'd be busy with the baby and have no time for him.

"That's why we have nannies. I'm all yours, Max," she said in a seductive tone and he kissed her. He loved his new baby, but he loved his beautiful young wife even more. And nothing was going to interfere with that. She wouldn't let it. Max was the priority in her life and always would be, she said. Hélène would have to wait.

*

Max was surprised when it took Julie a lot longer to get pregnant the second time. In his fantasies, she would have a baby every year. The reality was different. She blamed it on his constant absences so they were never together at the right time for her to conceive. Then she said that her doctor wanted her on the pill for a while to regulate her periods before she got pregnant again. And Max wondered if she was actually afraid to go through another delivery. It all slowed them down, and she stayed on the pill for a year. But he was so insistent about another baby that she finally relented. Hélène was three when Julie got pregnant with their second child, and would be four when the new baby was born. Max was determined to have a son this time. And all Julie wanted was to have a Caesarean section—she started negotiating it with her doctor when she was two months pregnant. She never wanted to go through a delivery like that again, especially without an epidural. Her doctor said they'd see how things looked when she was further along, so she went shopping for an obstetrician who would promise to do it, and finally found one.

Hélène was an adorable little girl by then. She had curly blond hair, huge blue eyes, she loved watching her mother get dressed up, and wearing pretty dresses herself. Her "Mamie Emm" as she called her, and Jakob was Opa, which was Grampa in German, made her beautiful little dresses with coats to match. People said she was the best dressed child they'd ever seen. And Mamie Emm visited her often and took the train to Greenwich to do so. She commented to Jakob when she got home that Julie was never there. She was always at a lunch, or an appointment, a fashion show, a charity event, or shopping with her sisters in the city.

"She's simply never around. I don't know when Hélène ever sees her." And Max was traveling more than ever. His empire was growing. He had added another oil well in Houston, and one in Oklahoma. He was continuing to buy land and develop it. They had written about him in *Fortune* magazine. He was one of the youngest, richest self-made men in the country, but there was no hiding the fact that he was never at home. Julie had gotten used to going to events without him, but she complained about it, and he tried to get back for the things that were the most important to her. But he told her he couldn't do it all.

Hélène was the joy of his life whenever he was in Greenwich, and he was grateful that his parents saw her often. Both of Julie's sisters had gotten married in the last three years, and moved to California. Her father wasn't well, so they were all busy and didn't see Hélène as often as the Steins. They were continuing their travels and cruises, but the light of their life was their grandchild, and she adored both of them.

They had just celebrated Hélène's fourth birthday with a pony for the children to ride at the party, and a clown, when her little sister was born two weeks later. Her birth was much less traumatic for Julie than Hélène's had been. She was able to orchestrate it the way she wanted. The baby was breech for the last month and they couldn't move it, so it would have had to be a C-section anyway. It was all very civilized, and scheduled on a convenient day for Julie. She never went into labor, she opted for general anesthesia instead of an epidural, and when she woke up from surgery they told her she had a beautiful baby girl. They named her Kendra, and Max was as much in love with her as he was with Hélène. He was thirty-eight years old and said to be one of the richest self-made men in America by then. Julie was twenty-nine, and more beautiful than ever.

She took longer to recover from Kendra's birth since it was a Caesarean, and she wasn't up to taking care of the baby while she recovered. But the same two nannies were still with them, and took care of both girls. And as soon as Julie was on her feet again, she was off and running. As a surprise, when the baby was four weeks old, Max took Julie on a three-week trip to Hong Kong and Japan. It was business for him, but the shopping was fabulous, and Julie had a ball. She loved being with him, instead of at home alone. He more than made up to her for the time he didn't spend with her, with lavish gifts, his constant generosity, and his kindness to her. She was the first to admit that he was a wonderful husband.

After they got back from their trip, Julie got busy chairing a big charity event, seeing friends, and she spent several nights a week in the city to be with Max. She even spent nights in the city when he was away, so she could go to social events without him and not have to go back to Greenwich late at night.

Her mothering style had upset Emmanuelle for four years by then.

"She's *never* with her children, and neither is Max. I see more of them than they do."

"They have a much bigger life than we did," Jakob

reminded her, always willing to make excuses for those he loved. "He's a very successful man with business all over the world. You can't expect him to be at home all the time with his kids."

"I understand that," Emmanuelle said reasonably, "but what is *she* doing? She doesn't have a job or a business. I go out there all the time, and she's never there. They're lucky they have such good children." Hélène was adorable, and Kendra looked like a baby in a magazine ad and was picture perfect.

"We're lucky too," he said, calming her down, but it disturbed Emmanuelle to see her grandchildren essentially ignored and neglected, except for their nannies. And she had come to realize how important they were, and how loving to the children. The two girls didn't lack for attention, what they lacked were parents who spent time with them. Julie treated them like accessories, like handbags she'd pulled out of the closet, forgotten about, and decided to wear from time to time. She loved showing them off when they had guests at the house, but Emmanuelle never saw her play with them, or read them a story. Julie was exactly what they had feared from the beginning, a very beautiful, very spoiled young woman, whom their son indulged, and she thought of no one but herself. She was a showpiece, but not a mother. Max was still crazy about her, five years after he'd married her. He wasn't home enough to see how little time she spent with their children. The nannies knew and tried to compensate for it, and so did Emmanuelle, but no one could replace a mother and father. And her grand-children had the attention of neither one.

*

When Hélène was seven and a half, and Kendra three and a half, their mother made an unpleasant discovery. It was an accident this time, although she had been prom-ising Max for two years to have another baby, but she could never bring herself to do it. She liked her life the way it was. She was thirty-two years old, Max was forty-one and at the peak of his career and still climbing, but she was always alone, and had learned to fend for herself socially. She didn't want another baby with a constantly absent husband, and had told him so. But somehow it had happened, and she discovered she was pregnant. The girls would be four and eight when the baby was born. She waited for Max to come home from a trip to tell him. She needed time to get used to the idea herself. And predictably, he was thrilled. It was everything he wanted. He was still hoping for a boy, and dreamed of a house full of children, which was becoming less and less likely, given how hard he worked. Julie loved her husband, but their life was different from what he had promised. She was tired of being a solo act, and three kids seemed like a lot to her. She said as much to him when she told him she was pregnant.

He promised he would slow down, that he'd spend more time with her and the girls, and she knew that he meant it when he said it, but it was a promise he would never keep. There was always some crisis happening somewhere in the world that he had to fly off to take care of, to save a deal, or a company, or some part of his business. It was who he was. And as much as she hated his being away all the time, she loved the perks and benefits of his success. She had everything she wanted, except her husband at her side.

*

The pregnancy with their third child seemed interminable. She was sicker than she'd been with Kendra, and she hadn't been sick with Hélène at all. This time it was different, and Max was sure it was because it was a boy. She had the option of a C-section because she'd had one before. She could have had a vaginal delivery but was adamant she didn't want one, or to go through that again. She scheduled the Caesarean a week before her due date. That way she could be sure that Max would be there. And maybe if they had a boy this time, it would be different. Maybe he would want to be at home more. Since Kendra's birth, she had realized that mothering was not her strong suit. She never knew what to do with her children, or what to say to them. She was a better wife than mother and always had been. And she didn't get a chance to be much of a wife to Max anymore. He was never there.

She hired two more nannies right before the baby came, a full-time one and a relief, so there would be two nannies with the three children at all times.

Everything went according to schedule. Except Max, and the baby. Max had promised to be home the day before her scheduled C-section. He was in Houston for an oil deal, and going on to New Mexico and Arizona for a series of land development deals, when she took an aerobics class with a friend and her water broke at midnight a week before. She was in Greenwich, and didn't know what to do. One of the nannies drove her into the city, to the hospital. She didn't want to go into labor again. She called Max before she left the house and told him what had happened, and asked him to come home right away.

"Baby, it's ten o'clock at night here. I'm in some shit town in Texas miles from an airport. I'll get there as soon as I can. Try to hang in. Don't let them do anything till I'm there." And when she got to the hospital, the doctor wanted to wait anyway. She wasn't in labor yet, and he said they could wait twenty-four hours before they did a C-section. But an hour later, she was in labor with the contractions tearing through her.

When the time came, they gave her an epidural which slowed things down for a while, but at seven in the morning, they told her they were going to do the

C-section, they couldn't wait. The baby was in distress, and so was she. She was waiting for them to roll her away, when the door to her room opened and Max walked in, looking harried and exhausted, and enormously relieved when he saw her in the bed. Her enormous belly was still in evidence, with monitors recording the contractions. She smiled the minute she saw him.

"You made it! How did you get here in time, all the way from Texas?"

"I think I just bought a plane. A crop duster or something. We landed at Teterboro. I love you, baby. I came as fast as I could." She nodded with tears in her eyes, and they came to take her away at that moment. The doctor told him what was happening, and said they'd be back in a few minutes once the baby was born. Julie was going to be awake for this one, since she already had an epidural in place, and then her doctor asked Max if he wanted to come with them and he said he did. They threw him a set of surgical pajamas, a mask, a cap, and paper booties for his shoes. He dressed in the bathroom of her room, and walked beside her as they wheeled her into surgery. He was holding her hand and she was squeezing his. She couldn't feel the contractions with the epidural, but the monitor showed that they were huge.

They put a drape up so she and Max couldn't see the surgery and told him to stand at her head. Everything moved quickly after that, two pediatricians from the nursery showed up, the labor and surgical nurses were there. They started the surgery without telling her, and she could feel them pulling at her but nothing more, and while Max was talking to her to distract her, they heard a cry, and their baby had been born.

"Is it a boy?" Max called over the drape and the doctor laughed.

"No, it's a lovely little girl. Congratulations, Mom and Dad." Max tried not to look disappointed and there were tears rolling down Julie's cheeks, and she wasn't even sure why. She didn't know if she was happy or sad, or what she felt. She had three daughters now, just like her own mother. But she had been such a good mother, and Julie had no idea how to be that. She felt overwhelmed as Max bent to kiss her and told her he didn't care if it was a girl. He was just happy it was a healthy baby.

They gave her something to make her sleepy after the surgery. They sewed her up, and she woke up in her room, with Max sitting by her bed. He was looking at her intensely and holding her hand. And he could see how sad she was, but he had no idea how overwhelmed she felt.

"I know I cut it too close this time, and I've been a shit husband. I'm trying to build something, Julie, for all of us, for our children and their children, so we never have to worry." He tried to explain it to her.

"You already did," she said in a whisper. "Don't we have enough?" But in his mind they never would. He wanted them to be secure forever, and he wasn't there yet. He had given himself until fifty to make all the money he could, and then he would slow down. He was forty-two years old, and had seven or eight years of intense work ahead of him. He couldn't stop now.

"I promise I'll be better, and I'll try to be home more. I mean it, Julie." She knew he did, but it was a promise he was never going to keep. He didn't know how, any more than she knew how to be a mother. "I want to spend more time with you and our kids." She nodded and went back to sleep.

They named the baby Daisy, and when they took her home five days later, the nannies and Hélène and Kendra had made signs and put up streamers and balloons to welcome their mother and baby sister. They were excited to see them both. Julie had the nannies take the baby to the nursery, and she went to bed. She felt depressed and overwhelmed. Max had been planning to be at home with them, but he had left for Houston the day before. They'd had a fire on an oil rig, and he had to be there. And there was a crisis in Wichita. Nothing had changed, and she knew it never would. The only thing different was that she had one more daughter now. She took a pill and went to sleep. She could hear children laughing in the hall as she drifted off, and wondered whose children they were.

Chapter 14

Daisy's birth was different from that of her two older sisters. Julie took a long time to recover from her second Caesarean, and she appeared to be suffering from some form of postpartum depression for the first three months. Whenever Emmanuelle visited the children, Julie was locked up in her bedroom, either with a "headache" or supposedly asleep. And it worried her mother-in-law. But once she finally recovered, she was off and running again. Emmanuelle hadn't laid eyes on her daughter-in-law in months, and Max was traveling constantly. Julie had been in the social columns without him a few times, at big charity events. Emmanuelle wasn't sure if there were problems in their marriage or not. But whatever was happening, her son was not being attentive to his family, and his wife was spending no time with her children, even less so since Daisy was born. She was a sunny, happy baby, and squealed with delight every time her grandmother came to visit.

After talking to Jakob about it at length, she finally convinced him to have lunch with Max and give him some fatherly advice. Daisy was six months old by then, and Emmanuelle saw the four nannies when she visited the children far more frequently than she glimpsed their mother. Their home was like a rudderless ship without the visible presence of parents with the three children. And Jakob didn't disagree with her. He called Max when he knew he was back in town, and invited him to lunch at the Four Seasons. He thought he might relax and open up more in a nice restaurant.

Max was looking tired and stressed and had lost weight. And the first thing he did when he sat down was order a martini. His father had noticed that he was drinking more the last few times he'd seen him, and he was concerned about that too. Max had never been a heavy drinker. But he did a lot of business deals over lunch, and most likely the men he did business with liked to have a drink or two. But Jakob didn't think it was a good sign that he ordered one while having lunch with his father. Max was clearly under a lot of pressure to keep all the balls in the air. He had created an empire.

While they waited to order lunch, Max said that he had a big oil deal in Texas that had just gone sour, and he'd lost some money on a bad land buy in Oklahoma. Someone had beat them to the punch and opened a bigger, better mall too close to the one they were building. Their market research had been inadequate. They'd scrapped the deal and he was trying to sell the land now.

Danielle Steel

"You probably can afford the loss," Jakob said quietly. "Is it all worth it, Max? No one needs that much money."

"Maybe I do," he said after they ordered, and he asked for a second martini, which didn't please his father either. "Isn't that what you taught me, Dad?" Max asked with an edge to his voice that had never been there before. "Didn't you and Mom teach me that there's never enough money, and you have to keep putting it away for a rainy day, or a war, or a Holocaust, or whatever comes?"

"It didn't rain that much for Noah's ark, if what I read about you in *Fortune* is true. You must have enough now to feel safe, and to keep your family secure."

"When did you ever feel safe?" Max asked him, and Jakob hesitated.

"That's different. We lived through a war. We lost everything. That's never going to happen to you. There's no war coming, Max. Your family needs you. You have a beautiful young wife who must be lonely without you. And your children will grow up faster than you think. Don't miss that. You'll regret it later." Max looked pensive, and his father didn't comment when he finished his second drink. His son was a forty-three-year-old man, and had a right to live the way he wanted, he just didn't want something bad to happen to him.

"I'm going to lose a fair amount of money on those two deals in Texas and Oklahoma." Whenever that happened, which wasn't often, it always scared him.

268

What if everything started sliding? He remembered his mother's warnings when he was young. His parents had always been worried about money.

"You'll weather it," his father said quietly. "You need to slow down a little, son, before you lose something more important."

"I just want to shore up these two deals, or compensate for them." He was like a gambler at the gaming table, unable to tear himself away. "I've given myself till I'm fifty, Dad. After that I'll slow down." He had said the same thing to Julie when Daisy was born.

"You'll miss a lot of time with Julie and the kids in the meantime," Jakob said seriously. "That's seven years away."

"She's got the home base covered," Max said confidently, and Jakob realized that Max had no idea that wasn't true. Julie had nothing covered, except her lunches with other women, and the charity events she organized. She spent as little time at home with their children as he did. Max just didn't know it. He wondered how you could live in the same house with a woman and know so little about her. She'd begun to look unhappy to Max's parents over the last few years. But Max was so busy flying around, he hadn't seen it.

They talked about other things then, some investments Jakob had made, a trip he and Emmanuelle were planning to take. Jakob was turning seventy and they were talking about taking part of a cruise around the world. It was hard to believe he'd been retired for fifteen years. Time went by so quickly. And Emmanuelle didn't want to be away from her granddaughters for too long, she was enjoying them immensely.

Max thought his father looked tired too. The travel they did frequently now was fun for them, but he'd gotten sick on the last trip. For the first time, the cruise had worn him out more than energized him. His time in the camp had taxed his health, and recently, Max thought Jakob looked older than his years. There was no telling what five years of starvation and beatings would do to you long term. He worried about both of them, although his mother seemed sturdier again. They took good care of each other, and always had. He was well aware that his parents were extraordinary people. He would have liked to have a relationship with Julie more like theirs, but he suspected that that kind of bond only came out of adversity, and not normal times. He couldn't envision Julie being able to survive what they had been through, or himself for that matter. He didn't have their fortitude either. He had creativity and ingenuity and courage in the business world, but that was far different from what they'd experienced. He had great respect for them because of it, no matter what quirks and fears it had left them with. In spite of their history, they were sane, strong, rational, honorable, kind people, and had always been a good role model for him. And nothing in their life had made them bitter, despite the war.

At the end of lunch, Max looked more relaxed and smiled at his father across the table. "Thanks, Dad, for the good advice. Did Mom put you up to this?"

"Not really. She worries about you, but I wanted to talk to you too. Life goes by so fast. I don't want you to miss any of the good parts, like with Julie and your kids. In the end, that's all that matters. The rest is nice, but it's less important." Max nodded, listening to him, and knew he was right, but he still wanted to give himself until he was fifty to continue building his fortune. He'd had a meteoric rise so far, and he knew he could spend more time with Julie and the girls, and should, but not yet.

"I'll try to ease up on the drinking too." His father hadn't mentioned it, but Max had seen his eyes when he ordered the second martini.

"Don't live by what we were afraid of, Max. There were reasons for our fears. You have to lead your own life. Just don't lose sight of what's important. Life can change in an instant. You never want to have regrets about what you didn't do."

"Do you have regrets?" Max had never asked him that before, and his father thought about it for a moment.

"Not really. I should have forced your mother to have more fun. But she was afraid to. We've made up for it in the last few years, she loves our cruises. And we probably should have had another child so everything wasn't focused on you. That can't have been easy for you."

"Sometimes it wasn't," he said honestly. "But you came out of what you lived through remarkably. I don't know how you did it."

"Neither do I," Jakob said quietly, "but we were lucky, we had each other. I'm not sure I would have survived it without her." They were both quiet for a moment, and then Max looked at his watch. He had a meeting in his office in twenty minutes, but he'd enjoyed the time with his father.

"We should do this more often, Dad," he said, smiling, as they left the restaurant. And his father had insisted on paying for lunch. It had been a special moment, and Max thought about what his father had said in the cab on the way back to his office. He wanted to go home and spend time with Julie that night, and put his arms around her. But at five o'clock he got a call. There was a deal he'd been trying to make in Chicago, and they wanted to see him that night. He hesitated for a moment, and then decided to do it. He called Julie and told her, left for the airport straight from work, and caught a seven o'clock flight to O'Hare. It wasn't what his father would have wanted him to do. But he had to do it. One more time. He could spend time with Julie and the girls that weekend.

Max flew from Chicago to LA, and was back in New York three days later, in time for the weekend. He had just walked in the door when Julie turned to him with a strange expression. He hadn't even had time to kiss her.

"Your mother just called," she said seriously, "your father's in the hospital. Something happened this afternoon. They think he had a heart attack. He's at NYU hospital." He went straight to the phone and called the emergency room, and they said his father was in cardiac ICU. He tried to speak to his mother, but she was with him and couldn't come to the phone. He looked at Julie in a panic.

"I don't know when I'll be back." He was already halfway to the door.

"Do you want me to come with you?" she called after him, and he hesitated for a moment and shook his head. He really didn't. He wanted to be alone with his parents. Julie had never been close to them, even after ten years of marriage to their son.

"Stay here with the girls. I'll call you." And then he was gone again and drove to the city as quickly as he could. He thought about his last lunch with his father on his way into town and everything he'd said. When he got to the hospital, he rushed to cardiac ICU. His father was hooked up to monitors, his eyes were closed and he looked gray, and Emmanuelle was standing beside him, holding his hand. Jakob didn't look like he was conscious, but he opened his eyes when Max walked into the room and nodded. He smiled almost imperceptibly and then closed his eyes again.

They tiptoed out of the room then so they could talk for a few minutes, a nurse was with him.

"What happened?" Max asked her.

"I don't know. We went to buy groceries, we were talking, and suddenly he just stopped and fell to the ground, unconscious. The paramedics came, and they put him in the ambulance. They said it was his heart, it stopped twice on the way to the hospital and they defibrillated him," she said. She was out of breath and looked deathly pale herself. She was sixty-eight years old, but she was a strong woman, and Max had always admired her for it. "His heart stopped again after we got here." He'd had heart problems before, not severe ones and not recently, but his health had suffered from years of hardship and malnutrition, just as hers had. But they'd always gotten through whatever happened to them, and Max had thought they always would. It had never occurred to him that one of them might die, or get sick. He had expected them to be there forever. He counted on them.

They went back to Jakob's room then, and stood next to him. He opened his eyes and looked at his wife, she bent down and kissed him, and he smiled, and then he looked at Max again, closed his eyes, and sighed. He looked strangely peaceful, and as they watched him, Max suddenly realized he had stopped breathing. An alarm sounded and a team of doctors and nurses rushed in to defibrillate him again. They pounded on his chest, massaged his heart, gave him a shot, and performed CPR. Nothing happened. His time had come. It was over. Somewhere it was written how long his life would be, and he had reached it. He was too young to die, but apparently not after all he'd been through.

Emmanuelle stood silently by, holding her son's hand as they worked on Jakob, but she knew. She could see it. She had seen death so many times before, although not recently. His spirit had flown. Emmanuelle looked devastated when the team stopped working on him. She bent and tenderly kissed her husband, and she and Max quietly left the room. Max put an arm around her shoulders to support her, but he found himself sobbing in her arms, like the child he had once been. It was she who supported him now, just as she had his father. They had been married for forty-five years, and hardly separated for a moment. They had shared every possible experience with each other, and had given each other strength and hope and the will to live in a death camp. They had the kind of love few people ever know.

"It was his time," she said gently as she and Max held each other. She didn't argue with it or fight or rail against it. She understood it, and he had gone peacefully. They went back into the room when the doctors had left, and stood on either side of Jakob's bed. But he was gone now. He looked as if he were sleeping. She bent to kiss him for a last time, and then she left the room, her back straight, her head high, and Max walked beside her. Somehow she knew that this was right and meant to be. It was Max who couldn't accept it, who didn't want to lose the father he had loved so much. They went back to his parents' apartment, and neither of them slept that night. In the morning, Max called the funeral parlor to make the arrangements. And then he remembered to call Julie and told her what had happened. She told him how sorry she was. She had lost her own father and knew what it felt like. He had died quickly of cancer a few years before and Max had been there for her. She wanted to do the same for him now, but he wasn't reaching out to her. She said she'd tell the girls when they got up, and then Max went back to his mother. She was sitting at Jakob's desk, and had pulled out a photograph of them on the day they were married, before they sailed for the States. They both looked like skeletons, and their heads were still shorn, but they looked so happy. They were smiling and their eyes were vibrant and full of joy. She was carrying a tiny nosegay of white flowers, and they were holding hands standing beside the Army chaplain who had just married them.

"It was the happiest day of my life," she said, as she smiled at Max and showed him the photograph. They had no money, and had just survived a war and a horror beyond belief, had lost everyone they loved, were wearing ugly cast-off clothes that didn't fit, and were about to follow each other to an unknown destiny in a foreign country, and she could still say it was the happiest day of her life. As Max looked at her, he noticed a photograph of his own wedding in a silver frame on his father's desk, and wondered if Julie would say the same, or if he would. He wasn't sure.

Chapter 15

Max stayed at the apartment with his mother for the next two days to help organize his father's funeral, and canceled all his appointments so he could be there with her. Julie came into the city to help them. She was quiet and respectful, and went out to get them lunch.

Emmanuelle told Max that she didn't want Jakob's funeral to be at the temple. She didn't want to be hypocritical about it. They weren't religious or members of the temple, and she knew he wouldn't have wanted that. So Max arranged to use the large nondenominational chapel at the funeral home for the service, and they found a Reform rabbi to officiate. Max wrote the obituary with the information his mother gave him. He was surprised by how much he'd never known before about his father's family in Vienna, their importance in the community, their bank, his accomplishments, his studies at university, the things he'd done, the people he was related to, the languages he spoke. All he knew about was the business Jakob had inherited from Izzie, his time in Buchenwald, and where he came from. But there was so much more.

Julie took the obituary to the *New York Times* office herself.

By the time they got to the funeral home for the service two days later, the flowers were perfect, there was a program for the service with a beautiful photograph of him, the music had been chosen, everything had been arranged. The chapel was full before they got there, and there were rows of people standing who had come to pay their respects. Julie had thought to bring two black leather guest books so people could write their names. And she had been very kind to Emmanuelle.

The service was dignified and traditional. It respected Jewish traditions and customs, without being overly religious, which was perfect for the man Jakob had been. There were dozens of people who had respected him profoundly from the business he had worked in, and there was an elderly German couple Max didn't know who Emmanuelle said had been sponsored by the same people and came over on the boat with them. There were people from every part of their life since they'd been in the States. Forty-five years of their history were represented and nothing from before. And the photograph Emmanuelle had selected for the program showed Jakob young and strong and healthy again after the war, smiling broadly. Emmanuelle had worn an elegant black suit she had copied from Chanel, a chic black hat Julie had gotten for her at Saks, and the diamond ring Jakob had given her twenty-five years before that had almost never left her hand since. He had teased her that he was going to buy her a fifty-carat diamond for their fiftieth anniversary, which wasn't far away. He had almost made it, and was months away from his seventieth birthday.

After the service, they went to the cemetery, just Max and his mother and Julie and the rabbi. He said a few words, read from the Torah, and they each poured a shovelful of dirt onto the casket as they had for Izzie. And then Max took his mother home and Julie went back to Connecticut. Emmanuelle thanked her for all her help, and Max stayed with his mother again that night. The next day he went back to work, and then finally went back to Greenwich that night.

But as the weeks went by, Max realized that his life had changed immeasurably. He was stunned by how much he missed his father. Although he was busy and didn't see him all the time, they spoke often and he valued his advice. His absence left a huge void where his loving presence had been, and he knew it did for his mother too. He tried to call her every day to see how she was doing, and she said she was fine, but her voice was small and sad. She felt as though half of her had died with her husband, and Max could hear it and didn't know what to say. There was no way to make up for a loss like that. They had been through so much together. She went to visit the children, which usually cheered her. And within a week of his father's death, Max was on the road again, and she could see that Julie was upset. She was used to it, but it had been bothering her more and more recently. Max knew he needed to spend more time at home, just as his father had said, and he'd meant to, but something always came up that was more pressing. It was hard to make time with his family happen, and he was worried about his mother now too, and didn't see enough of her.

Two months after his father's death, he went to play golf with a man he'd been doing business with. They went to an exclusive club in Greenwich and someone he scarcely knew made a snide remark implying that Julie was having an affair.

He waited for the right moment when they were alone that night and he was shaking when he asked her. As much as he traveled, he had never cheated on her, and now suddenly he remembered his father's words and knew he'd been right. He asked her point-blank if she was having an affair, and she ardently denied it. He didn't know if she was telling the truth, and it opened the door to a deeper conversation between them that was long overdue.

"I wouldn't do that to you," she said and looked as though she meant it, "but you're never here, Max. Half the time, you're not even in the city I think you're in. Sometimes you're in three cities in a day. I can never count on you to go anywhere with me. We never do anything together. We don't even go out to dinner. You're either gone, too tired, or I'm in the city at something you were supposed to come to and didn't. You're like a phantom husband. You care more about your business deals than you do about me."

"That's not true." He tried to deny it but he knew it seemed that way, not only to others but, more important, to her. "I can't just give it all up and retire. I'm too young to do that. I want to put more aside for us before I do."

"Can't you slow down a little?" she asked, pleading with him, and the look in her eyes tugged at his heart. "Your girls don't even know you. Hélène is going to be nine, and you don't go to any of her school events. The other fathers do." She made him feel like a total heel, and he realized it looked that way to everyone else, and maybe he was.

"I'll try to do better," he promised her and meant it, and they made love that night for the first time in months. Talking made a difference, but he also knew that he had to deliver more than promises this time. For the next month, he tried to do everything he said he would, he even went to a science fair at Hélène's school and she was thrilled. He visited his mother in New York too, and took her to lunch. She was more nervous than he'd seen her in a long time. Jakob had balanced her and calmed her when she got anxious. Now she had no one to curb her fears and they had grown again. She wasn't worried about a war anymore, or an imminent Holocaust, but she was worried about her son, his marriage and his health, and how little time he spent with his daughters.

"Let me worry about all that, Mom. That's between Julie and me."

"She doesn't say anything to you, she just goes out on her own. She's never there when I visit the girls."

"Her mother has been sick." He made excuses for her, but wondered if it was true that she was out all the time, especially when he was away. She had never been a stay-at-home mother the way his had been. They had help for that, a lot of it, but he was suddenly curious about whether or not she ever picked Hélène and Kendra up at school, or took them to ballet or the dentist. He had no idea if she did.

A week later, a series of crises pulled him away again. He felt guilty every time he left now, but he had an empire to run. He was horrified to realize, three weeks later, that he hadn't seen his mother in a month. He dropped by to see her at the apartment, and was shocked by how pale she was. She looked like a ghost.

"Are you feeling okay, Mom?" he asked, and she insisted she was.

"I've been having problems with my stomach again. I lost a little weight." He hadn't noticed that she was thinner too. "It's the same old stuff. I've had it ever since the camp." It had almost killed her once before until she got it under control through sheer grit, but she was frailer now and Max suspected that without his father to cook for, she wasn't eating much. He promised himself he'd take her out to dinner once a week and he tried, but most of the time she refused him and didn't want to go out, so he dropped by for a cup of coffee after work instead. He had the frightening feeling that she was fading away. Without Jakob, she had no anchor, and no purpose to her life. She went out to Greenwich to visit his children, but a few weeks later Julie told him that she hadn't been to see them recently, and he went to see his mother the next day.

"Something's wrong, Mom. You have to go to a doctor." Her clothes were hanging off her, her face was gaunt, and she looked gray. She promised to see her physician. When she did, they sent her for tests, and since she'd listed Max as her next of kin, they called him with the results. She had advanced stomach cancer which had metastasized, and leukemia. Max closed his eyes and felt the room spin around him when he heard the words.

"Can you operate?" he asked the doctor.

"There's no way we could. It's spread pretty much everywhere. We can't take out her stomach, and the leukemia has weakened her. We can transfuse her, which might give her some energy back, but her condition is severe, Mr. Stein. I didn't want to tell her. I thought you should know first."

"Is there *anything* we can do?" Max asked, sounding desperate.

"Very little, except make her comfortable. She says she lives alone since she lost her husband. You'll want hospice nurses with her eventually." Max couldn't believe what he was hearing. This couldn't be happening to his mother, who never let anything beat her. But alone, her life had no purpose now. She had lived for Jakob, and her son.

"Please don't tell her," Max said in a hoarse voice, wondering how he could talk her into moving in with them so they could take care of her, but he didn't think she'd do it. A few days later, she told him the results they had given her, which were not the real ones.

"The doctor called with the test results. He said I'm anemic. I guess I need to eat spinach and liver," she said, neither of which she liked.

"Why don't you come stay with us for a while, Mom? Our cook can feed you so you don't have to cook. The girls would love it, and so would we." She thought about it for a moment, but she was happy in her own apartment with all her own things around her.

"Maybe for a weekend," she said after thinking about it. "I don't want to bother Julie or be intrusive. You two need time to yourselves."

"We'd love it," he insisted, and she said she'd let him know. But two weeks later she had a hemorrhage in her stomach and wound up in the hospital. They gave her three transfusions and kept her for several days, and after that she agreed to come to Greenwich for a week. She was too weak to go home alone, and didn't want nurses.

She stayed two weeks in the end, and they didn't know it, but they were her final weeks. The stomach cancer had moved so quickly that she went steadily downhill, coupled with the leukemia. She had a wonderful time with the children, and ate her meals with them until she couldn't get out of bed anymore in the last few days. She and Max had a long talk the night he came back from a trip, about how much she loved him and her grandchildren. She fell asleep while he was sitting with her, with a smile on her face, holding his hand, and she died in her sleep that night. The end had come swiftly and gently, and had been a blessing for her. She didn't have to go back to the hospital. She had died with her family around her, and Julie had been very kind to her. They had never been great friends but she was a respectful daughter-in-law, and she helped Max make the arrangements.

He couldn't believe what had happened. Four and a half months after his father's death, he had lost both his parents. They had been the mainstay and foundation of his life, as he had been the hub of theirs. He had never expected to lose them so young. His mother was only sixty-eight years old, and his father had been turning seventy. Their war experiences had taken too great a toll and cut their lives short, long before their natural times. They had valiantly withstood the punishment of Buchenwald, but it caught up with both of them in the end, and Max had the feeling that his mother no longer wanted to go on without his father, and didn't want to upset him by saying so. She had suddenly opened her mental floodgates and allowed herself to be swept away by forces she could no longer resist without him. They were unable to survive without each other. In a sense, theirs had been a perfect love, and he would have liked to experience one like it. What he had with Julie was far more earthbound and superficial, and never as deep. What his parents had shared was of another dimension, and he was sure they were together again. He said as much to his children, and told them that Opa and Mamie Emm were in Heaven now, together. And he believed it.

His daughters had all been baptized Episcopalian, at the insistence of Julie's parents. They'd never had a formal baptism with friends and godparents—it had been done by the minister of their church with only Julie and her parents present. Max hadn't attended. The children had no formal religious education. They knew that their father was Jewish and their mother wasn't. Telling them that Mamie Emm had gone to Heaven was the only religious thought he had ever shared with them. Hélène had always been fascinated by the fact that her grandparents were

Jewish and always said she wanted to go to temple one day. Max was sad that Daisy and maybe even Kendra were too young to remember her and Hélène was the only one who would. He wished his mother could have lived many more years to watch her grandchildren grow up and for them to get to know her.

They buried Emmanuelle in the same cemetery where they had buried Jakob. They had a small service for her, but kept the service and burial private and, knowing his mother, Max felt sure she would have preferred it that way.

He fell into a melancholy sadness for weeks afterward. The loss of both his parents hit him harder than even he would have expected. He suddenly questioned what kind of son he had been, and saw all the ways he'd fallen short. He remembered how ashamed of them he had been as a boy because his parents were different, and had accents when they spoke English, his father with his very educated, cultured Austrian accent, and Emmanuelle's French accent which stayed strong. She and Jakob always spoke French to each other, although Max spoke to her in English despite his still fluent French. But he had wanted an American mother so badly and tried to pretend she was. Now he felt that he hadn't been there enough for them, but at least they had each other, which had always been such a close relationship that sometimes he felt left out.

He spent several days packing up his parents' apartment. He kept boxes and boxes of things that were sentimental to them and brought them back to Greenwich. Albums, photographs, letters, favorite books. He put their furniture in storage to deal with later. His parents had left everything to him, including Jakob's fortune. He would have preferred to have his parents than their money. And Jakob had left a large amount to each of his granddaughters.

Max had so many regrets now that it distracted him from everything else. He went back to traveling all the time, just to keep moving and to escape the haunting voices in his head that reproached him for everything he had done wrong. And he drank more than he should and knew it. He hardly talked to Julie while he mourned his parents. He felt as though he had been in an emotional freefall since his mother's death and couldn't find the ground under his feet. He forgot Kendra's birthday, and then Hélène's, and missed her birthday party after promising to be there—instead he was at a meeting in Houston and didn't come home. He forgot his own birthday and the people Julie had told him she'd invited to have dinner with them. He was in a daze from which he couldn't seem to waken, but he remembered to light the Chanukah candles for his children as his mother would have. He had brought them back with him to Greenwich after she died. He had put the apartment on the market, and had an offer on it a month later, which he accepted. He suddenly felt steeped in the past and lost in the present.

When he forgot his anniversary with Julie, their tenth, which made it even worse, there was a chasm between them that neither could reach across. All communication was down between them. She knew he was devastated about his parents, but she couldn't get near him to comfort him, or even talk to him, he was in too much pain. All she had left were three children that she could barely handle without the help of nannies they preferred to her anyway, and a husband who was never there. Both of her sisters had married and moved to other cities, her own mother was dying, and she had never felt so alone in her life. She waited till the day after the anniversary he'd forgotten to give him the news that she knew would blow the lid right off their life.

He was reading through a stack of memos and messages his office had dropped off for him. He had just come back from Houston that afternoon, and she walked into his study, stood across his desk from him with a grim expression. She felt sorry for him and his grief over his mother, but she had problems of her own.

"I'm pregnant, Max, and I want an abortion," she said in a monotone. He thought he hadn't heard her right at first, and he looked up, surprised and confused.

"What did you just say?" She thought the children had

gone to bed, but the door was open, and Hélène's room was right next door.

"You heard me." She could barely remember the last time they'd made love, except it had been after a talk when he'd promised her things would be different and he'd try to stay home more. She had believed him, and nothing had changed.

The doctor had just told her she was three months pregnant, and if she wanted to have an abortion, it would have to be very soon. She wanted to do it right after Christmas.

"Is it mine?" he asked her with an icy expression, which was the ultimate low blow, and the meanest thing he'd ever said to her.

"Obviously," Julie said just as coldly. "I don't know what you do while you're flying around the country, but I don't screw around at home. I'm three months pregnant and it's yours." She had been planning to tell him about the baby on their anniversary, but his not coming home had made the decision to abort easier for her, and she knew it was the right one. She looked at him with an iron resolve. "We already have three children you never bother to spend time with, and to be honest, I don't see enough of them either. Your mother said that to me once or twice and she was right. The last thing we need is a fourth. We hardly have a marriage anymore, we don't need another child we can both ignore. Having Daisy was a mistake. This one would be a joke."

"Julie, please." He stood up from his desk when he realized she was serious. "You can't do something like that. If you're pregnant, it was meant to be. I just lost both my parents, and I've been half crazy over it, with regret and guilt, and your mother is very sick. We can't kill our baby. We have wonderful children, and I know I'm a shit husband right now, but I love you." He tried to put his arms around her, and she pushed him away.

"I can't handle another child," she said, being honest with him for the first time. "I don't think I even had postpartum depression last time, I just didn't want another kid. We should have stopped at Hélène, or at most Kendra, when you decided you wanted to be the richest man on the planet and forget about us."

"I'll slow down. I'll stop traveling as much. I promise. Hire another nanny, hire ten of them if you want. I don't care. But you can't have an abortion. Don't kill our baby. That's a life inside you that's part of both of us."

"There is no 'us,' Max. I don't even know who you are anymore. What's worse, I don't know who I am. But I know who I'm not. I'm not the young girl you married who wanted to do anything you wanted me to, just to keep you happy, and have six kids. I'll go crazy if we have another child. I'm not cut out for this. I'm a lousy mother. I hate everything about my life, and I'm tired of being married to a man who's never here."

"Are you telling me you want a divorce?" He looked

shocked as he stood across the room from her, afraid to move near her again. She was on the verge of hysteria, something inside her had snapped, and she knew it too. When she found out she was pregnant again, it felt like a death sentence to her.

"I don't know what I'm telling you, except that I'm not having another baby, and I'm going to have an abortion this week. I don't have time to wait. I could have done it without telling you, but I thought you had a right to know." She also wanted to punish him for all the times he was never there, and she knew this would hurt. It was the ultimate rejection, worse than a divorce. She didn't want to have his child. "I'm not going through all that again for a baby that neither of us want."

"I want it! I want you! I love our daughters, and I'm sorry I'm not here enough. One day, we'll all be glad I did this. Our children and their children will be secure forever."

"I don't care, and maybe you won't either. Maybe they'd rather have a father who shows up once in a while and remembers their birthdays. Hélène cried for hours when you didn't come home for hers after you said you would."

"I forgot," he said, looking morbidly remorseful.

"I know you did, just like you forgot Kendra's and your own and our anniversary. You don't care about any of us. I looked like a complete idiot when you didn't show up for your birthday dinner, which wasn't even a surprise. Several people asked me if you'd left me. This baby is just another problem we don't need."

"It's a baby, it's a human being, it looks like one. It's sucking its thumb right now. You've seen the sonograms. How can you kill a child?"

"Because you're killing all of us, and you don't even know it. All you care about is making more money and your goddamn business deals. It's an addiction, like gambling or drugs. Work is your drug of choice." And as she said it, he remembered he was going to London, leaving on Christmas night, and he hadn't told her yet, but how could he leave her now? He really did care about her and their children, he just had too much on his plate to balance it all to everyone's satisfaction, even his own. It reminded him of what his father had said at lunch. As usual, he was right. And now he was about to lose something he cared about much more than a business deal— his baby, and maybe his wife. She didn't look far from walking out, and maybe after the abortion, she would. She looked capable of it now.

"You should have stayed single, Max. You could have had a girl in every city all across the United States, and wouldn't have had to bother coming home to us at all."

"I *want* to come home to you, all of you, even our unborn child." He said it with feeling, but she no longer believed anything he said. He hadn't kept a promise to her in years.

"No, you don't. This is just another baby who'll turn into a child you'll ignore, unless it's a boy."

"Is it?" he asked with a gleam in his eye, and she shrugged.

"I have no idea. I didn't try to find out. I don't want to know what sex it is when they kill it," she said harshly, but she felt like she was fighting for her sanity and her life. She couldn't do it again.

"I'm begging you," he said with real feeling in his eyes, "don't do this. At least think about it."

"I have. I was going to tell you about it on our anniversary. But as usual, you didn't show up. That made the decision easier for me. But even if you had shown up, having this baby would be a huge mistake for both of us, and definitely for me."

"I'll do anything you want if you have it. If it were in me, I couldn't kill a part of you. I love you, Julie. And I'm sorry things haven't worked out the way we wanted. My work life turned out to be a lot more demanding and complicated than I thought. But I still want you and our family. You mean everything to me." She didn't answer him and just looked at him with despair from across the room.

"I'm not the wife I thought I would be either," she said sadly. "I didn't know it when we got married, but I'm not cut out to have all these kids. They like the nannies better than they do me and they're probably right. I'm not a good mother to them. I'm a better wife to you, or I would be if you came home more often."

"Please think about it," he pleaded with her again. "I have to go to London for two days and I can't get out of it, it's too big a deal and there are too many people involved. Just think about it while I'm gone. Give me another chance. I'll do everything I can not to disappoint you. I may slip once in a while, but I'll spend all the time I can at home. I give you my word."

"Your word is worth nothing around here," she said quietly and walked out of the room. He sat in his study alone for an hour thinking of everything she had said, and poured himself a stiff drink. He wanted to do everything he could to convince her not to have an abortion. And finally he turned off the lights and went to their bedroom, and the door was locked. It was the first time she had ever done that to him, and he walked quietly down the hall and upstairs to one of their guest rooms, and slept there that night, thinking about the baby growing inside her, and praying he could convince her to keep it.

Neither of them knew it, but Hélène had heard everything they said to each other. And she wanted her mother to keep the baby too. It wasn't right to kill it. She wanted to tell her that she would help take care of the baby. She helped the nannies with Daisy all the time. But she knew she wasn't supposed to be listening, and she was nine years old and they wouldn't pay attention to what she said. She didn't know why they were so angry at each other. Maybe that was why he was always away and she was always out, because they thought they had too many kids. But at least she knew her father loved her mother if he wanted her to have the baby. She would just have to see what would happen next, but her mom couldn't kill a baby. That would be terrible. And maybe the police would take her away and put her in jail if she did.

Hélène closed her door very softly and slipped back into bed and said a prayer that God, or her dad, or someone would make her mom stop being so angry and do the right thing.

Chapter 16

Max tried to talk to Julie before he left for London on Christmas night, but she refused to discuss the pregnancy with him. They had spent Christmas with the children, and put a good face on it for them, but she avoided him whenever they weren't around. He continued to sleep in the guest room until he left. He didn't want to push her, and she made it clear that she wanted to be left alone. She was still furious about the anniversary he hadn't come home for and the birthday dinner she'd given for him that he'd missed, and there was nothing he could say or do to make up for it right now.

As he rode to the airport from Greenwich, he felt as though his whole life was coming apart. His parents had died, his wife wanted to abort his baby, and their marriage was hanging by a thread. He knew that none of the things she'd said to him were wrong. He'd been neglecting his children and his wife, and his mother had told him that Julie was never around. She clearly felt overwhelmed by the family he had wanted, and she hadn't bargained for a husband who would be gone most of the time and didn't share the responsibility of three children with her. It was too much for her alone. Her own support system had fallen apart. The father who had indulged and protected her was gone, her mother was dying, and her sisters were three thousand miles away now. And she had a husband she never saw, and children she had no idea how to take care of.

Max was planning to look up his old friend Steve in London and was thinking of talking to him about it. Steve had moved to London years ago and was working for an investment bank there, and he'd had troubles of his own. He had married an English girl and gotten divorced a few years before. And he'd written recently that he was getting married again. Maybe he'd have some insights about how to calm things down. But Max already knew he was failing as a husband and father, and he wasn't even sure he'd been adequate as a son. Everything in his life was going wrong. He didn't even know if Julie would have the abortion before he got back. And as much as he wanted to, he had no right to stop her. As she had pointed out to him that morning in the five minutes they had spent in the kitchen alone, her body was her own, even if the child she was carrying was his.

*

He had dinner with Steve the night before he left London and he didn't have any magical solutions to share. His first wife had been a model, and she'd cheated on him with his best friend. The divorce had been expensive but simple, and easier because they had no kids and had only been married for three years. The woman he was about to marry was forty, a barrister, and had two children of her own. And he was hoping to have a child with her. It was a marriage that made sense. He'd already lived with her for three years so there were no surprises there. He was sorry to hear that Max and Julie were having trouble, but he wasn't too surprised given the way Max worked.

"You're going to have to spend more time at home if you want it to work," Steve said simply. He told him that Jared had gotten divorced too, and Andy was married to a doctor he'd gone to school with. They lived in Texas and had four kids. Max had lost touch with the other two, but he and Steve called each other from time to time. It was nice spending an evening with him before he went home. He was still his closest friend although they hardly ever saw each other.

His flight was delayed at Heathrow and he got in late. The house was quiet when Max got there, and their bedroom door was unlocked, which he took as a good sign. It was two in the morning, and Julie was sound asleep. He showered and changed into pajamas and slipped in quietly beside her. She was already up when he woke up in the morning, and he couldn't find her anywhere. The nanny feeding the children in the kitchen said she had gone to see her mother, who wasn't doing well. And she didn't come back until late afternoon.

He spent the afternoon playing with the children, and helped Hélène assemble the dollhouse she'd gotten for Christmas. She seemed unusually subdued and she agreed with everything he wanted to do. He wondered if she sensed what was going on. Kendra was her usual exuberant self. She was always full of bright ideas and announced at breakfast that she was going to write a book, and Daisy was pounding on a cooking pot with a spoon that someone had handed her. Julie looked serious when she walked in.

"How's your mother?" he asked her in a subdued tone after he left Hélène with her dollhouse and went to find his wife.

"Not well," she said tersely and left the room again. She was dying a slow painful death and since Julie's sisters no longer lived nearby all the difficult decisions and painful tasks fell to her, although she spent hours on the phone with them. It was a hard time for her. Her mother was in the final stages of cancer now, and he was relieved his own mother had gone quickly, and hadn't had to live through that.

Julie left for the city early the next morning and he wondered if she was going to the doctor to have the abortion. She hadn't said a word to him the night before. She went to bed and turned her back to him, and in the morning she was gone. Waiting to hear her decision was killing him, and he'd heard nothing from her while he was in London, which didn't seem like a good sign.

He spent the morning returning calls, and had lunch with the girls in the kitchen, and at two o'clock he saw Julie drive up. He heard her come in, and go straight to their bedroom. He joined her there a few minutes later with a worried look.

"Are you all right?" he asked her, wondering if she'd had the procedure, but she was standing in her dressing room and looked at him.

"I'm keeping the baby," she said in a flat voice. "I had a sonogram this morning. The baby's fine." He felt a wave of relief wash over him as she said it, and he walked over and tried to put his arms around her but she turned away. "I saw it on the sonogram. It was too hard to do anything about it after that," she said matter-of-factly. "You were right. I'm having another sonogram in four weeks, and we can find out the sex then, if you want." She said it as though they were ordering furniture or drapes. She wasn't happy about it, but she knew she was doing the right thing, and they had enough nannies to take care of another baby. There were two on duty at all times. She had turned into a baby machine for him. But all she had to do was carry them and give birth to them, she didn't have to take care of them. It made him sad to see how unhappy she was, and he hoped she'd warm up to the idea if things got better between the two of them.

"Thank you," he said quietly, and she nodded and walked past him. She had put on jeans and a sweatshirt, and he saw then that the baby was already growing and she couldn't close her jeans. It made it seem that much more real.

She only spoke to him when she had to for the rest of the week, but he stuck around. And they stayed home on New Year's Eve. He vaguely remembered that she had wanted to have friends over, but apparently hadn't done anything about it, or canceled it after the birthday dinner fiasco. He didn't dare ask which. They had dinner together in the kitchen, after the children went to bed and the nannies to their rooms.

"I saw Steve in London," he said to make conversation with her, and she looked interested for a minute. It was the first time she'd actually let him talk to her in a week.

"How is he?"

"He's fine. He's marrying that woman he's been living with for years. I haven't met her, but she sounds nice and he's crazy about her. They're going to try to have a baby, which may not be so easy since she's forty. He seems happy." He spared her the news of Jared's divorce and Andy's four kids, both of which seemed like dangerous subjects at the moment given the situation they were in. But he was grateful that she was having his baby. He noticed that she hadn't bothered to dress for dinner, even though it was New Year's Eve. The cook had left food in the refrigerator for them, and he saw that she was barely eating and wondered if she was sick from the pregnancy. "How are you feeling?" he asked her cautiously.

"Fine," she said dully. "I haven't been sick at all this time, which is how I missed it until now. The doctor said that might not be a good sign, but everything looked fine on the sonogram. At least it's not twins," she said and he smiled. He would have loved that but didn't dare say it to her. It wasn't his body that was going to be occupied by another human being for the next six months, and go through surgery again in the end, since after two Caesarean sections, she'd have to have one for sure this time, which was another reason why she didn't want another child. It had taken her a long time to recover from the last one.

"I'm glad you feel okay at least." Their conversation was awkward and stilted, but it was hard to come back from where they'd been before he left for London. "I put Hélène's dollhouse together for her yesterday, and she was very quiet. Do you think she heard us the other night?"

"I hope not," Julie said, looking worried. Hélène was normally quiet anyway, but he had found her unusually so. "I guess we should be more careful about that. She always watches me like a hawk when she thinks something's wrong." She was mature beyond her years, and liked the company of adults. Kendra just liked the company of anyone who would talk to her. And Daisy was too young to know. "I guess they'll be happy about another baby," she said, sounding depressed about it, which made him feel guilty again. The baby was due in June, and if she didn't cheer up, it was going to be a long wait for both of them. The news was still fresh and had been a shock to her. She had thought that she was through having babies after Daisy, and now she was starting all over again.

"Is there anything I can do to make this easier for you?" he asked her gently, and she shook her head with tears in her eyes.

"There are probably going to be hard times ahead with my mom, but not for too long. The hospice nurses came yesterday. She wants to die at home."

"I'm sorry," he said and meant it, realizing how far they had drifted apart.

"Yeah, me too. And with my sisters in Santa Barbara and LA, they're not much help. But there's very little I can do for her at this point, except show up every day. She sleeps most of the time now." The subject was a dismal way to spend New Year's Eve, but so was their relationship, and there didn't seem to be anything he could do about that either. She made it very obvious that she didn't want to be close to him, and when she finished eating she rinsed her dishes and put them in the dishwasher. He was going to offer her some champagne and then remembered that she couldn't drink. She left the kitchen without saying anything to him, and went to bed with a book, and he went to his study and poured himself a drink. The house was quiet, and he sat in a comfortable chair thinking about everything that had happened in the past year. He thought of his parents, and wondered what his mother would have told him to do. Probably leave Julie alone until she came around on her own, if she ever did.

He went to bed before midnight, wished her a happy New Year, turned over and tried to go to sleep and lay awake for a long time, until she turned off the light without saying anything to him. It was going to be a long six months until the baby came.

They hardly spoke to each other for the next month. He traveled but less than usual, and he made a point of being around on the weekends. She went to the city several times a week, and daily visited her mother, who was slowly fading away. And a month later, Julie handed him an envelope when she came back from the city. She wasn't smiling and he was afraid to open it for a minute. It crossed his mind that she might be serving him with divorce papers. Anything was possible. She hadn't warmed up at all.

"What's that?"

"Pictures for you. I had the second sonogram today."

He smiled as she said it, and he started to open the envelope. "You got your wish. It's a boy." He looked at her with amazement and stood up and put his arms around her. He didn't care how angry she was at him, he was even more grateful to her now. It mattered to him. He didn't want his father's family name to die out. He was the last one left, and now he would have a son. He took the images out of the envelope and stared at them. You could see the baby's face, and as Julie watched Max look at them, she smiled for the first time in a long time. "I hope he looks like you, and your father. It's too bad he's not here to see him, he'd be pleased."

"Yes, he would," Max said, smiling at her. "My mother would be too. Thank you." She nodded. "I guess we'll have to tell the girls pretty soon." It was starting to show, and she thought Hélène had noticed and Kendra would soon too. "They probably won't be happy it's a boy."

"They'll get used to it," he said, looking delighted. "We need some guys on our team here," he said, looking more relaxed, and she laughed for the first time in a month.

"Well, don't expect me to have two more to even out the score. I'm done."

"I think you've made that clear," he teased her. "I'm just grateful you haven't tried to kill me in my sleep." She laughed again, and they were both relaxed as they left the room. They told the girls that night when they were having dinner with the nannies, and Max and Julie sat down with them for a few minutes. Julie didn't like eating with the children, she said they made too much noise. But they told them about their baby brother and Hélène looked relieved. She didn't know what her mother had done about the baby her father said she was going to kill. But she hadn't done it. She had prayed about it every night since she'd heard them, and her prayers had been answered. And Kendra said it was too bad it was a boy. She wanted to know if she could take him to school for show-and-tell. One of her classmates had brought in a guinea pig to show them, and she thought a baby would be better, which made her father laugh. It had turned into a good day after all. Julie might not have forgiven him, but she was talking to him again at least. The atmosphere lightened in the house after that. And then got tense again, when he had to start traveling more in April to close a deal.

He tried to explain it to her, but it was just more of the same to her. He'd made a real effort to be around more for three months, and now he was back to the same old tricks. The only big change he had made was that he had bought a plane, instead of buying occasional time shares or flying commercially. He said that this way he could get around more easily and wasn't dependent on the airlines. It was a big expense, but he could come home from wherever he was.

He asked her if she would go to a big political dinner with him in the city. One of the land developers he was negotiating with had invited him, and he wanted Julie to join him. He warned her that it might be boring, but he didn't want to go alone. The event was in two weeks at Gracie Mansion and it was supposed to be a glittering affair. A lot of important politicians were coming up from Washington, and major political donors. Julie was always good at events like that and charmed everyone.

"I don't have anything to wear." She was already almost seven months pregnant and bigger than she'd been before at the same stage.

"Then buy something." He smiled at her, hoping she'd go with him. The truce between them had remained tenuous, but things were holding for the moment. She was impressed he'd bought a plane, if it meant he'd come home sooner and more easily. Or maybe it just meant he'd leave more often. She didn't trust him anymore, and had made that clear.

"I'll see what I can find," she said tentatively. And much to her own surprise, she found a dress she liked and said she'd go. It flowed in all the right places and was made of sky blue sari fabric, and she looked spectacular in it. At first glance you couldn't even tell she was pregnant.

The night of the event, she looked exquisite when she put it on. They dressed at his New York apartment that they still used for a night in town. She looked like a princess when she walked into Gracie Mansion on Max's arm and he looked very proud, and then left her chatting to the mayor's wife while he talked to the group of developers who had invited him, and came back to her just in time to walk in to dinner. He got her seated at their table, and then went off again to talk to a senator, as the man on her other side introduced himself. His name was Richard Randall, which rang a bell with her although she wasn't sure why. He was tall and slim, with a thick crop of white hair, and he looked very elegant in his tuxedo. He had a slight Southern accent. And then she remembered who he was. He was a major oil tycoon from Texas who lived in New York part of the time, had been a financier in the past, and had houses all over the world. He had been on the covers of both *Time* and *Fortune*.

"Your husband's busy tonight," he commented with a wry smile.

"Do you know him?" she asked.

"No, but I've been watching him work the room since you got here, he's an enterprising guy. I was hoping to use it as an opportunity to talk to you, but the fates have been kind to me tonight. Or maybe just our hostess, since I'm seated next to you. That's a lovely dress you're wearing." He saw on closer inspection that it was the same color as her eyes. She wondered for an instant if he had noticed that she was pregnant and hoped he hadn't, and then felt foolish for thinking it. What did it matter? She thanked him for the compliment and let it go at that. He was a charming man, and very good-looking. He looked to be somewhere in his early sixties, and appeared athletic and vital.

"Are you interested in politics?" he inquired in a voice the others at the table wouldn't overhear.

"Sometimes," she said honestly, "not always."

"That's how I feel about it. At one time, I thought I'd like to be in elected office, but you couldn't pay me to do it now." He seemed confident and worldly, and told her he lived in Hong Kong and London part of the year, and it made her feel very boring. She was just a housewife from Greenwich with three small children, and a fourth on the way. It made her long for the days when she went out all the time. And he had already pegged her correctly as the neglected wife of a very ambitious man. "I've read about your husband. I used to run that hard. I got over it. I don't do that anymore."

"What cured you?" she asked as he flirted with her subtly, but not so overtly that anyone would notice or her husband could object if he glanced at their table and saw them talking. Randall was as smooth as silk.

"Three wives who left me," he said in answer to her question, and she laughed.

"I'll have to mention that to my husband," she said in response.

"Don't bother, men like him don't get it till someone lowers the boom on them. I didn't. I was a bad husband to all three of them, and I deserved it when they left me. They're all happily married to other people now." He said it with an easy smile.

"Do you have children?" She was curious about him. He was intriguing, and there was something wonderfully sophisticated and grown up about him.

"Five," he answered, "all older than you are. I was young when I got started. They're nice people. I don't see much of them. I wasn't a good father either. But I'm on friendly terms with my ex-wives now. It's hard to build a big career and spend time with your family at the same time. The two aren't compatible. You've probably discovered that by now." She nodded, feeling slightly disloyal to Max as she did, but Richard Randall seemed to understand perfectly the situation she was in. The band struck up then and he asked her to dance. She was startled when he did, but she accepted, and he led her onto the dance floor until they were ready to serve dinner, and he got her back to her seat three minutes before Max arrived at the table, apologizing profusely for leaving her alone for so long.

"I've been boring your wife shamelessly while she waited for you," Richard said. He introduced himself and Julie saw that Max was impressed. He knew exactly who he was. And when Richard got up to talk to a friend he'd seen at another table, Max whispered to her.

"Do you know who he is? He almost ran for president once. But he backed out before he could be nominated. He's a really big deal guy. What did you talk to him about?" He asked her as though there was no hope that she could hold a conversation with him, and she answered him honestly.

"His wives and kids."

"I think he's been married a couple of times. One of them was a major movie star. We should try to get to know him. I'd love to have lunch with him sometime."

"I'll try to work it out for you," she said, and he didn't catch the sarcasm in her voice. So far, Richard Randall was her conquest, not her husband's, and Max was very full of himself after circulating among the political figures there that night. Julie noticed that Richard Randall stayed in his seat most of the time, and they all came to him. But it was interesting to know that he'd almost run for president. She was flattered to be seated next to him. Max kept leaving the table between courses, to talk to people he thought were important, and it gave her a chance to talk to Richard about art and life, marriage and travel. He said he had a boat he kept in the Mediterranean and was planning to use that summer. And he asked her what her plans were. When he asked her, it depressed her. She didn't want to tell him that she was having a baby she desperately hadn't wanted. But as they had danced several times, she was sure he had noticed that she was pregnant.

"We haven't made any plans yet." She'd be recovering from her third Caesarean section. The thought of it sank her spirits, and he saw it in her eyes, and patted her hand gently.

"To everything there is a season. We all have our challenges and down times. You never know what life has in store just around the corner. Like my sitting next to you tonight. You made my evening, Julie." She was touched when he said it, and they exchanged a smile as Max returned to the table for dessert, and then he sailed off for one last conversation. Richard looked her in the eye, and then laid a pen down on the table next to her place card. "What I'm going to ask you is extremely improper, and I'd be thrown out of any decent club for doing it, but if you write down your phone number, I'd love to call you sometime. Maybe we can have lunch." She was stunned at first and then she smiled at him.

"Now you just made my evening. I'd love that." Maybe they could be friends. It was presumptuous to think so, but she liked the idea of seeing him again. She jotted down her phone number quickly and he slipped the card discreetly into his pocket. And after Max returned for the last time, Richard stood up, shook hands with both of them, thanked Julie for a most enjoyable evening, and left the table.

Max looked disappointed that he had never had a

chance to talk to him, he had gotten up so many times. "He's a powerful guy," he said, visibly impressed by him.

"You were busy tonight," Julie said noncommittally.

"There were a lot of people I wanted to see here. It was a great opportunity. That's why I wanted you to come with me. Randall didn't give you his card, did he?" he asked her and she answered truthfully.

"No, he didn't." She didn't tell him that Richard had described Max's behavior perfectly, and had ended the evening by asking for her phone number, and she had given it to him. It was the perfect antidote to feeling fat and boring and like a suburban housewife. He had made her feel glamorous, fascinating, and seductive, none of which she believed herself to be, although she liked her new dress and it somewhat concealed her blimplike figure, or at least enough so that the first question everyone asked her wasn't "When is the baby due?," which always made it seem like she wasn't capable of any topic of conversation or activity other than giving birth.

"You looked very pretty tonight," Max complimented her as they took a cab back to the apartment. She had noticed Richard leaving in a limousine a few minutes earlier. It wasn't his vast fortune and success which fascinated her—that's what Max was interested in. For her, it was the man himself, the one who had flirted with her and had been bold enough to ask for her phone number even though he knew she was a married woman. For the first time since she'd been married, she felt like she had a secret. She'd probably never hear from him, but it had been fun to play femme fatale for a minute, before she wound up in the delivery room again. She hated that image of herself, which was how Max saw her now, as a baby-making machine, and she felt as though she had lost herself in the process. But Richard Randall had found her anyway.

She felt like Cinderella when she took her dress off. She had enjoyed dancing with Richard, and she was thinking about him while Max slept innocently next to her that night. She only felt very slightly guilty.

They both got up early the next morning. Max went to his office to call Europe. And she drove back to Greenwich. She stopped to see her mother on the way, and she was heavily sedated. Julie drove home then and stopped in the kitchen to discuss menus with the chef, and Barbara, their youngest nanny, was taking Daisy out for a walk in her stroller before her morning nap.

Julie was putting away her dress from the night before when she heard the phone ring and answered it herself. The voice was familiar with the soft Southern drawl. "I was afraid I had dreamed you last night. What are you doing for lunch today?" It was Richard. Her heart gave a leap when she heard him.

"Unfortunately, I'm back in Greenwich." She sounded disappointed.

"That's not exactly on another planet. What about lunch at Terra, unless you're afraid to be seen with a man of somewhat dubious reputation? Although I've been fairly well behaved lately. Age is catching up with me." He didn't look as though it was, he was very dashing, and she wanted to have lunch with him.

"I think I can handle that," she said bravely, not sure what his intentions were. She was hardly in any condition to have an affair with him, so he couldn't have that in mind. Maybe friendship? Or innocent flirtation? She was up for either one.

"One o'clock? I'll get in my chariot right now and meet you there. It might be a little blunt to have me show up at your front door and pick you up."

"I'll be there," she promised, hung up, and dove into her closet. She didn't want to wear some enormous muumuu-like dress that would spoil the sophisticated effect of the night before. But she didn't have a lot of great maternity dresses. She was so unhappy about the pregnancy that she wasn't going anywhere and hadn't bought anything and was making do with what she had. But she had one chic navy top she could wear over jeans with high heels, which was appropriate for Greenwich. She was dressed and ready in time with freshly washed hair and carefully applied makeup, and met him at the restaurant on the dot of one. She arrived just in time to see him pull up in a black Ferrari, get out, and hand the keys to the valet, and he spotted her immediately. He looked delighted to see her, and the mood was just as flirtatious in broad daylight as the night before. There was no mistaking her belly, and he politely ignored it. He had asked for a quiet table, and as soon as they had ordered lunch, he told her how happy he was to see her.

"I thought about you all night, Julie. I know it's a terrible line, but I mean it. There was magic in the air last night, and I still feel it today." He looked into her eyes, and she suddenly had a terrifying fear that he was some kind of pervert who went around pursuing pregnant women, but he didn't seem like it. She decided to be honest with him, even if it made her sound disloyal to her husband. She wasn't sure how loyal she wanted to be to Max these days, or if the situation he had put her in was even kind or compassionate to her.

"I feel it too," she said in a soft voice, "although that must sound crazy to you." She looked down at her lap briefly and then back at him and he understood.

"That's not going to be there forever, is it? Unless it's some kind of unusual growth. Things happen at odd times in life, for unknown reasons, in unexpected ways." He had summed it up succinctly, and then he asked her a blunt question. "Are you happy about this baby?" She was quick to shake her head.

"No, I'm not. I was devastated when I found out I was

pregnant. I was going to have an abortion but I couldn't do it."

"I had that feeling last night. You would have mentioned it if you were pleased about it. The dress was terrific, but I figured it out when I was dancing with the two of you," he said and she laughed.

"It's a little hard to miss."

"Next hard question. I'm not known to beat about the bush. Do you love your husband? He seems like a nice guy, but I know how men like him treat their wives, until someone teaches them a lesson. I had to get the lesson three times before I figured out that I wasn't good husband material while I was working that hard. You're in luck. I'm retired, more or less. Men like us never retire completely. But we're tough to love while we're neglecting our women. I was guilty of it too."

"You have him pegged, to a tee. And in answer to your question, I'm not sure if I still love him. We've been married for ten years, and he's been good to me. Beautiful house, he's a generous man. He has a good heart and he's an honest person, and I think he means well, but he's a shit father and a lousy husband, and some of it is my own fault. I let him turn me into a baby machine because he wanted the illusion of a big happy family, only to discover after three children that I'm not cut out for motherhood. I don't know what's wrong, but I just don't have it in me. They still feel like someone else's children. And now this one. I felt coerced to have the second one and the last one was an accident. It's my own fault for letting it happen. I can't even remember when we did it, or why for that matter. And he's no better at parenting than I am. We never spend time with our kids. They think the nannies are their mothers, and they should be. They're much better parents than we are. We have four of them."

"They're only better at it because they get paid to be. So what are you going to do now?" he asked with considerable interest.

"I haven't figured it out yet. I know I'm supposed to be all dewy-eyed about the baby and motherhood is supposed to overtake me at some point, but it never does. I don't even want to hold them when they arrive. It's like being possessed by another human being. And after they're born, I feel totally overwhelmed by them. And I have no idea how to bring up four children, especially with a husband who's never there, and never will be."

"He might be one day, for another set of children with a new wife. Or maybe not. I'm sixty-two and I'm not paternal yet. I never got that gene either," he said honestly, "and my children know it. Some of them have even forgiven me for it and think I'm fun to have at a dinner party, two of them actively hate me, and I don't blame them. I was never around and didn't want to be. And I'm not interested in grandchildren either." He was being totally honest and so was she. She felt she could say anything to him and be herself.

"That's how I feel. They're sweet. My oldest daughter is nine and she's sensitive and caring, like her father used to be. My second one is a pistol, bright and funny and independent, and the littlest one is in diapers. But they still don't feel like they're mine. And I got incredibly depressed when I had the last one. I'm not looking forward to that again, or a baby in the house. They just make me feel guilty."

"It'll probably be worse this time," he said and she was sure he was right. "It doesn't sound like you have the parenting gene either," he said pensively, "and it's much too soon to say so, but with all due respect to your young ambitious husband, you and I sound like a match made in Heaven. I have to admit, I don't feel sorry for him, and it's been done to me too. The only ones I feel sorry for are your children, who will need to find a parent some-where along the way who actually wants to be with them, which you don't and neither does he. My children all got lucky with their step-parents, fortunately, which probably saved them. So what are we going to do about this? We have time to think about it. But unless you tell me that you're madly in love with your husband and want ten more children with him, I'm not going to let you go easily. It took me too long to find you." She was bowled over and didn't know what to say, as he reached across the table, held her hand in his, and her eyes filled with tears. She felt as though he had just saved her. He really was the handsome prince, or her knight in shining armor. It seemed too good to be true. "Don't cry, I'm not going anywhere. We'll figure it out together." She felt as though she was dreaming. It was the opposite of the nightmare she'd been living. "I suggest we take it slow, for a while, and see where this leads, and figure it out as we go along. How does that sound to you?"

"Perfect," she said, as two tears rolled down her cheeks and he brushed them away gently with his fingertip. "This must seem shocking to you. I think I might be falling in love with you, while carrying another man's baby."

"I'm not easy to shock anymore. I have a friend who got in a similar situation years ago. The woman left her husband for him after she had the baby, and they've been happily married for thirty years." She thought about it for a moment after he said it. "I have neither a fetish for, nor an aversion to, pregnant women. As long as I don't have to bring up the baby. You wouldn't want me to. I'm not good at it. But it sounds like you aren't either." She nodded agreement.

"I'd have to give up my children, wouldn't I?" She had gotten his drift all through lunch.

"With me, yes, you would. I did a lousy job with my own kids. I don't want to do a lousy job with yours. If we do something about this mad infatuation of ours," he smiled at her as he said it, "we'd be talking about an adult life between two people who love each other, in total freedom, in various cities around the world. I have no problem with you visiting your children whenever you want to, I just don't want to live with them. I can't stand the mess and the noise, the arguments, the fights about what they can and can't do, their dangerous friends and unsuitable partners, the alcohol and drugs they want to experiment with and you don't want them to. It's a nightmare. I can't go through it again. And you aren't even there yet with one in diapers and one not even born."

"You make it sound even worse than what I'm going through now."

"Trust me. It is. Some people love it. I just don't happen to be one of them. It took me a long time to figure that out. You're way ahead of the game. And you're honest about yourself, which I like. I can't stand people who pretend they're good parents, and really aren't. That's what damages the kids."

"I don't suppose their mother walking out on them will do them a lot of good either," she said, looking worried, especially about Hélène, who would think it was somehow her fault. She was such a responsible child, and willing to carry everyone's burdens, including her mother's.

"No, but it leaves them room for someone else, who might do a better job of it and really love them. I'm not sure that people like you and I really can love our children. We're not terrible people, but there's something missing in us." She nodded. It was exactly what she felt about herself, and she loved his honesty about it. It no longer made her feel subhuman for the emotions she couldn't conjure up. "I've given you a lot to think about," he said quietly, and she nodded again.

"Yes, you have." It had been the most amazing lunch of her life. He had come to some very rapid conclusions, but so many of them sounded right.

"When can I see you again?" He didn't want to leave her. Now that he had found her, he wanted to keep her close to him.

"I have to go to the city tomorrow," she said cautiously. She had to go to the doctor for a routine test.

"Perfect. I'll figure out someplace quiet for lunch and call you in the morning. If we're going to get tired of each other, we might as well find that out now," he said as they stood up, and he smiled down at her. "And in case you're wondering," he said softly, "I've fallen in love with you, you should know that. I would kidnap you right now if I could." He gently touched her hand as they walked out. She hardly knew him, but she felt as though she belonged with him, and she was in love with him too. There was no hiding from it and she didn't want to.

He walked her to her car when they left the restaurant and stood next to her for a minute. The attraction between them was so powerful it took her breath away. He was the strongest, most magnetic, decisive, exciting man she had ever met. He watched her get in the car and then leaned down next to her and gently brushed her lips with his. "See you tomorrow," he said gently. "And for the rest of our lives, I hope." Then he stepped back and walked to his Ferrari, and waved as she drove away. They were both smiling, and when she got home, she couldn't stop grinning. She wanted to dance around. She put on some music and thought about him. She didn't know what was going to happen or if anything would come of it, but just for now, it was the best day of her life. She felt as though she'd been saved.

Chapter 17

As he promised he would, Richard called her in the morning, fortunately right after Max left for work. He was flying to Albuquerque on his new plane for a meeting at lunchtime. And Julie felt like a free woman when she drove to New York. She had an appointment with her doctor at three o'clock, and she had agreed to meet Richard at noon at an Italian restaurant in Tribeca, where she was unlikely to see anyone she knew, but she didn't really care. They weren't doing anything immoral or illicit yet, they were just having lunch. Or that was what she told herself as she drove into town. She was wearing a chic black dress and felt glamorous despite her incongruous shape, which seemed absurdly inappropriate for a date with a new man. The dress was short and showed off her legs, and she had worn high heels, and was wearing a black wool coat, with her blond hair loose and long.

He was waiting at the restaurant and kissed her as soon as she arrived, and she looked up at him with a broad smile. Overnight he had become her safe haven, her escape from a life she had come to hate and a man she was beginning to think she no longer loved. Richard was the embodiment of excitement, love, and hope. He was a welcome change from a neglectful husband, and three children to whom she had too little to give.

They talked about a hundred different things at lunch and avoided talking about the future. They wanted to savor the present first, and had set down the ground rules the day before. They didn't need to know more yet, except about each other, and how they felt being together. He made her laugh as she hadn't in years. She could no longer even remember when her relationship with Max had felt like that, if it ever had. This was grown up and mature, two adults who wanted to be together and knew the reasons why. Part of it was sexual attraction in spite of her condition, and part of it was emotional and a need to fill a void in their lives. Richard said he hadn't been in love with anyone in a long time. For Julie, he was an odd combination of best friend and a man she wanted to love, and thought she could. He was everything Max wasn't. He had been financially secure all his life— Max was running from a life of poverty, and had been deeply marked by his parents' fears while he was growing up. She knew he would never stop running, and trying to shore things up, while their marriage was dying at his feet, or already had.

Richard told her that he had an apartment in Tribeca

nearby. He wanted her to see it, but said he didn't want her to think he was trying to seduce her on their second date. He wanted to be respectful of her and give her time to think things out. He was free, she wasn't, and the situation was a great deal more complicated for her. He said his apartment had a view of the Hudson River, and she was curious to see it, and she felt comfortable going there with him for a few minutes, before she headed uptown for her appointment.

"I promise I'll behave," he said when he told her the apartment was two blocks away, and they walked there in the April sunshine arm in arm while he told her stories about his boyhood and made her laugh. She hadn't laughed like that in so long. He was fun and easy to be with, and she never questioned the fact that he was openly poaching another man's wife. Being with him felt so good and it was what they both wanted. They were so well suited to each other, and so much alike. They kept discovering things they had in common, in art, in the books they liked. In her lonely years with Max, she had discovered literature and art. They enjoyed the same cities in Europe. He promised to take her to Venice one day on his boat, which was currently in the South of France.

The building he lived in was a restored warehouse with a single loft apartment on every floor. It had a posh industrial feeling to it, typical of Tribeca and the areas around it that were becoming increasingly fashionable, but hadn't quite gotten there yet. The Meatpacking District was nearby, and so was SoHo. They rode up to the top floor in the freight elevator, which opened directly into his apartment, and she found herself standing in what looked like a contemporary art gallery, with deep, comfortable white couches scattered around the room, sculptures by important artists, and a Calder mobile hanging from the ceiling. A circular staircase led to his bedroom with a balcony, and there were tall windows which showed off his river view. It had been done by a famous decorator, and he had an entire wall of rare books. The kitchen area was black granite, and the whole place had a cool, crisp masculine feel to it. It was very sleek and sophisticated, just like him. In a way the apartment defined him. It was a world in which children wouldn't be comfortable or welcome and didn't belong. It was exactly where she wanted to be and who she wanted to be with, she thought as he showed her around.

"Welcome to my humble abode," he said, joking again as they walked in, and he tossed the keys on the granite counter. The marble, glass, and chrome surfaces were in sharp contrast to the comfortable couches, which enveloped you as soon as you sat down. He invited her to sit on one of them, and she laughed as she sank into it.

"You're going to need a crane to get me up again," she warned him, and he sank into it with her, and gently put his hand up the skirt of her dress with a questioning look to see if she would stop him, but she didn't and she didn't want to. "I have a feeling we're going to get in trouble," she said, her words muffled by his lips as he kissed her.

"Not if it's what we both want," he said, running a hand below her belly with nimble fingers that found their way further down, and then he stopped to look at her, with tenderness and a question in his eyes. "I don't want to do anything you don't want to, Julie." But she didn't want him to stop, and a moment later, they couldn't, and he pulled off her coat, and gently lifted her dress over her head. Her breasts were full and her belly large, and the rest of her shapely and slim. "You are the perfect sculpture of what womanhood should look like," he said, and they kissed as she peeled off his clothes and they lay naked together in the embrace of the couch. And he was infinitely careful as he made love to her and they artfully found positions that worked, and she had never known pleasure like it before. It felt like hours before they stopped, and he lay for a long time inside her, and then made love to her again. Then he looked at her, worried for a minute afterward, and moved gently away from her. "I don't want to deliver a baby in my apartment. Maybe we should take it easy for a while." She lay sated in his arms, and had completely forgotten her appointment and no longer cared. They walked upstairs to his bedroom then, and lay on his bed and looked at the river, and she didn't want to leave him again.

"I think you might be habit-forming," she said in a husky voice. She felt as though she belonged there, and they finally got up and walked downstairs in all their naked glory, or they would have made love again.

He had an enormous shower, and they stood in it together with the water running over them as they kissed.

"How am I going to live without you this summer?" he asked as he looked at her and watched her get dressed. He had told her he was meeting friends in Europe who were joining him on his boat, but she had a baby to give birth to, and there was no way she could come. "I don't want to be around when all that happens," he said simply. "I don't want to confuse you. You have to figure this out for yourself." And with everything going on in her life, June was going to be the right time for him to leave, and she knew she had to do some serious thinking. This was not a small decision, about whether or not to leave a husband and four children for a man she barely knew just because her instinct was telling her they were meant to be together, and he was saying the same thing. But she didn't doubt what she was feeling. Everything about it felt right to her, and to him too.

And from then on, she drove in from Greenwich and they met at his apartment almost every lunchtime and after-noon. They had a whole secret life together, and they went to galleries and museums and movies, exhibits he wanted to show her. They went to the theater one night when Max was away, and she stayed at Richard's apartment instead of her own. It was beginning to feel like home to her. They spent every possible moment together in April and May, and as the weeks wore on, she started to worry about his going away.

"It's going to be awful without you," she said miserably.

"It's going to be even worse for me," he said seriously. "You're having another man's baby, and you may fall in love with Max all over again and decide to stay with him and your children." And he wasn't going to try to convince her to leave. He wanted her to come to him on her own.

"That's not going to happen," she said, about falling in love with Max. "I love you, Richard. I just want to be sure I'm doing the right thing." He nodded and said he wanted that for her too, but what he wanted was for her to come away with him and share his life. He had an apartment in Hong Kong and a flat in London and a permanent suite at the Ritz in Paris. He had an enviable life and he wanted to share it with her. "What if you get tired of me one day?"

"That's not going to happen either. It's far more likely that you'll get tired of me. One day you may decide that I'm too old." He was twenty-nine years older than she was but she could no longer imagine not loving him.

"Would you ever want to get married?" She was curious, not planning.

"If that's what you want. I don't care either way. Maybe four is my lucky number," he said, smiling at her. He was easygoing about everything and wanted to please her, and they made love every day, although he was increasingly careful. Her due date was only four weeks away, and he didn't want the baby to come any sooner. He wouldn't be able to see her for a while after it came. And they had agreed that after he left, they wouldn't see each other again until she'd made up her mind. He didn't want to put pressure on her. And he was willing to wait as long as it took. "Within reason, of course. I don't want to wait until this one leaves for college," he said, pointing at her belly. He had already told her he didn't want a long-standing affair with a married woman. Her circumstances were exceptional now, for both of them, and it had just happened, but once the baby was born, she had to make a decision. It wouldn't be fair to anyone if she didn't, and she agreed. She didn't consider what she had with Richard an affair—it was their future, she said to him. "I hope so," he answered.

She was worried that Max would be at home all the time now with his new plane, and she'd have less opportunity to see Richard. But Max fell into his old routine rapidly, even with his own plane. He was gone constantly again in May. His promises were forgotten, and he went from one city to the next, without coming home in between. He would call her to check in, and explain that his plans had changed again, but she no longer complained. And he found her peaceful and happy when he did come home, and thought she was adjusted to the baby, and was basking in the glow of impending motherhood. It was a relief to see her in such good humor. She was even pleasant with him, although they never made love in this pregnancy. She didn't want to have sex with two men. Her body belonged to Richard now, and her womb to her husband. It was the only part of her he still owned, but that would end soon. And Richard constantly marveled that her body hadn't been marred by four pregnancies. She had the body of a young girl.

And even though the baby wasn't his, Richard worried about her. "It's getting awfully big, isn't it? What does your doctor say?" She smiled at his concern.

"That it's a big baby. The others were too, though not as big as this. Probably because it's a boy." He had noticed how much bigger it had gotten in the time they'd been together. "You'll call me afterward, won't you, so I know you're all right? Whatever you decide?"

"Of course." She dreaded his being away, and so did he. But there was no way around it and it was just as well. It would have driven her crazy if she knew he was nearby and she couldn't see him.

Before he left, there was a profile of him in *The New*

Yorker, and she found it on her desk when Max was home. For a minute, she panicked as he handed it to her and wondered if he'd had her followed.

"I don't know if you remember him, but that's the man you sat next to at dinner at Gracie Mansion. Interesting guy."

"I remember him," she said weakly, and breathed again. She told Richard about it later and they laughed.

"Poor guy, he has no idea what's about to hit him. At least I hope it will. He deserves it for neglecting you shamelessly, but he probably won't admit that to himself for a long time. Most men don't. I didn't either when it happened to me. His ego will take the hardest hit." She suspected it was true. He thought he owned her, and had designed their life to suit himself, and had told himself it suited her too.

And then June came, and Richard and Julie had only days left together. It made them both feel desperate. She came to see him in the city every day, and she was tired, so they rarely went out, except for lunch occasionally. But most of the time they stayed home, and then she would drive back to Greenwich, stop to check on her mother, and go home to her children. But they wore her out now and were too exuberant, and too noisy.

Mercifully, Max was out of town on Richard's last night before he left for France, so she could spend it with him. They lingered in bed for as long as they could, kissed constantly, and she went to the airport with him so they could be together until the last minute. He held her tightly in his arms at the gate, and closed his eyes, just feeling her and loving her. Neither of them cared who saw them.

"Come back to me," he whispered to her. "Don't leave me, Julie." She knew what he meant as he held her.

"I won't. I love you. Take care of yourself. I worry too. Be careful on the boat." He smiled then.

"It's not a rowboat, I promise." And she laughed. She had seen photographs of it in the apartment. It was a two-hundred-foot yacht with a crew of eighteen.

"You could still get hurt or fall off."

"I'll try not to. And you take it easy now. Don't do too much. Rest." She had two weeks left before her Caesarean, which was scheduled for a week before her due date. "And don't forget how much I love you." He had to leave her then to catch his flight. He kissed her a last time and walked onto the plane as she waved at him, and stood there for a few minutes after. She watched the plane taxi away and take off, and then she drove home to Greenwich, and was surprised to find Max in the kitchen. He looked worried as soon as she walked in.

"Where were you? I got in this morning and I came home to check on you instead of going straight to the office." He'd been gone for a week, and if she still cared, she would have been furious. He'd been away constantly for two months, which had worked out perfectly for her and Richard.

"I had the usual tests at my doctor's. They test for all kinds of stuff now at the end," she said casually.

"It won't be long now," he said, beaming, and put a proprietary hand on her belly which made her flinch. "I can't wait to meet him."

"Me too," she said and went to lie down in their bedroom. She wanted time to herself to think about Richard. She had a big decision to make. He was going to be away for two months, but she was planning to tell Max her decision long before then. She just wanted to get through the birth first, and try to think clearly.

Max came in then to shower and change clothes and go back to town for a business dinner. He said he'd be home late, and he might stay in the city and would sleep at the apartment. She didn't answer. "Are you okay? You're very quiet." She'd been so happy lately and now she seemed sober.

"Just thinking."

"Worried about the delivery?"

"Not yet. I will be. It's a good thing it's a C-section. He's huge." Max had noticed it too.

"How's your mom doing?" he asked delicately.

"Same. She's still hanging on. They have her very sedated. It's better that way. Thanks for asking." They were strangers now, living at the same address and having a baby together. She wondered if he'd make it to the delivery this time. And for a minute she was sorry it wasn't Richard's baby. But as he'd said, it wasn't what they were good at, or what he wanted.

She had a quiet evening after Max left. She saw the children for a little while. Hélène came and visited her in her room with the nannies' permission. She said something about wanting to be the baby's godmother because she'd been praying for him.

"What kind of prayers?" Julie asked her.

"Oh, you know, just nice prayers, like asking God to take care of him until he gets here and we can take care of him."

Julie thought that was sweet and thanked her for it. "But you can't be a godmother because Daddy's Jewish, and they don't have godmothers." Hélène looked disappointed.

"Why don't we go to church or temple?"

"Because Daddy doesn't go to temple, and I don't go to church anymore, at least not very often."

"Maybe one day I'll be Jewish like Opa and Mamie Emm. She said it was important to remember what happened in the war, so people don't forget about being Jewish. I think I'd like to be Jewish." Julie thought it was an odd thing to say, but she was a sensitive child, and thought about things very seriously, and had been close to her grandparents. Julie felt momentarily guilty for not taking the children to church from time to time, which was yet another thing she didn't do with them. There were so many. But Max always said it would confuse them.

Max stayed in the city that night and Julie went to bed early, and the phone woke her at six A.M. She wondered if it was Richard calling from Paris. He was staying at the Ritz for a few days before he headed south and met the boat in Monaco. But it wasn't. It was the hospice nurse at her mother's, she had died peacefully a few minutes before. There had been no warning or time to call Julie to come over, but she had already said goodbye to her mother many times. And they were all ready. The nurse said she had called her sisters too. Julie called them then, and they were both flying in that afternoon. They had already made all the decisions for the funeral and knew their mother's wishes. They'd had time to talk it over with her while she was still lucid. She had even told them what music. Julie was sad but it had been coming for so long, she felt peaceful about it. She called Max then to tell him, and he told her he was sorry. All of their parents were gone now. In a way, Julie was glad; she wouldn't have to deal with anyone's reactions except Max's if she left him for Richard. Their parents' opinions would have been an added burden.

She went to her mother's house a little while later, and the funeral parlor had already taken her away. The obituary had already been written, and she sent it off by messenger to the *Times* and the local papers. She called the florist, and set everything else in motion. Her mother wanted white lilies, and by the time her sisters arrived late that afternoon from California, everything had been organized. They had flown in together.

"OhmyGod, look at you, you're huge!" her older sister commented, and her younger sister chimed in too. It reminded her that they would have opinions about what she was doing too. But it didn't matter to her what they thought. She was the one who had to live her life, with a husband who was never around and four children she knew she couldn't manage and didn't want to. Her sisters each had two children which was all they wanted, and their children were still very young so they hadn't brought them. Julie had told Hélène and Kendra that morning that Grandma had gone to Heaven to be with Grampa.

"Will they see Opa and Mamie Emm?" Hélène had asked her. She was asking complicated religious questions these days. "Or would they be in a different part of Heaven because they're Jewish?"

"I'm not sure," Julie answered, "I think you have to ask your father." She had no idea what he'd want to tell her.

*

Everything went smoothly for Julie's mother's funeral, and Richard sent an enormous bouquet of white orchids to Julie at the house with a card that just said, "Love, Richard," which she put in her pocket when the flowers arrived. Everything about the funeral had been exactly what her mother had wanted. Her sisters stayed with her at The Orchards, and they talked about putting their parents' house on the market since none of them wanted it, and they no longer lived in the area, and Julie didn't need it. Everything had been left to the three of them, divided equally, so there would be no arguments over the estate, which was a blessing. And there was plenty for each of them. Money, antiques, jewelry, art.

They had already looked at her mother's furnishings, jewelry, and possessions to express their preferences, and divided them amicably. All three of them were rich women, and had been since their father died.

And when they left to return to California, they wished her luck with the C-section, and told her to call as soon as she had the baby.

Richard had called several times from France too. He was on the boat by then, and communication via sat com was more difficult, but he said he would call anytime they were in port, where it was easier. And he wanted to hear from her when the baby came too. He was concerned about her.

"I'll have Max call you," she teased him.

"That's not funny."

"I'm sorry. I may be a little out of it for a day or so after the surgery."

"I wish somebody could call me." But they both knew that wasn't possible, and she didn't want to say anything to her gossipy sisters, who would want to know everything, and then pass judgment about what she was doing. And there was a part of her that still wasn't sure about her decision. She knew she loved Richard unreservedly, but she wasn't sure what was the right thing to do about her children. She was trying to assess whether she had an obligation to them for life, no matter how disconnected she felt as their mother. Maybe that was just her problem, not theirs, and she had no right to make it theirs by leaving. She knew it would affect them deeply. What did it say about you if your own mother left you? Julie wasn't sure. She thought about it every day, and hoped the answer would become clear. She knew she didn't want to sacrifice Richard for her children. That was too much to ask. She thought it would be easier to leave them for him.

*

Max did what she expected two days before the delivery. He announced that he had a big meeting in Houston, another in Phoenix, and one in Albuquerque that he couldn't miss, but he promised he'd only be gone for two days, and back in time for the scheduled C-section the following day, after he got back. He was cutting it close, he always did.

"It's before your due date anyway, so the baby isn't going to come early and you won't go into labor."

"Are you trying to convince me or yourself?" she asked him crisply. "Should I remind you that Daisy came two weeks early and I went into labor before the scheduled C-section? Or should we just stay in Fantasyland about it, so you can feel okay about leaving this close to my due date?"

"I made it back last time, and I will this time," he said stubbornly, "and I have my own plane now."

"You made it by about two minutes," she reminded him, and he looked uncomfortable, but he kissed her on the top of her head and left. He hadn't really kissed her in months, and she didn't miss it. She just didn't feel the same way about him anymore. She wouldn't have anyway, but especially not since Richard.

She didn't go to aerobics class this time or swim in the pool for several days before the surgery. She didn't want to do anything she shouldn't. But two days before the scheduled date, there was a full moon and her water broke at midnight and she went into labor minutes later. The baby was in a hurry. She had Barbara, one of the nannies, drive her into the city, and there was no traffic, so they drove quickly. The pains were two minutes apart by the time they got there. By now she knew what she was dealing with and there were no surprises. She just had to grit her teeth and get through it until they reached the hospital, and since it had to be a C-section, they'd give her an epidural for sure, or general anesthesia, which she liked even better. She didn't call Max this time. It was all going too fast, and she knew he couldn't get back from Houston or Albuquerque in time. She knew all the signs, had Barbara run in to get a nurse as soon as they reached the hospital, and she had called her doctor before they left.

"I'm ready to push," she said to the nurse through clenched teeth, trying not to. Daisy had been born in even less time than that, but fortunately this one was slower.

"Aren't you a scheduled C?" the nurse said. Many of the nurses knew her by now, after three children. She felt like a cow dropping calves.

"Apparently nobody told my son that." Julie was gripping the arms of the wheelchair and wishing Richard was with her, not Max. He'd have control of the situation in minutes.

"We've got the delivery room ready for you," the nurse reassured her.

They helped her onto a gurney and whizzed her into surgery where the doctor took one look at her and knew she was already fully dilated and the baby was huge. A nurse attached a monitor to her belly, and as she did, they saw the baby's heartbeat plunge for the length of the contraction, and then come up again, and drop sharply again with the next one.

"We're going in now," the doctor said to the anesthesiologist, who was standing behind Julie and put a mask over her face. "I think we have a cord problem," he said to the attending staff but Julie was already woozy, and seconds later she was unconscious as they made the incision as quickly as they could, and pulled the baby out seconds later. His face was a deep blue and there was no sound in the room as the doctor massaged him and a nurse quickly unwound the cord that was wrapped tightly around his neck and had tightened with each contraction. A few more and he would have strangled, and as she loosened the last of it the baby let out a loud wail and everyone in the room breathed and the doctor smiled. "Good one. How many times?"

"Six times around his neck," the nurse answered, referring to the umbilical cord, as the baby continued to scream and his face went from purple to bright red and his mother never knew how close she'd come to losing him. They weighed him, and he was ten pounds four ounces.

"A big guy," the doctor said as he stitched Julie up. "This is her fourth. She'll be back again in a year or two," he said confidently. "We love repeat business," he said and they all laughed. Everyone was in good humor once the baby was safe and the pediatrician put him in an incubator which they did with all big babies. They sent him to the nursery to be cleaned up and dressed and have his vitals checked again. And after they cleaned Julie up, she was on the way to the recovery room half an hour later. She was shaking violently from the delivery when she woke up and threw up from the anesthesia and the nurse gave her a shot of Demerol for the pain from her incision. Julie felt like a soldier who'd been sent into battle too many times.

"Oh God, I feel awful," she said to no one in particular.

"I'll bet you do, honey. The shot will kick in in a minute," the recovery room nurse told her. And when it did, she went back to sleep. When she woke up, they told her about the cord around the baby's neck and how lucky it was that she was in the hospital and they could get him out quickly, and she lay there wondering how she would have felt if something had happened to him. Terrible, probably. And guilty. But he was fine.

"Would you like to hold your big boy?" the nurse asked her and she shook her head.

"No, I hurt too much."

"Where's his daddy? Is he downstairs in your room?"

"No, he's in Chicago or Houston or someplace, I can't remember where. He'll be back sometime." The nurse didn't comment, and Julie drifted back to sleep again and woke up in a private room. She remembered she had Richard's number in her purse then, and had the nurse get it for her. She wanted to talk to him. She had told him she'd call him. She tried to focus on the numbers but the call wouldn't go through. The operator told her you couldn't dial internationally from the room phones, so she couldn't talk to him. So she called Max instead. He answered immediately.

"Anything happening?" He sounded excited and hopeful.

"I had him a few hours ago. Ten pounds four ounces. He had the cord around his neck six times but he's fine now. Simon Jakob Stein is waiting to meet you." She tried to sound happy about it, but she didn't, because she wasn't. She didn't love his father, and the poor innocent baby was just another noose around her own neck.

"I'll be home in a few hours, and, baby, you're fantastic and I love you."

"I love you too," she said, and hung up as rivers of tears flowed down her cheeks. She felt like she was in jail again.

Chapter 18

Max walked into the hospital as though he owned it and his wife had just given birth to Jesus Christ. He walked into Julie's room, found her sound asleep, and went straight to the nursery to see the baby. A nurse held him up and Max gestured to take him to the room, and he and the baby arrived simultaneously and woke Julie up. The nurse tried to hand him to her but she couldn't sit up. She was in too much pain from the incision, and Max took him instead.

"He looks like a sumo wrestler," she said from a prone position, and Max looked like he was about to burst and tears of joy ran down his cheeks.

"I wish my parents could have seen him. My dad wanted a grandson so much. But he loved the girls too." He settled into a chair holding the baby, and Simon looked around and seemed satisfied with his surroundings and went back to sleep in his father's arms, while Julie stared at him trying to figure out how a baby that size could have fit inside her and was grateful she hadn't had to push him out. He was the biggest newborn she'd ever seen, and the biggest in the nursery at the moment.

Max set him down gently in the bassinet in the room then, without waking him. He took a small square box out of his pocket, and helped her open it. She was still groggy from pain medication and she stared at the enormous emerald ring Max slipped on her finger.

"I don't deserve it," she said, feeling guilty.

"Of course you do," he said and kissed her. She turned her face away from him then and closed her eyes. All she could think of was Richard.

*

They let them go home four days later. She could still hardly walk or stand up straight, but she wanted to go home to her own bed and she was dying to talk to Richard. She hadn't talked to him for five days.

The nannies helped her into the house, got her undressed, and eased her into bed. The incision felt worse this time, and Max took Simon to meet his sisters. They were happy to see him, and Hélène fussed over him like a little mother. She had all the instincts her mother didn't. But Julie hurt too much to deal with the baby, and he cried a lot. He was hungry and guzzled his formula every two hours.

Max took the girls out for ice cream that afternoon, and Julie called Richard on the boat. She had taken a pain pill but she was coherent enough to call him. It took him a long time to come to the phone. He'd been having dinner on deck with friends but hurried to the phone when they told him she was on the line.

"Julie? Are you okay?" He sounded worried.

"No, I feel like shit and I miss you. I had the baby, I just wanted to tell you I'm okay."

"Oh, sweetheart, I'm sorry. Did everything go all right?" She sounded awful, but she had come through it.

"Ten pounds four ounces."

"I thought so. My second son was that size. I think that's why she divorced me, aside from the fact that I was a crap husband and father," he said, and she groaned.

"Don't make me laugh! The incision is killing me. I miss you so much."

"I miss you too. Now rest and get better, and give me good news when you're not stoned on pain pills."

"I love you," she said weakly.

"I love you too. Call me whenever you want. And I'm so glad you're okay. You'll feel better in a few days." She started to cry as he said it, she was on a roller coaster of emotions. Between her hormones, the pain pills, and the residual anesthesia, she was a mess. He could hear it and knew what it was like. "It's all right, sweetheart, you're going to be fine soon. It's over now. You can get on with your life, and mine, I hope," he said and she smiled through her tears.

"Thank you."

"Get some sleep."

He went back to dinner, and there was no way he could tell the people he was dining with that he'd just had a call from the woman he loved, who had just given birth to her husband's baby, and he was hoping she would abandon her husband and children for him. It was too sordid for words, or sounded that way. And more than a little decadent.

In Greenwich, Julie was lying in bed crying and she wasn't sure why. All she knew was that she loved Richard and she wasn't sure what to do. Max was so happy with the baby, she didn't want to spoil it for him. It was all so confusing, and Hélène kept coming in to check on her and brought her little treats. She was worried about everyone, her mother, her father, the baby, and Simon meant the most to her since she was convinced her prayers had kept them from killing him, and she was glad they hadn't. She kept holding him and looking at him and kissing him. He was her baby now too.

Max stayed home for a week after she got out of the hospital, and he had a mohel come to do a circumcision with a rabbi. Hélène had a long talk with the rabbi, and he said afterward what a bright girl she was with a strong interest in Judaism, and he told Max that she should be taking Hebrew lessons to prepare for her bat mitzvah one day. Max nodded and thanked him and gave him a check for him and the mohel. He was not about to send his daughters to Hebrew classes just because he got his son circumcised. Max's involvement in his religion, like his parents' and his own upbringing, was cultural and minimal, not profound, and if Hélène had a deep religious calling she could pursue it later, not at the age of nine. He considered himself a Jew in name only. He was proud of being Jewish, and honored what his parents had suffered, but he had no interest in the temple and what went on there, and wasn't sure what, if anything, he believed in.

*

He went in to check on Julie several times, and she was asleep. He noticed that she seemed to feel worse this time. She was in a lot of pain and taking strong medication. Five days later, the depression set in, and she started to cry all the time. He left the next day for a two-week trip, and he wouldn't have admitted it, but he was relieved. The baby was beautiful but all the fuss that went with it, with the nannies and Julie and his daughters, was more than he wanted to deal with right now. He sat back in his seat on the plane and was delighted to have left it all behind to get back to business again, in the world where he felt the most at ease.

For Julie, the worst was just beginning. She was depressed all the time. The children came to visit in her bedroom and annoyed her. Kendra bounced on the bed, and Daisy wanted her mother to hold her, and cried every time she couldn't. Simon was colicky or hungry or all of the above and screamed constantly, she could hear it all the way down the hall from the nursery, and Hélène looked mournful and worried as soon as her father left on his trip. The nannies got them out of her room as soon as they could, but it was never soon enough for Julie. Invariably, they broke something or messed something up, or took something they weren't supposed to, and Hélène always lingered, with an anxious expression.

Julie was still in pain from the incision so she stayed in bed and felt trapped in her room. She felt like she was in jail with the nannies and children, and Max didn't bother to call for four days and claimed it was because of the time difference, which she knew was bullshit. She felt like her life would forever be a constant merry-go-round of children and nannies and the same husband who was never there. She felt overwhelmed, as though someone were drowning her, but walking out on them seemed selfish and cruel. And staying was torture for her. When Richard called her, she told him she was trying to do it right and think about it and be fair to the children, and maybe her job as a mother was to sacrifice her life for their well-being.

"You're not going to do anyone any good as miserable as you are," he said sensibly, "you're going to resent them for everything you gave up for them. But you also need to wait for your hormones to settle down. You're not thinking straight right now. Just give it time. The offer still stands, and will stand for a long time. We'll talk when you feel better. It sounds like you need to get out of the house."

"I feel like I'm in prison," she said, sobbing, and as he listened, he thanked God he was out of the baby business. He had forgotten how emotional it could be, and how unpleasant.

She felt even worse when Max came home from his trip, and she flinched every time he came near her. She saw how happy he was about the baby, and she felt nothing for him or the child. It was like there was a piece of her missing and always had been. She was a mess of emotions, and every time someone screamed "Mommy" and ran down the hall to her, she winced and wanted to lock the door to her room. It was as though there was something profoundly wrong with her and she knew it.

She was up and dressed by the time Max came back. She couldn't drive yet, so she had various members of the household drive her, and she found every excuse she could to get out, just to leave the house and get away from them all for a while. She had stopped calling Richard, which made her feel even worse, but she wanted to try to feel something for Max and the children, if there was anything there, but there wasn't, just a giant void where her feelings should have been. Everyone kept telling her how beautiful the baby was, but each time she tried to pick him up, he threw up on her and they both smelled disgusting.

There wasn't a single part of the whole experience she was enjoying, except for the spectacular emerald ring Max had given her after she gave birth to Simon, but she felt too guilty to wear it. She was in love with another man. She couldn't take a big piece of jewelry from Max just because she'd had his baby. And she knew he was saving his mother's big diamond ring to give her one of these days, and she didn't want that either. She didn't want anything from him. She just wanted to be left alone, and spent most of her time in her room, crying every time she told herself that this was her life forever and she had to stand by Max and their children. All it did was make her want to run away.

"How are you doing?" Max asked her one night when they went to bed. He could tell that she was depressed again and had been since the hospital, and he wasn't sure what it was about, other than hormones, and the "baby blues."

"I don't know. It's just all so overwhelming. We have so many kids now and they need so much attention." There were two in diapers who cried constantly, and two who talked incessantly, and the nannies wanted her attention too. She felt as though everyone was bleeding her dry.

"Well, we can't send them back," Max said unsympa- thetically. "You'll get used to it." And as he looked at her, he remembered what his mother had said, that Julie didn't seem like the kind of girl to have a lot of children, or even be a serious wife to him, and for the first time in his life he wondered if he had married the wrong woman.

He remembered the strength his parents had given each other, the wisdom they had shared, the faith they had in each other's abilities, the encouragement, the support. They had even given each other hope in a death camp, and Julie couldn't handle having four children with four nannies to help her. She was drowning in a teacup, as his mother would say. He needed a woman with guts, like his mother, but he'd been so in love with Julie when he met her, he hadn't wanted to see it. Julie was a woman to have fun with, she was decorative, but she wasn't sturdy, and she was exactly what his mother had said—she wasn't made to be the mother of many children or stand by her man while he built an empire for her. For the first time he felt despair lying next to her. It was a terrible feeling, and he turned over so she wouldn't see the tears in his eyes. On her side of the bed, she was crying too, and he knew it, and he didn't even want to reach out to comfort her. They had little compassion left for each other. They were two totally different people, two puzzle parts that no longer fit and never had, living under one roof.

He turned back to her for a minute. "I forgot to tell

you. I'm leaving for Seattle in the morning. There are some great opportunities there, and then I have meetings in Southern California." She didn't say a word for a minute, and then she nodded.

"Have a good trip." He couldn't tell if she was being sarcastic or sincere, and he wasn't even sure he cared which anymore. He hated to admit it, but he felt nothing for her.

*

Six weeks after he'd left, and a month after the baby was born, Richard called her from the boat. They were at the dock in Monte Carlo and had just come back from Sardinia, and he sounded serious on the phone.

"I can't stand it anymore, Julie. I know I said take all the time you wanted, but I'm going crazy. I miss you. I don't want to pressure you, but I have to see you. I'm flying to New York tonight from Nice. I get in around midnight, and I want to see you tomorrow. I just want to touch you and hold you and see your face." He sounded desperate and she was touched. She felt the same way, but she didn't know if seeing him was the right thing. She still hadn't made a decision and she was feeling worse every day.

"I'm kind of a mess," she said hesitantly. She looked pasty and pale, and she hadn't lost all the baby weight yet, and she was morbidly depressed.

"I don't care if you're a mess. I love you. I haven't seen you in six weeks. Just see me for an hour or two, and then I'll leave you alone until you figure things out. You're like the air I breathe, I need you."

"I need you too," she said sadly. And she didn't need Max and her children, but she thought they needed her. "Are you coming just to see me?"

"Yes, I am," he said honestly. It was frightening to let himself be that vulnerable, especially to a married woman, who might still decide not to leave her husband and children. And he knew he was asking a lot of her, but he couldn't take on four kids, two of them babies, with joint custody, and a fleet of nannies and a possibly irate husband. He knew himself well enough to know he couldn't handle it and they'd wind up hating each other. He wanted her to himself and on her own. And she knew it, he had told her. "I'll fly back tomorrow night after I see you."

"That's it? Just one day to see me?"

"I'll stay two if you want, or forever. You're the boss here. I had guests arriving tomorrow. I just canceled them. I want to come and see you. Is that a deal? Ten A.M. tomorrow at my place? Is Max in town?" he asked as an afterthought.

"No, he's not. He went to Seattle, and I forget where after that. I think he's gone for another week."

"That makes it easier." He wanted to ask her to meet him at the apartment when he arrived that night, but he didn't want to frighten her away. Anything but that.

"I'll be there tomorrow," she said softly, and lay on

her bed afterward, thinking about him, and just knowing he was coming, she felt different. She got up and washed her hair and did her nails. She looked in her closet to find something to wear and discovered that her clothes fit better than she thought. She'd been so distraught that she hadn't been eating and had lost most of the baby weight. There was a little left on her hips but that was all. Not nursing, she lost it faster.

She wandered around the house for the rest of the day and night, and at midnight she knew that his plane had touched down. She was awake for most of the night, slept fitfully for a few hours, and got up at six o'clock and showered and dressed and had a cup of coffee in the kitchen. Barbara was having a cup of tea. She had just given Simon his six o'clock feeding, and was wearing her uniform. Max liked to have the nannies dressed properly to take care of the babies and not slopping around in jeans and T-shirts. His father had been formal too, and always dressed impeccably for every occasion.

"I'm going to the city," she told the nanny before she left. "I'm not sure when I'll be back." She didn't know when his plane back to France was leaving. If everything went okay, she'd drive him to the airport and then come back to Greenwich, but it could be fairly late.

"Have a nice day," Barbara said as the door swung shut, and Julie could hear the baby upstairs crying. She ran to the car and looked at herself in the rearview mirror. She suddenly felt like herself again, knowing that she was going to see Richard. She was wearing makeup and heels, and her hair looked nice. She'd worn a dress she'd forgotten about in her closet, which fit her perfectly. It was a sky blue silk, the same color as the sari she had worn the night she'd met him. She felt like a woman again, not just a drudge who got left behind every time Max went away.

She pulled up outside his building in Tribeca at nine-fifty, waited politely for ten minutes, and announced herself to the doorman. "Mrs. Stein to see Mr. Randall." He called upstairs and waved her to the elevator, and when the elevator door opened, he was standing there in his apartment in white jeans and a black T-shirt and black espadrilles, with a deep tan and his mane of white hair. Without a word he pulled her to him and kissed her. She looked at him afterward and they were both smiling and she knew in that instant what the answer had to be, what it had been all along since the moment she'd met him.

"The answer is yes," she whispered, and he swept her off her feet, twirled her around, and set her down gently so he didn't hurt her. Then they raced each other up the stairs, straight to his bed, where Julie celebrated her freedom.

Chapter 19

She'd had the nannies keep the children busy out of the house for two days after she got back. They went to a park nearby with waterslides, and a fair that had come through the area with rides and cotton candy and popcorn and ice cream, so she had time to pack what she wanted in peace. She could have the rest of it sent later. She took what she needed for the next few months, for city, boat, and beach. She went through her jewelry, and took some of that too. And she left the emerald ring Max had just given her in its original box with a note that she appreciated it and couldn't accept it, and put it on his desk. There were six suitcases in all, and she sent them to Richard's apartment in a town car. He called to tease her about them when they arrived.

"I'm going to get a hernia carrying all your luggage!" But he was thrilled. The sight of her bags coming off the elevator was the happiest sight he'd ever seen.

She waited until the day the children went to the fair and even made them take the baby. The nannies slathered him with sunscreen. She knew Max was coming home that night. He could explain it to them however he wanted to. She had left a letter for him and one for each of the children on his desk. There was no way to say what she was feeling that he would understand. They were so different. Too different, and they always had been. He just didn't want to see it. She didn't have to pretend to be what he wanted anymore. She was thirty-six years old and she had to be herself now, even if that wasn't what he needed or wanted. She had to be free.

She walked around the house for a last time, and took the framed photographs of the children. She knew that there was nothing she would miss. Her life in that house had been an imprisonment. She and Max wanted none of the same things. She closed the front door behind her and never looked back.

She left her car there and took a town car into the city. She had the money she had inherited from her parents. She didn't need anything from Richard or want anything from Max. She felt light and unencumbered as they drove into the city, and she walked into Richard's apartment with the key he had given her. She was wearing jeans and a navy blazer and flat shoes for the flight. A car was picking them up in an hour to take them to the airport.

"Ready?" he asked her. She smiled at him and he kissed her before she could answer.

"Yes," she said breathlessly.

He held the door open for her and they got into the elevator with all her bags and the new doorman helped them when they got downstairs.

"We're leaving on a trip," he said, giving him a sizable tip. She wasn't going to use Max's name anymore. She had made that decision, and wanted her maiden name back. His name had served her well, and she had tried to measure up to it, but it didn't fit her and it never had. She was Julie Morgan again, which was who she wanted to be.

They got in the SUV the limo company had sent for them. Richard kissed her as they drove away.

*

Max knew he should have called Julie from Wichita, but he didn't. He'd gone to Arkansas after that, and made a quick stop in New Orleans, and then he went home, three days late. But he'd been busy and moving fast. He expected her to complain about it, but he didn't want to call her from every stop. He took a town car from the airport, and got home just after midnight and let himself in. The house was quiet, as he expected it to be. Everyone was sleeping, even Simon. It wasn't time for his night feeding yet. He had seen a light in one of the nannies' rooms, who was waiting for him to wake up. And he didn't know what it was, but he sensed something different when he walked into their bedroom, and Julie wasn't there.

He could hear the clock ticking on his nightstand, and noticed that things had been moved. The stack of books on hers had been put away. Her alarm clock was gone. Her desk had been cleared. He got an eerie feeling as he looked around the room. He walked into her closet and her clothes were there but whole sections were missing and a lot of her shoes. It was weird. Where was she? Had she gone to visit her sisters in California to recover from the baby? The apartment in New York? She hadn't said anything to him. She was mad at him all the time these days over something or nothing. She still resented having the baby, but she'd get over it. Simon was five weeks old.

He walked into his study and saw that there were five letters on his desk. One to each of the children, and one to him.

He tore his open and started to read it standing up, but he had to sit down. He thought his heart was going to stop. She had gone crazy. She didn't mean it. She was depressed, or it was a postpartum symptom, and for a minute her words swam before his eyes, and he thought he might faint.

Dear Max,

This is a hard letter to write and for you to read, I know. Simply put, I can't do this anymore. I never should have. We both tried. I'm sure you did too. I'm not the woman you married, or thought you married, or wanted to marry. You deserve that person, but I'm not it. You wanted to fill the house with babies, and for me to be the wife and mother of the year. I'm not a mother. I should have realized it sooner but I didn't. We have beautiful children. But we are strangers to each other and probably always will be. I don't have a mother gene. It's not in my DNA. You will be a better mother and father to them, I hope, than I could ever be. You'll need to stay home more, to be there for them, and guide them. That's who you wanted me to be. Now you'll have to be that for them.

I don't want to be your wife anymore, or their mother. I'm not coming back. I won't lie to the children. I'd like to see them if you'll let me from time to time. But I can't be a mother to them. I don't have that to give. And I can't be the kind of wife you want and need. I hope you find that person one day. You deserve that.

You've built an empire. Your family is secure. Now enjoy what you've built and share it with someone. You need more than deals in your life, and so do I. I can't be married to someone who's never here.

I'm going to Europe for a while. I'll let you

know where I am. You can contact my attorney,
the same one my father used. I am giving you
custody of the children. Take good care of them, I
know you will. And most of all, take good care of
yourself.

I am truly sorry it didn't work out, and that
I'm not the person you wanted me to be.

Love, Julie

Max sat staring at the letter and read it four times. He
didn't understand. It wasn't possible. Decent people
didn't do things like that, or maybe they did. Maybe the
real decency was in telling him she couldn't, instead of
being a fraud. She wanted out. From him, from their
kids. He had no idea how to explain it to them, although
she had, very simply. She didn't want to be a mother. She
was gone. He couldn't guess where she'd gone, or with
whom. He was going to call her sisters in the morning
and ask them. Someone had to know where she was. And
he wanted her back. She was his wife and the children's
mother, she couldn't just quit. But she had.

He lay awake all night, and read the letter again
several times. His children had no mother now. It all
rested on him. And he realized how wrong he had been
to push her into what he wanted. He had hoped for
someone like his mother, who was faithful to the end.
But Julie wasn't his mother. She was an entirely different

person. And she had had Simon only for him, and given him back five weeks after he was born. This was the kind of thing that women did who left babies on doorsteps with notes pinned to them. But there had to be a damn good reason for it. And for her there was. She couldn't be who he had forced her to be.

He was part furious, part terrified, and part sad. He felt suffocated by the responsibility she had just handed him, to be everything to their children, mother and father. She had stepped out of the ring and withdrawn from the fight, and given him back the prize. He could tell that she wanted nothing from him. And she didn't need it, after her parents died. She had her own money. And then he saw the box with the emerald ring on his desk. He hadn't noticed it before, and tears rolled down his cheeks when he read her note. He knew now how wrong he'd been to push her to have the last baby. Maybe that was what had done it, one child too many, but other women had accidental children and faced up to it. Julie had handed it all back to him, their life, their marriage, and their kids. He wanted to make her come back, but he didn't know how to do it. She had slipped right through his fingers and swam free. Like a prisoner tunneling to freedom. He had no idea she was planning this, and he had no idea where to find her. He had a strong feeling she didn't want to be found by any of them, even her kids.

He read the letters Julie had left for the children as the sun came up, and they made him cry. Three of them were to be given to the children when they were older, those to the three younger ones. The one to Hélène was similar to his but in simpler terms.

Darling Hélène,

I know this won't make sense to you right now. But one day maybe it will. You are a wonderful person and a wonderful daughter to me and your father. And nothing that is happening is your fault. You didn't do anything wrong.

Sometimes we make mistakes, because we love someone or are not honest with ourselves. I want to be honest with you and myself. I can't be a good wife to your dad, the kind of wife he wants. And I'm not a good mother to you, or your sisters and brother. I don't know how to be a mother, and I don't want to be. Some people aren't meant to be mothers, and I'm sorry I figured that out so late.

I am going away now, and your dad is going to take good care of you. And you please take good care of him too. I would like to see you sometime, but probably not soon. Maybe we can be friends one day and you will understand why I could not be a wife to your dad and a mother to all of you.

I love you,
Mommy

He had no idea how he was going to explain this to them, especially Hélène. How did you tell a child that their mother got up and quit and walked away? It was going to scar them forever to be rejected by her. Somehow he was going to have to find a way to hold them all together, and help them grow up without her. If he could talk her into coming back, he would. But he didn't even know where to find her.

He had an overwhelming sense of failure as he waited for his children to wake up. He knew it was his fault for forcing Julie to be something she wasn't. His own parents had been married for forty-five years, and his wife had dumped him after eleven. He had imposed a life on her she didn't want, and lacked judgment in understanding who she was, and now he had four children to bring up on his own, and no idea how to do it alone. It was as though she had died. And he felt like he had too.

He was sitting in the kitchen looking bleary-eyed when Barbara came in with the children. Simon was still asleep in his bassinet, and Daisy said she wanted "popcakes" for breakfast, which were pancakes, and Barbara reminded her that she'd had them yesterday. She'd even had Mickey

Mouse "popcakes." He asked her quietly to get something for Daisy to eat and take her back upstairs, he wanted to have a few minutes alone with Hélène and Kendra, and she could see immediately that something serious had happened. He looked ravaged, and she could smell brandy coming from his pores. It had been a long night for him and it showed.

His two older daughters looked at him with terrified eyes as Barbara carried Daisy upstairs with a box of cereal, some milk, and a banana, and a bowl to get her started. She waved goodbye as they left and blew her father a kiss, and he had to fight back tears. How could Julie do this? It was so wrong. But not for her.

"Did something happen to Mommy?" Hélène asked him in a strangled voice with a face that went sheet white.

"Is Mommy dead like Grandma and Mamie Emm?" Kendra asked, starting to cry before he could even answer. He put Kendra on his lap, and put an arm around Hélène.

"No, Mommy's not dead," he answered immediately. "She's fine. But she's done something unusual and a little crazy."

"Is Mommy crazy?" Kendra stopped crying and was interested in that.

"Not really crazy. But sometimes grown-ups do things that are hard to understand. Mommy decided that she doesn't want to be married to me anymore. And she thinks she doesn't want the responsibility of being a mom. She thinks it's too hard for her. So she's gone away for a while, maybe for a long time. I don't think she'll come back to live with us. She says she'll come to visit us, but she's not going to live with us anymore. It looks like we're on our own." He didn't know how else to say it.

Kendra shrieked and started to cry again with her arms around her father's neck. "I want Mommy to come back. She can't go away forever." It made his stomach turn over as he held her while she cried. "I want her to come back now!"

"So do I. But that's not going to happen. We just have to be brave about it." There were tears in his eyes as he said it, and he didn't feel brave at all. He wished he knew how his parents would have handled a situation like this. He had no clue what he could say that wouldn't make things even worse.

"Are you getting divorced?" Hélène asked in a choked voice.

"I don't know," he said honestly, "it sounds like it. That's what she wants."

"Was she mad at you when she left?" Hélène wanted to know, and he shook his head.

"Not that I know of. I don't even know when she left. She left us all letters. When I came home last night she was gone."

"Are her clothes gone?" Hélène was being systematic about it.

"Some of them."

"She's been crying a lot lately, and before Simon was born too. I think she's been sad for a long time."

"I think you're right," he admitted. "I was very stupid. I didn't understand that, or how sad she was. I thought she'd get over it. Instead she ran away. I don't think running away is a good thing to do. I think you should stay and face things and work them out. But Mommy didn't do that. She ran away." He wanted his kids to get some life lessons out of this about what kind of behavior is okay and what kind isn't. "And grown-ups get divorced sometimes when they don't get along. But they should never ever leave their kids."

"Are you going to divorce us, Daddy?" Kendra asked him. At five, the concepts were more simplistic.

"I am never, ever, ever, *ever* going to divorce you, or run away or leave you." He held up his right hand in a pledge. "That's a solemn promise from me to you. And you guys can't run away either. If you have a problem with something, we can always talk about it and try to fix it. We don't run away from each other." Both girls nodded. It didn't say a lot for their mother, but he didn't want her setting that example for her kids. He thought that what she had just done to her children was not only mean and despicable, but it was also somewhat deranged. A mother should never abandon her children.

"I should have helped her more," Hélène said quietly. "Maybe she would have been happier."

"This has nothing to do with you, Hélène, or any of you. It's very important that you understand that. You did everything you could, you're great kids. Some moms and dads just don't do what they're supposed to, and that's what happened here. Mommy was not supposed to run away, but that has nothing to do with you."

"But she did," Kendra said to sum it up with her hands held out. "Are you mad at her, Daddy?"

"Kind of," he said honestly. "But I'm mostly sad, for me, and all of you."

"Will we be okay?"

"We'll be very okay, we just have to help each other. I'm going to try and be mommy and daddy to all of you."

Kendra frowned at that. "Are you going to wear Mommy's clothes?"

"No, I'm not. But I'll have to learn to do the things she did for you."

"The nannies do everything for us," Kendra said, and they all knew it was true.

"Well, that's good, and that won't change."

They talked about it for a while, and then Max told Kendra to go upstairs and check on Daisy and the baby, and when she left he handed Hélène her mother's letter. She read it and tears filled her eyes and ran down her cheeks as his heart ached for her. She looked up at her father when she finished it and she was sobbing as he pulled her tightly into his arms.

"It sounds like we're never going to see her again. Why did she leave us, Daddy?" She was hiccupping on her sobs, but trying to be brave.

"I don't know," he said honestly, and he was crying too, for his daughter's loss, not his own. He couldn't bear to see her in pain. He knew that Julie's leaving would mark her forever. "I guess I screwed everything up for all of us. I traveled too much and she got lonely. I think we'll see her again, I just don't know when, and it could be a while." Hélène nodded and wiped the tears off her face. "We just have to be big guys about this. I know it feels terrible, but there's nothing else we can do." It was like a death, but he didn't say that to them. They had lost their mother, the one person who should never abandon a child, and she had.

He had tried to call her on her cellphone all night and it had gone to voicemail. He had left her a million messages and she hadn't called him back. And he doubted that she would. She had cut the cord to all of them.

He and Hélène made breakfast for her and Kendra. After that he called Julie's sisters. They didn't know where she'd gone either and they were shocked at what she'd done. Not that she had left him, that happened with couples, but the fact that she had abandoned her kids and didn't want to be their mother anymore was unthinkable, even to her own sisters.

"Poor kids," her younger sister, Belinda, said, "she wasn't happy about the last baby, but that was as much her fault as yours. If she felt that strongly about it, she should have had her tubes tied. You don't just walk out on four kids." She was furious with her sister. They both were, but it didn't change what she had done. It was the kids who were going to pay the price. He wondered if it was her way of getting back at him and punishing him, by hurting their children. But if that were the case, she was truly sick. He didn't think it was meant to be punitive, for any of them. She wasn't an evil person, she just wanted out. And that was exactly what she'd done, stepped out of her role as wife and mother and walked away. She had broken their children's hearts and he knew he would never forgive her. And she had injured his and returned it, like the emerald ring sitting on his desk.

*

As Max was explaining the situation to the children, and after that to the nannies, Richard and Julie had just gotten to Richard's boat, which was tied up at the dock in the old port in Antibes. It was a brilliantly sunny morning, and the yacht was gleaming. They had everything spic-and-span for him. He had the crew put her luggage in one of the guest cabins as her dressing room, and she would be sleeping in the master cabin with him. They were going to leave the dock at noon and head toward Italy. He wanted to take her to Portofino, and Corsica, and Sardinia after that. They were served coffee and croissants for a late breakfast, and Richard was standing with an arm around her as they started up the motors and the elegant yacht pushed away from the dock and motored out of the port, mindful of the small boats around her.

The sea was as flat as glass and the air was fresh as they caught a breeze as they picked up speed and he looked down at her with love and gratitude in his eyes.

"No regrets?" he asked her, worried for a moment. She could have changed her mind at any moment, but she hadn't. She was sure of what she'd done.

"None," she said, and he kissed her as they headed out to sea. Her prison sentence was over. She was free.

Chapter 20

A week after Julie flew to Nice with Richard, Max received the papers that Julie's lawyer had filed to begin divorce proceedings, at her request. She had her lawyer simply mail them to him, since she didn't want him to have the humiliation of a process server. There was no hostility on her part. In addition, she had signed a document relinquishing custody of their four children, granting sole custody to Max. He sat staring at the papers in his hand. She was serious about this. Their children now belonged entirely to him.

The first month was hard on all of them. Max had trips set up and had to travel, although he canceled those he could. And he was startled by all the things he had to pay attention to now. He had to go to ballet recitals, and school fairs, order school uniforms for Hélène and Kendra, which he asked the nannies to do. He tried to redistribute the responsibilities, and he realized that, as his mother had said, Julie hadn't done much with or for the kids and was rarely at home before she left. Practically, with four nannies, he was covered, and they had plenty

377

of other help in the house. But he had a two-year-old who had no idea where her mother had gone and kept looking for her in every nook and cranny, and calling for her at night. Kendra started wetting her bed, and Hélène had nightmares. And he had a two-month-old baby who needed more than nannies, he needed a mother and father to love him, or at least one of them. So Max gave him his bottle and held him every chance he got. He wore him on his back or in a sling around the house.

Max thought he was doing a lousy job at first, and he knew he drank too much. He would drink half a bottle of scotch at night after the kids went to bed, and Hélène would tiptoe out of her room late at night and find her father dressed, with the lights on, passed out on the couch in his study, with a bottle of Johnnie Walker Blue next to him. She would cover him with a cashmere blanket and turn off the light. She did it for many months until he finally started to go to bed at night in his pajamas again, turn off the light, and not leave a whiskey bottle next to his bed. It was a hard adjustment for all of them, and impossible for them to understand why Julie had done it, and even incomprehensible to him. He put her letters in the safe for the younger children, and promised himself he'd give her letters to them one day when they were older, no matter how angry he was at what she'd done to them, and to him.

He still tried to call her on her cellphone and left her

messages, and he thought Hélène did too, but Julie never returned the calls or answered her phone, and eventually her lawyer called him and said that Ms. Morgan did not wish to receive messages from him or the children, and if she wanted contact with him she would do so through her lawyer. He didn't have the heart to tell Hélène, but he never left a message for her again. He was bitter about Julie for many years, and he had a hard time trusting women. His anger and bitterness came through his pores.

When Steve MacMillan called him from London, and asked him to be best man at his second wedding, he was stunned when Max refused. He told him what had happened with Julie, and he said that the best advice he could give him was not to get married and not to try having babies with the woman he wanted to marry, and to run like hell and head for the hills. The one thing Julie appeared to have shattered forever was his belief in the institution of marriage. His parents had been the rare exception, but other than that, he no longer believed in marriage and wouldn't encourage anyone to try it. The only thing Max Stein believed in after Julie left was his kids.

Steve apologized to him for the call and was sad for his old friend. He wasn't the same man anymore, and probably never would be again.

Chapter 21

By the time Hélène was entering her junior year in high school, seven years after her mother had abandoned them, Max had his life, work, household, and children pretty much in control. He ran a tight ship.

The same nannies had stayed with them, and lived in the same house, the kids had moved on to the next schools appropriately. Their life hadn't fallen apart, as all of them had feared at first, but they'd had a hell of a time for the first year or two, and maybe Max most of all. He'd finally gotten control of his drinking and didn't pass out drunk on the couch every night, with Hélène ministering to him, and covering him with her favorite cashmere blanket. He still traveled almost as much for business, but his trips were of short duration, he stayed in constant contact with the kids while he was gone, and if there were any kind of serious problem, from a high fever to a run-in with a teacher in school, he flew home. He was not the father he had been when he was married to Julie, he was twenty times the father, and ten times the man. He had learned from his mistakes.

Julie had delivered what she'd promised when she left them. She had seen them six times in seven years. It was agony for the children the first time they saw her, and Kendra and Hélène had begged her to come back. Daisy just stared at her, confused, and Simon didn't know her. And Julie was visibly uncomfortable, looked at them like strangers and didn't stay long, and hadn't seen them for a year after that. For a while, Max hated her for it. But it was easier the next time, they had fewer and fewer expectations. She called them once in a while but not often, and usually at Christmas, and they had all been shocked to read in *The New York Times* that she'd gotten remarried a year after she left them, as soon as the divorce came through. They'd had no hint of it until then.

It made the front page of almost every newspaper when Richard Randall married an unknown woman named Julie Morgan. Max was livid when he read it. He would have liked to know if the romance was recent, or if she'd been cheating on him with Richard before she left, after they met at Gracie Mansion when she was pregnant with Simon. But there was no way to find out. The article said that they had homes in London and Hong Kong, an apartment in New York and one at the Ritz in Paris, and they were building a house in Sardinia, and they had a two-hundred-foot yacht in the Mediterranean where they spent their summers, mostly in Italy or Greece.

Max was curious about whether she had traded him and their children in for Richard. But she'd kept her distance from her children ever since she left, and had very little contact with them. Max was there when she visited the children, to support and protect them. And he and Julie hardly spoke to each other. He was too angry to say more than a few words. She was leading a glamorous jet-set adult life now with a handsome older man, and she was not going to soccer matches, ballet, or the orthodontist. She clearly had no desire to be her children's mother anymore, just as she had said. She had been honest with them, and herself. Max had been bitter about it for years. After five years, he had finally started to calm down. After seven, he was almost happy about it. Almost.

His children scolded him for it when he was bitter. He couldn't pass a happy couple on the street, anyone kissing or holding hands, hear about a wedding or talk about a date, without making acerbic comments about what fools they were and how someday they'd regret the relationship they were engaged in. It had become a cause célèbre with him.

"Dad, you have to *stop*!" Hélène would yell at him when he did it. "People are going to think you're weird. You sound like you have Tourette's about romance, or you're paranoid or something."

"I'm not paranoid or weird, I got burned."

"You have to let it go. It's been seven years."

"I can hang on to it for as long as I want. I'm officially a bitter old man now. It's part of my identity."

"First of all, you're not old, you're fifty-one, and second of all, you're still hot, but you're never going to get another date if you keep talking like that."

"I have lots of dates," Max said, looking defensive.

"Yeah," said Kendra, who was twelve now, "*first* dates. When was the last time you had a second date? No one will go out with you again. You have a chip on your shoulder the size of the Empire State Building."

"Maybe that's a good thing to have."

"Yeah, right," Kendra said and walked away. They were used to his angry, nasty comments about romance, and indirectly about their mother, but the women he occasionally invited out to dinner were not. And just as Kendra said, they almost never went out with him for a second date, not that he cared.

"I like first dates," he continued the argument with Hélène, who had just turned sixteen, and kept her siblings in good order as the senior member of the team. They were down to two nannies for Daisy, who was nine now, and Simon, who was seven. Daisy was the self-appointed family eccentric and thoroughly enjoyed it. She couldn't wait to be old enough to get pink hair, a belly-button ring, and a tattoo. Simon was seven, and loved everyone he met. He was the easiest child on the planet and his sisters doted on him. They all took care of each other. Simon had just entered second grade, and Daisy was taking remedial reading. They had just discovered that she was severely dyslexic, but she didn't seem to mind. She had taught herself to play the piano by ear and loved everything about music and particularly rap. She gave a great imitation of Snoop Dogg, including the bad language, which drove her father insane.

They'd all turned out to be truly good kids and very different. They had their own personalities. Hélène, deep and calm, reminded Max constantly of his mother. She was seriously engaged in the study of Judaism and went to a Reform temple every week on her own. She read everything she could lay her hands on about the Holocaust, to learn more about what her grandparents and their contemporaries had gone through, and she knew every fact available about Buchenwald, where they had been and met. She wanted to work for some kind of museum about Judaic art or a Holocaust museum. In essence, she wanted to be her grandmother when she grew up. Mamie Emm was her role model in life. And Kendra's hero was her father. She wanted to help him run his thriving land development empire when she grew up, and she loved everything involving numbers and business. Daisy wanted to be anything that involved music, preferably African American and a rapper. And Simon just wanted to be happy. He wanted to be a policeman or a fireman, he hadn't decided which, or maybe a baseball player, or a vet, depending on the day.

And even though Max was sure it would affect them in some way forever, none of them seemed to have suffered deep psychological scars because their mother had abandoned them. It was far from an ideal situation, but they had weathered it surprisingly well, in great part thanks to Max, who had stepped up to the plate after Julie left, and Hélène was an enormous help.

Even Julie's sisters had been outraged, but they lived in California, too far away now to see much of the kids or be of any real assistance. They sent greetings from time to time. They weren't in touch with their sister either. She had dismissed all of them, but worst of all her kids, with the exception of her rare visits to them. As far as her ex-husband was concerned, it was an unforgivable crime, particularly if she'd dumped them to run off with an even richer guy. She had been married to Richard for six years, and she looked happy when they saw her.

The only place where Max could see that it had affected them was that none of his children seemed to believe in marriage. Hélène said she didn't believe in it because it never worked and you'd just wind up with a broken heart. Kendra, the family math whiz/financier/economist, said marriage was stupid and expensive and you had to pay alimony and who cared about being married anyway. Daisy said she definitely wanted to get married and she wanted to have fifteen bridesmaids in rainbow colors with matching tattoos, so her mother's genes were in there somewhere, given the number of bridesmaids, or she wanted lots of babies and no husband. And Simon said he wanted to marry one of his sisters, which one varied according to the day, and in response to which, they all made a face and said "yeegghhhhh." None of them had boyfriends yet, which was a great relief to their father. But all in all they were doing well, everyone was getting good grades, except Daisy, who was battling her dyslexia.

Since all their grandparents were gone, the only living relative they had in their lives was their father. They went to three different schools. Hélène was in high school, Kendra was in middle school, Daisy wanted to go to music school but was in lower school with Simon. So they had pickups and drop-offs and after-school activities, which kept Max busy when he was in town, and the two remaining nannies busy full-time when he wasn't.

That he hadn't had a serious relationship in the last seven years had kept Max's home life simpler. As Kendra said to her older sister, "We love him, but no one else will put up with him. He has to stop bashing women because of Mom. They must think he's a total jerk." But the truth was he'd been gravely wounded, and he was no longer even sure if he had loved Julie, or just the illusion of her he'd created. In either case she was gone. He had dated other women after the first few years, but hadn't had a serious relationship and didn't seem to want one. He said he was too busy with his kids.

They all had dinner together every night, unless someone had a school event, a birthday party on the weekend, or their father had a business meeting. Dinner was considered their sacred time, which Max had established as a house rule as soon as Julie left. He figured it would stand them in good stead in the future when they wouldn't want to eat at home or with him anyway. So he was enjoying them while he could.

They were having dinner and eating tamales, enchiladas, and chili rellenos when Kendra looked across the table at her father and reminded him that she had signed him up for Career Day in her class the next day.

"Oh shit!" he said. "I forgot completely."

"And don't tell me you're going out of town because I'll have to kill you. Everyone is looking forward to what you have to say." She was in seventh grade.

"I'm sorry, sweetheart, I totally forgot. I've got a meeting but I'll postpone it. I'm glad you reminded me. What am I supposed to say?"

"Tell them how much money you make," she said and her father frowned at her. "I'm just kidding. I don't know, tell them how you buy crappy land and turn it into shopping malls."

"That's not exactly a career most people want to pursue."

"It's fine. We've got a female police detective, a horse trainer, a mystery writer, a dentist, a textile designer, and you."

"That's a weird mixture of stuff," her father said with a dubious look.

"They're all either parents or friends of someone. The mystery writer sounds pretty cool, the dentist sucks but is someone's father, the textile designer is a friend of our art teacher, the detective is a class mother, and I don't know who the horse trainer belongs to, and we're calling you a land developer/business tycoon."

"I should tell them how my father started out as a runner in the diamond trade and wound up owning the business. That would be a lot more interesting."

"I think they'd rather hear about you."

"It's kind of scary standing up in front of a bunch of kids. What if they boo me?" He was only half teasing her and she laughed.

"I'll beat them up for you if they do." She took karate twice a week and was getting good. "The police detective is hot by the way, she works undercover on the vice squad and she's divorced."

"She'd probably shoot me if I get cranky."

They all got up from the dinner table shortly after that and Kendra reminded him that he had to be at school in her classroom at ten o'clock sharp, and he promised to be there. The last seven years had been rewarding for him. He had gotten much closer to his children, so maybe Julie had done him a favor by leaving after all, although he never looked at it that way. And he worried about the effect it could still have on their children one day. But so far everything had turned out okay.

*

As promised, he drove to Kendra's school the next morning, and got there a little early. He was nervous about his presentation and had outlined what he wanted to say, but he didn't want to embarrass Kendra, who thought he walked on water, and he wanted to keep it that way until she became a teenager and decided that he was really a jerk. He'd been lucky with Hélène so far. She was charitable and gentle and protective and always defended him. Her teen years had been easy, which he knew was rare. She had tried to step in for her mother since she left.

He made a few phone calls in his car, and noticed an attractive red-headed woman smoking a cigarette in front of the school. She smiled at him as he walked by. He saw that she had a good figure and was wearing a black miniskirt and high heels, and other than the short skirt, there was something about her that reminded him of his mother. Then he walked into the school and found

Kendra's classroom, and saw a bunch of rowdy kids and a group of anxious-looking adults. The woman who'd been smoking the cigarette was the last to walk in and smiled at him again. He saw his daughter watching him and he pretended to ignore the smoker and decided she must be the vice squad cop since the miniskirt was very short, but she had fabulous legs.

The teacher called the class to order, and introduced their guests. The students applauded and the presentations began promptly so everyone would have enough time, and he discovered that the miniskirted smoker was the textile designer and not the vice squad cop.

The horse trainer went first and had some very interesting things to say. She told them some tricks about horse breaking, and the kids really liked her. The dentist went next and was predictably a dud but he handed out free toothbrushes, which went over well. And the textile designer went next. She whipped out a piece of fabric and a small box of paints, and right before their eyes she showed them how she tested designs and colors on the fabric. She said that she was originally an artist, but had gotten intrigued by the paint splatters on her smock, and made more money with those than her paintings, and they all laughed at that. As soon as she spoke, he realized by her accent she was French, which explained the cigarette and the sexy skirt. They all applauded her, and he was next, and felt like a total dullard after her.

But he explained how he had been told that if you bought really bad land that no one could grow crops on in rural and agricultural areas, you could build huge shopping malls, which those areas needed desperately, and the profit you could make was fantastic. He told them the different places he went to, and showed them some before and after photos he had brought with him. The shopping malls were very attractive. "And then you can sell the shopping mall and make more," he explained. They were impressed, especially when he told them that sometimes you could make four hundred times your investment.

"And it's exciting to turn some really dead-looking place into a fun, appealing location where everyone wants to hang out." And that was his presentation.

In the end, all of the presentations were well received, and the kids enjoyed it and so did he. The teacher thanked them all for coming and served donuts and cupcakes to the class and the guests. Kendra came over and hugged him.

"You were great, Dad."

"You're prejudiced," he said and hugged her back.

"I thought it was very interesting too," the French textile designer said with her accent, and, not knowing why he did it, Max volunteered in French that his mother was Parisian, and the designer looked surprised.

"You speak perfect French," she said, still in French.

"Thank you. I learned as a child. I don't get to speak it much anymore."

"Was your father French too?" They were still speaking French and Kendra looked mildly embarrassed.

"Austrian. Viennese."

"You speak German too?"

"Only a few words."

And then other people came up and chatted with him, and a few minutes later, they all left and he told Kendra he would see her that night. He saw the designer again outside the school and they chatted as they walked to their cars. "Your daughter is very pretty," she complimented him. "And she's very proud of you."

"I'm very proud of her too. Two years from now she'll hate me. I'm enjoying it while it lasts." She laughed at what he said.

"Is she your only child?" She was curious about him, and he didn't know why, but he was curious about her too. There was something very familiar about her, maybe because she was French. It was a style he knew well, a way of moving the head, or doing her hair. Frenchwomen were different.

"No, I have four children," he answered her question.

"Oh! I'm impressed."

"And you?"

"No children." He nodded and they had reached his car, and she looked at him strangely, reached into her bag and handed him her card. "If you ever need a textile designer." She smiled at him, and she had wonderful green eyes and red hair.

He took out one of his own cards and handed it to her for no reason at all. "If you ever need a land developer in Oklahoma or New Mexico," he said and she laughed. She liked him, he could tell. "We should have gotten a card from the dentist. That's more useful."

She smiled and waved and crossed the street to her own car, and he saw that she drove a tiny battered Fiat. And he looked at her card when he was in his car, and saw that she had an address in Greenwich and one in the city. He checked her out on Yahoo! when he got back to his office and saw that she had impressive credentials from the Sorbonne in Paris and the Beaux-Arts, and had taught at both, and at the Fine Arts Department at Yale, so she obviously knew what she was doing and had talent. He put the card back in his wallet.

And Kendra mentioned her that night at dinner. "She was hot, Dad."

"Actually, she was nice more than hot. We happened to walk out together and she said you're very pretty."

"She was just buttering you up, making a play for you. Are you going to ask her out?"

"Don't be silly, of course not." But in his study later that night, he thought about it, took her card out again, and saw that she had an email address.

He wrote her a quick email in French that read, "Enjoyed meeting you today. Great presentation. *À bientôt!*" which was "until soon" and signed his name and then felt like an idiot after he pushed send. He felt like a schoolboy with a recreation yard romance. But while he was still feeling silly about it, she responded, also in French.

"I enjoyed it too. You're welcome at my studio anytime."

And feeling even more daring and dumber yet, he wrote back "Lunch?" and she responded "Delighted!" And he sat there grinning. It was the most ridiculous thing he'd done in ages. And then he got more precise.

"Greenwich or the city?"

"The city tomorrow? I'm at my studio there Mon, Wed, Fri, Tues/Thurs in Greenwich. Come to my studio at 12:30."

He didn't say a word to Kendra about it at breakfast the next day, but he was excited when he left for work. He hadn't had a date in a while and she was an attractive woman and had a certain sexy style the French called *"chien,"* which was a compliment.

Her studio was fascinating. She had fabrics and designs everywhere, graphics and things drying. She said she did some industrial design and a lot of fashion, and she actually ran a real business. She had four young assistants working for her, doing things with paints and color blocks and silk screens. She showed him around and then he took her to Le Bernardin, a very fancy French fish restaurant, thought to be one of the best in the city. His parents had loved it and he had taken them there often. And the service was excellent.

"This is a very elegant lunch for a simple artist," she said, lowering her eyes and flirting with him a little, as Frenchwomen had developed into an art for centuries, and it made him smile.

"My parents used to love this restaurant, although my father preferred wienerschnitzel to fish. But my mother loved it."

"They're not alive anymore?" she asked cautiously, and he shook his head.

"Unfortunately not, they died younger than they should have, and they had one of those marriages where one can't survive without the other. My mother died within a few months of my father and they were both too young, in their sixties. They'd been married for forty-five years."

"That's impressive. They set you a good example."

"Not exactly." He looked tense for a moment. "My marriage ended after eleven. I'm divorced."

"Oh, I'm sorry." She looked genuinely sympathetic. "And you?"

"Never married. My parents were less romantic than yours. They stayed married, but my father behaved very badly and had a million mistresses and my mother was miserable. It never held much appeal for me after that. I've had two long relationships, but never married. I couldn't see the point of legalized torture after what I'd seen with my parents. Parents like yours are a gift." She smiled at him.

"They were very special."

"They came here after the war?"

He nodded, and hesitated for a minute. It was a heavy dose of truth for a first date, if it even was one. "They met in Buchenwald, they both lost their entire families and came to the States after that." She winced as he said it and instinctively touched his hand. And as he looked into her eyes, it was like looking into his mother's and he realized that it was the green eyes that were so familiar, and she had a warm sympathetic look that touched him.

"They must have been very remarkable people."

"They were."

"I grew up in Paris after the war, in the fifties, and there were many people like them, but so many didn't come back."

He nodded. "One of my daughters, the oldest one, wants to work at one of the Holocaust museums after college. It's incredibly moving."

"Yes, it is." She was pensive about it, and it was a warm conversation. "My family wasn't Jewish, but they lost so many friends. It's really inconceivable that in civilized societies such a thing can happen."

"My mother spent her entire life convinced it would happen again."

"Many people feel that way," she said, and then noticed the time and jumped. "Oh dear, I have a meeting in twenty minutes." So did he, but he was having much more fun with her.

"I'm glad we had lunch together. I felt very bold writing to you last night," he confessed.

"I'm glad you did." She looked at him warmly.

"Would you like to have dinner with me and my children some weekend?"

"I'd love that," she said after he paid the bill and they both got up. "And thank you for this very elegant lunch." They had spoken French the entire time and both enjoyed it.

He walked her out to the sidewalk and she hailed a cab and he walked back to his office. He had a warm feeling about her, like an old friend. Her name was Pascale Boyer and he knew his mother would have loved her. There was something very genuine about her.

*

She sent him an email that night to thank him for lunch and he invited her to Sunday dinner at the house. He had no idea what his kids would say, but she was so warm and friendly it was hard to imagine they'd object. He didn't tell them until Sunday morning. He made pancakes and eggs and bacon for everyone, and he had to make Mickey Mouse pancakes for Simon and Daisy. He mentioned Pascale as they were finishing breakfast, and Kendra looked up at him in surprise.

"Isn't that the woman who gave the presentation with you, Dad, at my school?" He looked faintly embarrassed and nodded. He had no secrets from his kids.

"It is. She gave me her card and I invited her to lunch. She's very nice."

"Whoa, Dad!" Kendra teased him and everyone laughed. "So how bad were you? Did you give her the speech that all women are cheaters and liars and end up dumping their husbands? That's one of your better ones. That usually has them running out the door on the first course."

"I've gotten better. We talked about your grandparents, my parents."

"Is she interested in the Holocaust, Dad?" Hélène chimed in with interest.

"Seems like it."

"Is she Jewish?" Kendra was intrigued.

"I don't think so."

"Are we?" Simon asked him.

"No, dummy. We're Episcopalian, the three of us girls," Kendra informed him, "you're nothing." Julie hadn't stuck around long enough to baptize him, and her parents were dead when he was born.

"Why am I nothing?" He started to cry. "I want to be something."

"I'm Jewish," Hélène corrected her sister.

"We're all Jewish culturally," their father said to them, "but not religiously, except Hélène, who wants to be Jewish and goes to temple. Your mom's parents had the girls baptized Episcopalian because that's what your mom is.

"And you can be whatever you want," he said to Simon, who stopped crying.

"I want to be Jewish, like Hélène. What are you, Dad?" Simon asked him with wide eyes.

"Jewish, but not religiously. I don't go to temple."

"Maybe I'll be everything," Simon said, thinking about it.

"That's a good thing to be." His father smiled at him and then looked around the table. "So is it okay if Pascale comes to dinner tonight?"

"Sure," Kendra said.

"Of course," Hélène seconded it, which was a good thing since he had already invited her.

The chef had left them lasagna and Max liked to barbecue on Sunday nights. Pascale arrived promptly at seven, with a chocolate cake, and Max introduced her to all his children, and everyone talked at once. They sat in the garden while their father barbecued. She was enjoying them. And Hélène talked to her about the Holocaust, and then they talked about colleges. Hélène was trying to decide where she'd apply senior year. Pascale said she'd taught at Yale and liked it, and at Brown, and in Paris at the Beaux-Arts.

"I want to go to college in Paris," Daisy piped up. "It's cooler there."

Pascale had fun with them at dinner and loved the diverse personalities. After they all left the table and went to their rooms, she asked Max about their mother.

"You have shared custody?" She had a feeling that he didn't and none of them had mentioned their mother at dinner, which had struck her. It was a delicate subject with him.

"No, I have sole custody." He sighed and looked at her. "This is where my children say I become a nutcase. I'll try not to. We had some bumps before Simon was born." He didn't want to go into them or say his wife hadn't wanted them. "And we came home one day when Simon was a month old, and she had left us each a letter basically saying that she quit. She didn't want to be a wife or a mother anymore. She gave me full custody. She's only seen them half a dozen times since, and that was seven years ago. She said she didn't want to be a mother, but figured it out after four kids. That's a pretty harsh thing to do to children, to be rejected by your own mother. I keep waiting for the other shoe to drop and for one or all of them to become serial killers, but so far so good. I have to be honest with you and I'll spare you the ranting and raving, but I'll never forgive her for it. She can dump me, but you can't do that to kids. She remarried a year later, a very important man she'd met before she left us. I don't know if that had anything to do with her walking out or not. I have no idea if she had an affair with him before she left, or if it started afterward. But I came home and she was gone."

Pascale looked deeply sympathetic, for him and the kids. "What a terrible thing to do to you and the children."

"Yeah, it was very rough at first, but it's worked out pretty well. I guess I really screwed it up for her to do that to our children." He looked grim as he said it, and she could see that he was still wounded.

"Non!" she said, sounding very French and put up a hand in objection. "That's not you! That's a woman with a terrible character flaw, a 'lack' in her, to do such a thing to her kids." She looked outraged. "You did *not* do that." She sounded like his mother again and he smiled.

"I don't know why, but you keep reminding me of my mother."

"Probably because I'm French." She smiled at him.

"Anyway, I was very bitter about it for a long time. I guess I still am to some degree. It's hard to trust anyone after that. I put a lot of walls up. But I had a part in it too. I was a bad husband. I was away too much of the time, and I neglected her and the kids. Oddly, my parents never thought she was right for me. I guess she was the wrong person. I was a little obtuse that it took me eleven years to notice. It makes me sound very stupid now."

"Or very loving and trusting," she said generously.

"Anyway, we're fine now, and I am too." But she could see that he was still gun-shy and wounded although he was very nice. "We were young, and she was very pretty. It takes a lot more than that to bring up kids." Pascale had checked him out on the Internet too and was impressed by his career and what he had built on his own from nothing.

They sat outside for a long time until it got chilly, and she didn't want to overstay her welcome. She finally got up to leave around nine-thirty. It was a warm October night.

"You have an amazing family," she said to him. "Your children are fantastic."

"I wish you could have met my parents." And then as he said it, a word came into his head that his mother had used about them. "They were soulmates. My father said he knew it the first time she stole a potato for him in the camp when she worked in the vegetable garden. She was a very brave woman. They would have killed her for it if they'd caught her."

"I'm sorry I didn't meet them." He nodded and walked

her to her car, and as she got in, he looked at her, thinking about the potato.

"Dinner this week?" he asked her cautiously, and she nodded. "I warn you, I've been a little bristly for the last seven years."

"You have good reason to be," she said quietly and patted his hand, and then she got in her car, waved, and drove off. He walked back into the house slowly.

"She's nice," Kendra said as she walked by. "Did you do okay, Dad?"

"I only insulted her twice," he said, laughing.

"That's a big improvement." And then she went back upstairs and he went to his study and thought about Pascale. He felt a connection to her, and somehow the potato had something to do with it, and the look in her eyes that was so familiar, as though they came from the same world.

Chapter 22

Max took Pascale to dinner that week at Jean-Louis, a small French restaurant in Greenwich, and twice the week after, and then she invited him to her small cozy apartment full of French things and made him coq au vin, which his mother used to make too. It was comforting to be with someone European who came from a similar culture even if she wasn't Jewish, which he didn't care about. Julie hadn't been either.

*

They continued having dinner together once or twice a week, and he invited her to go ice skating with his children when the weather got colder. They had fun with her. They all went to the city together another time, and she became a frequent guest at their home for dinner on weekends. He was enjoying her company and felt at home with her, but he also felt stuck. He had been so burned by Julie that he couldn't get past that. There was nothing about her that he didn't like or didn't trust, except he knew that if he let himself care about her, his heart would be at risk and she could smash it to bits, and she could sense what he was going through. He was a man on a ledge afraid to jump. But she was in no hurry and she enjoyed his company and his kids.

He invited her to their Chanukah celebration and Hélène lit the candles and sang the prayers, and then they had a feast. Hélène talked colleges again with Pascale. She was leaning to Princeton, and had the grades to get in. And Kendra, who worshipped her father, said she would go to Harvard just like him and he reminded her that she'd better get the grades. Pascale gave the children little Chanukah gifts. She had painted designs on some of them herself for the girls, and she bought a tie for Max.

He smiled when he saw it. "My mother used to make all my father's ties. She was a fantastic seamstress. Much to my chagrin, she made all my clothes until I was about thirteen. They were much nicer than anything my friends had, and I hated it. I wanted scruffy clothes like theirs, not little navy blue suits." He smiled at the memory. "It's funny how the things that embarrass us as children become tender memories."

He invited her to a movie that weekend, and when he took her back to her place, she invited him up for a drink. They lit a fire in the fireplace and she had champagne for him, and they sat in front of the blaze and talked about her childhood in Paris. Her mother had been an art history professor at the Sorbonne, and her father owned a restaurant where he picked up women constantly, and slept with all the waitresses. "I hated him for it. My mother was such a good woman. It's why I never married. I didn't want someone like him." He nodded, thinking about Julie and the marks she had left on him. He had tire tracks on his heart where she had run over him, although he admitted that part of it had been his fault, for forcing her into a mold that didn't fit her. His parents had been smart enough to see it, and he didn't want to and had refused to accept reality until she ran away.

"I've always wanted to have a relationship like my parents'. Maybe you have to go through something terrible together to have a bond like that. You realize what's important. I've never known two people closer. They were soulmates," he said, as he had before. He looked into the fire and then turned to look at Pascale. "I feel that way about you sometimes," he said, feeling safe with her.

"So do I," she said and he leaned over and kissed her. It had taken him two months to dare to take the risk, but once he did, he couldn't stop kissing her and she was a passionate woman and neither of them could stop. The floodgates had opened, and he picked her up and carried her into her bedroom and set her down gently on the bed. He looked at her, waiting for her to stop him, questioning if he should stop himself but he didn't want to.

He felt a powerful bond with her and he wanted all of her, her heart and her soul and her mind and her body and everything about her he loved. They made love for hours in her cozy bedroom and lay in each other's arms totally spent afterward. He still didn't know what had made her seem so familiar to him when he had seen her at the school. But there was something undeniable between them, a link of some kind. He had never had that with Julie, and he knew as he held Pascale that he could trust this woman, she wasn't going to hurt him, and he would never hurt her. He wanted to protect her from all harm. She made him feel like a better man.

"I love you, Pascale," he said and she told him she loved him too. They had had it all in one night, their first kiss, making love, and their admission that they loved each other. He stayed very late, and he didn't want to leave her now that he had found her. He had never met a woman like her and knew it instinctively. "My mother always said you know when you've found the right person. I never understood that. I think I do now." All the puzzle pieces had quietly slipped into place seamlessly.

*

Max and Pascale continued to date discreetly through the winter. They went away for the weekend together when the two older girls were busy, and the nannies had things to do with the little ones. They stayed at his apartment in New York occasionally. He still owned it, but hadn't used it in several years. He had an extremely comfortable life and she fit into it perfectly, and they brought out the best in each other.

He was taking the children to Aspen for spring break and he asked her to join them. The children didn't object when he told them, and he got her her own room so they looked respectable, but he slept in it with her every night. He had learned to ski over the years, but she was a fabulous skier and skied with the children, and they put Daisy and Simon in ski school. They were a nice family together, and by summer the answer seemed obvious to him. He asked her to marry him in June and she hesitated.

"I don't think I believe in marriage. It never works out the way people hope. I don't want to spoil what we have."

"It turns out well sometimes. Look at my parents."

"But look what they went through to get there."

"We've had our share of bumps before we met each other," he reminded her. "You had two bad relationships, and I had a bad marriage." She didn't disagree.

"Let me think about it." He was disappointed she was so hesitant, but he respected her wishes. He never again wanted to force someone into what they didn't want to be or do.

That summer they rented a house in Maine, and she came with them again. Hélène was going into her senior year in high school, and Kendra eighth grade. Daisy was working hard on her dyslexia with Pascale's help, and Simon looked more like a boy now than a baby. Max still couldn't understand how Julie could live without seeing her children, how they were growing up, what they were doing, and not being with them every day. He would never understand it.

"There's a piece of her missing," Pascale said simply when they talked about it.

"The pieces of her missing are her children," Max said sternly.

"She doesn't have room for them. It's a defect in her," Pascale insisted. It seemed so obvious to her.

They all hated to go home after the summer vacation, and Pascale seemed like part of the group now. She fit in naturally. It felt strange whenever she wasn't there.

The night they got back to Greenwich, she stayed to help Max cook dinner on the barbecue and they were laughing about something when she turned to him. "This is silly. I don't want to go home. I want to be here with all of you, forever. If you still want me." She looked at him cautiously.

"I thought you'd never say yes," he said with relief. "Let's get married soon." He was fifty-one years old and she was forty-four and he didn't want to waste any more time. "Can you put up with four kids?"

"They're our greatest blessing," she said, smiling at

him. They told them the news at dinner that night. It was a natural evolution. She belonged with them now.

"Can I throw roses at you when you marry Daddy?" Daisy wanted to know.

"Of course," Pascale told her, "and Simon can carry the rings if you promise not to lose them. Kendra will be our bridesmaid, and Hélène is the maid of honor."

"We need a witness old enough to sign the registry," Max commented. Hélène was not quite seventeen, which wasn't old enough. "And a minister or a rabbi to perform the ceremony, and someone to give the bride away."

"I can give myself away," she said simply. "And we can find a minister easily if a rabbi won't do it because I'm not Jewish, and we'll find someone to sign the registry." Only minor technical details remained. The big issues were clear.

They got married three weeks later at The Orchards on a beautiful fall day. Pascale wore a white Chanel suit and she had taken the girls shopping for new dresses. Max got Simon slacks and a blazer. Max looked handsome in a new dark blue suit. A minister performed the ceremony, and a Reform rabbi gave a blessing, as Max looked at them. They were a family again. He knew that this time he had found the right woman. All she wanted was a plain gold wedding ring. She said she didn't need a diamond or an engagement ring. And Daisy got her wish and threw rose petals at them after the ceremony. It was a perfect day. It had taken seven years to find her, after Julie left, and a lifetime before that, but it had been worth the wait. And Max knew with total certainty that Pascale was there to stay, and this time, his parents would approve. He could feel them smiling and happy for him from wherever they were.

Epilogue

"Good Lord! Do we have enough food here?" Max laughed as he walked into the kitchen. Hélène and Pascale were in charge of the dinner. They were celebrating Chanukah and Max's birthday. He was turning sixty-three. The girls were all bringing their boyfriends home and the house was bursting at the seams, and they had enough food to supply an army. He walked out again and left them to it. Kendra had just arrived from San Francisco with her boyfriend, Charlie. They had an idea for a startup and wanted to set it up there. She was twenty-five and had just finished Harvard Business School in June. She still wanted to work with her father, which was her lifelong dream, but she wanted to try to get their fledgling startup off the ground first. It was the first time Max had met Charlie and he seemed like a bright boy, and Kendra was crazy about him. He was twenty-six and had gotten his MBA at Harvard with her. They were sweet together. Pascale liked him when she met him too.

Hélène had come home the night before. She had her

dream job as an assistant curator at the Holocaust Museum in Washington, D.C. She'd spent a year as an intern at the Holocaust Museum in Berlin, and now she was back and loved Washington and the museum. And she was doing what she had promised her grandmother she would do one day, keeping the memories alive so no one would forget. Her boyfriend, David, was thirty-two and Jewish. He was a resident at Georgetown University Hospital, and Pascale had told Max she could hear wedding bells. Hélène was twenty-nine. There was no risk of that with Kendra. She was still much too young and focused on her career to settle down yet.

Daisy had just turned twenty-one and was in her last year at the Conservatory in Paris. Her boyfriend was French and he'd come home with her. Her hair was shocking pink, her boyfriend's blue; they played in a band on the weekends, and had just made a CD with Daisy playing guitar and Sylvain on drums. She was studying music composition at the Conservatory. Sylvain was twenty-nine and loved her just as she was, and she was thinking about staying in Paris for another year to take advanced courses.

And Simon was in his sophomore year at Harvard at nineteen, and wanted to go to law school after he graduated. He was the most conservative of the group, and he was dating a girl from Greenwich who was at Boston University so they could be close to each other. Every time Max looked at him he could see his father staring back at him, they looked so much alike.

They all came down before dinner, looking handsome and well dressed, and Max could see the family thread in each of them. Hélène looked like her grandmother, Simon like Jakob, Kendra wanted to follow her father's path in business and learn at the feet of the master, as she put it. Hélène had fulfilled her promise to her grandmother to keep the memories alive and had just gotten permission to do a special exhibit on Buchenwald, with a reunion of the survivors. Simon was going to Harvard like his father, and Daisy felt an irresistible pull toward Paris, and wanted to also study music in Vienna at some point. Each of them were following the footsteps of those before them in some way, and had found good people to travel with them, and Max had found happiness at last with Pascale. They'd been married for eleven years—as long as he'd been married to Julie—but it was so different.

Hélène lit the Chanukah candles as she did every year and they sang the prayers together, their voices raised as they stood together in memory of those who were no longer there, who had suffered, who had learned, who had gone on, and left joy and wisdom and memories behind. Max smiled at his children and held his wife's hand. He was still handsome and healthy and strong and he and Pascale loved each other. They were a family.

In His Father's Footsteps

Max had followed in his father's footsteps in his own way, his children would follow in his, and each would forge their own path, in honor of the past, in hope for the future, making new footprints of their own.

Danielle Steel

Have you liked Danielle Steel on Facebook?

Be the first to know about Danielle's latest books, access exclusive competitions and stay in touch with news about Danielle.

www.facebook.com/DanielleSteelOfficial

THE GOOD FIGHT

A PASSION FOR JUSTICE . . .

The daughter of prominent lawyers, Meredith McKenzie is destined for the best of everything: top schools, elite social circles, a perfect marriage. Spending her childhood in Germany as her father prosecutes Nazi war criminals at the Nuremberg trials, Meredith soaks up the conflict between good and evil as it plays out in real time. When her family returns to the United States, she begins blazing her own trail, determined to become a lawyer.

Encompassing the remarkable people Meredith meets, the historic events she witnesses, and the sacrifices she must make, this is the story of a woman changing her world as she herself is changed by it. *The Good Fight* is an inspiring historical novel with resonance for our own times.

Now available in paperback

PURE HEART. PURE STEEL.

TURNING POINT

ONE MOMENT CAN CHANGE EVERYTHING . . .

Bill Browning heads the trauma unit at San Francisco's busiest emergency room. With his ex-wife and daughters in London, he immerses himself in his work and lives for the little time he can spend with his children. A rising star at her teaching hospital, Stephanie Lawrence has two young sons, a frustrated husband, and not enough time for any of them. Harvard-educated Wendy Jones is a dedicated trauma doctor, trapped in a dead-end relationship with a married cardiac surgeon. And Tom Wylie's popularity with women rivals the super medical skills he employs at his medical centre, but he refuses to let anyone get too close, determined to remain unattached forever.

These exceptional doctors are chosen to work in Paris on a unique project with their counterparts in a mass-casualty training programme. But after an unspeakable act of violence, their temporary life becomes a stark turning point: a time to make hard choices – with consequences that will last a lifetime.

Coming soon in paperback

PURE HEART. PURE STEEL.

LOST AND FOUND

HAVE YOU EVER WONDERED 'WHAT IF'?

Madison Allen is a renowned, career-driven photographer. Sifting through old photos in her fashionable Manhattan apartment, she falls. The fall results in more than a broken ankle – it changes her life.

Consumed by old memories and with a forced pause in her demanding schedule, Maddie embarks on a road trip. She hopes to answer questions about the men she loved and might have married in the years after she was left alone with three young children. Maddie sets off to reconnect with three very different men – one in Boston, one in Chicago, and another in Wyoming – to know once and for all if the decisions she made long ago were the right ones.

With each new encounter, Maddie's life comes into clearer focus and a new future takes shape. *Lost and Found* is a deeply felt story about love, motherhood, family, and fate.

Available for pre-order

PURE HEART. PURE STEEL.